"Are you sure you're all right, J.J.?"

Simon framed her face with his hands, searching her eyes.

"I'm fine. I should have got the guy but he caught me off guard. I thought the place was empty. If you hadn't gotten there when you did..." She trailed off, still shaken.

"You'd have shot him. I just moved things along a little more quickly."

"You saved my life," she whispered, thinking that it was getting to be an all too common occurrence.

"Again..." Simon smiled, his train of thought following hers. "But then you'd have saved me too if the situation had been reversed."

"Yes." Jillian nodded, thinking that she should break the contact, but not actually willing to do it. "I would have."

"Which is why we make a perfect team," Simon whispered, bending his head closer to hers. For a moment, she thought he was going to kiss her, and by God, even though she knew it was a mistake, she was going to let him...

Raves for Dee Davis's A-Tac Series

DEADLY DANCE

"What an intense and thrilling read!"
—USAToday.com

"Davis brings in the suspense and romance in good, equal doses." —*RT Book Reviews*

"A dynamic suspense that fans will surely enjoy."
—RomRevToday.com

"A great addition to this exciting series. Ms. Davis keeps each book fresh and new. This is a wonderful series and one I recommend to anybody who loves action with their romance." —NightOwlReviews.com

DEEP DISCLOSURE

"The bullets are flying in this fast-paced, high-octane, romantic adventure. Don't miss *Deep Disclosure*—it's Dee Davis at her best!"
—Brenda Novak, *New York Times* bestselling author of *In Seconds*

"Davis creates a compelling, entertaining story line, action-packed and full of mystery, suspense, and an unlikely romance. Readers will not be able to put it down; this is a real page-turner."

—*RT Book Reviews*

"Dee Davis brings a pulse-pounding tale of romantic suspense in *Deep Disclosure*...This is the latest in Davis's series about hunky special operatives and the danger surrounding them, and they all continue to bring in the heat and the action."

—*Parkersburg News and Sentinel* (WV)

DESPERATE DEEDS

"Delightful...The perfect weekend or vacation read. The fast-paced story takes you through an intriguing game of cat and mouse as protagonists solve the crime, save the world, and, of course, fall in love."

—*RT Book Reviews*

"Five Stars, Top Pick! This series is fast-paced and action-packed. This book is a keeper. I, for one, cannot wait to see what Ms. Davis will bring us next."

—NightOwlReviews.com

DANGEROUS DESIRES

"Rich in dialogue [with] a strong heroine and intricate plot. Full of twists, turns, and near-death encounters, readers will consume this quickly and want more."

—*RT Book Reviews*

"Danger, deception, and desire are the main literary ingredients in Davis's high-adrenaline, highly addictive novel of romantic suspense."

—*Chicago Tribune*

DOUBLE DANGER

DEE DAVIS

FOREVER

NEW YORK   BOSTON

Copyright © 2012 by Dee Davis Oberwetter

Forever
Hachette Book Group
237 Park Avenue
New York, NY 10017

www.HachetteBookGroup.com

Printed in the United States of America

First Edition: December 2012
10 9 8 7 6 5 4 3 2 1

OPM

Forever is an imprint of Grand Central Publishing.
The Forever name and logo are trademarks of Hachette Book Group, Inc.

The Hachette Speakers Bureau provides a wide range of authors for speaking events. To find out more, go to www.hachettespeakersbureau .com or call (866) 376-6591.

The publisher is not responsible for websites (or their content) that are not owned by the publisher.

To Alex,
for everything you do

PROLOGUE

Afghanistan, Pakita Province

"I can see the target," Simon Kincaid said, his attention on the cluster of buildings directly below them.

"Any movement?" Avery Solomon asked. As the commander of A-Tac, a black-ops division of the CIA, Avery was in charge of their mission. And Simon could think of no one he'd rather follow into a red zone.

At the moment, the team was zeroing in on a suspected terrorist encampment in a hidden valley in the Afghan mountains. It had taken the team three days to hike into the hidden basin after a midnight airdrop courtesy of an Air Force Black Hawk.

"Nothing at all. In fact, the place looks deserted. Which seems odd considering the intel." Simon frowned, lowering his field glasses. "This would be a lot easier if we had a full set of eyes and ears."

"Yeah, well, the mountains block satellite access," Avery said. "I'm afraid we're going to have to do this the old-fashioned way."

Simon had to admit that given the choice he'd rather have all the bells and whistles Langley's technology could provide. But there was also a rush in depending only on boots on the ground. That and a bitter sense of foreboding. The last time he'd walked into a situation like this one, it hadn't ended well. Simon closed his eyes, fighting memories, his leg aching in protest. The truth was that the raid in Somalia could never truly be relegated to his past. Hell, he carried it with him every goddamned day.

"You okay?" Avery asked, his gaze probing, as usual, seeing too much.

"I'm fine," Simon said, fighting irritation. It wouldn't do to snap at his boss. Besides, he'd moved on, and this was just another mission, the similarities to his past irrelevant. "Just a little concerned about the lack of activity down there."

"I'll second that," Drake Flynn said, materializing beside them. When not tasked with an operation, Drake was an archeologist by profession, which meant he was an expert at extractions—both living and dead. "Tyler and I scouted the far perimeter, and we didn't see any signs of life."

"Which means they were tipped off," Tyler added, dropping down next to Simon and lifting her field glasses. Tyler was the unit's munitions expert. A whiz with all things ordnance, she also taught English at Sunderland, an interesting dichotomy to say the least. "Or maybe our intel was wrong."

"Not a chance," Nash Brennon, the unit's second in command, said with a frown. "More likely it's a trap."

"We certainly can't ignore the possibility," Avery agreed. "But we've also come too far to turn back now."

Their intel had identified the hidden compound as being run by a fanatic named Kamaal Sahar. Sahar, an elusive son of a bitch, had been tied at least indirectly to several terrorist attacks occurring in the Middle East over the past five years. And, there was also intel connecting him to the Consortium, an organization seemingly bent on facilitating international terrorist agendas, most likely for their own financial gain.

A-Tac had had its share of run-ins with the organization. Most of them before Simon came on board. But he'd been present for long enough to know that they were a viable opponent, a direct threat, not only to the unit, but to the nation. And as such, an enemy that had to be destroyed—whatever the cost.

"So how do you want to proceed?" Nash asked Avery.

"We go in. But cautiously. Even if this isn't a trap, there could be civilians present." His gaze moved from his number two to the scattered buildings below.

There were maybe half a dozen, most of them looking the worse for wear. Living in Afghanistan, especially in this province, meant existing in the middle of a war zone. One that the majority of the world's population most likely didn't even comprehend.

The village was situated around a square, a dilapidated fountain in the center. On the far side, one of the structures had a hole in the roof, the result of mortar rounds. And nearest to them, two more buildings had also been damaged. At the far end, a storefront with rooms upstairs seemed to have minimal damage and the two-story building next to it showed no visible signs of attack. Unlike the other structures in the town, it was constructed of stone, making it look out of place amid its mud-stuccoed neighbors.

Throughout the region, U.S. forces had constructed buildings in an effort not only to shore up support for allied troops but also in a somewhat misguided attempt to improve villagers' lifestyles. Problem was that said villagers weren't always so keen on having their lives changed. And even when they accepted the modern additions, often the insurgents managed to take down new buildings almost as quickly as they were erected.

"I'm thinking, if there's anything to find, it'll be in the stone building," Avery continued, breaking into Simon's thoughts. "It's the most defensible place in the village."

"Copy that," Nash said. "But to access it, we're going to have to come in hot. Until we reach the first building, there's nothing down there to give us cover. Which doesn't bode well if you're right and there are civilians."

"So what we need is a distraction," Simon mused. "Something to hold their attention long enough to allow us to get into town and gain cover."

"I might be able to help there," Tyler said, reaching into her bag to produce a cylindrical grenade.

"Flashbang." Drake grinned as he looked down at the weapon. First developed in the 1960s, nonlethal stun grenades were meant to incapacitate combatants, using sound and light to disorient. "That ought to do the trick. But how do you intend to put it into play? Even a professional ballplayer hasn't got enough of an arm to launch that thing from here into the village."

"True enough." Tyler nodded, pulling a second grenade from her duffel. "But if I use those boulders on the far slope for cover, I just might be able to get close enough. And if the grenades detonate on the far side, all the better for you guys coming in from here. If anyone's down there, they won't be able to formulate a coherent thought, let alone attack someone. It should buy you a few minutes."

"And you really think you can make it down there without being detected?" Avery asked, clearly considering the idea.

"Yeah. Piece of cake." She slid the grenades into pockets in her flak jacket. "And if things go south, you'll still have your distraction." Her smile belied the seriousness of her words. "Just give me a few minutes to get into place."

"You get the hell out of there as soon as you release the grenades," Avery instructed. "Radio when you're in place." Avery tapped the earbud tucked inside his ear. "And if you can't get back to us, then head for the rendezvous."

"Copy that," Tyler said, already in motion.

"All right, people, let's make ready," Avery said, as he watched Tyler disappear into the scrub as she worked her way over to the far slope. "We want to make sure Tyler's efforts count for something."

The team moved into action, checking both weapons and gear. Everyone was silent, left to their own thoughts, and Simon felt the familiar rush of adrenaline that always accompanied a firefight. The enemy might be different, as well as his comrades in arms, but the battle was always the same. Us against them. And no matter how many wins or losses, it seemed there was always another fight just around the corner.

It was never-ending.

Which was just as well, because Simon was good at fighting. Hell, pure and simple, he lived for it. A win was worth whatever losses they might sustain. It was the greater good that mattered. At least that's what he told himself in the middle of the fucking night when his mind was filled with thoughts of the dead. People he'd loved and lost.

Goddamn it.

"I'm here," Tyler said, her voice sounding hollow across the distance of the mountain basin. "Thirty seconds until detonation."

"Copy that," Avery acknowledged, as he nodded for everyone to get ready.

Below them, the little village erupted with white light and the roaring reverberation of Tyler's flashbang.

"Go," Avery mouthed, his voice lost in the fury.

Moving on instinct and adrenaline, Simon headed down the rocky slope, his feet skimming across the rock-strewn ground, his focus on the closest building. They had maybe fifty yards left to cover. A second explosion sounded below them. Tyler still at work. Somewhere in the distance, Simon thought he heard the sound of machine-gun fire.

His thoughts flew to Tyler, but then he pushed them aside. Nothing mattered except the objective. Take the village and neutralize any terrorists they might find.

He was the first to hit the rock fence that surrounded the closest building. A barn maybe. It was crudely built, and the roof was badly in need of repair. He slid to a stop on the left side of the building and cast a quick look over his shoulder as he inched forward. Nash and Drake were right behind him, Avery bringing up the rear. The sound was abating now, the smell of magnesium-laced smoke drifting on the air.

As Nash slid into place beside him, Avery and Drake moved into the barn itself. After a silent count of three, Simon cautiously peered around the corner. Dust, kicked up in the wake of the grenades, swirled around the fountain. Silence stretched through the village, deep and deadly.

Simon hesitated a heartbeat and then swung into the square. Nothing moved. "We seem to be clear," Simon said into his com unit's mic.

Nash followed right behind him, Drake and Avery stepping out of the barn just ahead. The wall fronting the barn offered a modicum of protection as they moved forward.

"Nothing inside," Avery said. "Looks like the place has been deserted for a while."

"So maybe this was a bum steer," Simon said, his attention jerking to a flash of movement on the far side of the square. "Or then again maybe not." He nodded in the direction of the motion, only to release a breath as Tyler's blonde hair caught the sun as she moved around the building's edge.

"It's clear over here," she said, her words echoing in his ear. "Nobody's home."

Nash moved away from the protection of the wall, and after lifting his hand to signal his intent, dashed across the dusty square to join Tyler on the other side, the two groups flanking the square now as they moved forward.

Still nothing moved, and Simon released a breath he hadn't realized he'd been holding. Maybe Tyler was right, and their intel was wrong, and this was just some godforsaken hellhole in the middle of the mountains.

They searched the next two buildings, again with nothing to show for it. The ravages of war were everywhere, from the damaged walls and rooftops to the abandoned signs of humanity. A faded photograph, shattered china, and a child's ball.

Moving more quickly now, intent on exploring the storefront and the stone structure, Simon led the way, gun at the ready. Avery and Tyler came next, staying low, moving almost in tandem on their respective sides of the square. Behind them, walking backward, Nash and Drake kept eyes on the rear, making sure there was nothing to threaten from behind.

Simon slowed as they neared the stone building, his senses going on high alert. There was still no noise, but something had triggered his attention. He motioned the others still, eyes narrowed as he swept his gaze across the windows on the remaining buildings. Nothing moved. But still he waited. And then after a slow count to ten, he took a step forward.

Bullets strafed across the square, sending dust spiraling into the air.

"Fall back," Simon shouted, not bothering to use his comlink. He dove for cover, another round of fire whizzing past his shoulder as he rolled to the relative safety of a building. "We've got a sniper." This time he spoke into his com unit, his eyes still searching the buildings in front of him for signs of life.

"Looks like we were right about the stone building," Avery said, pointing to a top window on the far left.

Sunlight flashed on something metal, and the curtains swayed ominously.

"Son of a bitch," Drake growled, moving to crouch beside them.

Across the way, Nash and Tyler were huddled behind an abandoned cart of some kind.

"You guys got a shot?" Avery asked. "Angle's impossible from here."

"Negative," Nash replied. "Besides, either he's moving or there's more than one of them. The first shots came from a different window." He motioned to a window two down from the one where they'd just seen movement. "I could try to ease my way around back."

"Won't work," Tyler's voice replaced Nash's. "There are windows on at least three sides. We make a move, he'll see, and odds are, he's got a shot."

"So what?" Drake groused. "We just call it a day and head back into the mountains?"

"Not likely," Simon said, his mind already working on the angles. "I can't get a shot from here, but if I can make it up to the second floor over there, I should be able to take the son of a bitch out. I'll just need covering fire."

"Well, whatever we do, I think sooner is better than later." Drake raised an eyebrow, his grin at odds with the grim nature of their situation. "The longer we sit on our asses, the more time the hostile up there has to call in reinforcements."

Avery nodded his agreement. "Simon, you'll go on three. We'll hold him off, and as soon as you're clear, I'll follow behind you."

"I don't need—" he started.

"Help. I know," Avery said, cutting him off with the wave of a hand. "But I can draw the hostile's fire better from closer in. And in order to get the shot, you're going to need me to get the asshole to engage. Otherwise he'll just move out of range."

Simon started to argue again, but stopped himself. Truth was he preferred a solo act. That propensity had become his Achilles heel in the SEALs. Hell, it had probably gotten Ryan killed. He blew out a breath and nodded, moving into place as Avery held up his fist.

One finger, two, and then three.

Simon dashed into the opening between the two buildings, the gunman above them immediately opening fire. Nash and Drake both responded with volleys of their own, and Simon just tucked and ran, feeling the ground beneath his feet reverberating from the shots.

In what felt like an eternal stretch of minutes, he made his way onto the rickety planking that served as a porch for the store-fronted building. There was a sporadic continuation of gunfire and then, like before, everything was quiet.

"Everyone okay?" Simon spoke softly into his comlink.

"Affirmative," Avery responded. "You in one piece?"

"Roger that," Simon said. "Moving into place now."

Turning his attention to the task at hand, he made quick work of searching the bottom floor, relieved that there were no surprise residents. Then, taking the stairs two at a time, he hit the upper floor just as the shooting began again in earnest as Avery moved into position.

Simon crossed to the window, kneeling so that his head was just barely above the sill. It took a moment to locate the gunman again. But after a volley from just below him, Simon saw the movement he was looking for—a flash as the sun hit the muzzle of the machine gun, three windows closer from where they'd originally spotted him.

Simon pulled his rifle from his pack and adjusted the scope. He'd come to A-Tac as a logistics man, but when Annie Brennon, Nash's wife, had announced that she was retiring, he'd taken on her duties as team sniper as well. He steadied his hand and closed an eye, waiting for Avery to work his magic.

"I'm engaging now," Avery said, a blast of gunfire from directly below Simon underscoring the words.

Unlike the previous window, the one the gunman occupied now was curtainless and open. All the better to take him down. Simon smiled as the man leaned into view, his gun trained on Avery.

Sucking in a deep breath, Simon squeezed the trigger.

The man's eyes widened and then he fell forward, half in and half out of the window.

"*Hooah*." The cry over the comlink came from Tyler. And Simon pumped a fist in response, his gaze searching the area for anything to contraindicate the idea that the shooter had been acting alone.

Everything was quiet, and with a sigh of relief, Simon headed down the stairs to join the rest of the team.

"Good shooting," Drake said as Simon stepped back into the square. "Got him in one. Don't think Annie could have done it any better."

"High praise," Simon acknowledged, his body still pumping adrenaline. "Gotta admit it was one hell of a rush."

"Now you sound like her, too," Tyler said with a laugh as she and Nash joined them on their side of the plaza.

"But swear to God, I don't see the point of such a risky maneuver if you can just blow the damn target."

"Yeah, well, sometimes you just don't need the overkill," Nash said, his tone teasing. "But in a pinch, I'll take whatever works. Hell of a shot, Simon."

"Any chance it's Kamaal?" he asked, rolling the body over so that they could see the face.

"There aren't any really clear pictures of the man," Nash responded. "But I'd say this guy is way too young."

"Pity, that." Simon nodded down at the dead man. "Would have liked to have taken him down."

"Another day," Avery said, coming up to stand beside them. "For now, let's just be grateful we got the shooter. For all we know, this guy called for reinforcements, and although I'd put money on us in a firefight I'd just as soon avoid one, if possible. So I'm thinking we need to move fast if we want to search the building."

"Roger that," Nash said. "So you think there's anything to find?"

"Only one way to know for sure." Drake grinned, then strode off for the building, the others quickly following.

At the door, they stopped, backs to the wall, as Avery reached out to open it.

"Wait," Tyler said, quickly feeling along the frame for signs that there might be some kind of booby trap. "It's clean."

"All right then," Avery said, "I'll go first."

The big man swung into the doorway, leading with his gun, and after calling "clear," the others followed him inside. The first floor was a one-room affair. Ratty furniture was scattered around with seemingly no thought to decoration. A sofa lay overturned, and a table had been flipped on end. Behind it, a fireplace smoldered, half-burned papers spilling out onto the hearth. Boxes littered the floor, and an open crate stood in the center of the room.

"Looks like weapons," Tyler said, motioning to an old Soviet stamp on the side of the crate as she peered inside. "I'm guessing, from the indentations, old PK machine guns." She lifted a bed of man-made straw to reveal what had most likely been a second layer of weaponry.

"A holdover from the Soviet/Afghan war?" Nash asked.

"That or maybe just old cast-offs." Tyler shrugged. "The Russian black market is full of serviceable but outdated equipment. And there are always people ready to buy."

"Like our boys here."

"Guy up here was packing a PK," Drake said, leaning over the stairway banister. Nothing to identify him. But there's crap all over the floor up here, too. Looks like whoever was using this building moved out on the fly."

"Leaving dead dude to hold the fort?" Simon quipped. "Talk about hazardous duty."

"Everyone fan out for a look," Avery said as he bent to pick up a torn piece of paper. "Maybe we'll still find something."

"Most of the paper is too burned for anything to be legible," Simon said, sifting through the singed rubbish. "But there's a notebook here that looks salvageable. The covers are toast, but the pages inside are relatively untouched." He held out the charred notebook. "Unfortunately, I can't read Arabic. Nash, what about you?"

"I can speak it fairly well," he said, taking the notebook from Simon and flipping through the pages with a frown. "But I'm not nearly as good at reading it. It'd take me a couple of days to make any sense of this."

"Doesn't matter." Avery shook his head. "We can get someone at Langley to translate when we get back."

"Well, it's definitely schematics of some kind," Nash said.

"So we've got weapons and diagrams." Avery frowned. "Seems to verify our intel that this was more than a simple village."

"Not to mention having their own personal sniper," Tyler added. "My guess is that he was finalizing clean-up with an eye to our arrival."

"And when forced into action, he started shooting."

"Yeah. And I'm betting it wasn't a voluntary assignment," Tyler said. "He had to have known it was suicide."

"Maybe he thought he could scare us off." Avery took the notebook from Nash, carefully stashing it in his pack. "Or maybe he thought it was a fast ticket to all those virgins."

"Well, wherever he ended up, maybe his hasty exit will play to our advantage somehow." Simon was back to sifting through the refuse in the fireplace.

"Damn well better," Avery said, "because it seems like lately, no matter what we do, we're always just a few minutes behind the ball. Anybody got anything else?"

"This count?" Drake asked, coming down the stairs holding out a small black box. "Looks like an external hard drive. I found it mixed in with some other destroyed electrical equipment."

"Don't know what you expect to get off that." Simon

wiped the soot off his hands as he studied the box in Drake's hand. "Looks to me like someone took after it with a hammer."

"I've seen Harrison resurrect worse," Avery said. Harrison Blake was the team's IT guru. "Hell, if we're really lucky maybe there's something on it that'll connect to the Consortium."

CHAPTER 1

New York City, Hospital for Special Surgery

S o on a scale of one to ten, how would you rank the pain?" Dr. Weinman asked as he probed the deep scars running across Simon's thigh.

"Three," Simon said, fighting against a grimace, pain radiating up into his hip. The long hike through the Afghan mountains plus the stress of the firefight had aggravated his injury, his pronounced limp causing Avery to send him to the orthopedist for a look-see.

"So a six." The doctor released the leg and scribbled something on his chart.

Simon opened his mouth to argue, but Weinman smiled. "Look, I've been patching up people like you for most of my career. Which means I'm more than aware that in your world, a three would definitely be a six for the rest of us. God's honest truth, probably more like an eight or nine."

"Apples to oranges," Simon said, his smile bitter. "The rest of you wouldn't have a leg full of shrapnel. So am I cleared for duty?"

"Yeah." Weinman shrugged. "You're good to go. There's no new damage. But I'm afraid as long as you insist on engaging in the kind of *work* you do, there's always going to be risk. And sooner or later, there's going to be additional injury. So it's not a matter of if, but when."

"Nothing I didn't already know," Simon said, jumping off the table to get dressed.

"I assume you're still working with the PT?" the doctor asked, glancing up over the top of his glasses.

"Actually, I'm not. With the new job, there just isn't time to come all the way into the city. But Sunderland has a great gym. And I've memorized the moves by now. So it's easy enough for me to work out on my own."

"Well, I suppose that'll have to do," the doctor said, still scribbling in the chart. "Just be careful not to push too hard. Do you need something for the pain?"

"No, I'm good." Simon shook his head as he shrugged into his shirt. The pain meds only dulled his brain, slowing his reflexes. And in his line of work, that wasn't an option. Besides, he prided himself on being tough.

"There's nothing dishonorable about managing pain," Weinman said, correctly reading Simon's train of thought.

"Look, I said I'm fine." Simon blew out a breath, forcing a smile. The doc was only trying to help.

And if Simon were truly being honest, he'd have to admit that sometimes, in the middle of the night when the pain threatened to overwhelm him, the pills were his only ticket to oblivion. But he'd seen what had happened to men he'd fought with when the meds had taken control. And he wasn't about to let himself go down that path. No matter how fucking much it hurt.

"It's up to you." Weinman shrugged, closing the chart

and rising to his feet. "But if you change your mind, I'm only a telephone call away."

"Good to know. But I'll be okay."

"All right then. We're done." Weinman paused, his gaze assessing. "Until next time." Leaving the words hanging, he turned and left the room, and Simon blew out a long breath.

The bottom line was that he knew he was on borrowed time. His injuries had been severe enough to force him out of the SEALs. And sooner or later, they were probably going to mean an end to his career with A-Tac, at least in the field.

But for now, he was determined to carry on. He was a soldier. Pure and simple. And just because he could no longer be a SEAL, he didn't have to settle for some piddly-ass desk job. A-Tac was as good as it got when it came to working counterterrorism. And he was lucky to have found a home there.

And he sure as hell wasn't going to fuck it up by letting his injury get in the way. Anyway, all that mattered now was that he was good to go. Which meant he could get back to Sunderland—and the hunt for the Consortium.

He walked out of the exam room, striding down the hall, ignoring the twinge of pain shooting up his leg. Compared to a couple of years ago, this was a cakewalk. And the way he figured, another year and it would hardly be noticeable. Everyone in his line of work lived with injury. It was part of the package. It just wasn't something most people could understand. Their idea of the fast lane was eating fried food on a Saturday night—his was perpetrating a raid on an Afghan terrorist encampment.

He waved at the receptionist as he walked through

the waiting room and pushed through the doors of the clinic. Dr. Weinman's offices were on an upper floor of the hospital, the corridor leading to the elevator lined with windows looking out over the FDR Drive and the East River. Outside, beyond the congestion of the highway's traffic, the river was flowing out toward the harbor. A tugboat, barge in tow, was making its laborious way upstream. Above the swiftly flowing water, the skyline of Long Island City stood illuminated against the bold blue sky.

It was the kind of day that made a kid want to skip school. And suddenly Simon was struck with the thought that everything was right with his world, the past firmly behind him and the future beckoning bright. It had been a long time since he'd felt hopeful about anything. Hell, with his past, who could blame him. But maybe it was time to move on. There wasn't much point in letting the past, or the future, for that matter, hold too much sway. Better to live in the now.

He laughed at the philosophical turn of his thoughts. Had to be the hospital. All that life and death crap. He stopped for a moment at the door to a large waiting room. Inside, a small army of nurses were triaging patients, most of them nonambulatory, with bleeding wounds and broken limbs.

But the blood was fake, and the moaning and groaning more about theatrics than pain. A disaster drill. He'd seen a notice in the elevator on the way up. Judging from the chaos ensuing inside the room, he'd have to assume it wasn't going all that well. Of course, if it been the real thing, the hysteria would have been much worse. But this was just play-acting, and thankfully, he didn't have a role to play. With a rueful smile, he turned to go, then stopped, his brain conjuring the picture of a blue-eyed blonde in green scrubs.

Frowning, he turned around again, certain that image must be wrong, that his mind had merely superimposed a memory onto a stranger. He rubbed his leg absently as his gaze settled again on the woman. She had her back to him, her sun-streaked ponytail bobbing as she talked to another woman also wearing scrubs. She was waving her hands, her slim fingers giving additional meaning to her words.

Even from behind, he knew that his instinct had been dead on. He knew the curve of her hips. The turn of her shoulders, the grace of her long, lithe legs. He recognized the way she stood, the way she moved. Hell, he'd have known her anywhere. And then she turned, as if somehow she'd felt his presence, her eyes widening in surprise and then shuttering as she recognized him.

His mind screamed retreat, but his feet moved forward, taking him across the room until they were standing inches apart. Behind her, out the window, he could still see the river, the blue of the sky almost the same color as her eyes.

"J.J.?" The words came out a gruff whisper, his mind and body still on overdrive as he tried to make sense of her being here in New York.

"I go by Jillian now," she said, her voice just as he'd remembered. Low and throaty. Sexy. "It's easier." There was a touch of bitterness in her words and a tightness around her mouth that he'd never seen before.

He paused, not exactly sure what to say. It had been a long time. And he hadn't thought he'd see her again. Memories flooded through him. The smell of her hair.

The feel of her skin beneath his fingers. An image of her standing with Ryan in her wedding dress, eyes full of questions, Simon's heart shriveling as he chose loyalty over everything else.

J.J. was Ryan's girl. She'd always been his. Since they were practically kids. And one drunken night couldn't change that fact.

Ryan was his best friend and he'd failed him—twice. Once an eon ago at a college party, and the second time, years later, in a compound in Somalia. He'd managed to avert disaster the first time, common sense and loyalty overriding his burgeoning libido. But in Somalia, he hadn't been so lucky, and because of his decisions, Ryan was dead. J.J. had lost her husband. And there was nothing Simon could do to make it right.

"I can't believe you're standing here," he said, shaking his head. "It's been a while since I saw you last."

"Four years," she replied, the words a recrimination.

"You look the same," he said, wishing to hell he'd never seen her. He didn't need this.

Again she laughed, but this time with humor. "You always were a flatterer."

"Yeah, well, I guess some things never change," he said, studying her face. There were faint lines at the corners of her eyes and mouth. And her hair was longer and slightly darker than before. But over all, she looked like the girl he remembered. Except for the smile.

J.J. had always been smiling. Or at least that's the way he'd chosen to remember her. The last time he'd seen her, she'd been anything but happy. He'd never forget the pain etched across her face as she'd accepted the flag that had been draped across Ryan's casket. Simon had promised to come by later that day. But instead he'd left town. And never looked back.

"You look good, too," she said, her eyes moving across his face. "So what brings you to the hospital?"

"Check-up," he sighed, rubbing his leg. "But it's all good. I'm healthy as a horse." And babbling like a fucking idiot. She'd always been able to reduce him to baser levels.

"I'm glad," she said. "I heard you left the team."

"Didn't have much of a choice." He shrugged. "But I landed on my feet, and I'm doing okay. What about you? You a nurse now?"

"Something like that." She nodded. "Speaking of which, I suppose I ought to be getting back to it."

"Right," he said, the silence that followed stretching awkwardly between them.

And then, with an apologetic shrug, she turned back to her "patients," and Simon forced himself to walk away. Hell, the past was better left buried. Hadn't he just been having that exact thought?

He stepped back into the corridor, and then, despite himself, turned for a last look. She was bending over a man with a rudimentary splint on his arm, her fingers gentle as she probed the imaginary wound.

Almost involuntarily, his gaze rose to the window, his senses sending out an alert. A high-pitched whine filled the room, the glass on the windows shaking. The sky disappeared as the window turned black. For a moment, everything seemed to move in slow motion. And then, all hell broke loose as the windows shattered and something rammed through the side of the building, the walls shredding like corrugated cardboard.

People screamed, and Simon called her name. "*J.J.*"

One minute she was standing there, eyes wide with confusion and fear, and the next—she was gone.

The air was acrid with the smell of smoke combined with the metallic odor of gasoline. Jillian's eyes opened as self-preservation kicked in. Visibility was almost nonexistent, the lights either blocked or extinguished. Neither of which made sense. She tried to push to her feet, but her body refused the order, and panic laced through her as she tried to figure out what was going on.

The last thing she remembered was Simon. Which was odd in and of itself considering how long it had been since she'd last seen him. She shook her head, trying again to move but finding her limbs still unresponsive. Despite the choking smoke, she forced herself to breathe, letting the rhythm of her rising chest soothe her into calmer thinking.

She was in the hospital. She'd been leading an emergency preparedness drill. And Simon had walked into the room. So at least she wasn't crazy. But then everything after that was a little more hazy. She remembered a whoosh of air followed by what had sounded like crumpling metal and shattering glass. A car accident of the nth degree.

But there was no way there'd been a car on the fifteenth floor of the building—which left only a couple of possibilities. The least being a bomb. The worst something on the scale of 9/11. She opened her mouth to scream, but smoke filled her lungs and she coughed instead, the inside of her throat burning with the effort.

She turned her head, trying to see. The smoke had thinned slightly, and she twisted up, stretching until her body rebelled, her muscles spasming with the effort.

Drained, she dropped back to the floor, but not before she'd ascertained that she was pinned underneath something. Heavy and metal, from the looks of it, although whatever it had been, it wasn't anymore. Again she tried to fill her lungs with air—this time breathing shallowly, mindful of the smoke.

"Help," she called, the word coming out somewhere between a whisper and a croak. She could hear people moving, screams filtering through the metal surrounding her. "Help," she cried again, louder this time.

"J.J.?" a voice broke through the barrier. *Simon.* "Is that you?"

"Yes," she called, her voice rising as she was filled with both hope and fear. The metal above her groaned and shifted, the pressure on her legs increasing. "I can't move. I'm stuck."

"Are you hurt?" he asked, his voice nearer now.

"I don't know." She shook her head, even though he couldn't see her. "But I don't think so. There isn't any pain." The fact wasn't necessarily a positive sign considering she was pinned, but panic wasn't going to help anything.

"That's good," Simon said, his voice more reassuring than she could have imagined. "Now we just have to figure out how to get you out of there."

She nodded. Again aware that it was pointless, but the movement made her feel more secure somehow. "What happened?"

"I can't say definitively," he answered as a piece of the metal directly to her left was yanked away. She could see the floor of the room, faint light filtering through the opening. "But it looks like a helicopter crashed into the side of the hospital. It came right through the windows. You're trapped underneath part of the fuselage." His head appeared suddenly just to her right, his green eyes filled with concern.

"What about all the people?" she asked, thinking of the staff and volunteers that had filled the room just before the collision.

"They're being evacuated. And emergency responders are on the way."

"How many dead?"

"Can't say for sure. The pilot and his passenger. And at least five or six others."

"Oh, God," she said, closing her eyes against the threatening tears. She'd been working with these folks for almost a week. Knew most of them by name and several well enough to think of them as friends.

"Yeah, but it could have been a hell of a lot worse."

There was a pause, and Jillian stiffened. "What?" she whispered, turning her head so that she could see his face. "What aren't you telling me?"

He hesitated for a moment, his expression grim. Then he reached out to grasp her free hand. She tightened the grip, waiting. "The helicopter's fuel tank was ruptured when it came through the wall." That explained the smell of gas.

"You're worried about an explosion." A shudder worked its way up her spine.

"Yes." The word was spoken quietly, lending it credence as it hung between them. "But I'll get you out," he continued. "No man left behind, right?" She thought she saw a flicker of something in his eyes. Regret maybe, although she wasn't sure why.

"Easier said than done. I can feel the fuselage. It's pinning me. And it's got to weigh a ton. There's no way you'll get it off me without help. And there's not time for that." She could smell the leaking fuel. Panic rose, but she shoved it down, her gaze locking with his, her decision made. "You've got to get out of here, Simon. There's no sense both of us dying."

"No fucking way." He shook his head.

"It's suicide for you to stay. Either the team of rescuers will make it up here or they won't. " She tried to keep her voice emotion-free. "I haven't got a choice, but you do."

"And I'm making it," he said, pulling his hand from hers, his face disappearing from the space he'd created. For a moment, she actually thought he'd left, but then another piece of the refuse was pulled free, his face red from the exertion. "Now if I can just find something to use for leverage."

"It's too heavy. Even you're not strong enough to get it off." She attempted a smile, but failed as the fuselage shifted again, the pressure robbing her of breath.

"I don't have to get it all the way off." He bent down, rummaging through the wreckage. "I just have to lift it enough for you to slide free. Do you think you can do that?"

She tensed her muscles, still not feeling any pain. "I'll give it my best."

"Can't ask for anything more." His answering smile was reassuring, and she nodded as he pulled a section of rebar free. "This should do the trick."

Working to insert the end of the rod underneath the fragment of the helicopter that had pinned her to the floor, he cursed, possibly in pain.

"Everything okay?" she whispered, almost afraid to hear the answer.

"Yeah, it's fine. I just burned my hand—the whole thing is really hot."

"Be careful."

He nodded, then grimaced as he tightened his hold on the rebar. "On my count."

She sucked in a breath as he counted down, muscles primed as he called "three." She could feel a little movement, but it wasn't enough. She still couldn't move. The pressure increased as he let go, and any hope she'd had evaporated.

The room was deadly silent now, the smell of fuel growing stronger.

"You need to go," she whispered, the pressure on her chest intense again.

He looked up, his gaze colliding with hers, the resolution there unmistakable. "One more time." He adjusted his stance, and then, with a second count to three, shoved against the rebar, the muscles under his T-shirt rippling with the effort.

At first there was little difference, a slight easing of the pressure, and then the metal groaned as it slid sideways. It wasn't much, but it was enough. Moving on a burst of pure adrenaline, Jillian slid from underneath the twisted fuselage. The resulting wave of pain was instant and intense, but she was free.

She rolled to a sitting position, fighting a wave of nausea, more than aware that their time was running out. The smell of smoke drew her eyes to the left and the fire burning near the twisted body of the helicopter, the flames licking toward the expanding pool of fuel beneath it.

"We've got to move now," Simon said, echoing her thoughts as he scooped her into his arms, and she fought against another wave of pain.

"I can walk," she argued, shuddering as she caught sight of a body, a nurse from the hospital, Gail something or other. The woman's eyes were wide, her mouth open in a silent scream, one leg twisted at an inhuman angle. Blood stained her scrubs and the floor beneath her.

"Don't look." Simon pulled her closer and headed across the room through the smoke to the elevator bank.

"Too late," she whispered, heart hammering as tears filled her eyes.

Behind them, the room seemed to shimmy and then erupt. The sound of the explosion reverberated off the walls, shards of metal and glass flying through the room like shrapnel as a giant ball of fire erupted from the center of the wreckage.

Heat buffeted her exposed skin as Simon ran into the comparative safety of the hallway in front of the elevators. His body blocked hers as the room behind them splintered into a fiery hell—the heated flames reaching out across the room with an intensity that melted the carpet beneath their feet.

Propping her between his body and the wall, he reached out with one hand to yank open the door to the stairwell. Then he shoved her through, slamming the door behind him, the sound accompanied by the sharp thwack of shrapnel against the metal on the other side.

"That was close," she said, suppressing another shudder.

"It's not over." The warning in his voice was echoed as the stairs shook beneath them. "Can you move on your own?" He shot a glance down the stairwell and then moved his gaze back to hers.

"Yes. I think so." She nodded, her feet already moving as he wrapped an arm around her, propelling them down the stairs. Above her head, she heard the shearing of metal and a tremendous crack as the landing broke away and fell in a hail of rubble onto the stairs just behind them.

"Keep moving," he yelled over the din, his arm tightening as he practically carried her downward, the sound of the collapse still roaring in their wake, a billowing cloud of smoke and dust enveloping them as they ran.

In what seemed like hours, but was probably no more than minutes, they'd covered the distance from the fifteenth floor to the first, Simon sweeping her back into his arms as they hit the bottom landing and burst through the doors into the pale rays of an October afternoon. There were first responders everywhere. Along with dazed people. Patients in beds, doctors in scrubs. People in crisis.

Her first thought was that she needed to help them.

But before she could put voice to the words, her vision went blurry, her mind fuzzy, and her last coherent thought was that, as impossible as it might seem, Simon Kincaid had just saved her life.

CHAPTER 2

Sunderland College, New York

W hat do you mean she's not there?" Simon asked, gripping his cellphone as he tried to hold his temper in check. The last time he'd seen J.J., she'd been huddled in the back of an ambulance, ready for transfer to another city hospital. They'd been separated after making it down the stairs, each of them being checked out and then Simon answering questions from the first responders.

Still, he should have followed up. Checked on her in person.

He'd told himself that she wouldn't have wanted to see him. But the truth was that he was a coward. He'd only just begun to put Ryan's death and the events surrounding it behind him. And J.J. only brought it all to the surface again, the memories still painful and raw. It was more than he was ready to handle.

"I'm sorry, sir," the nurse said, her voice pulling him back to the present. "Ms. Montgomery was released shortly after she arrived."

"Fine." His voice was clipped as he disconnected, his anger directed more at himself than anyone else. He'd assumed the docs would have at least kept her overnight. Which meant he'd still had time. But now...hell, now she was gone. Which was a good thing, surely. J.J. was fine. And preliminary findings had ruled the crash a horrible accident. End of story.

"Checking on the woman from the hospital?" Harrison Blake asked as he stopped next to Simon in front of the professor's elevators in the Aaron Thomas Academic Center.

The building, which housed the college's renowned think tank, also sat atop the underground complex that served as headquarters for the American Tactical Intelligence Command. A-Tac. The elite CIA unit was made up of not only experts at covert activities but also some of the top academicians in the country. Simon considered himself lucky to be a part of it all.

"Yeah." He nodded as Harrison used his key to activate access to the elevator. "I just wanted to make sure she was okay," Simon continued. "Which obviously she is, because she's been released."

He hadn't told anyone about his history with Jillian Montgomery, her new name making it more difficult to connect the dots even if someone was inclined to do so. He'd shared some of his past with Hannah Marshall, A-Tac's intel specialist. But everyone in A-Tac had secrets, so none of them was in the habit of probing too deeply. At least not without invitation or provocation. And Simon wasn't inclined to provide either.

"Well, she's damn lucky you were on site," Harrison said, with a shrug.

They stepped into the elevator, and Harrison lifted

the Otis Elevator plaque to insert a second key. For the most part, students were turned away by the sign at the elevator. And without a key, even if they tried to take the elevator, they'd only have access to a suite of offices on the top floor that conceivably served as a professors' lounge. Of course, with the proper keys, the elevator took occupants down to the sub-basement levels and A-Tac's operational center.

"Yeah, well, it's over now." Simon frowned, pushing thoughts of J.J. out of his mind. "Any idea why Avery called a meeting?"

"No. Just that it's important. I figured it was probably something to do with the stuff you guys brought back from Afghanistan. Maybe the brain trust at Langley found something when they translated the notebook you recovered."

"Have you had any luck with the hard drive?" Simon asked. Harrison was the unit's computer forensics specialist. One of the best Simon had ever worked with.

"Not yet." Harrison shook his head. "Damn thing was obliterated. I'm not sure I'll be able to pull anything intelligible off it. But I haven't given up yet. Sons of bitches tried to destroy it for a reason."

The elevator doors slid open, revealing a large reception area, another ploy to fool students who somehow managed to make it this far. Of course, entering here was a sure ticket straight to Avery's office. Besides serving as A-Tac's commander, he was also the dean of students, and his reputation as a hard-ass, in both incarnations, was well earned.

Harrison slapped his palm against the bust of Aaron Thomas, a Revolutionary War hero who served as A-Tac's unofficial mascot. A spy for the American side, he'd also been a political philosopher of the day and, as such, a teacher. And in that way, his life and times served to mirror the twin objectives of A-Tac.

A section of the far wall slid open, and the two men walked through the opening into the heart of the beast, so to speak. Harrison grinned. "Hannah always says it reminds her of the bat cave."

"Well, you've got to admit, we've got a lot of the trappings," she said, appearing at the doorway to the war room. Hannah Marshall was the unit's intel officer. Her glasses today were a deep magenta, a contrast to the purple streaks in her spiky hair. "We were just wondering if you guys had found something better to do."

She linked arms with Harrison, pulling him over to the large table that dominated the center of the room. At the front, Avery stood deep in conversation with Nash, his expression grim. Simon wondered what had the big man so upset. It had to be something pretty damn serious. He'd learned over the past year that nothing much fazed Avery.

On the right side of the table, Tyler sat next to Drake, the two of them laughing at something, the light glinting off Tyler's hair. The sight triggered the memory of J.J. standing in scrubs, blue eyes wide as she recognized him. Then, like some kind of montage, his mind moved to another picture, a younger J.J., lips swollen from his kisses, her sweet breath fanning across his face.

He shook his head, clearing his thoughts as he moved to the opposite side of the table, feeling, as usual, like the outsider. It was stupid. He'd been through hell with these people. But in their line of work, friendship came at too big a cost. It was a lesson learned in the heat of battle and not easily forgotten.

When it came to an operation, he'd give everything he had, but no matter how much he liked the people he worked with, it was safer to keep them at arm's length. The price for anything more was just too damn high.

He dropped down into a seat. Hannah and Harrison had moved to the front of the table, both opening laptops. The room had several computer stations around the periphery and a large screen above Avery's head on the far wall. There were monitors built into the table as well, the room's equipment state of the art.

Nash joined Simon on his side of the table, frowning across it at Drake. "I've got to say you're not looking too good."

"No shit." Drake sighed. "Truth is, I haven't slept in two weeks. Doctor says it's teething." Drake and his wife, Madeline, had a six-month-old, Brianna—named in honor of Harrison's sister. "I love my daughter more than I ever could have imagined, but, I'll be honest, I think I'd be better off bunking somewhere else for the duration."

"Like eighteen years?" Nash smiled with a fatalistic shrug. "Trust me, it's worth the pain. I'd give anything to have had those early days with Adam."

"Yeah, I know. I'm just blowing hot air. Although I have to say I'm not sorry Madeline and Bree are off to California to visit Alexis." Alexis was Tucker's wife. The two of them spent most of their time in Redlands although they had a house here at Sunderland too.

"Yeah, Annie and Adam were stoked about the trip, too," Nash acknowledged. "Although I think the promise of going to an Angels game played a large part in Adam's excitement."

"Hey, what can I say, the kid has great taste in base-ball teams. And although I'll definitely miss my wife and kid, I'm looking forward to some down time. I'm telling you, Simon," Drake said with his usual easy grin, "if you value your sleep, think long and hard before you have kids."

"Not an issue." Simon held up a hand to underscore his words. "I don't think I'm exactly father material."

"That's what I said." Drake laughed as he propped his chair back against the wall. "And look at me now."

"So where's Tucker?" Simon asked, with a frown. Tucker was Drake's brother. And, like Simon, a fairly new member to the team.

"Off with Owen. NSA business," Tyler said. "The two of them are thick as thieves these days." Owen was Tyler's husband, and he worked for the division of NSA tasked with policing the other intelligence agencies. It didn't always make him the most popular guy on the block. But he seemed like a stand-up guy, and Tyler loved him, so Simon figured he was okay.

"All right, people." Avery cleared his throat, signaling a beginning to the meeting, and Simon sat forward in anticipation.

"So what's with the summons?" Drake asked, raising an eyebrow. "You got a new assignment for us?" He sounded so hopeful that Simon hid a smile. Fatherhood was definitely taking a toll.

"Possibly," Avery said. "Or maybe I should say an old one."

"The Consortium." Nash's expression darkened, the two words hanging in the air almost like a challenge, everyone's mood sobering in an instant.

"Again that's a maybe," Avery repeated. "At the moment, we haven't got anything tangible to tie them in to any of what I'm about to tell you. Hell, we can't even prove for certain that what we found isn't just some kind of cosmic coincidence."

"Well, for the record, my gut is telling me it's anything but," Hannah was quick to add.

"Your hunches I believe in." Drake's smile was tempered with a wry twist of his lips. Hannah had been part of the team who'd gone off book to rescue Madeline and Drake from a Consortium trap in Colombia. Flying the helicopter, no less.

"So what have we got?" Nash prompted, pulling everyone's attention back to Avery.

"The guys at Langley are still working on the notebook we uncovered," Avery said, nodding at Hannah, who hit a button and pulled up the image of a burned page. "But they've managed to decipher at least part of it. Something that I think you're all going to find relevant in light of recent events."

Hannah hit another key on the computer and the page dissolved into a newer version, the enhanced image courtesy of Langley's forensics department. She adjusted slightly, and the diagram became clear.

"Holy shit," Simon whispered, his eyes riveted to the screen. "Is that what I think it is?" The diagram was a blueprint. The layout exactly the same as the hospital floor where the helicopter crashed. He could see the doctor's office, the hallway, the waiting room, even the windows—it was all there.

"Sure as hell looks that way." Avery turned so that he, too, could see the schematic on the screen above him.

"Especially when you take a look at the second diagram we found."

Hannah hit a button and another image appeared on the screen next to the first.

"It's a map," Drake offered.

"Yeah, but of what?" Tyler asked, still studying the newest projection.

"This will help," Hannah said, hitting another key. The scribbles on what looked to be streets cleared, the words in English now.

"It *is* the hospital." Simon frowned up at the screen. "The East River and the FDR are clearly marked. I can see York Avenue and Seventy-first Street. And the blank space between Seventieth and Seventy-first, that's the hospital. Son of a bitch."

Everyone was leaning forward now, eyes riveted to the screen above them.

"There's also a notation on the blueprint." Hannah used a pointer to highlight Arabic words at the bottom of the diagram. "According to the guys at Langley, it reads fifteen east, southeast."

"That's the location of the floor where we were hit." Simon felt a shiver of trepidation, or maybe forewarning, work its way up his spine. "Fifteen east. And the windows in the waiting room faced south and east. They were mapping the goddamned hospital."

"Exactly." Avery crossed his arms, his gaze moving to encompass them all.

"So what's with the name?" Nash asked, still looking at the blueprint. "My Arabic sucks, but that definitely looks like a name. Yusuf, right?"

"Yes," Hannah said. "But so far we haven't been able

to tie it to anyone specific. Unfortunately, it's a common name, and without a surname, it's almost impossible to ID him. Although I'm still digging."

"Maybe it's just a doodle," Drake suggested.

"Yeah well, doodle or no, I'm thinking it's got to mean something," Simon said. "Maybe this Yusuf orchestrated the crash somehow. Or was at least part of the planning. I'm assuming we're no longer considering it an accident."

"Not definitively, no." Avery shook his head. "All we can say for certain is that the documents we found seem to indicate that the crash was planned. Although we still can't ignore the initial investigation. The teams involved found evidence that definitely supports the idea that the crash was indeed an accident."

"But evidence can be manipulated," Tyler said, her eyes narrowing as she studied the screen.

"And there's no way some dude in the Afghan desert was just farting around drawing the schematics for the exact place where a helicopter happened to crash. There's got to be something more to it." Drake was leaning forward now, hands flattened on the table.

"Especially when you add in the encampment's possible connection to Kamaal Sahar and the Consortium," Nash said.

"Which is why they're reopening the investigation." Avery crossed his arms over his massive chest.

"They?" Tyler asked.

"Well, us, technically. But we've been ordered to work with Homeland Security on this one."

"Because that went so well last time," Drake said, shooting a look in Nash's direction.

"Well, to be fair to Homeland Security, Tom was CIA when he screwed things up." Nash frowned, the memory obviously still rankling even after all this time.

Tom Walker had been Nash and Annie's handler back when they'd worked operations in Eastern Europe. He'd gone on to a high-level job with Homeland Security and used that power to try to railroad Annie. Simon hadn't been there when it happened, but according to Hannah, not only did Avery get the man to admit his complicity in Annie's predicament, he also got Tom punted so far down the ladder that he was lucky to still have a job in intelligence.

"Yeah, but it was his position at Homeland Security that made your life hell," Hannah reiterated. "Yours and Annie's."

"Well, we're fine now." Nash's eyes softened for a moment as his thoughts clearly moved to his wife, and Simon couldn't help but wonder what it was like to know that someone cared enough to always have your back. "And we can't hold the entire organization responsible for Tom's actions. They were actually pretty decent once the dust had settled."

"And you handed them Kim Sun on a platter," Tyler said.

"Yeah, well, it's all old news. And I say, if working with Homeland Security gives us a better chance to catch these bastards, then I'm in."

"Good," Avery said, his expression inscrutable. "Because it's non-negotiable. If nothing else, we need them so that we can maintain our cover."

"So when are we going to meet this liaison?" Harrison asked.

"Should be any minute now." Avery nodded toward the door to the hallway. "I left her in my office. She had to take a call."

"She?" Drake queried, his eyebrow back in play.

"Yes. She was on site when it all went down. Which means she and Simon will be able to hit the ground running."

"Me?" Simon felt a frisson of worry trickle through him. Surely he was jumping to conclusions. J.J. couldn't be with Homeland Security. He replayed their conversation in his head, realizing that at no time had she said exactly what her role in the drill had been. When she hadn't corrected him, he'd just assumed she was a nurse.

"Seems logical, considering you were there and that the two of you have already met." Avery's voice seem to be coming from somewhere far away, the world suddenly moving in slo-mo. The door swung open, and a woman in jeans and a mouthwateringly tight T-shirt strode into the room, blonde ponytail swinging.

Jesus, God. *J.J.* Shit. He was screwed.

Simon leaned back against the wall as Avery introduced J.J. to everyone. He still couldn't bring himself to think of her as Jillian. It was like turning her into some kind of stranger. But then again, maybe that's exactly what she was. Just because he'd known her a lifetime ago didn't mean that he knew her now. He watched as J.J. smiled at Drake, reaching out to shake his hand.

Jillian Jane Montgomery. Named for her two grandmothers. Her mother, a product of the Deep South, had actually called her Jillian Jane. J.J. had hated it. He and Ryan, best friends since grade school, had met Jillian at college orientation, and the three of them had been thick as thieves from that moment on. Ryan had actually been the first to christen her J.J. And it had caught on quickly in the way that sort of thing always did.

When she'd married Ryan and become a Jackowski, it had only seemed more fitting. Hell, Ryan had even teased her that she could go by the moniker Three-J had she been inclined to a career as a rapper. Simon remembered her laughing at the notion, striking a pose, cap turned backward, finger brushing her nose. They'd had some good times, the three of them.

But now Ryan was dead, J.J. had a new name, and he was—hell, he'd moved on, too. And her being here didn't change any of that. Whatever they'd shared in the past, bottom line, he'd killed it.

"So now that everyone knows everyone else," Avery said, pulling Simon from his tumbling thoughts, "we need to get to work. And the first thing we have to do is find something concrete to refute the evidence that this was an accident."

"What do we know so far?" Drake asked, tipping his chair back against the wall again.

"The flight originated from the Downtown Manhattan Heliport at the East River Piers," J.J. said, glancing down at an open file folder she'd laid on the tabletop. "The helicopter is owned by Aerial Manhattan. The company's been around for almost twenty years, and their reputation is solid."

J.J. nodded to Hannah, who hit a key on her computer and the company's logo flashed up on the screen. Simon marveled at how easily she'd assumed a leadership role. Not that he should have been surprised. In college, she'd always been right there in the thick of things. Meeting every challenge they'd set for her. Just one of the guys. Until she wasn't...

But then she'd married Ryan, and, well, in truth, the three of them hadn't spent as much time together after that. But she'd seemed to fall into the role of military wife with the ease and grace with which she did everything else. And to hear Ryan tell it, their life had been pretty damn close to idyllic.

"They provide myriad services," J.J. continued, "a lot of it generated by Wall Street. They offer travel for executives and delivery of time-sensitive documents. And with the downturn of the economy, they've also started offering high-end tours of the city."

"So what was the reason for this particular flight?"

"According to the flight manifesto, the helicopter was booked for a flight over Manhattan. Basically thirty minutes seeing the city from on high."

"I'm guessing that cost a pretty penny," Drake said, the words preceded by a low whistle.

"So what do we know about the guy who booked it?" Tyler asked.

Hannah flashed another picture up onto the screen. A middle-aged balding man with the paunch to match. "Meet Eric Wilderman."

"He's an insurance executive out of Des Moines, Iowa." Again J.J. checked her notes. "He was here for a conference and booked the tour online. We've got confirmation that he did indeed attend the conference, along with nothing suspicious in his background. Basically, just your average businessman."

"Which of course is exactly what you want when home-growing a terrorist," Tyler said.

"True enough, but this guy's jacket is clean. He was born and raised in Iowa, was a finance major at Iowa State. Married once early on, but it ended in divorce. No kids. He owns a house in the suburbs that's almost paid for. Relatively no debt. And nothing to indicate that he could be bought."

"Considering we only just found out that this might not have been an accident, you seem to know a lot about this guy." Simon wasn't sure why he'd made the statement. It was certainly something they'd have done had they been investigating from the beginning. But it somehow didn't sit right to know that J.J. was already one up on them.

"I have pretty much the same information," Hannah said, clearly following Simon's train of thought. "In fact, when we compared notes earlier, it was pretty much a draw."

"Sorry." Simon shook his head, wishing he'd just kept his mouth shut. "I didn't mean to start a pissing match."

"Look, I just hit the ground running when I got home from the hospital." She shot him a look, and he ducked his head, angry at himself for letting her get to him. "I got a call from my superiors telling me that I'd been assigned to work with you guys. They faxed me everything they had on the crash."

Simon swallowed a curse. It was bad enough that J.J. was here as a liaison, but now it looked as though she had already wormed her way into Hannah's and Avery's good graces. He knew he wasn't thinking rationally, but he didn't want his old life bleeding into his new one. And now, with her here, it was already happening.

"What about the pilot?" Harrison asked, cutting into the building tension, real or imagined.

"According to information from Aerial Manhattan," Hannah replied, "he's been an employee for just over eight years. Before that he flew Black Hawks for the army. Served in both Iraq wars, received commendations for valor and was discharged honorably."

"Super." Simon shook his head, blowing out a long breath. "So we've got Mr. Middle America as a passenger and GI Joe as the pilot. Not a lot of room to support a terrorist plot."

"But we've still got the diagram of the hospital and the map found in the middle of the Afghan mountains. In what we believe was a terrorist encampment funded by the Consortium. I'd say that's worth digging a little deeper," Nash said. "So, Avery, where do you want us to start?"

"Well, first off, we'll be moving headquarters to the brownstone in Manhattan."

"Beats a hotel," Drake said. "So what do you want us to do?"

"I'm thinking you, Nash, and I can help Tyler check the scene and see if there's anything the original investigators missed." Avery pushed away from the table, his gaze encompassing the entire group. "And then follow up with the FAA. They've commandeered a warehouse nearby to examine the wreckage in more detail."

"Hannah, you and Harrison will set up shop at the brownstone. The usual array of equipment. And Simon, you'll be working with Jillian."

He stood up, avoiding J.J.'s startled gaze, but relieved to see that he wasn't the only one feeling unsettled. "What do you want us to do?"

"Head to the city and start with the ME. I want to

verify that the people in the helicopter were really who we think they were. And ideally, once you've all had the chance to examine the various pieces of the puzzle, we'll have a clearer idea of what the hell happened. And, if it proves to be an act of terrorism, who was behind it."

CHAPTER 3

City Morgue, Midtown Manhattan

The crash victims had been sequestered in a separate lab at the city morgue, the idea being to keep the bodies together in one place until the autopsies and investigation had been completed. White plastic sheets had been set up around the perimeter, and though they added an antiseptic feel, the air was still permeated with the chemically infused stench of death.

In the course of his career, Simon had seen his fair share of bodies in the field. But seeing someone lying on the slab, y-shaped Frankensteinesque stitching adorning his or her chest, was more disconcerting somehow.

The bodies were on tables aligned neatly in two rows, death forced into some semblance of macabre order, several autopsies clearly in progress. In a corner, perched on a stool, a gray-headed woman with wire-rimmed glasses was multitasking, studying something underneath the lens of a microscope while eating what looked to be a pastrami sandwich.

"Sorry," the woman said, swallowing a bite of her food as they walked into the room. "I wasn't expecting you for another half hour or so." She laid the sandwich on a table and brushed the crumbs from her face. "I have to grab lunch when I can. I'm sure you understand." With an apologetic smile, she pushed off the stool and strode across the space to meet them, extending a hand. "Lydia Rochard. I've been put in charge of the autopsies."

"What's the final body count?" Simon asked after introductions had been made.

"I've got nine here. And there are two more still on the critical list at the hospital." She nodded at the bodies around her. "But obviously we're hoping this is it."

J.J. had moved to one side, her gaze locked on the body of a young woman half covered with a sheet. "I knew her," she whispered, the words more of a reflex than anything else. "She had two kids. One of them still a baby."

"Sorry," Lydia said, pulling the sheet over the woman. "I didn't realize you were acquainted with the vics. If it helps, she was caught by the helicopter's rotor. She died instantly."

J.J.'s face shuttered, and Simon laid a hand on her arm, but she pulled free, her shoulders straightening as she faced Lydia and the body. "So was that true for most of them?" She gestured toward the shrouds lining the room.

"Yes, fortunately," Lydia said. "Most of the victims were either caught directly in the path of the helicopter or sucked out of the windows. There's nothing anyone could have done," she said, her sympathetic gaze landing on J.J.

J.J. shivered, crossing her arms over her chest, no doubt remembering just how close she'd come to dying herself. Then she sucked in a breath and lifted her head, eyes clearing as she obviously pushed the memory aside. "So, have you autopsied the pilot and his passenger?"

"I started on them first," Lydia said as she ushered them through the plastic sheeting to the back of the room and two sequestered corpses on tables. "But I've got to tell you, there wasn't enough left to ID them visually. They were both burned pretty badly. Although the vic in the passenger seat was wearing a watch inscribed with the initials E.W."

"Eric Wilderman."

"It isn't conclusive, but it's a start," Lydia said.

The canvas-covered mounds looked innocuous enough, but Simon had seen the explosion firsthand so he had an idea of just how badly the bodies would have been disfigured. "Was there enough to get DNA?"

"Yes. And I've sent it off for verification. For obvious reasons, the specimens are a priority, and the lab is working as fast as they can, but unfortunately it still takes time."

"So which is which?" J.J. asked, her face devoid of emotion, but her fingers clenching into fists as she clearly fought against her unease.

"This was the pilot," Lydia said, tilting her head toward the closest body. She reached out and pulled the sheet back. Simon's stomach roiled, and J.J. bit back a gasp. "You want me to cover him back up?"

J.J. shook her head, her hand still covering her mouth. And Simon marveled at her strength. "So do you have a cause of death?" she asked.

"Blunt force trauma." Lydia nodded. "You can actually still see the point of impact here." She pointed to the man's skull, most of the skin burned away, and a deep indentation just above one eye socket. "I'm guessing it happened when they hit the building. He was most likely thrown against the instrument panel. Truth is I'm surprised he wasn't tossed right through the window."

"Might have saved his life," Simon mused, hoping the poor bastard hadn't suffered too much.

"Not likely," Lydia said.

"So he died instantly?" J.J. asked.

"Unfortunately, no. There was evidence of smoke in his lungs, which means he was alive when the fire started, and I understand that wasn't until sometime after the crash."

"Yeah. About fifteen minutes or so." Simon couldn't pull his eyes from the mutilated body.

"But I thought you said it was blunt force trauma?" J.J. frowned, her puzzled gaze catching Simon's.

"It was," Lydia confirmed. "Or more accurately, a brain bleed caused by blunt force trauma. When a person takes a blow to the head, the brain moves within the skull in the direction of the blow, for the most part, absorbing the shock. But if the blow is strong enough, the brain is slammed, quite literally, into the wall of the skull." She jerked her head back to demonstrate. "And then in worst-case scenarios, it rebounds off the other side." She swung her head forward. "Which causes tremendous bruising and swelling."

"Hematoma," Simon said, his eyes back on the body.

"Right. In some cases, the swelling itself can be lethal. But if the hematoma breaks or tears, then the brain is going to fill with blood. And unless there's immediate medical care, chances of survival are nil."

"But when I checked the guy, he was already dead,"

Simon said. "Before the fire started. So how did he wind up with smoke in his lungs?"

"Could be a couple of things." Lydia shrugged. "There may have been a smaller fire in the helicopter on impact. Maybe electrical. And that would be the source of the smoke. I should be able to verify that with more testing. But it's equally possible that the pilot was still alive when you checked. He'd have been unconscious and, considering the impact, quite possibly in a coma. So for all practical purposes, he'd have looked dead."

"So you're saying that if I could have gotten to him, I could have saved him?"

"Not with that kind of brain injury." She shook her head. "He was dead the moment his brain began to bleed. There's nothing you could have done."

"But he was in the middle of a hospital," J.J. whispered to no one in particular, the horror in her voice reaching something deep inside him.

"Doesn't matter. He didn't have a chance." Lydia reached out to cover him up. "Sometimes there's just nothing we can do."

"Did the autopsy show any signs of a struggle?" Simon asked, already pretty sure he knew the answer. "We think it's possible that his passenger forced him to crash the helicopter."

"If that's the case, then I think maybe you have it backward," Lydia said, moving over to the other body. "If there was coercion involved, I'd say it was this guy that was on the wrong end of that stick."

"I don't understand," J.J. said, her confusion mirroring his own.

"It's pretty straightforward," Lydia said, pulling back

the sheet to reveal an equally mutilated body. "I've got postmortem bruising consistent with his position during the crash. And look at these gashes," she pointed to a portion of the man's arm that was relatively unburned, "there's no sign of blood loss. Bottom line, this guy was already dead when the helicopter slammed into the hospital."

"Son of a bitch," Simon said. "That sure as hell changes the game. Looks like GI Joe might not have been as red, white, and blue as we were led to believe."

Although Jillian had flown in helicopters as part of her training at Homeland Security, she'd never actually been to a heliport. Of course she'd seen this particular one in many movies, and in truth, it looked pretty much the same in person as it did on the big screen. A giant L-shaped slab of concrete jutted out into the mouth of the East River, fronted by a parking lot and a two-story building just off the FDR.

She and Simon had come to meet with Aerial Manhattan's owner about their newest discoveries concerning the crash, in particular any insight he might have into Nicolas Essex, the pilot. Something that might point to the man's involvement with what now appeared to be a deliberate assault on the hospital. Drake Flynn was on his way to Essex's apartment with the same goal. Hopefully, between the three of them, they'd hit pay dirt.

The families of the people lying in the morgue deserved answers. And the first step was to find out what role Nicolas Essex had played in all of this. The wind off the river was brisk, and Jillian grabbed the end of her ponytail to keep her hair out of her face as they walked toward the heliport offices. Definite downside to long hair. She'd considered cutting it when she'd taken the job with Homeland Security. One more way to make herself into someone new. But in the end, she'd settled for pulling it back.

Once, a long time ago, Simon had teased her that it was her crowning glory. She'd held the compliment close long after he'd stopped being a permanent fixture in her life. Maybe because no one else had ever said anything like that to her before. Or maybe because she was a glutton for self-flagellation.

She shook her head, pushing aside her thoughts. She wasn't going to let him get to her. Not now. Not after fighting so hard to get to this point. Simon represented everything that she'd sworn to walk away from. And she sure as hell wasn't going to let go of everything she'd gained for the faded memory of a man who'd walked out of her life without looking back. This was just business. Or maybe it was some kind of cosmic test. Either way, she was determined to get through it without letting the past rear its ugly head.

"So what's the director's name again?" Simon asked, his voice cutting through her thoughts.

"Alan Neiman," she said, checking her iPad for verification. "He founded the company. He grew up in Flatbush. Never went to college. Was drafted and did a couple tours in Vietnam, then he was stationed stateside until he retired and founded Aerial Manhattan."

"And they're headquartered out of here?" Simon held the door open as they stepped into the lobby of the building, a sign posted on the wall directing them to a suite in the back.

"No," Jillian shook her head, still reading on her tablet. "Their main offices are in Brooklyn. But this is where most of their flights originate, so they keep an office here as well. The manager is actually Neiman's son. Gideon."

"And I'm guessing you have a dossier on him as well." Simon grinned as they stopped outside the doors leading to Aerial Manhattan.

"I do," she acknowledged, closing the cover on the iPad, "but I can tell you right now that it's pretty uninteresting. Started with Aerial out of college, worked his way up to running the heliport office. Been with the company almost eleven years. No record and nothing that would flag him as a person of interest."

"All right, then, let's do this," Simon said, his fingers cupping her elbow, the warmth sending a fission of electricity pulsing through her, his nearness making her shiver in anticipation of something that could never— *would never*—be.

God, she was a fool. One night out of her life. One stupid, incredible night, and she'd given her heart to a man who didn't want it. And to make it all the more reprehensible, she'd turned around and married his best friend. A man whose anger and jealousy had destroyed any chance they might have had at happiness.

It wasn't Simon's fault. Intellectually she knew that. But she'd also been devastated when he hadn't come to her rescue. As always, in the end, he'd chosen Ryan. And now . . . now she was having trouble just standing close to him, the memories, both good and bad, threatening to tear her apart.

Inside the office, he let go of her arm, and she forced her thoughts away from the past. A man rose from behind a desk, identifying himself as Gideon Neiman. After introductions, he ushered them into a small conference room. The man standing at the far end of the room turned immediately, and Jillian recognized Gideon's father, Alan, from the photo in their file.

"I appreciate your meeting with us on such short notice," Simon said, as they all took seats around the table, Neiman at the head, his son on his right.

"I'm happy to do it," Neiman replied. "Although I'm not sure what else we can tell you. We've both been interviewed by the NYPD and the FBI, as well as having the FAA hovering—excuse the pun—at every turn. I'm afraid there's nothing new to offer."

"We're not part of the original investigation," Jillian said, opening her iPad to her notes.

"I don't understand." Gideon frowned, shooting a look at his father. "I thought this had been deemed an accident."

"Actually, we're taking a second look at that," Simon said, leaning back as he studied the two men. "There have been some developments that are calling the original determination into question."

"What kind of developments?" the older Neiman asked.

"Most of it is need to know, unfortunately." Jillian smiled. "But we're hoping you won't mind going over a few things again with us."

"Should I be calling a lawyer?" Gideon asked, reaching into his pocket for his cellphone.

"I don't see why," Simon answered with a frown. "Unless, of course, you have something to hide."

Gideon opened his mouth to respond, but Jillian waved him off. "There's nothing to be concerned about, I

promise. We're not interested in either of you. Or, as far
as we know, your company. We're actually here to talk
about Nicolas Essex."

"Nicky?" Gideon said, his surprise evident. "Surely
you don't believe he's involved with this? I've known him
since I was a kid."

"We have some evidence that seems to suggest that
Mr. Essex may have been involved in what happened."

"I don't believe it," Alan said, his eyes narrowing.
"There's no way Nicky would be involved in anything
that even remotely resembled treason. If he had a hand in
the crash then I can assure you it was an accident."

"But he was a seasoned pilot, Mr. Neiman," Jillian
said, her gaze on the older man. "And there was nothing
about the weather or, according to your statement to the
police, the helicopter that would have been problematic.
Add that to our information and we come full circle back
to Mr. Essex."

"Captain Essex," Neiman corrected, his gaze shrewd.
"And I can guarantee you the boy had nothing to do with
this. His father and I fought in 'Nam together. Hell, I
practically raised him. Not to mention the fact that he's a
decorated war hero."

Jillian swallowed, fighting her own emotions. In her
experience, decorated war heroes weren't always what
they seemed to be. "So you've never had any reason to
be concerned about Captain Essex's state of mind?" she
asked, focusing on the conversation at hand. "No signs of
uncontrolled anger, detachment, loss of interest—"

"I'm more than aware of the symptoms of PTSD, Ms.
Montgomery," Neiman said. "And I can tell you unequiv-
ocally that Nicky didn't suffer from it."

"I agree," Gideon said. "We were close. I'd have noticed if something was wrong."

"What about the day of the crash? Anything happen that was out of the ordinary?"

"No." Gideon shook his head, his gaze cutting to his father's. "But I told you, I've already been over all of this."

"So humor us," Simon said. "We wouldn't be bothering you if we didn't think it was important."

"It was a routine day." Gideon sat back, blowing out a breath. "I came in around nine. Nicky was already here."

"And it's just the two of you?"

"Usually. Although I have an assistant that comes in three days a week. But she wasn't there that day."

"What about mechanics?" Simon asked.

"We share them with the others who use the heliport. They're actually employees of the city. It's regulation." The elder Neiman shrugged. "I've got my own mechanics, of course, but they don't handle routine maintenance. And there was no one here the day the helicopter crashed. Just my son and Nicky."

"And everything seemed normal?"

"Yeah," Gideon said. "Nicky took a couple of Wall Street bigwigs for a run in the morning, and then he had the tour in the afternoon."

"With Eric Wilderman."

"Right." Gideon nodded. "I checked him in myself. And if you ask me, he's the one you should be looking at."

"Is there something specific that makes you say that?" Simon asked.

"No. Just that the little guy seemed off somehow. I don't know. It's not something you can put into words."

"But there wasn't anything about that in the original

report," Simon prompted, his brows drawn together in a frown.

"No one asked. I didn't even think about it, really. I mean, they were so sure it was an accident."

"You said Wilderman was little. What exactly did you mean by that?" Jillian asked, pulling Eric Wilderman's photo up on her iPad.

"Just what I said. The guy was real small. Five-five max."

"And just to be clear, you're referring to Eric Wilderman, right?"

"Yes," Gideon said, confusion playing across his face. "Eric Wilderman, the man who signed up for the tour." Simon leaned forward, clearly at a loss as well.

"Can you give me a description?" Jillian said, looking down at Mr. Wilderman's photo, his balding pate glistening in the sunlight.

"Um, he was short. Like I said. And kind of wiry." Gideon looked over to his father, who shrugged. Gideon sighed and then scrunched up his face as he tried to remember. "He had dark hair. Cropped short. But not like a buzz cut. And more than a few days' growth on his face, but it wasn't a full beard. More like he just hadn't shaved in a while."

"What about ethnicity? White, Asian, Latino?"

"I don't know. Nothing really. I mean, I guess, white. He was definitely American, complete with a midwestern nasal drawl."

"How about his clothes?" she prompted, Simon showing signs of comprehension now.

"Expensive. The suit had to have cost a couple thousand. And the shoes. Oh, and there was a watch. A Rolex or something like it. It was big and definitely expensive. I remember being surprised. I mean he was an insurance salesman, right?" He shot an apologetic look at his dad, and J.J. lifted the iPad so that they could all see it.

"Is this the guy?" she asked.

"No. He didn't look anything at all like that. Who is that?"

"Eric Wilderman," Jillian said, alarm bells ringing. "No one showed you this photograph, I take it?"

"Like I said"—this from the elder Neiman—"everyone thought it was an accident. They were far more interested in our maintenance records."

"Did you confirm his identification?" Simon asked.

"Yes, of course," Gideon said, looking something close to befuddled. "I have to for insurance purposes. I always check the driver's license. I've got the form right here." He reached over to a pile of papers sitting in front of his father, and, after rifling through a file, handed Jillian a handwritten form.

She quickly checked the information against the file she had on Wilderman, aware that tension was rising as the men awaited her response. "It matches what we've got for him. The address, the phone numbers. Even the license number is the same. At least on paper it was Wilderman."

"So you actually saw the driver's license, right?" Simon asked Gideon.

He nodded. "Absolutely. And I can promise you the photo was of the guy I described. The one standing in my office. Not the one in your photo."

There was a moment of silence as everyone digested this newest information.

"What about interaction between Essex and Wilderman?" Simon asked finally. "Did they seem to know each other?"

"Not from what I could see," Gideon said. "But I wasn't with them very long. I took Wilderman, or whoever he was, out to the helipad and introduced him to Nicky, but then I got a call so I left."

"Everything seem normal at takeoff?" Simon continued to probe.

"Yeah, nothing out of the ordinary...except," Gideon paused, clearly considering his words, "there was a glitch in communications, but it was only for a second or so. I didn't really think anything of it. I mean they took off okay, and everything seemed fine until we got the call about the crash." He shrugged, looking over at his father, who reached out to squeeze his arm.

"It's fine, son," Neiman said. "No one is questioning your part in this. They're just trying to understand what happened."

Jillian looked to Simon, who nodded at the two men reassuringly. "We appreciate your cooperation," he said, pushing to his feet. "And we'll get back to you if we need anything else."

"You're thinking that this man, whoever he was, might have been behind the crash," the older Neiman said, his gaze assessing.

"It's possible." Simon shrugged. "It's certainly something we'll be looking into, you can rest assured."

"And Nicky?" Gideon asked. "Are you convinced now that he's innocent?"

"At this point, we can't rule anyone out."

CHAPTER 4

You don't really consider the Neimans suspect, do you?" J.J. asked as they walked toward the front desk of Eric Wilderman's hotel.

"I meant what I said. We can't rule anyone out. But no, I don't actually think they were involved."

"And the captain?"

"Him, I haven't ruled out," Simon said, with a shrug. "But the switched ID for Wilderman seems like the bigger red flag of the two."

"But if he was dead at takeoff?" J.J. queried.

"I know. None of it really makes any sense. Seems like every answer only creates more questions."

"Well, maybe Drake is having more luck."

They stopped in front of the desk, flashed J.J's ID, and waited for the manager.

"So does it feel odd?" J.J. asked, shooting a sideways glance in his direction. "Working together like this, I mean?"

"I suppose it's a little weird," Simon admitted, drumming his fingers on the counter. Hell, of course it was weird, fucking crazy weird. Half of him wanted to fall prostrate at her feet, apologizing for all the pain he'd caused, and the other half wanted to take her into his arms and kiss her until neither of them could feel anything but each other. But he wasn't about to admit either one. "But it's not like this is the first time we've been joined at the hip."

"Yes, but this is different," she pressed.

"You mean because Ryan isn't here." The words came out of their own accord, and a shadow flashed across her face. He cursed himself for being so insensitive. Of course, she missed Ryan. Hell, he did, too. It was bad enough that he'd played a role in her husband's death. The least he could do was try not to remind her of the fact.

"There is that," she said, her voice quiet, her expression indecipherable. "But I was going to say that, in college when we were all so close, the only thing we were worried about was finding the cheapest place to buy beer. Now we're chasing terrorists."

"Slightly more risk, I suppose." Simon grinned. "But some of those bars were pretty dicey, if I'm remembering right."

She smiled, the gesture not quite reaching her eyes, and he felt another wave of guilt.

"You never did say how you got into this game," he asked. "I mean, the last time I saw you, you were—"

"A grieving widow?" She tilted her head, the movement familiar as her hair draped over her shoulder. "Let's just say I needed to be my own hero. I'd followed in Ryan's and your footsteps for too damn long. It was time to stand on my own two feet. Make my own move."

"Yes, but Homeland Security?" He frowned.

"Maybe I just figured what was good for the gander..."
She shrugged. "Why? You don't think I'm up to it?"

He remembered a clear summer day. The three of
them at the lake, perched high up on a cliffside. He and
Ryan had been debating the best place to launch into the
lake. Arguing about it, actually. J.J. had just laughed at
them and jumped. Fearless. As always.

"No." He shook his head, fighting the urge to reach for
her, angry at himself for having the need. "I've always
thought you could do anything you set your mind to."

Their gazes met and held for a moment, and Simon
almost forgot to breathe.

In front of them, a tall, thin man with a scraggly goa-
tee approached the desk, clearing his throat to announce
himself, his face composed but his eyes sparking with
curiosity. Bastard clearly saw way too much. "I understand you have questions about one of our guests?" he
asked.

"Yeah," Simon said, still reeling from something he
couldn't even put a name to. Pushing aside his tumbling
thoughts, he glanced down at the man's nametag. "We're
trying to verify that Eric Wilderman is, in fact, a guest at
your hotel, Mr. Kent."

J.J. smiled, extending the wallet with her credentials,
her hand trembling slightly. At least he wasn't alone in his
confusion. Kent blinked once as he examined them and
then handed them back with a flourish.

"According to our records," the manager said, glancing down at a computer screen embedded in the desk,
"Mr. Wilderman is still registered. He checked in a week
ago, for the National Insurance Convention."

"But the convention ended three days ago, correct?" J.J. asked, glancing down to check her notes.

"Yes," the man acknowledged, "but the rate is good a week before and after, as long as the days are an add-on to the convention itself. New York is a primary tourist destination, and we find it's more enticing to people if we allow them to stay beyond their conferences."

"And were you, by any chance, the one to check Mr. Wilderman in?" Simon asked.

"No." Kent shook his head. "According to the record, it was Shannon Gates. Shannon?" The manager called over to a red-headed woman at the next terminal. "Can you spare a moment?"

She nodded, clicked something on her computer, and then turned her attention to the three of them.

"These people are with Homeland Security." For obvious reasons, Simon wasn't able to use his own credentials. Since A-Tac, for all practical purposes, didn't actually exist, he was allowing J.J. to take the lead, using her credentials as cover. "And they're investigating, Mr. Wilderman, one of our guests."

Fear flittered across the woman's face. "Should I be concerned?"

"No." J.J.'s voice was reassuring, and the woman relaxed. "We're just hoping you can identify a photograph for us." She laid her iPad on the desk. "Is this the man?"

Shannon studied it for a moment and then sighed. "I think I remember him. But you have to understand that we have so many people coming through here. It's hard to remember anyone specifically."

"Maybe you could check with the convention people,"

Kent offered. "The organizers are still here. They're packing things up. In fact, the guy in charge is standing over there by that table." He gestured toward a man in jeans and a sweatshirt.

"Thank you." J.J. smiled. "You've been most helpful."

"But before we go, we're also going to need to check Mr. Wilderman's room," Simon said. "Which means we'll need a key."

Shannon shot a look at her boss, who was already shaking his head. "I'm afraid that's simply not possible. We take our guests' security very seriously."

"Even after they're dead?" J.J. asked, her tone brooking no argument.

"Oh, dear. You're saying that Mr. Wilderman is... well, that does change things, I suppose," Kent said, swallowing uncomfortably.

"If there's a problem with your superiors, they can take it up with mine." J.J. leaned forward, tilting her head provocatively as she held Kent's gaze. "I promise I'll make sure they know you considered every option." She smiled at him then, her blue eyes conspiratorial. "I can't tell you how much your help means to me."

There was a beat, and Kent swallowed again. J.J.'s smile widened, and, having been on the receiving end of her beguiling entreaties many times, Simon knew that the manager was a goner.

Kent sighed and then nodded at Shannon, his gaze still locked on J.J. The other woman slid a card through the machine and handed it to him. He in turn handed it over to J.J., his fingers lingering over the transfer. Simon bit back a smile as the two of them headed over to the table where the insurance guy was packing boxes.

"I should have known you'd pull out the big guns," he said when they were out of earshot.

"What can I say? It was for a good cause." She grinned, and for a moment, it actually seemed like old times.

"No kidding."

J.J. shrugged, her smile fading as they approached the man at the table, and the sense of camaraderie vanished. They quickly introduced themselves. The man identified himself as Brian Childs, the executive director for the insurance organization sponsoring the convention.

"We already know that Mr. Wilderman was registered for the convention," J.J. said. "What we need now is verification that this is him." She held out the photo on her iPad. "We figured you might be able to ID him for us."

"Sure," Childs said. "That's definitely Eric. We've know each other for years."

"And you saw him here at the convention?" Simon asked.

"Absolutely. I had drinks with him on the first night." The man frowned, his expression confused. "Is Eric in some kind of trouble?"

"We're just looking into some anomalies. Nothing for you to be concerned about," J.J. responded, her tone dismissive. "Did you spend any more time with Mr. Wilderman?"

"No." Childs shook his head. "I've been running like crazy all week. I saw him across the room a couple of times. But I'm afraid that's it." A woman walked up with a teetering stack of boxes. "If that's all?" he asked, his attention already turning to his colleague.

J.J. nodded, and they walked toward the elevator bank. "So at least we know that the real Wilderman was at the hotel," she said as they stepped into an open car.

"But if he was here, who the hell was at the heliport? And where is Mr. Wilderman now?"

"With any luck," J.J. said, "in his room. Although if he was involved in all of this, I figure that's pretty unlikely."

"Agreed." Simon frowned as the two of them stared at the changing numbers over the door. The smell of J.J.'s perfume filled the elevator, the sharp, sweet scent taking him back. It had all seemed so simple then. The three of them against the world. And then... hell, he wasn't going to let himself go there. This was about business. The past was just that—past.

The doors slid open, and they stepped out onto the fifth floor, J.J. thankfully oblivious to the turn of his thoughts. They walked in silence as they made their way down the hallway, slowing as they reached Wilderman's door.

"So this is it," she said. "How do you want to handle it?"

Simon pulled out his gun. "You armed?"

She shook her head.

He swallowed a grunt of dismay. "But you know how to handle a weapon?"

"I've been trained. I've just never had any reason to carry a gun. Until the other day, my disaster scenarios were just drills."

"Well, you need to start carrying one now." Simon reached down for the gun he carried at his ankle. "Until then, take this." He held it out, and to her credit, she took it without hesitation, checking the magazine and releasing the safety. "I'm going to knock, and I want you to identify yourself as housekeeping."

"Packing heat," she added, the corners of her mouth tilting up into another smile.

"He won't know that from your voice." Simon returned the smile and then reached out to knock, the sound seeming overly loud in the quiet hallway.

"Housekeeping," J.J. called. There was no answer, so Simon knocked again. "I don't think there's anyone here," she said, lowering her weapon as Simon slid the key down the lock, his gun still at the ready. Motioning her to stay behind him, he opened the door and swung inside, his gaze moving over the empty room.

"Looks clear," he called as he moved to check the closet and bathroom, then lowered his gun.

"I was right," J.J. said. "He's gone."

"At least for now. But there's still luggage. Most of it unpacked."

"So maybe he wanted us to believe he hadn't left." J.J. bent to look through the open suitcase.

"Or maybe he's just out in the city somewhere playing tourist. Totally oblivious to the fact that someone has been using his name."

"Except that they had his watch." J.J. frowned, biting her lower lip. It was a habit he remembered well. Something she did when she was thinking. "Remember the coroner said that it had his initials."

"Could have been a plant," Simon said, rifling through the clothes hanging in the closet. "Neiman also said that the guy was wearing an expensive suit. Most of this stuff looks like it was bought right off the rack."

"In the old days, you wouldn't have known Armani from Men's Wearhouse." She looked up at him, her gaze teasing.

"I still don't." He laughed. "But the label on this sports coat says Sears. And even I know that doesn't qualify as high-end."

"So we've got a guy who presents himself as Wilderman but doesn't actually make an effort to look like the guy. Physically or economically. Doesn't make a lot of sense."

"Probably didn't have to." Simon shrugged as he walked over to check out the nightstand. "I mean, Neiman only has to verify the identity of his passengers. If there's nothing suspicious, he'd certainly have no reason to dig further."

"I suppose you're right," J.J. said. "And since most of Neiman's customers are well-heeled, our pseudo-Wilderman would have wanted to look the part. Maybe you're right, and the real Wilderman was clueless. His computer is still here." She motioned to a laptop sitting open on the room's small desk.

"Doesn't make sense that he'd have left it behind if he was trying to hide something."

"Unless it was on purpose," she said as she hit a button to turn it on. The machine whirred to life and then stopped, presenting the blue screen of death. "What the hell?" She frowned at the screen and hit one key and then another. "There's nothing here. This machine has been wiped clean."

Simon walked over to have a look. "Well that's weird."

"Yeah, and, unfortunately, it puts the spotlight clearly back on the possibility that Wilderman had some kind of active role in all of this."

"Didn't you say that he booked the tour online?" Simon asked.

"Right. Your guy, Harrison, was working to try to trace it back to an IP. But I'm guessing we're looking at it."

"Wouldn't it be easier to take the thing with you rather than go to the trouble of wiping the hard drive and leaving it behind?"

"Maybe Wilderman's trying to mess with our heads," she said, her attention shifting to something by the edge of the bed.

"Well, it's working." Simon walked over to the window and pushed back the draperies to look out the window. "Not exactly a room with a view." Directly across the way, maybe seven or eight feet away, was a crumbling brick wall. And below, a rubbish-strewn walkway complete with an overloaded Dumpster directly beneath the window.

"Simon," J.J. said, pulling his attention back to the room. "Come look at this."

He crossed over to where she was kneeling beside the bed, using a hotel pen to lift the nap of the carpet. "What have you got?" he asked, bending down for a better look.

"I'm pretty sure it's blood," she said. "And it looks like there might be more over there." She nodded toward the floor by the window and a small brown stain on the carpet.

"Son of a bitch," he mumbled as he knelt to examine the new discovery. "I think you're right." Frowning, he stood up, examining the window more carefully. "There's another spot here on the curtains."

She joined him, pulling out the fabric for closer inspection. "There's more here." She pointed to a spot higher up. "But there's no cast-off. And nothing to indicate a struggle. So what the hell happened?"

"God's truth, it could be from anyone," Simon said. "I mean, we have no way of knowing how old it is. Or even if it is, in fact, blood."

"Yes, but look at the window. It's unlatched. And unless I'm seeing things, there's another stain here on the sill." She pointed to a streak of what appeared to be dried blood.

Simon looked down at the Dumpster, his mind suddenly moving into high gear. "We need to check the passageway between the buildings."

"I'm not following," she said, sliding open the window and leaning out for a better view below.

"I'm saying that if I had a dead body in a hotel room and a Dumpster right beneath the window..." he trailed off as she pulled back inside, spinning around to face him.

"You think Wilderman, the *real* Wilderman, is down there? In the Dumpster?"

The walkway between the hotel and the building next door smelled like dead fish... or something even worse. Trash was scattered everywhere, a derelict cardboard box pushed behind an empty crate a sign of someone's home away from home. Jillian could hear rustling in the refuse as they moved. Rats, most likely. She suppressed a shudder, following Simon as they made their way toward the Dumpster.

As they drew nearer, Simon waved her back, and despite being annoyed at his efforts to protect her, she had to admit that she was grateful for the reprieve. Uncovering the body of a missing man wasn't exactly on her list of fun-time activities. Still, she'd meant what she'd said earlier—she'd damn well play her own hero.

And it was that thought that spurred her forward.

"So, any sign of him?" she asked, fervently hoping for a negative answer.

"Unfortunately, yeah," Simon said, his mouth tightening. "And it's not pretty."

She took a step backward, and then forced herself to advance again, rising on her tiptoes to see inside. Simon was right. The bin was half covered, which had shielded their view from above, but from this angle, the man was in plain sight, his body sprawled across the Dumpster, eyes open.

"Looks like a single shot to the head," Simon said, pointing to a black ringed hole near Wilderman's temple. "Execution style. I'm guessing, from the size of the hole, it was small-caliber gun. So either he knew his killer, or the guy was a pro. Either way the killer knew what he was doing."

"Then why not dispose of the body in a less public place?"

"What's easier than a Dumpster? The trash is emptied through a chute." He pointed to the metal-rimmed opening through the brick wall. "So no one from the hotel is going to be checking. There's no traffic in this passageway, except maybe for the homeless, and even if they found him, they most likely wouldn't have called it in. And the thing is emptied mechanically, probably twice a week."

"Which means he hasn't been dead more than a few days."

"Seems probable, but the ME will be able to narrow that down."

"So Wilderman would have ended up in a landfill somewhere. But still, there was at least a small chance someone would find him and call the authorities."

"Maybe they didn't care. Or maybe they figured that,

by the time someone found him, it would have been harder to identify him." Using a stick, Simon carefully lifted one of Wilderman's hands.

"Oh, God." Jillian fought for control as her stomach threatened revolt. The ends of the man's fingers were ragged and torn, bite marks already obscuring his prints.

"Between the rats and decomp, IDing him would have been difficult at best. Especially if no one was looking for the guy."

"But surely..." she started, and then stopped, remembering Wilderman's dossier. "He didn't have any family." She blew out a breath, her eyes falling to the dead man's face. "There was no one to miss him."

"Makes him an ideal target." Simon shrugged.

"So, what, you think that someone used his computer to book the helicopter trip, and then stole his identity to make the flight? But that doesn't fit with the idea that Captain Essex was flying the helicopter and that the fake Wilderman was already dead."

"I'll admit there are a hell of a lot of unanswered questions. But there's no doubt that this is Wilderman. And the fact that he's dead seems to support the idea that he's involved somehow."

Jillian nodded and pushed up for a closer look, steeling herself as she studied the body. "Look at his wrist," she said, nodding toward Wilderman's left arm. "There's a tan line."

Simon moved closer, squinting as his gaze followed hers. "From a watch. I'll be damned. So the watch we found was probably his."

"Except that it doesn't quite jibe with the clothes from Sears." Jillian frowned.

"So maybe it was a gift. None of this really makes any sense."

"So what do we do now?" she asked.

"We call in backup and then meet with the team to regroup."

CHAPTER 5

Köln, Germany

B oss, we've got a problem."
  Michael Brecht looked up from the papers he'd
been studying, a chill of premonition running down his
spine. "A-Tac."

"Yes." Gregor nodded, his craggy face impassive. He'd
been working as Michael's right-hand man since Alain
DuBois's unfortunate accident. Wrong place. Wrong
time. Too much information. It was the risk that came
with working for the Consortium. "They're starting to put
the pieces together."

"I thought you told me that we'd covered our tracks.
Left nothing to find." Even as he said the words, he knew
that in the face of Solomon and his relentless band of
legitimized thugs there was no such thing.

"I did. And at the time I believed it." Gregor crossed
his arms as he dropped down into the chair opposite
Michael's. "The crash was ruled an accident. But we had

no way of knowing that there'd be an A-Tac operative on site. It was pure coincidence."

"There is no such thing." Michael grabbed the rubber ball lying on top of the desk, squeezing as he tried to manage his anger. It always came back to A-Tac. And Solomon. "They must have found something in Afghanistan."

"But Kamaal sent in people to sanitize before they arrived. There shouldn't have been anything to find except for the things we'd intended."

"Well, obviously there was something more. And now, as you so succinctly put it, they're assembling the pieces. It won't be long before they confirm that the crash wasn't an accident. Which means we need to rethink our next step."

"You want to call it off?" Gregor asked, his gaze unflinching. "In light of everything that's happened, maybe it would be for the best."

"For whom?" Michael asked. "Certainly not the Consortium, and therefore, by definition, for you or for me. We've spent too much time to abandon our plans now. We'll just have to revise them a bit. Improvise."

"And do what exactly?" Gregor asked.

Michael's fingers tightened around the little ball. "Set it up so that we can use A-Tac to make the brass in Manhattan believe one thing is another." Michael opened his hand, the ball rolling across the desk and onto the floor. "They'll think they've stopped us, and we'll be back on track with no one the wiser."

"Okay, so we've got a dead guy who books a flight over Manhattan and winds up in a Dumpster outside his hotel with a single shot to the head." Simon paced nervously across the small office in the back of the FAA-procured warehouse where Tyler and her bomb team were going over the debris from the crash.

Jillian's nerves were strung almost as tightly. In a matter of days, she'd seen more dead bodies than most people saw in a lifetime. And yet somehow, Wilderman's had been the worst. She hadn't even known the guy, but something in the callous way he'd been discarded struck a chord deep inside her. Still, despite the grisly discovery, they were no closer to putting the pieces of the puzzle together.

Which was why they were here now, comparing notes—trying to find the pattern in all of this. Everyone was present except Drake, who was on his way, and Nash and Tyler, who were still in the main room of the warehouse examining fragments from the helicopter.

"And we have another guy," Avery said, continuing Simon's thought, "pretending to be Wilderman, who winds up dead before the helicopter even takes off."

"Which leaves us with Captain America who, for reasons clear only to him, conceivably kills our impostor and then rams his chopper into the hospital." Simon stopped moving for a moment, the crease between his eyes evidence of his frustration.

He looked older and more battle-weary than she remembered. And he was clearly favoring his leg. Although he made every attempt to hide the fact. There was a part of her that wanted to reach out—to comfort him, to let him know that he wasn't alone. But the days when she'd been close enough to get past his barriers were long gone. He'd torpedoed any chance the two of them had ever had. Now if only her heart would accept the fact.

"Well, if that's true," Simon allowed, pulling her attention back to the conversation at hand, "I'm thinking that he might have been the one who killed Wilderman. He'd have been strong enough to have dumped the body into the bin. And if they were really working together, then Wilderman probably wouldn't have expected Captain Essex to take him out."

"Well, I did manage to trace the initial reservation back to an IP, and it definitely was Wilderman's," Harrison said. "But it's easy enough to clone an address. So it's still possible that the original flight reservation wasn't actually made from his computer."

"I don't suppose there's any chance you can work your magic on Wilderman's computer?" Jillian asked Harrison.

"Absolutely," Hannah answered for him with a smile. "Harrison is pretty good at finding something in the middle of what looks like nothing."

"It just takes a little time." Harrison grinned, his gaze landing on Hannah, the love there so palpable that Jillian felt a pang of longing. "But I'm not sure that knowing for certain is going to tell us anything. Even if it was his computer, it's still possible that someone else was using it, with or without his knowledge."

"So we've got nothing." Jillian shook her head, trying to make sense out of the tangled evidence they'd accumulated.

"Well, there is the dead man," Simon reminded her.

"Three actually," Avery added. "Two of them named Wilderman."

"But if both of the Wildermans were killed around the time of the crash, then why the ruse in the first place?" Harrison asked.

"Seems like no matter how you look at it, Essex is the key."

"If he is, then he's managed to keep all signs of it out of his life," Drake said as he strode into the room, Nash following behind him, talking on his cellphone. "I've been over his place with a fine-tooth comb, and there's nothing. From what I could gather, the man was well respected and liked. He doesn't have debts. There's no sign of any kind of radical leanings in his background. Hell, he was a bona fide military hero."

Jillian's thoughts immediately jumped to Ryan. If she'd learned anything, it was that appearances were often deceiving.

"Maybe it wasn't terrorism. Maybe it was suicide?" Hannah suggested.

"It's a valid suggestion, except when you add in the switcheroo with the Wildermans," Drake said.

"I agree," Simon added. "Seems more likely that Essex was working with the real Wilderman. What if Essex was planning to walk out of the crash alive and hang everything on the other guy in the helicopter? Maybe killing Wilderman was an attempt to tie up loose ends. Leave Essex as the sole survivor."

"Nice theory," Tyler said, appearing in the doorway, carrying something in her hand, "except that I found evidence of a bomb planted on board the helicopter." She tossed a charred metal tube on the table, a filament wire extending from one end. "I found pieces of the casing and wiring, and it looks to me like it was rigged to go off immediately after the crash."

"So, what? You think it was an effort to achieve maximum damage?" Jillian asked.

"Not likely," Tyler said, shaking her head. "The charge was a small one. Basically a moderately sophisticated version of a pipe bomb. So I'm guessing it was meant to take out what was left of the helicopter. Along with anyone inside."

"They wanted to destroy the evidence." Avery leaned back in his chair, eyes narrowed in thought.

"And make sure everyone in the chopper was dead," Drake added.

"Meaning, one way or another, no one was supposed to come out of the crash alive," Harrison said.

"Exactly," Tyler concurred. "So while it's still possible that Essex planned to survive, that would have to mean that he didn't know the device was there."

"Which would make him a pawn in all of this." Simon crossed his arms over his chest, leaning against one corner of the table.

"Except that he was flying the helicopter," Jillian reminded them.

"Only it turns out that he wasn't," Nash said, stepping into the room as he pocketed his cell. "That was the ME. She got the DNA results. And the guy flying the helicopter wasn't Essex."

"So we've got two people masquerading as someone they're not?" Drake asked, his confusion mirrored on everyone else's faces.

"Actually, no." Nash shook his head. "Just the one. Turns out the body in the back of the chopper was Essex. He was dead before the helicopter ever left the ground. The watch was a plant. Meant to throw everyone off. Had the crash been deemed an accident, I doubt anyone would have dug any deeper."

"And if we hadn't found the notebook in Afghanistan, that's exactly what would have happened," Avery said.

"So the pilot was the fake-Wilderman?" Harrison asked.

"Looks that way." Nash nodded.

"Did the DNA ID him?" Tyler asked.

"Interestingly enough, we did get a hit, but I'm not sure how much help it'll be. Guy was ex-Army."

"Let me guess, another bona fide hero?" Jillian hadn't meant to say the words out loud, but fortunately no one, not even Simon, had a clue to her real meaning.

"Actually, no," Tyler said. "Dishonorably discharged. But he had experience flying a chopper, which explains a lot. He seemed to attract trouble. He's got a rap sheet a mile long, but no known affiliations with terrorist organizations. My guess is that he was simply a hired gun."

"So what was his name?" Hannah asked, already pulling out her tablet.

"Mason Dearborn."

"Seems to me there has to be more to it than that," Drake observed. "I mean, I understand wanting to use someone who couldn't be tracked back to the source, but this was basically a suicide mission, so, if the guy wasn't a zealot, then how exactly did they convince him to fly the bird?"

"Maybe we were right the first time," Jillian said, "and he thought he was going to walk out alive. Although now, considering all the body switching, it sounds a little far-fetched."

"You're sure there were no known connections to terrorists?" Avery asked. "Maybe the guy's a recent convert."

"I'm searching now," Hannah nodded. "But so far, I'm not finding anything beyond the usual. Petty theft that blossomed into armed robbery. Possession of a controlled substance. Crystal meth. He's been in jail a couple of times, but always manages to get out on parole."

"Looks like he might have been involved in the illegal sale of firearms at one point," Harrison said, hitting a key on his laptop. "Here's his picture." He turned it around so that everyone could see. The man was young, not more than twenty. Dark hair, and as described by the Neimans, definitely on the short side.

"When he was running guns, was he working on his own or maybe in conjunction with someone else?" Avery asked.

"Hang on a minute," Hannah said, "I'm looking." She scrolled through the document on her tablet and then nodded in satisfaction. "According to one of the original arrest reports from the gun-running charge, there was speculation that Mason was working for Emmanuel Rivon."

"Well, there's a nasty little memory." Nash's face tightened with anger.

"Who is Emmanuel Rivon?" Jillian asked.

"A low-life scumbag that almost took out Annie," Drake said, his eyes narrowing with the memory. "He was a Bolivian national who operated a coffee conglomerate and used the business to cover travel in and out of questionable countries. Including Afghanistan. He was connected to several terrorist organizations."

"You said 'was,' " Jillian prompted.

"Yeah." Nash nodded. "Annie killed him. He was holding our son hostage. And as far as I'm concerned, the bastard got better than he deserved."

"You'll get no argument from me," Harrison said, "but if Hannah's right about the association, it could mean that Mason was still connected to Rivon's organization somehow."

"But you just said Rivon was dead."

"Him, yes," Hannah said, scrolling through a program on her tablet. "But not so much the organization. It's being run now by Rivon's younger brother, Emilio."

"And if Mason was working for Rivon," Harrison continued, picking up on Hannah's thoughts, "it's possible Emilio would have kept him in the loop."

"Which in turn," Hannah smiled over at Harrison, "might be the link to his becoming involved with a terrorist plot."

"So do we have an address on this guy?" Tyler asked.

"According to my sources, he's been living here in the city, on the East Side," Hannah said. "Fourteenth and Second Avenue. Near Union Square. I'm uploading the addy to your tablets now."

"Got it." Simon nodded, his smoky green eyes alight with excitement as his gaze met hers. "What do you say the two of us head over there and have a look?"

Jillian started to protest, to say that she'd be better off staying here and helping Harrison or Hannah, anything that kept her away from him and the memories of their shared past. But then his eyes flashed with something more than excitement. Something she recognized as a dare. Squaring her shoulders, she stuck out her chin.

"All right then," she said, pleased to note that her voice actually sounded almost normal, despite the butterflies in her stomach. "What are we waiting for?"

CHAPTER 6

Second Avenue at Fourteenth Street acted as a dividing line of sorts. To the east, scrubs-clad personnel worked at the long row of hospitals that stretched along First Avenue. And to the west, the jeans and T-shirt set inhabited the area surrounding Union Square, students from NYU mixing with tourists as they mingled together along the crowded streets.

Mason Dearborn's apartment was on the third floor of what had once been an elegant brownstone built sometime in the early 1900s. Unfortunately, although still well-appointed, it had been cut up into box-sized apartments somewhere along the way, the rusting metal fire escapes standing testament to the fact.

Squeezed between a bodega promising the city's best bagels and a neon-lighted Indian restaurant, the building's entrance was now an enclosed affair that had once been an open stoop. At the top of the stairs, Simon pressed the buzzer for the owner who also served as the super. They'd already tried calling several times with no response. So it wasn't all that surprising when no one answered.

"What now?" J.J. asked, crinkling her nose in distaste at the littered vestibule housing the call box. "The door is locked."

"I could probably jimmy it," Simon said, studying the ancient lock. "But it might be easier if we just wait for that guy." He nodded toward a man almost at the bottom of the inside stairs. In short order, he'd crossed the small lobby and yanked open the door without giving Simon and Jillian a second glance. "What did I tell you?" Simon grinned as he caught the door and motioned her inside.

"Smooth." She smiled up at him as they headed for the stairs, and his gut clenched, past and present blending together.

And as before, it was as if no time had passed, the two of them still in college with nothing more important to worry about than which kegger they were going to attend. Then the light shifted, and J.J. was a stranger again—Jillian. The little lines at the corners of her eyes and mouth a reflection of everything that had gone down since. With one reckless decision, he'd gotten Ryan killed and destroyed her life. It wasn't something that could be washed away by happy memories.

They climbed the stairs in silence, heading for the third floor and Dearborn's apartment. Just past the second landing, Simon's earpiece sprang to life. "You guys in yet?" Drake asked. He was positioned in the small yard behind the building at the bottom of the fire escape. Backup in case something went wrong.

"Just heading down the hall now," Simon replied as they turned into the narrow passageway. The walls were covered with pale gray paper, a fluorescent bulb at the end of the hall flickering off and on, its incessant humming filling the space.

"It's still got good bones," J.J. observed, as they came to the end of the hall, adorned with a stained-glass window.

"It must have been something before they tore it all up to make individual apartments," Simon said. "I've always wanted to fix up a place like this."

"Yeah, well, trust me," Drake's voice echoed in his ear, "remodeling isn't all it's cracked up to be." Drake and Madeline had been working hard to rebuild their house after part of it was destroyed by an explosion.

J.J. reached out to knock on the door. There was no answer.

"Any movement from your end?" Simon asked Drake.

"Nada. If there's someone in there, they're sitting tight."

"So we go in, right?" J.J. asked, already reaching for the doorknob.

"Better to check first," he said, reaching up to run his fingers around the door frame and threshold. "You never know when someone's left a little welcome gift." He stepped back, giving the door a final once-over. "Looks clear. No trip wires. It is locked but I should be able to get it open." He pulled out a small case with picks and set to work, the old lock yielding easily. "We're in."

"Nice to see our government dollars at work," J.J. said, her eyes crinkling with amusement. "I figured an ex-Navy SEAL would be more of a ram-the-door-down type."

"It's not all guts and glory," he shrugged, drawing his

gun as he pushed the door open. "Sometimes I find a more understated approach works better."

"And besides, contrary to popular belief," Drake quipped into the earpiece, "ramming a door hurts."

Moving slowly, Simon swung into the apartment, J.J. on his heels, as they checked for signs that someone was there. "Front rooms are clear," Simon called after they were sure.

"Back, too," Drake said, walking into the living room. "Fire escape led right to the kitchen window. I figured I'd be more useful up here."

"Roger that," Simon said, eyes still on the room. "Doesn't look like anyone's been here recently."

"Well I suppose that depends on how you define 'anyone.'" Jillian bent to scoop up a black and white cat who was peeking out from behind a potted plant. "This little guy is definitely in residence." The cat purred as J.J smoothed a hand along its fur. "And I'd say his presence lends support to the idea that Dearborn wasn't planning on making a permanent exit. I can't imagine he'd have purposely left the cat on his own." She cradled the animal, rubbing between its ears. With a contented sigh, it snuggled closer. *Smart cat.*

"I wouldn't have figured a guy like Dearborn for an animal lover," Drake said, frowning as he turned to survey the apartment. "Doesn't fit the profile. Especially not a cat. Actually, the whole place feels a little too put together, if that makes any sense."

"It is kind of cozy," J.J. said, still cuddling the cat.

Simon frowned, giving the room the once-over again. He'd been so intent upon identifying any threat that he hadn't really given the contents much thought. But now that he was, he had to agree there was a decidedly unmasculine feel to the place. A large bookcase in one corner was overflowing with books, two overgrown houseplants completely blocking the bottom two shelves.

Across the way, an overly ornate Victorian-looking sofa straddled the corner, red velvet pillows thrown across the seat cushions. A worn leather armchair sat adjacent to the sofa, with a heavy-legged coffee table positioned between the two. A large volume, proclaiming to be the *History of Art*, lay on the table, its white cover adorned with a bust of an Egyptian pharaoh.

The walls were hung with an eclectic collection of art, but even to Simon's untrained eyes, they looked nicely arranged and well...at least a couple steps up from "Dogs Playing Poker." There wasn't a beer can or pizza box in sight. And no sign of a TV of any kind. Hell, there were even fresh flowers on the table.

Drake walked over to a small antique desk and punched a button on the laptop sitting there. It whirred to life, the wallpaper depicting an art gallery in Soho.

"You're right. Something about this doesn't feel right," Simon said, moving over to examine the computer. "I mean, it wouldn't surprise me if Dearborn was using some kind of cover, but this seems a little extreme."

"Having taste is extreme?" J.J. asked, her eyebrows raising as she continued to stroke the cat.

"Considering the state of the building and Dearborn's background, I'd have to say, yes. It feels a little off."

"It's not looking like there's anything here either," Drake said, as he paged through the computers files. "There's no password protection at all. And the files are mainly business records for the gallery on the screensaver."

"There was no mention of an art gallery in Dearborn's files," J.J. said, moving over for a better look at the monitor. "What about email?"

"There's nothing here. He must be using an online account. Although the browser history has been wiped clean." Drake frowned. "If this is an alias, it's a damn good one. Either that or the dude's just a neat freak."

Behind them the door rattled, and Simon pivoted, pulling his weapon, Drake following suit. J.J. stepped back, still holding the cat.

"Who the hell are you?" Simon asked, leveling his gun at a man standing in the doorway. He was wearing pressed khakis and a starched, button-down shirt with an argyle sweater. His red hair was thinning but neatly combed. Drake had nailed it with neat freak.

"I think the more relevant question, since you're standing in my apartment, holding my cat," the man said, his eyes locked on Simon's gun, "is who are you?"

"But since I've got a weapon," Simon replied with a shrug, "I'd say my inquiry still trumps yours."

The man swallowed, Adam's apple wobbling as he clutched the doorknob. "Norman Lester."

"And this is your apartment?" Simon repeated, waving him inside. Lester moved slowly, his legs quivering ever so slightly.

"Yes. It is." His eyes moved from Simon to Drake and then back to Simon again. Then his gaze dropped again to the gun, his fingers twining together nervously. "And for what it's worth, I don't have anything worth stealing." Despite his shaking hands, his voice was steady, and Simon had to give the guy props for not soiling his pants on the spot.

"This isn't a robbery, Mr. Lester," J.J. assured him, releasing the cat, who immediately crossed the room to twine around Lester's ankles.

"Then I don't understand." The man shook his head, confusion playing across his face. "Why have you broken into my apartment?"

"We were actually under the impression that it belonged to someone else," J.J. said, her gaze shooting to Simon, who nodded his approval. Unless he'd completely lost his touch, there was no way Norman Lester was involved in the helicopter crash. "We're with Homeland Security."

"You won't mind if I ask for some identification?"

"Not at all," J.J. replied, holding out her wallet with a beguiling smile. "We're sorry for the intrusion, but according to our records, this apartment belongs to Mason Dearborn."

"Actually," Lester said, visibly relaxing as he handed back the wallet and both Simon and Drake lowered their guns, "he doesn't own it, he rents. And I'm subletting the apartment from him."

"So the two of you are friends?" Drake asked, leaning back against the desk.

"No," Lester protested with a wave of his hand. "I never even met the man."

"But you just said that you were subletting the place." Simon motioned for Lester to sit, and he dropped onto the sofa gratefully.

"I am. But the whole transaction was done through the super. Who actually owns the building, which makes it perfectly legal." He shot them a worried look. "I never saw Dearborn at all. I only know his name because it was on the lease I signed."

"And the owner never indicated why Mr. Dearborn was in need of a sublet?" J.J. asked, perching on the arm of the chair.

"Something about traveling for business. I wasn't really all that interested, to tell you the truth. I just wanted to sign the lease and get on with it."

"So how did you know the apartment was available?"

"My cousin. He knows the super." The cat leaped up onto the sofa, settling into Lester's lap.

"So when did you take possession?" Simon asked.

"Almost two weeks ago."

"And you're already moved in?" Drake's frown deepened. "We moved back into our house over a month ago, and we're still living out of boxes."

"I know it's a bit odd," Lester admitted, "but I like everything in its place. I worked pretty much nonstop, and as you can see this place is small. And there are still a few boxes in the closet." His smile was tentative but genuine.

"So I don't suppose you have a forwarding address for Dearborn?" Simon asked, pretty sure he already knew the answer.

"No." Lester shook his head. "I'm afraid I don't. I just pay the owner directly." He chewed on his lower lip for a moment, studying the three of them. "So what is it exactly that Dearborn's supposed to have done?"

"He's involved in a case we're working on," Simon said, not trusting Lester enough to share more than that.

Lester nodded, still clearly trying to make sense of all of it. "So should I be worried? Am I in some kind of danger?"

"If you're telling us the truth," Simon said, "and you

truly have no connection with Dearborn other than this apartment, then no, I don't think there's any reason to worry."

"But you were in here with guns. So this guy is obviously not someone to be taken lightly. What if he comes back here? Or one of his contacts shows up?"

"There's no reason to believe anything like that will happen." J.J. was quick to reassure. "And we can make sure that someone keeps an eye out, if that'll make you feel better."

"Definitely," Lester said, his Adam's apple bobbing again. "I don't want any trouble."

"I don't suppose Dearborn left anything behind?" Drake asked. "Furniture, books, papers, anything like that?"

"No. The place was empty. In fact, he paid to have the place painted and cleaned. They were incredibly thorough. The apartment was spotless."

"And completely sanitized, I'm guessing," Simon said, frustration cresting. "We'll still want to have our tech team sweep the place. Just to be certain."

"Of course," Lester agreed. "Whatever you need." He was looking almost excited now. "I just can't believe any of this is happening." He glanced down at the newspaper lying on the table, his eyes widening as he saw the headlines. "Hey, this is about the helicopter crash at the hospital, isn't it? But I thought it was an accident? That someone had just made a really bad mistake. But you're from Homeland Security and so it's got to be connected. Right?"

"We're just investigating," J.J. said.

"Oh, my God," Lester breathed, his voice turning raspy. "Dearborn's a terrorist."

"Mr. Lester," Drake said, a note of steel creeping into his voice, "if you want to protect national security and, in addition, make sure that you are not putting yourself in further danger, you'll keep your speculations to yourself. We don't want to alert the people we're searching for that we're on to them."

"Which is why you're telling the press it was an accident." Lester nodded. "I promise I won't say anything."

"And if you think of something that might help," J.J. prompted, holding out a business card.

"I'll call." Again the man nodded, looking so earnest that Simon felt like he'd fallen into a Frank Capra movie.

"Good." J.J. smiled as they all stood up. "And we'll be sending over our forensics team."

"Like on *CSI*." Lester's face was still alight with excitement.

"Something like that." Drake pulled his phone from his pocket. "I'll call it in now. They should be here in half an hour or so. We'll need you to stay put."

"Oh," Lester said, sinking back onto the sofa. "By myself?" The man looked hopefully up at J.J., who shot a questioning glance in Simon's direction.

"No worries. Drake will stay with you," he said.

Drake, standing behind Lester now, rolled his eyes but nodded his agreement.

"Thank you." Lester sighed. "I don't think I could have handled waiting on my own. To think that I'm living in a terrorist's apartment, and that I touched his mail."

"I thought you said you didn't have anything of Dearborn's?" Simon felt his pulse rate increasing.

"I don't have anything," the man shook his head. "But I did. There was some mail. Nothing important. Just a few bills and a flyer or two. But one never knows. Of course I'd have sent them on to him, but like I said, I didn't have a forwarding address."

"So what did you do with them?" J.J. cut in, her frustration matching Simon's.

"What?" For a moment Lester looked confused, then he shook his head. "I'm sorry, I'm afraid this is all just a bit overwhelming."

"The letters, Lester?" Simon prompted.

"Right. The letters. I put them in a Duane Reade bag, and I took them downstairs to Sanchez. I figured he'd have an address."

"Sanchez?" Drake asked, fighting to keep his voice calm. "You're talking about the super?"

"Yes," Lester said.

"And did he have a forwarding address?"

"I don't know." Lester shook his head "He wasn't there when I went down. So I just left the bag hanging on the door." He ducked his head, his tone apologetic. "I'm sorry. I had no idea that they might be important."

"When did you leave them there?"

"Yesterday morning. I was on my way to my art gallery."

"And you haven't talked to Sanchez since?"

"No. I haven't seen him at all. But then it's not like we're friends."

"Which apartment is he in?" Drake asked.

"He has the whole first floor. The entrance is just beyond the staircase."

"You stay here with him," Simon said to Drake. "J.J. and I will head down to Sanchez's."

A few moments later, they were standing in front of

Carlos Sanchez's apartment, only this time there was no reason to knock. The door was open, the frame splintered from the force of the entry.

"Stay behind me," Simon warned as he pushed into the room, gun at the ready.

Inside, everything had been tossed. Chair cushions ripped, tables upended. The drawers in a file cabinet in the corner were open, folders spilling out onto the floor.

"Looks like someone beat us to the punch," J.J. said, kneeling to examine some of the scattered file folders. "Any sign of Mr. Sanchez?"

"No, but I'll check the bedroom," Simon said, already heading that way. The hallway was short, lined with photographs. Most of them of a smiling man Simon assumed to be Sanchez. A couple of them had been knocked off the wall, the glass shattering on the wooden floor. Simon stopped to examine a smear of what looked to be blood. Apparently there'd been a struggle.

Still holding his gun, he stepped into the bedroom. Like the living room, the place had been tossed, but the focal point here wasn't the mess. It was the man splayed across the bed, blood spatter on the wall behind the headboard looking like some kind of macabre decoration.

"Is he dead?" J.J. asked, coming to a stop in the doorway behind him.

"Certainly looks that way." Simon crossed to the bed to check for a pulse, confirming what they already knew.

"Any way to know how long?"

"Not without an ME." He shook his head. "But if I had to call it, I'd say he's been here well over a day. So we couldn't have done anything to stop it, if that's what you're thinking."

"How'd he die?" she asked.

"Single shot to the head."

"Just like Wilderman," J.J. said, her shoulders tightening as she forced herself across the room to examine the body.

"Not exactly. Wilderman was killed at close range. This was a longer shot. Maybe from the doorway."

"How can you tell?" she asked.

"The spatter." He waved at the blood on the wall behind the bed. "The direction and size of the droplets can tell you a lot. I'm guessing Sanchez was trying to get away." He pointed to a window near the bed. "Probably looked back as he reached the bed, and the shooter took the shot."

"And then he fell backward onto the bed." Jillian nodded as she considered the idea. "Are we sure it's Sanchez?"

"Yeah." Simon pointed to the name stitched across the man's uniform.

"That doesn't really mean anything. These people have played fast and loose with bodies before," she reminded him.

"Except that he's in all the photographs. The ones in the hall and the one over there." He nodded at a framed picture on the wall over the bureau, the shot showing Sanchez in the aft of a boat, holding up one hell of a sea bass.

"So we're too late." She sighed. "With Sanchez dead, and the place tossed, I'm guessing the letters are long gone."

"Yeah, well, maybe you're giving up too easily," Simon said, reaching down to pull something wedged between the headboard and the wall. "Lester said it was a Duane Reade bag, right?" He stood up, holding out the sack with a triumphant grin. "Looks like it fell off the nightstand. Maybe in the struggle."

J.J. reached for the bag and, with a quick intake of breath, pulled it open. "They're here." She smiled at him, holding out the small stack of envelopes. "And they're clearly addressed to Dearborn."

Simon flipped through the stack, noting that Lester had been right, there was nothing out of the ordinary here. But when he reached the last one, he stopped. A sticky note covered the address, a handwritten message scribbled in pencil.

"What have you got?" J.J. asked, pushing closer, the smell of her perfume enveloping him. He blinked, pulling himself from the sensory onslaught, concentrating instead on the words Sanchez had written on the Post-it.

"It's the forwarding address. For Dearborn." Simon looked up, his gaze moving to the dead man on the bed. "Sanchez came through after all."

CHAPTER 7

'm not sure I want to go in there." Jillian eyed the apartment doorway nervously. "So far, everywhere we've gone, we've uncovered a body."

"I can't say that I blame you," Simon said, with a small smile. "But it's part of the job description."

"Speak for yourself." She laid a hand on the railing, looking down into the shadows.

They were standing at the top of a small flight of steps that led down to a basement apartment near the corner of Pearl and Fulton. The address on the sticky note in Sanchez's apartment. According to records Hannah had found, it was owned by an eighty-six-year-old retiree named Alden Ayers. Except that Alden had been dead for almost three months, a coronary that had taken him to the ICU and then the morgue. With no known relatives, the estate, such that it was, had been lost in a shuffle of red tape and inertia.

All of which made it the perfect place for someone with something to hide.

Dearborn.

Except that he was dead.

"If you want to wait up here," Simon said, "I totally understand."

"No." She shook her head. "You're right. I need to see this through."

"J.J., nobody is going to blame you for wanting out. No matter how much training you've had, there's no way to prepare for something like this."

She bristled at the protective note in his voice. She didn't need someone to take care of her. Not even Simon. Hell, particularly not Simon. "Yeah, well, I'm not afraid, if that's what you're getting at. And it's *Jillian*." She lifted her chin and headed down the stairs, reaching for Simon's gun. She wasn't sure she'd ever get used to the feel of the weight in her hands, but considering the things she'd seen, she was damned sure she wasn't going in unarmed.

At the bottom she stopped, waiting for Simon, who had also drawn his weapon.

"Looks like it's open." He nodded at a dark sliver of space between the frame and the door. "Doesn't look forced." He inched forward, using the barrel of his gun to push it wider. "And there's no sign of a booby trap."

"It's almost like an invitation." She frowned as Simon stepped inside, and then, with a slow exhalation, she followed.

The room was dark, and it took a moment for her eyes to adjust to the low light. Simon flipped on a table lamp, the pale wash of light doing little to illuminate the room. But it was enough for her to make out the furniture. All of it well past its prime. There was a large lounger in one corner with what looked to be a TV tray in front of it. Across from the chair was a television console straight out of the fifties. She'd seen one like it once on a trip to the Smithsonian as a kid. And sitting against the wall, adjacent to the TV, was a floral sofa covered in plastic.

"Looks like Mr. Ayers wasn't big on redecorating," Simon said. "This place looks like something right out of *Leave It to Beaver*."

"Without the benefit of Barbara Billingsley." She ran her finger along the top of the console, leaving a line in the dust that coated the top. "I don't think anyone has cleaned in here in years. Which makes it unlikely that Dearborn actually spent any time here. Maybe this was just a decoy."

"What do you say we check the rest of the place out before we jump to any conclusions?" His voice held a hint of censure, and she bristled again.

"Sure. Whatever." She shrugged, holstering her gun, disliking the feel of it against her skin.

Simon walked into the small bedroom. Like the living area, it looked like a museum piece. A dusty, dirty one.

"I told you there was nothing," she said, already turning to go.

Simon flipped the switch, and a floor lamp flashed to life, the light spilling out over a long folding table. Clearly new. Simon smiled, a look of triumph flashing in his eyes. "Oh, ye of little faith."

The table was covered with tools and rolls of wire, along with a length of metal pipe and some plastic tubing. Several open boxes sat on the floor by the chair. Even in the dim light, it was obvious that everything was clean and new.

"This one is full of projectiles," Simon said, reaching into one of the boxes and producing a handful of small spiked pieces of metal.

"If I'm not mistaken, this one used to house explosives." She pulled back the flap so that Simon could see the empty containers inside.

" 'Used to' being the operative phrase." Simon leaned in for a closer look, his breath grazing her hair, his scent tantalizingly familiar. Sensory memory danced across her skin, and she wondered for the millionth time what it was about this man that called to her so deeply. No matter the distance between them, he was still always a part of her somehow. She pulled back, angry at the turn of her thoughts as she forced herself to focus.

"So you think this is where they made the bomb Tyler found in the helicopter?"

"It's possible. The length of pipe and the wiring would seem to support the idea. But these containers are used for plastique. And the pipe bomb in the chopper used black powder."

"Meaning there's another bomb?" Jillian felt a chill run down her spine, the memory of the heat and acrid smell of the explosion at the hospital threatening to swamp her.

"Looks that way." Using a handkerchief, Simon bent to pick up something on the floor. And as he moved out of her line of sight, Jillian saw a flash of light reflected against one of the rolls of wire.

Frowning, she moved closer, thinking at first that she'd imagined it, but then it flashed again. She reached for the spool, moving it out of the way, her mind screaming caution as she caught sight of a small black box taped to the wall behind the table. A small amber light in the bottom corner flashed on and then off again.

"Simon," she said, trying to keep her voice calm. It was probably just a charger of some kind.

"I see it." He stepped forward, using the tac-light on his gun to illuminate the box. In the light, Jillian could see what the shadows had blocked. A timer—ticking downward. Ten...nine...

"Run," Simon yelled, grabbing her hand as the two of them sprinted from the bedroom into the living room, out the front door, and up the stairs, taking them two at a time. As they reached the street, a young man in a khaki flak jacket, carrying a backpack, took off running. Simon started after him, but before Jillian could follow, the apartment exploded, flames shooting out the front window and curling up the stairs, a cloud of ash and smoke gushing out onto the street.

Momentarily blinded, Jillian tripped, the heated smoke filling her lungs as her knees slammed into the asphalt. For a moment, she was too stunned to move, and then suddenly Simon was there, yanking her upward, pulling her out into the middle of the street away from the now burning building.

"You okay?" he asked.

"I'm fine," she said, gasping the fresh air, her eyes moving to the still visible figure of the man running down the street. "Go on. We can't afford to lose him. I'll be right behind you."

He searched her face for a long minute and then sprinted off after the man, both of them heading for the river. With one last, deep breath, Jillian followed, grateful for the grueling training she'd completed when she'd accepted the job at Homeland Security. Besides, the son of a bitch had almost killed her. And she damn well was going to be there when Simon caught up to him.

The man was fast. Simon had to give him that. They'd been running full out for almost a block. And to make matters worse, the traffic on Water Street was considerably heavier than Fulton. Plus the bastard had caught the light, which meant that Simon was left to dodge traffic, bouncing off the fender of a taxi in the process, his bad leg sending a streak of pain shooting up to his hip

Gritting his teeth, he vaulted over a parked car, swerving to miss a lady with a baby carriage. He'd lost ground, the man almost disappearing into the surging crowd of tourists heading for the South Street Seaport.

The perfect place to detonate a bomb.

This part of Fulton had been made into a pedestrian mall, the street lined with high-end retailers. And beyond that, beneath the FDR Drive, the old fisherman's warehouses that had turned into restaurants and shops. And finally there was a large open wharf, housing Piers 16 and 17, where two Circle Line cruise ships sat ready and waiting, as well as a restored clipper ship. And everywhere, tourists. People completely unaware of the potential danger heading directly at them.

The crowd had slowed the runner's progress, but it was impeding Simon's as well. He swerved to the far side of the sidewalk where it was less crowded, increasing his pace, careful to keep the guy within sight as he worked to close the distance between them.

There were too many people here to risk a shot, better to try to catch up and incapacitate him somehow. Not an easy task, but the stakes were high, and Simon wasn't about to give up without a fight. Ahead, the man zagged to the left, into a sidewalk café. Like Simon, he'd realized that it would be easier going.

But just as the runner was picking up speed, a waiter stepped out of the restaurant, carrying several plates on a large tray. The two men slammed into each other, food and cutlery flying. Adrenaline surging, Simon sprinted forward, but as he reached the first table, the man with the backpack sprang to his feet again. Turning, he made a run for the far side of the café, pushing over tables, leaving an obstacle course in his wake.

Concentrating on staying upright, Simon dodged both people and the fallen furniture, but by the time he was free of the café, the man with the backpack had managed to pull ahead of him again, the crowd surging around him, providing cover.

Simon fought against frustration and anger, his breathing coming in gasps as his leg throbbed. He pushed through the pain, forcing himself to try to close the distance again. The overpass loomed above him as the two of them dashed from the sunlight into the heavy shadow of the FDR. The man sprinted across the street that fronted the wharf and out into the sunlight ahead.

In front of Simon, a large group of tourists stopped as their guide pointed to the warehouses sitting underneath the bridge. Simon pushed his way through the group, screaming for people to move. In any other city, the commotion would have raised all kinds of alarms. But this was New York, and people, even tourists, tended to take it all in stride.

Once free of the tourists, Simon wasted valuable

seconds slowing down, his eyes sweeping the wharf until he spotted the khaki flak jacket moving along the side of the pier toward a café overflowing with people.

Jesus. If the man detonated now . . .

Years of training kicking in, Simon assessed his options, choosing a gangplank that led up and onto an empty tourist vessel. Ignoring the crew's cries for him to stop, he sprinted along the deck, running above and parallel to the man with the pack. Leg screaming in protest, Simon pushed himself harder, his lungs burning with the effort. Just a few more feet.

For a moment, he thought the guy was going to pull away from him, but three women in high heels holding margarita glasses came out of nowhere, forcing the guy closer to the side of the ship.

Sucking in a deep breath and summoning every ounce of his strength, Simon leaped from the side of the boat, tackling the man from above, grateful that he hadn't hit anyone else in the process. The two of them drove to the ground, hitting hard, but the man with the flak jacket was nimble, slamming his fist into Simon's jaw as they rolled over, each of them fighting for control.

Simon tried to pin him to the pavement, but the guy was strong and managed to break the hold, though not before Simon got in a punch, satisfied to feel his fist connect with the side of the man's head. The guy went limp, and just for a moment, Simon thought he'd managed to knock him out.

But before he could secure a hold, the man was moving again, this time flipping them over, breaking free and pushing to his feet. Simon grabbed the guy around the ankles, but the man managed to regain his balance, taking a swing at Simon, who ducked to avoid the blow. The move gave the man the opening he needed, and with a grunt of satisfaction, he pulled free again.

Simon scrambled to his feet, but the man had already managed to skirt the crowd, running back the way he had come. A couple of yards away, Simon could see the backpack. He hesitated, torn between retrieving the bag and giving chase. Seconds ticked by, and then J.J. appeared from out of nowhere, scooping up the backpack and yelling for him to go.

Adrenaline surged, and Simon ran after the man, who was just rounding the edge of the wharf to head back under the FDR. Simon's leg and jaw throbbed in rhythm to his pounding feet. And he was gratified to see that the man was favoring his right leg as well. Gritting his teeth in determination, Simon pushed himself forward, forcing himself into an out-and-out sprint.

As he passed under the highway, the shadows of the bridge overtook him, and he blinked, for a moment losing sight of his quarry, but then he saw him, heading down the street toward one of the old warehouses, one that hadn't yet been turned into a high-dollar tourist trap.

As the guy dashed inside, Simon slowed, pulling his gun. If there was going to be a showdown, he wanted to be prepared. At least the guy had lost the backpack. Still, he'd proved himself a formidable opponent, and Simon knew better than to make the mistake of assuming he could easily obtain the upper hand. Never underestimate the enemy.

Even after the gloom of the highway overpass, the warehouse seemed dark, most of the casement windows high above him obscured with soot and grime. A single beam of light fell across the floor like a white gash, streaming from a broken windowpane on the east wall. Off to his left, near the door, Simon could see a stack of crates fronted by a large iron pillar, rust leaching into the paint, making it look like some sort of macabre barber pole. The cement floor was wet and cracked. And the place smelled of salt, sea, and dead fish.

Ahead, somewhere in the shadows, Simon heard a footfall. Calling on years of training, he pushed aside fatigue and pain, moving on silent feet to crouch behind the stack of fallen crates. Momentarily secure in the relative cover provided by the wooden boxes, he peered out into the darkness. At first he thought the man was gone, or that he'd managed to find a place to hide, but then the guy stepped into the beam of light near the far wall.

Seeing an opening, Simon grabbed his gun and pushed to his feet, but his elbow caught the edge of a crate, and before he had time to react, it fell, slamming into the concrete floor. The man jerked around, whipping open his jacket, the light hitting the explosives taped to his torso.

Everything shifted into slow motion, Simon trying to gauge the distance as he leveled his gun. Too far, even for him. But from where he was standing, he could see the man's craggy face split into a grin as he lifted an arm, his gaze reaching for Simon's across the expanse of the warehouse. And then, in what was probably less than a fraction of a second, the man pressed his thumb onto something he held in his hand.

The warehouse was suddenly swallowed in an eruption of light, the man disappearing as a massive ball of fire mushroomed upward, ripping through the warehouse's roof as if it were made of paper. Above him,

Simon heard concrete and metal buckling and groaning as the explosion tore through the overpass.

And then as his mind struggled with the reality of what was happening, the fireball expanded, rushing straight at him. In its wake, windows shattered and the floor buckled, giant pieces of concrete crashing to the ground.

Simon's brain was screaming for him to run, but his feet seemed to have forgotten the drill. Then suddenly, something hit him hard, driving him to the ground behind the pillar and the fallen crates. The roar of the blast and the heat of the flames rushed past, searing the wooden boxes and melting the paint on the pillar, but then it was gone. Debris from the building and the overpass still rained down from above, but despite all of that, he was alive.

Next to him, something groaned. And his mind shifted into gear. Not something—someone. *J.J.*

She lay next to him, one arm still thrown protectively across his shoulders. She'd been the one to push him to safety. She groaned again and then shifted beneath the rubble of a crate. Alarmed, he sat up, pulling bits of debris off her. Dazed, her gaze moved to his face.

"You okay?"

"Yeah. I'm fine. But what the hell did you think you were doing coming in here like that? You had to have seen him. Seen the bomb." He knew his anger was irrational. But he couldn't seem to stop himself. "Christ, J.J., you could have been killed."

"Well, you *would* have been killed if I hadn't come." Her voice was colored with an emotion he wasn't sure he could identify, but there was something in her eyes that held his. Something that suddenly seemed more important than breathing. He leaned forward, not sure exactly what he planned to do, losing himself in the azure depths of her eyes.

But then a piece of metal clattered to the ground, startling them both—the moment evaporating, almost as if it had never been there.

And as the sound of sirens filled the air, he stood up and held out his hand.

"You saved my life."

"No big deal." She shrugged as she pushed to her feet, ignoring his outstretched hand. "I was just returning the favor."

It was exactly what he would have said had the situation been reversed. And considering their past, it was better that they keep it professional. The moment of—whatever the hell it was—was best forgotten.

CHAPTER 8

"Be still or you're going to have a scar," Hannah said, taking another stitch as Jillian winced.

"At least it's not anywhere anyone is going to see it." The gash was just above her waistline. About three inches long. Deep and fairly jagged. And just at the moment, despite an anesthetic, it hurt like hell. Actually, if she were being honest, everything hurt. From the top of her head to the tips of her toes. But she wasn't about to admit it. Not even to Hannah, who on the whole had been pretty sympathetic.

Jillian had spent the last couple of hours at the bomb site with the team. Answering questions and dealing with the fallout. And then finally, she and Simon had been allowed to come back to the brownstone, where she'd opted for Hannah's care over losing another four or five hours at the emergency room.

At the moment, she was sitting on a stool in the kitchen while Hannah worked. Simon had disappeared upstairs, presumably to change clothes and take a shower. They hadn't really had a chance to talk about what had happened. But Jillian figured that was probably for the best.

"Yeah, well, if you ask me," Hannah was saying, drawing Jillian's attention back to the present, "you should have gone to the hospital and let them stitch you up. I've got rudimentary training, thanks to a couple of training courses and Lara. But at best, this is nothing more than a field dressing."

"It's just a cut." Jillian shrugged. "I would have done it myself, but I couldn't see it. And you can bet your ass Simon isn't up there calling a doctor for himself."

Hannah shot her a look over the top of her glasses, the frames a pale green with multicolored stripes. "It's not a competition. From what you've said, it sounds to me like the two of you are lucky to be alive. Simon in particular."

"It was closer than I would have liked." She closed her eyes as Hannah took another stitch. "I've had the training, and I'm more than qualified to be here. It's just that when I took the job with Homeland Security, I didn't figure on being on the front line."

"So what made you do it?" Hannah asked. "Take the job, I mean. Simon said you were interested in medicine back in the day. Homeland Security seems like a pretty significant change of course."

For a moment, Jillian hesitated. There were parts of the story she simply wasn't ready to share. Especially not with a friend of Simon's. But there was no reason to cut Hannah off. She was just trying to be friendly and keep Jillian's mind off the pain. So, with a sigh, she settled for a partial truth.

"I gave up the idea of medical school when I got married."

"That was right after college?" Hannah smiled. "Simon doesn't like talking about his past all that much. But when it was clear the two of you knew each other, he told us about the three of you in college. Your husband's name was Ryan, right?"

"Yeah. We sort of got married on the spur of the moment." An understatement. "He and Simon had just enlisted, and I guess I was feeling left out." And hurt. "So when Ryan asked, I said yes."

"Sounds less than romantic." Hannah's gaze was probing for a moment, and then she turned back to her work. "Sorry, I didn't mean that the way it came out."

"That's okay. We were really young and impulsive." And just like her mother, Jillian had traded all of her dreams for a wedding ring and the wrong man.

"But surely you still could have gone to medical school?"

"Not without amassing a world of debt. And I couldn't do that to Ryan. Not just starting out. I figured there'd be time enough later. Pretty unrealistic, I guess."

"Life is about trade-offs." Hannah shrugged, taking a last stitch. "Sometimes it pays off. Sometimes not. So how did you adjust to life on base?"

"It was hard. I mean, Ryan and Simon were gone most of the time."

A blessing in hindsight, but in the beginning, she'd felt so alone. And when Ryan was home, it hadn't always been pretty. She winced at the memory. Relieved that Hannah would think it was because of the physical pain.

"I know what you mean. I've always said that military spouses have the hardest job."

"I tried to keep busy. I took some nursing courses and

volunteered at the base clinic. It wasn't med school, but it was something. At least until..." Her mind flashed on the image of Ryan's funeral. The flag-draped coffin. Simon in his service dress uniform. She'd wanted to reach out to him, but all she'd been able to think about were the awful secrets being buried that day.

"I'm so sorry for your loss," Hannah said, her eyes full of sympathy, and Jillian took comfort even though Hannah didn't truly understand. "It must have been really awful. Especially to lose Ryan like that."

"You think you've prepared yourself," Jillian said, still fighting the memories. "You imagine the worst over and over when they're gone. But then when the officers show up at your door, it's nothing at all like what you imagined." She could still see them standing there. Her thoughts rushing immediately to Simon. Praying that he be alive. That he be unhurt. And then the guilt had hit her. Ryan was the one who was dead. And no matter what he'd done, who he'd become, he was still her husband. And she'd...

"You okay?" Hannah asked, her eyes kind behind her glasses. "Am I hurting you?"

"I'm sorry." She shook her head. "Just tough memories."

"I shouldn't have brought it up."

"It's okay. It's part of the reason I'm here actually. Because of what happened in Somalia, Ryan died a hero, and the Navy brass figured the best way to promote the success of the war was to trot out the hero's widow."

"You."

"Exactly. And it didn't hurt that my father was a general. Army. Two tours in Vietnam and, after that, a career with the Pentagon. So essentially, I became a commodity.

Paraded about to smile and shake hands. Anything for the greater good. Believe me, there were days I wanted to run away screaming." The paradox had almost killed her, actually. Celebrating her husband as a hero, while trying to deal with the memory of the man who'd almost destroyed her.

"But you didn't," Hannah said, tying off the surgical thread, "because you're a strong woman. I've seen you in action. Or at least I've seen the aftermath." She spread some ointment on a bandage and carefully placed it over the newly sutured wound. "And besides, it takes one to know one." She grinned, her smile making her look impish. "So is that how Homeland Security found you? All that greater good bullshit?"

"More or less." Jillian nodded, grateful to be back on safer ground. "The director of Homeland Security and my father go way back. I ran into him at an event. And after catching up on old times, he mentioned that he was looking for someone to be a part of his disaster training program. Someone to coordinate the department's efforts to keep the nation's first responders ready for anything."

"And he thought you were the right person for the job."

"I don't know. I guess. Between the premed and nursing classes, I had enough medical background to fill the bill. But I suspect his friendship with my father had a lot to do with it. As I said, they're pretty tight."

"And your father was worried about you."

"Something like that," she shrugged. Her father had seen it as a way to enhance his reputation. In his mind, wives and daughters were meant to be displayed. Accessories to be used to their greatest advantage. "Anyway, there was also the whole widow of a hero thing—it played well in the press and meant that I was openly received by most everyone I needed to work with."

"But Avery said you'd been trained as an agent."

"I was. It was part of the deal. The director figured that if the disaster drills ever became reality—"

"Which, as we proved with the helicopter crash, is a *when* not *if*," Hannah interjected.

"True." Jillian shifted on the stool. "Anyway, in that kind of situation, obviously I needed a different skill set."

"And did you make the right decision?" Hannah asked. "Accepting the director's offer?"

"Well, in the middle of training, I had some pretty serious doubts. It was a tough nine months. But I also realized just how badly I needed a purpose in my life. Something separate from Ryan and the Navy. And I'm not the kind to back down from a challenge. So yeah, I think I did the right thing." She laughed, surprised at how easy it had been to talk with Hannah even if she'd only shared a revised version of the truth. "Probably more than you wanted to know. I'd say it was the drugs, only you haven't really given me anything but a local."

"Blame it on my curiosity," Hannah said with a smile. "There aren't that many women in our line of work, and I'm always interested in what brought them to the party. And let me be the first to say how grateful we are that you were out there today. Without your quick thinking, we might have lost Simon. And he's become very important to all of us."

It was a sentiment Jillian shared, for better or worse, but she wasn't willing to talk about it with Hannah, no matter how friendly the woman was.

"All right," Hannah said, thankfully not pushing for

anything more. "We're all done here. But I want you to promise you'll see a doctor as soon as things calm down."

Jillian lifted both hands in supplication. "I swear. I've already got an appointment. Follow-up from the helicopter crash. It's been a hell of a week."

"No kidding," Simon said, appearing in the doorway, leaning against the frame, his voice washing over her like some kind of tonic. "You okay?"

"Couple of stitches." She pulled her shirt into place as Hannah cleared away the medical supplies. "You?"

"Nothing a good stiff drink won't cure." He walked farther into the room, his limp more noticeable than usual.

"You're sure you shouldn't see a doctor? I mean, after everything you've been through."

"Talk about the pot calling the kettle black," Hannah said with a laugh as she walked out of the room.

"She has a point." Simon had moved closer now, standing only inches away, his breath warm against her cheek. "You were injured to start with. And now..." he trailed off, looking at the bloody gauze in the trashcan.

"I told you it's just a cut and a few stitches. Nothing to worry about. But your leg—"

"Is going to be just fine." He brushed a strand of hair back from her face. "Thanks to you."

"I already told you it was nothing." Her brain was telling her to move. To widen the distance between them, but the rest of her wasn't listening, concentrating instead on the cadence of his breathing and the silvery flecks in the depths of his eyes.

"Like hell." He leaned closer, framing her face with his hands. She tried to ignore the feel of his skin against hers, but memory surfaced, and she caught her breath, waiting. "You've always had my back, J.J."

"I just reacted in the moment," she whispered. "I saw what he was going to do, and all I could think was that he was going to hurt you. And I couldn't bear the thought of losing you."

The minute the words were out, she regretted them. But he took them as an invitation, his lips closing on hers, the heat of contact setting her nerves on fire. And for just a moment, she allowed herself the pleasure, opening to him, their tongues touching, tasting. Drinking deeply. Sharing a passion born of fear and relief and other emotions she wasn't willing to put a name to, the past and the present blending together, the horrors of the last few days receding against the power of their attraction.

In the circle of his arms she felt safe.

And trapped.

She'd been here before. And she knew the cost was too high. She'd only just found herself again. And she'd sworn that she wouldn't let anyone take that away. Not even Simon.

Especially not Simon.

She pushed away, rubbing the back of her hand against her lips. "I'm sorry. We can't. I can't." The words were low, almost a whisper, but he reacted as if she'd yelled them, stepping back, his expression impossible to read.

"I'm the one who should be sorry. I took advantage—"

"No. I was right there with you. It's just…" she trailed off, unsure of what to say. There was so much standing between them.

"Ryan," he said, having no idea just how right he

actually was. "I know. And like I said, I was out of line.
I promise, it won't happen again."

She nodded, knowing it was the right decision, and
yet wishing somehow that it could be different. And as
he turned to walk out the door, she reminded herself
that loving a soldier came with a high price. She hadn't
lied when she'd told Hannah that losing Ryan had been
far worse than anything she'd ever imagined. What she
hadn't said, however, was that on the day the soldiers
had stood at her door, when she'd been so frightened for
Simon, she'd also wished Ryan dead. And the guilt still
clawed at her, refusing to let her go.

"Okay, people," Avery said, settling in at the head of
the large table in the brownstone's war room. The whole
team was gathered there. Harrison and Hannah in one
corner, huddled around their computers. Nash and Drake
flanking Avery on the right side of the table with Tyler
and J.J. on the left, their blonde heads bent together as
they whispered about something.

Simon settled at the far end of the table, his gaze still
on J.J., who was smiling over at Avery now. She'd certainly managed to make herself an integral part of the
team in short order. Not that he begrudged her the fact.
She'd already proven her mettle, saving his ass in the
warehouse. Hell, maybe that was the problem. He was
supposed to be the one doing the saving.

Or maybe it was just the fact that he'd let his emotions get the better of him and kissed her. What the hell
had he been thinking? Even if there wasn't the ghost of
Ryan standing between them, there was still the matter
of behaving in a professional manner. He sure as shit

wouldn't have kissed Drake for saving his life. He shook his head, clearing his thoughts. J.J. had always managed to get under his skin.

But her heart had always belonged to Ryan.

A small voice at the back of his head reminded him of a crisp spring night at an off-campus party, but he ignored it. It had always been Ryan. And even if it hadn't, she'd sure as hell picked him in the end. And now, thanks to his own arrogance, she'd lost Ryan forever.

Same song. Millionth verse. He'd been out of line. And he wasn't going to let it happen again. Not that he had a choice. She'd made it pretty damn clear how she'd felt about things. And now—well, now she could hardly look him in the eyes.

He was a first-class shit, no question about it.

And yet, truth be told, he wasn't actually sorry he'd done it. She tasted just exactly the way he'd remembered. Her lips soft and pliant. And if things were different...

But they weren't. And there was a hell of a lot more at stake than his libido. He blew out a breath and forced himself to focus on Avery.

"Bottom line," Avery was saying, "it looks like we've had two terrorist attacks in a matter of days. And the only culprits we've been able to directly tie to the events are dead."

"But we can't know for certain that the second bombing was meant as an actual attack," Nash said. "It's possible that Simon and Jillian interrupted the bomber, and he fled the scene, detonating only when he had no other choice."

"Well, even so, I don't think that lessens the impact," J.J. said. "The warehouse was destroyed, the FDR overpass seriously damaged, and at least eight people lost their lives."

"So we're damn lucky that Simon and Jillian got there when they did," Tyler said.

"Don't look at me." J.J. shook her head in protest. "Simon is the one who tackled the guy and then chased him into the warehouse."

"Yeah, well, you're the one that kept me from getting blown to hell." He waited, hoping that she'd finally look at him, but instead she lifted a shoulder, her attention still on Avery standing at the front of the room.

"Look, the point is that without the two of you being on the scene, things might have been a hell of a lot worse," Hannah said. "If that guy had detonated in the actual seaport... There were literally hundreds of people present."

"But what if the seaport wasn't the target?" J.J. asked. "What if the guy wouldn't have detonated at all if we hadn't arrived at the apartment and spooked him?"

"At least from my perspective," Tyler said, resting her chin in her hands, elbows planted on the table, "I'd have to say the seaport was the target. First off you have the proximity of the apartment. It's not practical to try to transport a bomb any great distance, no matter how portable."

"Especially with the city on alert after what happened at the hospital," Nash agreed.

"And second, you have the fact that the guy was wearing the bomb. You saw the vest, right?" Tyler turned to Simon.

"Oh, yeah." He nodded on a sigh. "Believe me, the image is burned into my head."

"Okay, so if he wasn't planning to detonate at the seaport, what the hell was he doing wearing the bomb?"

"Testing it?" Hannah suggested. "For weight or something?"

"It's possible," Tyler admitted, "but not likely. Even the most dedicated zealot isn't going to want to lounge around in the thing. Even for a test. You're lucky the damn think didn't go off when you tackled him, Simon. Besides, there's also the fact that the apartment was rigged to blow."

"They could have triggered it," Harrison said, glancing up from his computer where he was studying something on the monitor.

"I'll certainly know more after I've had time to go over the site, but from the way you guys described it, I'm thinking it was more likely that it was already set."

"Meaning that the attack was already in play before Simon and Jillian ever arrived," Avery said, leaning against the edge of the table.

"On first blush, I'd have to say that that seems the most likely scenario. But the pieces still don't fit together in any kind of coherent whole. Even if we agree that we've got an organized, disciplined group of players ready and willing to sacrifice for the cause—"

"Or not so willing in the case of Dearborn," Drake inserted.

"We've still got completely different MOs. The first, hijacking a helicopter to crash into a hospital with a very limited population, and the second, a suicide bomber set to take out a major tourist hub."

"So they're escalating." Nash shrugged.

"Yeah, maybe, but there's still got to be some kind of

plan or pattern. Some logic to the progression, and I'll be damned if I'm seeing it." Tyler blew out a breath, clearly frustrated.

"Another thing that feels off about all of this," Hannah said, her eyes narrowing as she considered her words, "is that there's been no chatter. Nothing to point at any of this happening. The whole reason for acts of terrorism is to take credit for the blow. And there's been absolutely nothing."

"Not to mention the efforts to cover everything up." Simon stood, needing movement to better order his thoughts. "First there was the switch with the real Wilderman. And then fake Wilderman and Essex, the pilot. And the second explosion in the helicopter to destroy evidence."

"And then there's Dearborn moving out of his old apartment to a new one that was wired for destruction," Drake continued. "Not to mention the guy in the warehouse and his one-way ticket straight to hell."

"It seems like they're more interested in covering their tracks than taking credit for any of their actions," Tyler agreed.

"Well, to some extent you'd expect that," Avery said. "In most situations with a plot this intricate, there's a hierarchy. And the people at the bottom levels rarely have knowledge of anything more than their small, unique part in the grand scheme of things. It's only at the upper levels that the big picture is revealed."

"That sounds familiar," Nash said, exchanging a look with Drake.

"Yeah, the Consortium is up to its old tricks. They've definitely got hierarchy down to a science."

"What about the backpack?" Hannah asked. "Was there anything inside?"

"No." Avery shook his head. "It was completely empty. No fingerprints. Nothing."

"Maybe it was meant to be a decoy?" Nash suggested.

"Your guess is as good as mine," Simon said, blowing out a breath in frustration. "Nothing these guys do makes any sense."

"What if these weren't terrorist attacks at all?" Tyler mused. "What if they're something else altogether? It's not uncommon for a criminal to use overkill to hide something much more specific."

"You're suggesting that this could be about taking out a particular person." Nash leaned forward, his brows drawn together into a frown. "Someone who was at the hospital and escaped and then was present again at the seaport."

"I already thought about that," Hannah said, with a shake of her head. "And I ran a cross-check against the list of witnesses from the seaport and the people present in the hospital the day of the crash. Except for Simon and Jillian, there are no matches."

"How about Dearborn's old apartment?" Simon asked. "Did the forensics folks find anything?"

"No," Drake said. "Lester was right about the apartment being cleaned. There wasn't anything at all to tie it to Dearborn. And they even checked the drains for hair. Not a damn thing."

"And the super's place?" Nash asked.

"Sanchez." Drake nodded. "Only he was the building owner, not just the super."

"Either way," Nash shrugged, "did the techs turn up anything?"

"Again, that's a negative," Drake said with a frown.
"The blood was Sanchez's, and there weren't any prints
besides his and a couple of tenants who've already been
cleared. They did retrieve the bullet, and they're checking against the one they found in Wilderman. But even if
it turns out to be the same, they ran it through the databases, and there was no match to a gun."

"Have we established time of death?" Avery asked.

"Not yet. The ME is working on the autopsy, but definitely less than twenty-four hours. Which puts him in the
bloody middle of all of this."

"Anything in his background that might link him to
the other players?" Tyler asked.

"Besides renting to Dearborn, there's nothing," Hannah said. "He wasn't exactly landlord of the year, but he
wasn't in any trouble either. And there's nothing in any of
his records that would signal involvement."

"My guess is that he just got caught up with the wrong
people, and they took him out. Another loose end."
Simon leaned back, crossing his arms over his chest.
"And considering he's the one that posthumously pointed
us to the apartment by the seaport, I'd say they were right.
We're just lucky they didn't find that Duane Reade bag."

"So has it occurred to any of you that maybe we're
being played?" J.J. sat back, her gaze encompassing the
entire group. "I mean, hasn't this all seemed just a little
too easy?"

"You wound me," Drake said with mock severity. "We
make it seem easy because we're so damn good at what
we do."

"I know." She smiled. "Believe me, the unit's reputation precedes you. But seriously, it's almost like we've

been playing connect the dots. First the watch, and then the dead guy in the Dumpster, and then identifying Dearborn. I mean, usually these kinds of cells recruit unknowns. Idealistic kids who are trained to be martyrs. But Dearborn doesn't fit that image at all. And then there's Dearborn's second apartment, the one that was coincidentally rigged to blow. The address was on a sticky note."

"She has a point," Simon said, warming to the idea. "It's almost as if they wanted us to walk into that apartment."

"And get blown to bits." Drake was frowning now. "Wouldn't be the first time the Consortium's tried to get rid of us."

"We don't know that it's the Consortium," Avery cautioned. "But I agree that something here doesn't feel quite right."

"So if the plan was for you guys to walk into the apartment on Fulton and get blown up," Hannah queried, "then why was the bomber still outside?"

"To make sure the job got done," Simon said with a shrug.

"Or maybe the point was to get us to follow him?" J.J. suggested, clearly not buying into the idea.

"That doesn't make any sense either." Simon shook his head. "The guy was definitely not waiting around for me. He was running full out. His intention was quite obviously to leave my ass behind and get on with the business of detonating his bomb."

"Maybe it was a two-part equation and the first half went wrong," Tyler said. "Maybe they did want to take you out with the apartment. But you got there too soon, so the guy didn't have the chance to get out fast enough."

"But why take the risk?" Hannah asked. "Why involve us at all if there's a chance that we could succeed in stopping the bomber?"

"Because they like playing games," Drake said, clearly still thinking about the Consortium.

"Everything we're saying is feasible," Avery said, "but unfortunately, all we know for certain is that we've got two attacks on the city. One successful, one not so much. And although I can't prove it, I can't shake the feeling that, whatever the reason, this wasn't the endgame."

"So we need answers." Simon dropped back into his chair, frustration rising.

"Maybe I can help with that," Harrison said, looking up from his computer. "I can't shed any light on what the ultimate plan might be, but maybe I've just gotten us a step closer to who is behind it. I've been digging around in Wilderman's computer, trying to find something that might help nail the people behind the attacks."

"But I thought the thing had been wiped clean," Drake said, one eyebrow shooting up in question.

"It was. But as I've said before, it's not that easy to completely erase a hard drive. And with the right tools and a little tenacity, it's still possible to find pieces of the original configuration."

"And you've found something," Avery said.

"Yes." Harrison nodded, a little smile playing at the corners of his lips.

"So go on and tell us already." Simon hadn't meant to sound so harsh, but he'd damn near been blown to hell only a few hours ago, so he deserved to be cut a little slack.

"I found a key logger."

"A program that remotely mirrors keystrokes," Drake said, remembering no doubt when one had been used to gain access to his whereabouts in Colombia.

"Right. But they can also be used to remotely access a computer."

"To make a reservation," J.J. said, her expression triumphant. "You found an IP for the person who made the helicopter reservation."

"I did." Harrison grinned, clearly enjoying the moment.

"And did that lead to an actual name?" Simon asked, still fighting aggravation.

"Yup," Harrison said, sobering. "According to my research, the IP connected to the key logger is registered to Norman Lester."

"Son of a bitch."

CHAPTER 9

That was Drake," Simon said, flipping his phone closed as they rounded the corner, approaching Norman Lester's gallery. "Lester wasn't at the apartment. And everything was pretty much the way it was when the forensics people left. Except that now his computer is gone. Along with the cat."

"Damn it." Nash stopped as they neared the gallery's door. "If he took the cat, I'm guessing that means he's making a run for it."

"And assuming he left right after the techs," Jillian said, "he's got a pretty substantial lead."

"Well, it's still worth checking the gallery." Simon shrugged, shooting a glance at Nash, who nodded his agreement. "There's always a chance he came here after clearing out. To pick something up or maybe to get rid of incriminating evidence. And even if he's not here, there might be something that will point us in the right direction."

"Okay, so how do you want to do this?" Jillian asked, her gaze catching Simon's, her heart leaping to her throat as she quickly looked away. It was the first time she'd actually met his eyes since the kiss. And just for a single second, all she wanted to do was kiss him again. Feel the heat of his mouth against hers, their breath mingling as their tongues tangled together. She blew out a sharp breath, forcing herself to clear her mind. What she needed to do was quit thinking with her fractured heart and concentrate on the here and now. On finding Lester.

"I'll take the back," Nash said. "You guys go in from the front. If we're lucky, we'll catch him by surprise."

"Copy that." Simon nodded as Nash sprinted around the corner for the alley running along the right side of the building. In some former incarnation, the place had been a factory. The windows were oversized, and the building was fronted with cast-iron ornamentation that marked it as mid–nineteenth century. Above the arched doorway, an awning was adorned with the word Passions, the name of Lester's gallery.

"You ready?" Simon asked, as he reached out to push open the front door.

"Actually, I think I might be getting used to this kind of thing," Jillian said, surprising herself with the pronouncement, her fingers moving to the gun tucked into her waistband. "So let's do it."

On the other side of the door, they found themselves in a small vestibule painted a soft mauve. A second arched opening led to the main gallery, a cavernous space broken up by artfully lit half-walls draped in scarlet velvet, each adorned with a series of paintings.

The walls, set at obtuse angles, were broken up with

narrow mirrors in elaborate gilded frames, each of them supported by the elegant rise of the building's cast-iron pillars. The result was an illusion of motion, the lighting designed to invoke the flicker of candles, the walls fading into each other as their reflections soared upward into the shadowy recesses of the vaulted ceiling, the pillars the only things seeming to keep them grounded.

"Jesus," Simon breathed. "This place reminds me of a surrealist version of some kind of Victorian whorehouse."

"Actually, there were brothels in this area once. So I guess the idea isn't too far-fetched. It's like we've stepped through to the other side of the mirror," Jillian whispered. "But someone's got to be here, right? The door was open, and the lights are on."

"Yeah, well, if Lester's somewhere in here, I'd say he's got the advantage." Simon drew his gun, his eyes sweeping across the room. "It's like a fucking maze. Nash, you getting this?"

"Roger that," Nash replied, his voice echoing in Jillian's ear. "Kind of sorry to be missing it actually. I've got nothing at all interesting back here. No vehicles and no sign of life."

"What about the Dumpster?" Simon asked, shooting an apologetic look in Jillian's direction.

"Nada. It's completely empty. As is the alley. There's a loading dock back here, but it's locked tighter than a drum."

"Well, that's certainly never stopped you before," Simon said.

"True," Nash answered, a hint of laughter coloring his voice. "So we'll see who gets to Lester first."

"If that's a challenge, you're on." Simon smiled,

already moving toward an opening between two of the blood-red walls near the center of the room.

Little boys and their games. Jillian followed Simon into the gallery, moving cautiously, the paintings seeming to jump out at her as she moved deeper into the exhibition. The artist, whoever he was, had a penchant for the macabre, the stark simplicity of the images making them all the more frightening. Whatever else Norman Lester was involved in, he knew his way around an exhibition. The paintings had been hung for maximum impact, forcing viewers into the artist's world whether they wanted to be there or not.

"This place gives me the creeps," Simon said, as they hit a dead end, a painting of a decapitated doll reflected against its red-velvet backdrop in one of the mirrors.

"Right there with you," Jillian agreed, moving slowly, gun raised, every instinct on high alert as she surveyed the area. As she turned back, Simon disappeared as he moved behind one of the mirrors. She followed, but when she rounded the pillar, he was gone.

Panic threatened for a moment, and then Jillian reminded herself that she had chosen this profession. If for no other reason than to prove to herself once and for all that she could handle anything that life could throw at her.

Squaring her shoulders, she sucked in a breath and moved farther into the maze of paintings and mirrors, her mind repeating the mantra that had gotten her through the darkness of the past few years. She'd never cower from anything again. Not ever.

"You guys there?" she whispered into the comlink, heart still pounding despite her resolve. There was a burst of static, and then nothing. Tightening her fingers on the gun, she looked up at the ceiling, using it as a guide to point her in the right direction. Simon would be heading for Nash, and he was coming in from the rear. So that's the way she'd go, too.

She rounded another corner, this time confronted with a giant canvas, the tortured souls captured there reaching out as if imploring her to rescue them. If nothing else came of this little exercise, she'd certainly discovered a skilled artist. Twisted maybe, but nevertheless still talented.

Ahead of her, just beyond a mirrored pillar, she heard someone moving. "Simon?" she said, careful to keep her voice low, afraid that anything louder would only alert Lester if he was indeed somewhere within the gallery.

"Over here," came the whispered response from just beyond the mirror, and she sighed with relief, only to find the area empty when she rounded the corner.

"Damn it, Simon," she spoke into the comlink, "this isn't funny. Where the hell are you?" Again static filled her ear, and the finger of fear returned to trace its way up her spine. Something behind her skittered across the floor, and she swung around, pointing her gun, her eyes searching the flickering gloom for some sign of Simon.

But everything had gone deadly quiet again.

"Nash?" she whispered, her heart beating a tattoo against her ribs as she took shelter behind the solid strength of one of the cast-iron pillars. "Can you hear me?"

"Roger that," Nash replied, his voice in her ear seeming abnormally loud after the silence. "I was afraid the comlink was down."

"I think maybe it was," she acknowledged. "But at least now it's back."

"Simon there with you?" Nash asked.

"No." She shook her head, even though he couldn't see her. "He was just ahead of me. But I lost him in this damn maze. Whoever set up this exhibit wasn't interested in casual visitors. There's no easy in or out. It's like being in a funhouse. Between the crooked pathways, the spooky lighting, and the ghostly reflections, it's hard to figure out which way is which."

"I'll second that," Simon said, pushing out from behind a swath of velvet, still leading with his gun.

"You okay?" Jillian asked, hating herself for sounding like she cared. There was no place in her life for emotion. At least not the kind that Simon seemed to bring out.

"Yeah, just got twisted around. To be honest, I'm not exactly sure how I got back here. But I'm glad I did." His smile was warm, and for a moment, Jillian let herself forget the things that lay between them, grateful just to have him nearby. "Any sign of Lester?" he asked, his question meant for Nash as well as her.

"No sign of him back here," Nash said, "but I've only just made it through the loading bay."

"I haven't seen anything either." Jillian leaned against the pillar. "But I heard something." She lifted her hand to point behind her. "That way. I would have said it was you, but you came from over there." She nodded at the velvet-covered wall to her left.

"All right," Simon said, "then we'll follow the noise. But I think we'll be better off with radio silence."

"Copy that," Nash said. "Signing off for now."

There was another burst of static and then silence.

"You think he'll be okay?" Jillian asked, still spooked by the noise she'd heard.

"He'll be fine. And we can always break the silence if there's an emergency." They started forward, Simon in the lead again. "Take note of the paintings. It's the only way to be sure you're not just going in circles."

"Wonderful." Jillian sighed as she followed him. "Nothing like some guy's nightmarish depictions of death to mark the way."

For the next few minutes, they walked in silence, trying to stay to the left—a trick she remembered from childhood to help traverse a maze. The gallery was eerily quiet. And Jillian's nerves stretched tight in anticipation each time they rounded a corner.

They passed a small table set in front of a canvas covered with roiling skeletons rising into a fiery sky. Something glistening caught Jillian's eye, and she stopped, bending to pick it up off the floor, but her fingers came away empty, covered instead with something wet.

Jerking her hand back, she lifted it to the flickering light, her stomach seizing as she recognized the liquid for what it was.

Blood.

She opened her mouth to speak, but realized too late that Simon had moved out of sight again. Although she was tempted to use the comlink, she knew that she risked being overheard. So instead, she inched her way around one of the mirrors, still keeping to the left, and then stopped, her stomach leaping into her throat.

As if it were springing from the canvas hanging on the velvet-shrouded wall, the body of a woman lay at the foot of a pillar. Cloudy blue eyes stared upward as if fascinated with the soaring ceiling above. But the blood pooling beneath her head made it clear that these eyes would never see again.

Jillian braced herself as she reached down to touch the woman's throat, already certain of what she'd find. No pulse. Whoever the lady had been, she was dead, the blood spattered, black-edged hole near her temple matching those Jillian had seen on both Sanchez and Wilderman.

"What have you got?" Simon said, startling her with his proximity. She'd been so absorbed with the sight of the body, she hadn't heard him approaching. "Sorry." He laid a hand on her shoulder, the feel of his fingers against her skin anything but soothing. "I didn't mean to startle you."

"I found blood," Jillian said, her eyes still locked on the body. "And then I found her."

Simon squatted to have a closer look. "She's dead," he said, stating the obvious. "And based on lividity, I'd say it wasn't that long ago."

"But we didn't hear anything." Jillian took a step back, letting her gaze sweep the area.

"Probably happened just before we got here." He reached out to close the woman's eyes and then gently searched the body. "Did you find anything to ID her?"

"She's wearing a nametag," Jillian said, pointing to the front of the blazer the woman was wearing. The lapel had been pressed against the floor until Simon had searched the body, his movements flipping the tag upright. "Sara Frazier."

"Doesn't ring any bells. But the tag is embossed with the gallery's name as well. So it looks like Sara worked for Lester."

"And got herself killed because of it. You want me to call it in?" Jillian asked, reaching for her cellphone, but Simon shook his head.

"There's no service in here. Must be all the iron. I think that's what was screwing with the comlinks, too. Hopefully we'll be able to call out once we catch up with Nash."

Simon turned to go back the way they'd come, but before Jillian could follow, a face flashed in the shadows off to her right.

"Simon," she warned, freezing in place as the other man seemed to materialize from the shadows. With a flicker of a smile, he lifted his gun, and Jillian's brain screamed in recognition. Lester. Reacting on instinct aided by pure adrenaline, Jillian took the shot, the bullet slamming not into flesh but glass, the man's reflection shattering with the force.

Footsteps echoed off to her right, and Jillian swung around, trying to find Lester and, more important, Simon. But the area, littered now with fragments of the mirror, remained empty, and Jillian strained for some sound to guide her.

At first there was nothing, and then the gallery reverberated with the sound of another gunshot. Terrified, Jillian ran forward blindly, her only thought to get to Simon. Rounding the edge of the nearest pillar at almost a dead run, she cleared the last of the velvet panels, her heart skittering to a stop as she broke into the open to see Simon clutch his chest and fall to the floor. Across from him, still holding a gun, stood Lester.

White-hot fury rushed through her as she leveled her gun and shot, the sound echoing through the gallery. Lester turned, and Jillian could feel the malevolence of his gaze as it settled on her. Again he lifted his weapon, and again she shot. This time, she hit the mark, a blossom of blood blooming across Lester's shirt as his gun fell from his hand.

For a moment, he held his ground, his eyes still locked on hers, and then he made a gurgling noise, blood running out the corner of his mouth. One minute he was standing there, and the next he was on the floor, and Nash was emerging from somewhere in the back of the gallery.

Fighting to breathe, Jillian ran to Simon, dropping to her knees as she reached for him, praying with everything inside her that he wasn't dead. She reached for his pulse, just as he groaned, his green eyes flickering open, his fingers closing around her hand.

"Thank God," she whispered, tears springing in her eyes. "I thought he'd killed you."

"Not a chance," Simon said, as she helped him to sit up. "I was wearing a vest, remember?" He pointed to the triangle of Kevlar that showed just beneath the neck of his shirt. "It hurt like hell, but I'm going to be fine."

"I killed Lester," she said, her breathing still coming in sharp little gasps. "I...I shot him..."

"I know." Simon nodded, slipping an arm around her as she knelt beside him. "And I'm grateful. His next shot would have been for my head."

She shivered violently, the reality of the situation setting in.

"Hey," Simon's voice was soft now, cajoling, his hold on her tightening. "I'm okay. And it's over."

"I wouldn't count on that," Nash said, coming over to stand beside them. "Lester was still alive when I got to him."

"But I shot him," Jillian repeated, her eyes darting over to Lester's prone body.

"That you did." The ghost of a smile crested in Nash's eyes. "And he's dead now. But before he died, he left us with a warning."

"What did he say?" Jillian asked, suppressing another shiver.

Nash blew out a long breath, his gaze encompassing them both. "It wasn't exactly coherent, but the gist of it was that this was just the beginning."

"Beginning of what?"

"Damned if I know," Nash said, "but, all things considered, I figure it can't be anything good."

CHAPTER 10

Köln, Germany

Norman Lester is dead," Michael Brecht said, snapping his phone shut as Gregor took a sip of his cappuccino. The little café was a favorite. Quiet and discreet. He'd spent many hours strategizing here at the table in the window. People wandered past, mostly tourists completely oblivious to the world around them. Which suited him just fine.

"What happened?" Gregor asked, his craggy face wrinkling as he frowned.

"The woman from Homeland Security shot him." It wasn't that he cared about Lester. He'd been nothing more than a pawn. A useful one, but still no one of true consequence. What irked him were the circumstances.

"The one who has been working with A-Tac."

"Yes. I hadn't thought her a true threat. But perhaps I underestimated her abilities."

"Or overestimated Lester's." Gregor shrugged. "I was never impressed with the man."

"He served his purpose."

"Still, it means that A-Tac is one step closer to figuring it all out. I've been fielding calls all morning. The council members are growing restless. And I don't need to remind you that we can't afford another failure."

"And by 'we' you mean me," Michael said, taking a sip of his espresso, the bitter brew matching his mood. "But not to worry. I'm not out of moves yet. Isaacs has a little surprise planned for the bitch who took out Lester."

"But isn't that just stirring the hornets' nest?"

"Precisely. We rile them up and then lead them on a merry chase. We can use Lester. After all, he's dead. Which means his network dies along with him. Why not use that to our advantage? Let A-Tac discover what Lester was really up to. While they're trying to make it fit with the other facts, we'll move forward with the real plan."

"And what about Isaacs? It was his network, too."

"Yes, but it's still been burned. Which actually makes him the perfect one to set the trap. And then when A-Tac takes the bait, we'll stop them once and for all."

Simon waited as the hospital doors slid open and then walked into the waiting room, grimacing a little as the ACE bandage hugged his ribs. Just a precaution, the doc had said. But he hated the idea that he needed any kind of support.

Across the room, he saw J.J. sitting with Harrison and Drake, the three of them huddled together, Harrison holding her hand. Despite the fact that Harrison literally worshiped the ground Hannah walked on, Simon felt an irrational flush of jealousy, and for a moment, considered turning tail and getting the hell out of Dodge.

But then J.J. saw him, her eyes going wide with questions, her lips tilting in the slightest of smiles. And damn it all to hell if he didn't suddenly feel right as rain.

"You're okay?" she asked, crossing the room in two strides, holding out her hands.

He took them, relishing the feel of her skin against his palms. "I'm fine. Just a bruise. Doc bandaged me up and said I'm good to go. What about you?"

"Nothing new to show. Just a little powder burn on my hand. Drake says it's an easy mistake for a beginner. And the doctor checked on Hannah's handiwork, but said that he couldn't have done any better himself. So I'm clear, too."

"You sure?" He searched her eyes, resisting the urge to lose himself in the blue depths. He'd been where she was. The first kill was never easy. No matter who was being threatened or how bad the person on the other end of the gun. Life was sacred. And nowhere was that more important than in a job like theirs.

"Yeah. I'm just glad you're all right."

"I'm relieved everyone is okay," Drake said, coming over to join them, Harrison on his heels. "Man, to hear Nash tell it, you were damn near a goner."

"Yeah, well, I'm here to tell the tale so something must have gone right." Simon grinned, thinking, not for the first time, that he was lucky to have landed here with A-Tac after losing his place in the SEALs.

"How's the leg?" Harrison asked, his expression uncharacteristically somber.

"No worse than usual." Simon brushed off the question, hoping that Harrison would take the hint. Truth was, he was hurting like hell. "So where's everyone else?"

"Nash is still at the gallery, working with the forensics team. Avery and Hannah are digging to see if they can find anything useful on Lester. And Tyler is still playing with explosives."

"At least some things are always the same. She find anything new?"

"Just confirmation of what we already suspected," Drake replied, perching on the back of a chair as the rest of them sat down in a corner of the waiting room. "The bomb in the helicopter and the one in the apartment were constructed similarly, one using pipe and the other a plastic box, but she says the mechanisms were the same. And they both used black powder."

"And the one in the warehouse?"

"Totally different animal," Harrison said. "Designed for more bang for the buck. The first two explosions were meant to cover evidence. Enough of a charge to destroy the area immediately surrounding the point of origin and start a fire that would consume most of the rest. The bomber in the warehouse, on the other hand, was wearing enough plastique to have taken out most of lower Manhattan. The only thing that kept the blast from being catastrophic was the fact that it went off in a warehouse underneath a ton of concrete."

"The overpass." J.J. nodded.

"Roger that," Drake said. "If Simon hadn't run the bastard to ground, there's no telling how bad it might have been."

"All the more reason we need to find out what kind of game Norman Lester was playing." Simon leaned back in the chair, ignoring the throbbing in his chest and leg. "Did we confirm the ID on the dead woman in the gallery?"

"Yeah," Harrison said. "Looks like it was a case of wrong place, wrong time."

"Or at least wrong time," Drake said. "Her name was Sara Frazier. She worked at the gallery. My guess is that she surprised Lester—maybe asked the wrong questions—and he took her out."

"Collateral damage." J.J. sighed, running a hand through her hair. "This thing just keeps on getting weirder and weirder. It's almost as if they're trying to be random. To keep us on our toes. But there has to be some kind of plan, right?"

"If we're dealing with rational people, sure. But who's to say that any of this is rational?" Simon shrugged. "What about Lester? You said Avery and Hannah were digging. But I'm assuming they haven't come up with anything yet?"

"No," Drake said, "but thanks to Jillian's quick thinking, at least we got his computer."

They'd found the computer, along with a suitcase and the cat, in an office on the second floor in the factory. Lester had been running a program to wipe it clean. But Jillian had managed to stop it before it could completely erase everything.

"I'm running diagnostics on it now," Harrison said. "Unfortunately, it's going to take a little time. But if it was important enough to dump the data, that probably means there's something there."

"What about the hard drive we found in Afghanistan?" Simon asked. He'd almost forgotten about the half-destroyed box.

"That one is a tougher nut to crack, but I'll get it, too." Harrison grinned. And Simon had no doubt he'd be able to unlock its secrets sooner or later. It's just that sooner seemed the better option.

"Which probably means we'd best be getting on with it," Simon said, pushing to his feet, trying, but not quite succeeding, to hide a wince.

"You're hurting," J.J. said, her hand immediately cupping his elbow as they headed to the exit. "We need to get you to bed."

"Now there's an invitation, if ever I did hear one," Drake said, and Simon watched as J.J. turned a rosy shade of pink.

"You know I didn't mean it like that," she protested as the automatic doors opened and the crisp New York night embraced them.

"Pity," Simon mumbled under his breath.

"What?" She tipped her head up, searching his eyes, but he shook his head.

"Nothing. Honest." Simon pulled his jacket closer as they headed to their SUV, the wind swirling around them. It was late, and for once, the city was fairly quiet.

"Yeah, well, however she meant it," Drake said, "I'd listen up. The woman knows how to use force when necessary."

J.J. flinched, and Simon reached out to squeeze her arm. "You didn't have a choice."

"I know," she said, nodding as Drake pulled out his keys and hit the button to unlock the SUV, the chirping sound filling the night. "But that doesn't change the fact that I killed a man tonight."

As she started to step off the curb, a taxi swerved between the four of them and the SUV. The taxi honked and started to pull away, but before it had made it more than a couple of feet, the SUV exploded, both vehicles disappearing in a cloud of shrapnel and flame, the sharp smells of gasoline and sulfur saturating the smoke-laden air.

"Everyone okay?" Drake called, already on his feet again and heading for the taxi.

"I'm good." Harrison, too, had risen, his face blackened from the smoke and ash. "Simon?"

"I'm fine. Where's J.J.?" She'd been right next to him. He frantically spun around, his heart pounding, fear racing through him like nothing he'd ever felt before. Scenes from the helicopter crash rushed through his head. And then he heard a moan.

"I'm over here," she called, her voice soft but strong. She was sprawled across the sidewalk, her jeans ripped at the knees, soot from the explosion staining her arms and cheeks.

"Are you all right?" Simon asked, running his hands down her body searching for injury.

"Yes." She nodded, clearly surprised by the fact. "I was heading for the car, and then a wave of fire and heat literally lifted me up and threw me over here. What happened?"

"It was a bomb. In the SUV. Probably detonated when Drake unlocked it."

"But I'm not hurt." She looked up at him with disbelieving eyes, her body starting to tremble. "I'm not hurt."

Simon ignored the little voice in his head screaming for professional detachment, instead pulling her close, brushing his lips against the top of her head as his gaze met Harrison's. "Whatever the hell is going on here, looks like Lester was right. It's far from over."

*   *   *

"Well, this is getting to be a regular habit," Drake said, as Tyler and Avery walked into the hospital waiting room. "Maybe we should just move the war room here."

"Not funny," Simon said, looking in the direction of the cubicles for like the hundredth time. Although she'd sworn she was fine, he'd insisted that J.J. be checked out anyway. She'd gone grudgingly and refused when he'd offered to accompany her. So now all he could do was wait.

"How's Jillian?" Avery asked, picking up on Simon's train of thought.

"She's fine," Harrison said. "Simon just wanted to be certain. The blast threw her to the ground, so we figured better safe than sorry."

"Definitely the right move," Avery said, his gaze settling on Simon. The big man, as usual, saw way too much. "I'm glad to hear she's going to be okay. Although you need to keep an eye on her. First kills can play hell with your head."

"I'm on it," Simon said, praying he was up to the task. And more important, that she'd let him in.

Avery nodded, then turned to look at Tyler. "So did you find anything on the SUV?"

"You're kidding, right? I've been here like maybe five minutes. And while I appreciate the confidence, I'm not a miracle worker. Not to mention the fact that we're stretched a little thin, what with four separate bomb sites and all. Still, based on my initial impression, I'd say that we're dealing with some kind of pipe bomb. Probably triggered when Drake opened the door."

"Thank God for the remote," Harrison said.

"And the taxi." Simon, who had been pacing back

and forth across the little room, stopped to settle against the back of a chair. "If that son of a bitch hadn't cut us off, we'd have been a hell of a lot closer when the bomb exploded."

"That son of a bitch is in there right now with second-degree burns," Avery reminded him.

"I know. And I'm sorry. I didn't mean it like that. It's just that, it could have been J.J." The minute the words were out he realized he'd said too much. "Or any of us. Hell, we could all be dead right now."

"But we're not," Drake said. "That's all that really matters. That and finding the people who did this. So if it was a pipe bomb, I assume you're expecting to find the same signature as the bomb in the helicopter and the one at the apartment on Fulton?"

"It seems likely," Tyler agreed, "but I won't know anything until I actually have a closer look, and right now, everything is literally too hot to handle."

"But if the explosion destroyed the apartment where they were making the bombs, then shouldn't that have been the end of it?" Simon asked.

"There could have been more than one location. Or even if there wasn't, it's easy enough to put together the kind of explosion they rigged for the SUV. Little bombs like that can be made pretty much anywhere. It's the bigger ones, like the one at the seaport, that need specialized equipment and special handling."

"Great, so now it could have been anybody," Drake said, throwing his hands up in the air in frustration. "For all we know, the attack wasn't even related."

"I'll know more when I've had a chance to look through the rubble, but I think I can safely say that it

was related. We just don't know how. Or more specifically, why."

"Why is easy," Simon said. "The bastards hate us. We
keep cutting them off at the knees."

"So if these guys are so bomb happy," Harrison
mused, "why not an explosion at the gallery or Lester's
apartment?"

"I don't think Lester thought either was in danger of
giving anything away. And he was right about the apartment. The forensics team found nothing." Tyler shrugged.
"And as to the gallery, so far Nash hasn't found anything
that might link to Dearborn, Wilderman, or any of the
other players."

"So what have you found on Lester so far?" Simon
asked, turning his attention to Avery.

"Nothing to tie him to the bombings yet, but Hannah
is still digging and Nash is still at the gallery. It's a big
place, maybe there's still something to find."

"But you don't think so?" Drake prompted, his gaze
on Avery.

"No. I don't. I think Lester was too smart for that. The
only hope we really have, evidencewise, is the computer."

"Still running diagnostics to try to restore it," Harrison
said. "But the presence of the key logger on Wilderman's
machine would point to Lester as a major player."

"Agreed." Avery nodded. "And his death might very
well mean that we're actually past endgame."

"With them on the losing side," Drake agreed.

"Yeah, well, I'd say trying to blow us up is a funny way
to end the chapter," Simon said.

"I meant the threat to the city. I'm thinking that it was
a one-two punch. First the hospital and then the seaport.

But we managed to avert the bigger of the two strikes, thanks to you, Simon. I'd say anyone else involved is probably running for cover right about now."

"So what about the SUV?" Simon asked.

"I'm thinking that the attack was personal. Someone who wanted payback for our thwarting their plans. And possibly for killing Lester."

"That would explain his dying comment," Drake said. "But somehow, I can't help but feel as if the other shoe is still waiting to drop."

"We should know more by the morning." Avery stood up as J.J. walked into the waiting room, her gait measured and her face pale. If there'd been any doubt that the night had taken its toll on her, there was none now.

"You okay?" Simon asked, rushing over to slide an arm around her, not caring what the hell it looked like. He just needed to touch her—to reassure himself that she was all right.

"Just a couple of cuts and a few new bruises," she said. "The doctor said I was lucky."

"I think we should all count our blessings tonight," Avery agreed. "And to that end, Jillian, I want you to go back to the brownstone. Simon will take you. You need some rest."

"But, I..." she started, then faded as she stumbled and leaned into Simon for support.

"You've been through a lot, and you need some down time. Nothing major is going to happen tonight," Avery assured her. "But if something breaks, we'll come get you. Okay?"

She nodded, pulling away from Simon, clearly determined to stand on her own two feet. And Simon felt a rush of something both possessive and proud. J.J.— *Jillian* was a force to be reckoned with. Although he had no right to feel either emotion. J.J. wasn't his. And no amount of wishful thinking on his part was going to change the fact.

CHAPTER **11**

The sitting room on the third floor of the brownstone was dark, which suited Jillian just fine. Her head was spinning, images of the carnage of the past few days running on an endless loop—the final scene with Lester, eyes widening slightly in surprise as her bullet ripped through him.

She'd killed a man. A man linked to two terrorist attacks, but still a living, breathing human being. And she'd shot him without a second's hesitation, her only thought to save Simon. And now she had blood on her hands. And like Lady Macbeth, she wasn't sure she'd ever be truly clean again.

She knew that it had been justifiable, but it didn't change the fact that in the moment, she'd been carried forward by rage. Emotion winning out over logic with lethal consequences. Was that how it had been for Ryan? His rage so powerful that it overcame any sense of love—of basic decency?

She'd been raised in a military family. And she understood that there were times when violence was unavoidable—even called for—but it had always been an abstract concept. Something affecting other people. Until it had become part of her everyday existence.

She'd always wondered why a woman wouldn't just walk away. Run for her life and never look back. But then she'd never understood the guilt. The shame. The feelings of complete worthlessness. Even with Ryan dead and buried, she'd still been trying to justify it. Find ways to forgive him. As if in doing so, she was somehow forgiving herself. But those days were behind her. She'd fought the darkness and come out on the other side. And she'd sworn it would never happen again.

So she should feel elated. She'd not only stood her ground, she'd fought the enemy and she'd won. Wasn't that why she'd joined Homeland Security in the first place? But instead, she just felt sick to her stomach, as if she'd stepped off of a precipice into an endless abyss.

She blew out a breath, wrapping her arms around herself, the lights of the building across the way twinkling in the deep shadows of what had to be early morning by now. She was supposed to be sleeping. But closing her eyes only made it worse. So she'd decided to go downstairs, offer her help. Harrison and Hannah were still working, trying to find something on Lester. Surely doing something beat the hell out of sitting here trying to keep from falling to pieces.

But despite her best intentions, she hadn't made it farther than the sitting room and the sofa, her eyes on the trees outside the window, her mind replaying the last moments of Norman Lester's life over and over again.

Behind her a floorboard creaked, and she felt a hand on her shoulder. Her reaction was intense and immediate. She jerked to her feet, twisting around, leading with a fist. But he caught her wrist before she could make contact, his fingers burning into her skin. Fear raced through her, and she fought to free herself, her mind still locked on the events in the warehouse.

"Easy, J.J.," Simon said, as the little voice in her head insisted that he wasn't here to hurt her. "It's just me."

"Oh, God," she whispered, tears filling her eyes. Confusion warred with her fear, and suddenly she just felt tired. As if all the life had been sucked out of her. She sagged, and Simon caught her, his strong arms supporting her as he helped her back to the sofa.

"I'm sorry. I didn't mean—" she broke off, the recent past blending with other, more painful memories. Ones she'd sworn never to share with Simon. Ryan had been Simon's best friend, and Ryan was dead. There was nothing to be gained by opening old wounds.

And yet, they'd been opened, the little voice stubbornly whispered. The minute she'd seen Simon again.

"Sweetheart, it's okay," he said, almost as if he'd read her mind. "Everyone deals with taking a life differently. But no one handles it easily. So you don't need to apologize for anything."

She sighed, relieved and disappointed all at the same time. She'd believed once that they were connected on some cosmic level. But she'd been a fool. A silly girl who believed in fairy tales and fantasy. Now, as a grown woman, she knew better.

And yet, sitting here, his fingers massaging her palm, his deep green eyes full of concern, she found herself doubting, some part of her wanting to give in to the comfort she knew he was offering.

"I'm just having trouble sleeping," she said, pulling her hand free, forcing herself to push aside her rioting emotions. "I keep seeing...him...you know, just before I...It's like a movie I can't turn off. It just keeps playing over and over again."

"I know this doesn't help," he said, his voice gentle, "but it will get better. And for what it's worth, you probably saved my life. Even with the vest, if Lester had gotten off a second shot—"

She shivered, the image of Simon lying on the floor of the gallery presenting itself front and center, and this time when he slid an arm around her, she didn't shrug him off. "Were you like this? The first time you had to kill someone?"

There was silence as Simon considered her words, the darkened room somehow making the question seem more intimate. "It was different for me, but yeah, I had nightmares for a while. Still do sometimes."

"Different how?" she asked, feeling his warmth seep into her.

"Well, it was the heat of battle for one thing. Bullets and mortar shells flying every which way. We were jammed up in a mountain pass. Cut off and waiting for help to arrive. You can't imagine how chaotic it is. Sometimes you can't even tell who's shooting at whom."

"Oh, my God, did you?" Her eyes widened as a horrible thought planted itself in her brain. "It wasn't..."

"No, not friendly fire. I didn't kill one of my own. Although it happens. More often than anyone wants to admit. No, the way we were situated, it was easy enough to tell friendlies from hostiles. It's just that the latter were mostly kids. Armed to the teeth and determined to take us out—but still kids. So that's who I see in my nightmares. A kid who was barely old enough to shave. He wanted me dead, and in my own way, I suppose I wanted him dead, too. So we fought. Each of us trying to win the day." He paused again, clearly remembering. "In the end, I made it out of there alive, and he didn't."

"But you had no choice," she said, surprised at how important it was to defend him.

"There's always a choice, J.J. And although I believe I made the right one—the only one, all things considered—it didn't make the idea of it any easier to stomach."

"So why did you keep doing it then? The incident you're talking about was years ago, right? And yet, you kept on fighting. Kept reupping and going back. Surely there was a moment when you wanted out?"

"There were a lot of times I wanted to run. Usually in the heat of a firefight, when leaving wasn't an option. But even if I could have left, I wouldn't have."

"Because you're an honorable man."

"I don't know about that." He shook his head, a muscle tightening in his jaw as he shifted, breaking contact. "We all have things in our lives that we'd change if we could. But I believe in what I'm doing. Whether it's on the front lines in Afghanistan or here on the home front with A-Tac, I honestly believe I'm making the world a safer place. At the end of the day, I'm a soldier. Which means that what I do is always going to be dangerous. And I'm always going to hold other people's lives in my hands. It's not an easy life, but it's what I've chosen. And I'm good at it. At least most of the time."

"I'd say more often than not." She sighed, tipping back her head so that she could see him better, the street light highlighting the strong line of his jaw. "You have to take comfort in the fact that you've saved far more lives than you've taken."

"But you know now that it doesn't work that way." His voice held a trace of bitterness, and she thought about how many years had passed since the carefree days of college. They'd both grown up. Simon into a warrior. And she ... well, she was still working on it.

"No. You're right." She sighed. "It doesn't. But if I had to do it all over again, I wouldn't handle it differently. I'd still kill him."

"And you'd still feel remorse. It's the one thing that sets us apart from serial killers and psychopaths. We care. And as long as that's there, then I think we have to believe we're going to be okay."

"But it'll never be the same. You can never go back to the way you felt before."

"No." He shook his head. "But that's not always such a bad thing either. I believe that things happen for a reason."

"Like Ryan dying." She could feel him tense, even though they were no longer touching.

"I should have qualified my statement." His words were clipped, pain coloring his expression. "I should have said *most* things happen for a reason." He looked down at her hands, his frown deepening. "You're not wearing Ryan's ring."

It was a straightforward question, but the answer was far from simple. "I ... just ... " She tucked her left hand under her leg, searching for the right words, a feasible

explanation. One that wouldn't demand that she bare her
soul. "It was easier. Seeing it there was just too painful."

Silence swelled, Ryan's specter floating between them,
creating a gulf she wasn't sure they could ever cross.
Maybe it was for the best. And yet, when Simon made the
move to go, she reached for his hand again.

"Stay with me, Simon," she whispered. "Please. I don't
want to be alone."

He nodded, reaching out to pull her into his arms,
his strength surrounding her. She closed her eyes, letting the cadence of his breathing soothe her. And from
somewhere out of the mists of memory, she remembered
another night—long ago.

College. Freshman year. She'd had a date for a dance
with an upperclassman. A jock. The kind of guy every
girl went wild for. She'd spent days finding the right dress.
And on that night, she'd spent forever getting ready, wanting to look perfect. Only he'd never shown. He'd gone
instead with another girl. She'd been devastated—and
mortified.

But Simon had found out somehow, and he'd come
to her dorm. He threatened to murder the guy. And then
he'd taken her to the dance. It had been the most wonderful night of her life—the upperclassman completely
forgotten. She could still feel Simon's arms as they'd
tightened around her, the two of them swaying to the
music, the scent of his aftershave surrounding her, his
breath warm against her cheek. He'd been her knight in
shining armor.

Jillian sighed, closing her eyes as she listened to the
steady cadence of his heart, the past and the present, at
least for the moment, seeming one and the same.

*   *   *

The sky outside the window was starting to lighten, which meant, of course, that it was almost time to get up and face the day. Simon looked down at J.J., still curled up against him, her hair splayed out across his chest.

He wasn't usually big on regret, but just at the moment, he was feeling more than just guilt. He was feeling as if he'd lost something he'd never really had in the first place. And she was still lying here beside him. He'd held her through the night, watching as she slept. Remembering the past. Wondering if he could have done something to make it all turn out differently.

But there was no pushing back the clock. Even though she'd reached out to him last night, Ryan's shadow still hovered between them. And when she woke, she was going to remember who he was and what his rash decisions had taken from her. His heart constricted at the thought.

Ryan and Jillian had been happy. That much he was certain of. Of course, he'd stayed away as much as possible, but he'd spent a hell of a lot of time holed up in Godforsaken places with Ryan, and his friend had been fond of talking about his wife and their life together. Hell, he'd been so proud of her. How well she'd fit in as a Navy wife and how he couldn't possibly live without her.

And Simon had smiled and agreed and never let Ryan know just how deep his jealousy had gone. How much he had wanted J.J. for himself. Jesus, he was a fucking bastard. He'd not only coveted his friend's wife, he'd sent him into an impossible situation and gotten him killed. And now . . . shit, now he was holding her as she slept, thinking about how badly he wanted to bury himself inside her.

What kind of man had he become?

One who wanted Jillian Montgomery, for the girl she'd once been and for the woman she'd become. It was as simple as that.

He reached out to tuck a strand of hair behind her ear, and her eyes flickered open. He knew the time had come for them to talk. He could see it in the shadow that chased across her face, but he couldn't bear the idea of breaking the spell, so instead he pulled her into his arms and kissed her. They might not be able to surmount the events in their past, but right now, in this moment, he was determined to keep reality at bay for at least a little while longer.

It was selfish. But he didn't care. He needed to feel himself inside her, to create something he could hold on to after all of this was over and she'd walked away. He'd made his choices—and there was always a price to pay, but that didn't mean he didn't wish it were different sometimes. Especially right now, holding J.J.

He pulled her closer, relieved when she responded in kind, her body pressing tightly against his. He kissed her lips, and then her cheeks, and the tender place on her neck that made her shiver. He ran his palms over her shoulders, letting them slide along the curve of her back, and across her ass, then up again until he cupped both breasts.

She moaned low in her throat, grinding against him, and he circled each nipple with the pads of his thumbs, delighting in the fact that she responded to him so quickly. With a little cry, she opened her mouth, their tongues tangling together as their desire took control. They thrust and parried—taking and giving, every touch ratcheting up the degree of pleasure.

He traced the line of her lips with his tongue, nipping the corners of her mouth, before trailing kisses along her cheek to the soft lobe of her ear. He bit against it, feeling her respond beneath his touch. He knew her so well, and yet he didn't know her at all.

There was something exciting in the idea. And frightening. He'd never allowed himself to depend on another person. To trust anyone on a level so intimate. And yet, here he was nearly unmanned by just the feel of her body moving against his.

Cradling her in his arms, he carried her into his bedroom and laid her against the sheets. Together, they pulled off their clothes, laughing in their haste, their need making them clumsy. And then she was reaching for him, her blue eyes clouded with passion, her body waiting and ready.

He straddled her, his gaze holding hers, as he allowed himself to simply drink in her beauty. And then she twined her arms around his neck, and he was lost. Bracing himself over her, he rubbed a knee against the moist juncture between her thighs and then bent his head to savor her breasts. Kissing first one, then the other. Teasing her with his tongue before finally taking her into his mouth and biting her nipple, her responsive cry almost his undoing.

He tasted the other nipple and then trailed kisses along her stomach, tracing the soft skin between her thighs, finally allowing himself the pleasure of tasting her, his tongue thrusting where he longed to follow, sucking and pulling, nipping and teasing until he felt her rise off the bed in her release.

He slid upward again, lying with his head cradled

between her breasts, content for the moment just to listen to her heartbeat. But then with a slow smile she moved, and they flipped over so that she was straddling him. Her fingers circled him, moving up and down, the sensations washing through him on a wave of pure pleasure.

She teased him with her hands until he couldn't stand another minute, and in one deft move he lifted her, thrusting inside her, the wet, hot moisture surrounding him. Grasping her hips, he moved her up and down, setting the rhythm. And with a tiny smile, she braced her hands on his shoulders, pulling upward so that they were almost disengaged and then slamming home again with a force that threatened to send him spiraling out of control.

But he wasn't ready to surrender, and bending his legs, he pulled up to a sitting position, cradling her against him, rocking slightly so that he moved inside her, the motion sending her squirming against him.

He smiled, kissing her cheeks and her eyelids, his hands cupping her breasts, his thumbs circling her nipples, each movement designed to move them closer to the edge. Then he kissed her. And with a moan, she pushed him back again, pumping hard against him, the exquisite pain building inside him until he was meeting each and every thrust with one of his own, the two of them driving together, reaching out for that moment of bliss.

And then it was there, the intensity electrifying, and he knew that even if he never had this moment again—he would cherish it always.

Jillian zipped her jeans and then pulled her sweater over her head. Simon was still sleeping, looking younger in repose. More like the boy she'd fallen in love with all those years ago. But last night had been an aberration—a one-off. A new memory for her to hold in her heart.

Yet even as she had the thought, she knew she had to let him go. There was too much between them. And she wasn't sure she was strong enough to deal with the possibility that if she told him the truth about Ryan, he might choose to reject her—again. Better to cut her losses now, get out before it had the power to hurt her.

"Going somewhere?" His voice was thick with sleep, and she shivered as she remembered the power of last night's shared passion.

"We need to get downstairs. There's work to be done. And people will talk." It sounded priggish, and she suppressed a smile. She wasn't at all worried about what the other members of A-Tac thought. She just knew she had to get out of this room before she let herself get in any deeper.

Simon sat up, the muscles in his chest rippling with the movement, his eyes dark with emotion, and she swallowed reflexively, taking an involuntary step backward.

"You're not going to solve anything by running away," he said, his gaze pinning her to the wall. "We need to talk."

She nodded, moving cautiously to sit on the end of the bed. Not sure that this was a good idea, but pretty certain that she didn't really have a choice in the matter, and besides, her legs probably wouldn't support her anyway.

"Look," he started, then stopped, staring down at his hands, clearly at a loss for words. The silence stretched for a moment, and then he sighed, lifting his gaze to meet hers again, the pain reflected there almost taking her breath away. "I know you blame me for what happened to Ryan."

"What are you talking about?" Surprise made her voice sharp. She hadn't expected him to say that. "I don't blame you."

"Well, you should," he said, his voice cracking with emotion. "Because I was the one who got him killed."

"He was killed by an enemy combatant. During the raid in Somalia. I have a letter. And they talked about it when he received the medal of honor. Bravery during a firefight."

"Well, there's more to it than that." He leaned forward, regret creasing his face. "A lot more."

She studied the line of his shoulders, the slant of his head, forgetting about her own problems for the moment. This was clearly eating him alive. She wanted to reach for his hand, to soothe him somehow. He was close enough that she could feel his breathing, but she dared not touch him. Not if she wanted him to talk.

"So tell me what happened."

"On paper it was a pretty simple operation."

"You're talking a Navy SEAL team," she said, working to keep the emotion from her voice. "Nothing you guys do is ever simple."

"True." She could see his face soften just a little as he smiled. "But this one shouldn't have been that hard. We were tasked with extracting two journalists being held hostage in Somalia. Just a quick in and out. Our recon indicated that the building was only minimally fortified. We came in on two choppers. Sixteen in all. It turned out there was over double that number waiting for us once we'd landed."

"I thought you said—"

"Yeah, famous last words. I still don't know how we

got it so wrong. But by the time we figured it out, we were already on the ground. I was in charge of the mission, which meant that once we realized what we were up against, it was my call whether we stayed or we aborted."

"And you chose to stay."

"The journalists were innocent. And they were women. And all I could think about was what might be happening to them. So I made the call."

"You couldn't have just left them. Not after coming so close."

"That was my logic. But I never stopped to think about what the cost was going to be. I was so focused on the objective that I forgot about collateral damage. I sent half of the men, with Ryan in charge, into the building, while the rest of us tried to hold the attacking enemy back. I figured it was our best option."

"So what happened?" she asked, still wanting to take his hand, to erase the pain etched across his face.

"There were more men inside. Almost as many as there were outside. We tried to close ranks, but I'd effectively split us in two. Somehow Ryan and his men managed to get the women freed. The two of them came running out the front of the building, bullets still flying everywhere."

"And Ryan?" she asked, not sure she wanted to hear it again, to relive the horror of his death. It only made her feel more confused and guilty. But Simon needed to say it out loud.

"He never came out. None of them did. And I didn't have the manpower to go in after them. Not with the journalists caught in the crossfire. They were my mission. So I made another choice. I left my men there to die. I sacrificed them to save those women."

"You did what you were charged with doing."

"We don't leave our men behind, J.J." Something in his voice reminded her of the boy he'd once been. Innocent. Untouched by the horrors reality held for those who dared to fight for a better world. And this time she didn't resist the urge, she took his hand in hers.

"You had no choice, Simon."

"Maybe not at that point. But yeah, I had a choice. I could have chosen my men. I could have aborted the mission the minute I realized that we were outgunned. But I didn't. I just couldn't take my eye off the prize."

"The prize was two women's lives. By your own words, two *innocent* women. What you did—what all of you did—was heroic. And had you done anything different, you wouldn't have been able to live with yourself."

"I can't live with myself now. Because of me, my best friend is dead. Your husband is dead. I did that, J.J. I made that choice."

"Well, you didn't make it in a vacuum," she said, anger flashing as she thought of Ryan. It always came back to him. "And you sure as hell didn't force him to go into that building. Even if you'd forbidden it, Ryan would probably have still gone in. He thrived on the danger. It's what he lived for."

"Yeah, but that's the point, isn't it? I was supposed to be the one who held him back. Who kept him from doing stupid things. But instead, I was the one who sent him in there. If I hadn't done that, he'd still be alive."

"You can't know that. Even if you'd decided to retreat, you still might have lost your men. The odds were against you the minute you landed. But if you'd pulled back then you'd have accomplished nothing. All those people would have died for nothing."

"But I killed Ryan." He bit the words out, and Jillian wondered if he'd ever actually said them to anyone besides himself.

"No. You didn't. Ryan died in combat. He died doing what he loved. It was a risk he willingly undertook every damn day of his life. And sooner or later, it was going to be his time. If not Somalia, then somewhere else. He was never the kind of man who would have been content to just die in his bed. It wasn't your fault."

He lifted his gaze to meet hers, looking so deeply she thought for certain that he would be able to see all of her secrets. But then with a sigh, he looked away, pulling his hand free, his face still tight with anguish.

"You have to find a way to forgive yourself, Simon." She watched as he gripped the pillow, the muscles in his shoulders tightening as he fought his demons. "You were just doing your job. Had the roles been reversed, Ryan would have done exactly the same." Only he probably wouldn't have been as conflicted.

There was significance in the thought, but she wasn't ready to try to figure out what it might mean. Instead she pushed off the side of the bed. "I don't blame you." She was repeating herself, but if nothing else, she needed for him to believe that. "I never did. Not for a single second."

"Then why..." he trailed off, his confusion tugging at her heart.

She sucked in a breath, wishing she were a stronger woman. Wishing that she'd made different choices all those years ago. But she hadn't. And she wasn't ready to admit that. To tell him everything. Truth was, she might never be. She hated herself for being so afraid. But it was better to close the door and walk away now. While she was still standing.

She squared her shoulders, hard-won self-preservation kicking in. "I can't do this, Simon. It's all too much. You. Me. Ryan. It's too complicated. And it hurts. I just can't."

She waited for him to say something. To try to stop her maybe, but he just looked so damn sad. And she knew then with absolute certainty that she was making the right decision. So she turned and walked out of the room.

CHAPTER 12

Simon walked into the makeshift war room still reeling from the night before and the words that had followed. They'd found each other again. Despite everything. And it had been even better than before, if that was possible. It had been everything he'd remembered and more.

And because of that—because of *her*—he'd found the courage to face his greatest fear. To admit the guilt he carried for his part in Ryan's death. It had almost killed him. But he'd said the words. Out loud. To J.J. And then he waited for her condemnation, but there had been none. In fact, she'd begged him to let it go. To forgive himself. She'd held his hand and reminded him all over again why he'd fallen for her all those years ago.

He'd actually felt a small glimmer of hope.

Then she'd walked out the goddamned door. And he felt as if he'd been sucker-punched.

Everyone was already gathered. Avery and Nash stood

by the fireplace talking. Hannah and Harrison were huddled over their computers. Half-eaten bagels and cups of coffee littered the tabletop, and Drake, Tyler, and J.J. were seated on the far side, their conversation animated.

Considering everything that had happened, Simon felt even more like an outsider than usual. Maybe it was just his lot in life to be once removed from the people he cared about. His latest attempt to reach out to someone had failed so completely that she couldn't even find the words to tell him why.

Walking the rest of the way into the room, he grabbed a bagel and a chair by Hannah.

"Glad you could join us, Kincaid," Nash grinned. "We were wondering if you'd make the meeting."

"Very funny," he said, feigning a laugh as he reached for the cream cheese. "You try getting shot at close quarters and see how spry you are the next morning." He'd meant the comment to be offhand, but for some reason it had the opposite effect, everyone sobering as Avery moved to the head of the table and Nash took a seat.

"So how are you feeling?" Avery asked, his dark eyes probing.

"I've been better, but then again I've been a lot worse." He wasn't actually sure about the latter, but it wasn't something he wanted to discuss. And Avery wasn't referring to his heart anyway. He was talking about Simon's leg. Which wasn't exactly working at full capacity. But he wasn't going to share that fact either. "Basically, I'm ready for whatever these bastards want to throw at us next."

He shot a look in J.J.'s direction, but she ducked her head, avoiding his gaze. One step forward, ten steps back. But damn it, he wasn't going to give up without a fight.

"You and me both, brother," Nash was saying, fortunately oblivious to the turn of Simon's thoughts as he
grabbed a pot on the buffet and poured himself a cup of
coffee.

"So now that we're all together," Avery said, "why
don't we get started? Tyler, now that you've had time to
look at the SUV, did you find a common signature for the
smaller bombs?"

"Nothing that would lead me to a specific individual,
unfortunately. And I did run the information through all of
our databases. But there are enough commonalities for me
to be certain that the same person was behind the smaller
blasts. I was also able to lift traces of the explosive used,
and the compound in all three was identical in structure—
which points to it all coming from one source."

"Like the apartment on Fulton."

"Affirmative." Tyler nodded. "I've got my guys digging for trace over there right now. Although confirming
place of origin isn't going to help when it comes to figuring out who actually did it."

"Well, Lester seems an odds-on choice." Simon took a
sip of coffee and then leaned back regarding the assem-
bled company.

"I'd have to agree, but there's no evidence to link him
to any of the bombings."

"Which isn't true when it comes to the shootings."
Sporting pale blonde streaks and a fairly modest pair of
tortoiseshell frames, Hannah lifted her head from her
computer with a smile. "We got the ballistics report on
Lester's gun. It's a match to all three murders. Wilderman, Sanchez, and Sara. So I'd say that it's safe to con-
clude that he's our shooter."

"So if Lester killed Sanchez," J.J. said, still avoiding Simon's gaze, "it's possible that the Duane Reade bag was a set-up. If he was working with Dearborn, why would he have done anything that would have given away the bomber's location—unless the plan all along was for us to find it and believe that the killer had somehow missed it when he took out Sanchez?"

"And if Lester, in effect, handed us the address to the apartment on Fulton," Hannah continued, "then we can be fairly certain that the explosion there was meant for us as well."

"But why would he risk the bomber's operation by sending us in just before what was meant to be a detonation at the seaport?" Nash asked.

"Maybe the bomber was already supposed to have been in place," Drake suggested. "That way the two explosions would have been almost simultaneous. One taking us out and another taking out the seaport and everyone in the vicinity."

"I don't know," Simon said, wheels turning. "If that was the case, and the timing was off, then why not take the opportunity to get the hell out of there? Even abort the mission if necessary?"

"Zealots, if that is in fact what we're dealing with," Avery answered, "aren't known for making logical decisions. The man committed suicide by bomb, after all. Not someone I'd expect to act rationally."

"Well, as usual, it seems that someone definitely has a hard-on for A-Tac," Drake quipped. "Or at least for Jillian, Harrison, Simon, and me. The bomb in the SUV was definitely meant for us. There's no other explanation."

"Now that I think about it," Hannah said, "it rules

Lester out as our bomber. I mean, we know he didn't have time to put it in place. Drake and the SUV weren't at the gallery."

"And he never left my sight when I was with him at his apartment," Drake added.

"So we know there's another player." Simon frowned. "And he's got to be tied to Lester somehow. What else have we got on Lester?"

"He comes from Arizona originally," Hannah said. "Went to college in New Mexico and majored in art. He moved to the city shortly after graduation and seems to have made a name for himself and his gallery among art patrons in the city. His finances don't show anything hinkey. He does travel a lot. But that's to be expected in his line of work."

"He's not on any watch lists," Avery continued, "and so far we haven't been able to tie him into any kind of international movement. For the most part, he's been pretty apolitical. He hasn't voted in the last three elections, but he's also never shown any kind of anti-American sentiment."

"So he's really good at covering his tracks," J.J. offered.

"Maybe not as good as he thinks," Harrison said, a smug smile indicating that he'd found something. "I think maybe I've found a couple of things on his computer. First off, I isolated the program he was using to operate the key logger on Wilderman's computer. It's pretty basic. And from what I can see, he only used it a couple of times. Once as a test run of sorts and then again to make the reservation for the helicopter tour."

"Yeah, but we were already fairly certain it was Lester

who was using the key logger; that's what led us to suspect him in the first place." Simon pushed to his feet, frustration making him restless.

"You said a couple of things," Drake prompted Harrison as Simon paced the back of the room.

"Right. I did find something else. According to an encrypted file I was able to recover, Lester has a storage unit in New Jersey. Which considering his line of work isn't all that interesting per se. So I did a little digging. And it turns out that although Lester paid the bills, the unit isn't listed in his name." Harrison paused, sitting back, his gaze encompassing them all. "Technically, it belongs to someone named Isaacs. Joseph Isaacs."

"Joseph," Simon said, shaking his head, and then the light bulb went off. "*Yusuf.* You think Joseph Isaacs is the Yusuf from the notebook."

"I think it's possible," Harrison admitted. "Of course it's also credible to assume that Lester is Isaacs."

"Actually it's not." Hannah hit a key on her computer, and the monitor on the wall above the credenza flashed a photograph of a group of men milling around at some kind of meeting.

"This is a picture taken at an art exhibition in Soho last year attended by dealers only. You'll note Lester is on the far right." Using the laser pointer, she highlighted Lester sitting at a table. "And next to him, at least according to the notations under the photo, is Joseph Isaacs." She zoomed in on the picture, highlighting the man's face. "I'm running facial recognition software to see if he's known by any other aliases."

"Did you find anything else?" Avery asked.

"Not much. The information is pretty sketchy.

Assuming I have the right man, he's a British national, an art dealer, although unfortunately not a very well-known one. I'm waiting for passport pictures from MI-6 to verify. According to immigration records, the British Isaacs has been in and out of the States over the past five years with some regularity."

"Everything on the up and up?" Tyler asked.

"There is nothing in the ICE records to make me think there's been a problem, but there are some entries without documented exit. Which raises a flag, although there are certainly legitimate explanations for that sort of thing."

"Where is he now?"

"That's the sketchy part. I can't find a record of his coming into the country any time recently. But I've got him leaving Britain about three weeks ago. And you know as well as I do that there are all kinds of ways to get in and out of the country under the radar, if one has the right resources."

"Like being a key part of a terrorist organization."

"Simon," Avery said, "any chance he could be the seaport bomber?"

Simon studied the photograph again, then shook his head. "No. The other guy was smaller and his hair was lighter and he had a scar." He traced a line across his cheek in demonstration.

"Well, whoever Isaacs is, he's not on our radar," Hannah said. "I ran his name through our computers, and nothing popped, so I'm running it using the Arabic now."

"That would be what?" Nash asked. "Yusuf Ishaq?"

"Among the possible variations," Hannah agreed.

"What about his relationship with Lester?" Drake asked. "Do you have anything more than the photograph?"

"No." Hannah shook her head. "I was actually lucky to have that—it came from a rather obscure professional publication. I've not been able to uncover anything else that connects him directly to Lester, beyond the storage unit, but I've only just started, and it's going to take a little time."

"Which we don't have," Simon said. "Even if this thing is over, whoever was behind it is going to be scrambling to cover their tracks. We've seen that already."

"And if there's still something on the drawing board," Jillian continued, "they're going to be even more motivated to go to ground."

"All of which means we need to get to that storage unit before someone beats us to it."

CHAPTER **13**

The storage facility in North Bergen, New Jersey, looked like thousands of others across the country. Eleven rows of low-pitched, cinder block buildings painted a bright white with flat aluminum roofs, each of the 576 individual cubicles fronted by a rolling steel door.

Harrison pulled the new SUV up in front of the building. The guy in charge had been only too willing to surrender a key to Lester's unit once Jillian had shown him her ID. It was amazing what one could accomplish with the proper credentials. She wasn't sure how A-Tac normally managed, considering that, for all practical purposes, they didn't actually exist, but she supposed they worked it out. Maybe they always roped in an official of some kind.

So far, she and Simon hadn't had any time alone together. Which in some ways was a relief. Last night had been amazing, and though she didn't regret any of it, she knew she'd made the right decision to walk away.

There was just too much standing between them. And considering the fact that he'd let her go, she was pretty certain he agreed.

She watched as he opened the door on the storage unit, his muscles rippling under the black T-shirt he wore, the edge of a tattoo showing just below one sleeve. For a moment, her breath caught in her throat as she remembered what it felt like to have those arms around her. His hard body, his sharp masculine scent.

Shaking her head, she pushed aside her heated thoughts. Better to let the feelings go and keep him at arm's length.

"Looks like the place is full of crates," Harrison said, his voice pulling her sharply back to the present. "Art, from the looks of it."

"Yeah, but from all over the place." Simon frowned down at the bill of lading of one of the crates. "This one is out of Ecuador. And the one behind it is from Paris."

"I've got one from Indonesia, here." Jillian skimmed the paper tucked into a plastic sleeve on the outside of the crate. "But it's going out, not coming in."

"Interesting," Harrison said. "So we've got two-way traffic."

"Yes, but none of that is particularly surprising for an art dealer." Jillian shrugged, moving to another crate to check its contents.

"No." Simon agreed. "But it would imply some degree of success. I mean, it can't be cheap to ship this stuff in and out of the country."

"Not to mention buying the art in the first place." Jillian frowned down at the crate's bill of lading.

"There's a lot of shit in here," Simon said to no one in

particular as he moved farther back into the storage unit, shifting crates as he walked.

"No kidding," Harrison agreed. "Must be at least twenty crates. Maybe more."

"Yeah, but something isn't right here," Jillian said, still frowning. "According to the bill of lading, this crate contains two paintings. Both watercolors. Which most likely means they're not very big. But look at this crate. It's huge."

"I see what you mean." Harrison nodded. "This one's the same. One painting. But still a large crate. Although I'd assume that for overseas transport something like a painting would have to be carefully protected."

"Agreed, but this still seems like overkill." Jillian picked up another bill of lading. "This one lists dimensions for one of the two paintings inside. Twelve by fifteen. Inches. And this crate has to be more than four feet long. And at least three feet tall."

"So why don't we verify the contents?" Simon appeared at her elbow, his breath brushing against her ear as he bent across her to retrieve a crowbar leaning against another crate.

It took a couple of minutes for him to pry the top off. But once he'd pulled the nails free, the wooden lid was easily removed. Inside, the box was filled with synthetic straw—a good six inches deep—and beneath that, carefully secured, the two listed paintings, both lying flat on top of a second layer of the straw.

"There's still a lot of crate underneath the paintings," Jillian said, as she carefully lifted the first painting out, laying it on a nearby crate. Simon took the second one, while Harrison removed the second layer of straw. Below that was a wooden barrier serving as a false bottom.

Using the crowbar again, Simon pried the piece of plywood free to reveal a row of machine guns. Russian made, if the markings were any indication.

"Son of a bitch," Simon said with a low whistle. "Looks like Lester and this Joseph guy were dealing a hell of a lot more than old paintings."

"It looks like there's another layer beneath these," Jillian said, pushing aside more straw, careful to keep from touching the actual weapons.

"Let's see what else they've been hiding in here." Simon picked up the crowbar again, in short order pulling the lids from several more crates. Each of them, like the first, held the listed artwork, but beneath that they found more weapons.

Grenade launchers, hand guns, assault rifles, even a crate full of C4. Some manufactured in Russia, some in Germany, and even a couple of crates with arms manufactured in the U.S., one headed for Nicaragua and another to Belgrade. Places where it was easy to get contraband into the country.

"Hey, I might have found something significant back here," Harrison called from behind a stack of unopened crates.

"Something more astonishing than the cache of munitions we've just uncovered?" Simon asked.

"Well, maybe not as astonishing, but quite possibly a hell of a lot more useful." Harrison stepped back into view, holding up his find—an iPad. "If this belongs to Lester or Isaacs, we just might have hit pay dirt."

He powered the little machine on. "Gotta love portability." The screen flashed blue, then rows of apps appeared. None of them looking all that interesting.

"Looks to me like some pretty normal shit. I see Angry Birds and a couple of news apps. Nothing helpful there." Simon shifted so that he could see better, the movement placing him directly behind Jillian, the heat from his body making it hard to think.

Harrison opened a program and scrolled down, nodding when he found whatever it was he'd been looking for. "This is Lester's iPad." He pointed to the name and then closed the screen, scrolling through the rows of apps until he came to a word-processing program. "Let's see what kind of documents he's got in here."

At first the program refused to open, demanding a password, but Harrison navigated out of the app and instead opened a browser. Then after typing in a URL and a password, he downloaded another application. In just a few more minutes, he reopened the program, and the box demanding the password was gone, a list of documents appearing in its place.

"Looks like more paperwork on the shipments. I suspect, if we go through them all, we'll find a document for each crate." He opened a couple, and together they skimmed through the two-page reports, each listing the artistic contents of the crates, as well as customs information and insurance estimates.

Simon whistled again. "I had no idea selling art could be this lucrative."

"Only if you can find the right buyers," Jillian replied, shifting slightly so that Simon had to step back.

"Yeah, well, I'm thinking the big money here isn't in the art." Harrison clicked open another document, this one listing the hidden contents of one of the crates. The machine guns. "Jesus, this stuff is worth a fortune on the black market."

"Any idea where it was coming in? Or going out, for that matter? My guess is that even with all the precautions to hide the contents, there'd still have been trouble if it came into the country through normal channels."

"According to this," Harrison said, "most of the crates were coming into a warehouse just outside of Jersey City."

"That's a big port." Jillian picked up another bill of lading. "I suppose it wouldn't be that hard for a shipment to skip through customs, with the proper amount of inducement, of course."

"American ingenuity at its best," Simon agreed.

"Well, according to Google maps," Harrison said, "the address listed belongs to a warehouse just at the edge of the port."

"Definitely a plus when you're trafficking in contraband." Simon pulled out his cellphone and began taking pictures of the crates and their contents. "I'm thinking our next move should be to hit the warehouse."

"Agreed," Harrison said, "but I think we should have backup. You guys head over there for a look, and I'll call Avery and have him send the cavalry. So stay put until he gets there, okay? I'll hang back here and finish documenting what we've found."

"I don't like leaving you alone," Jillian protested. "And without a vehicle."

"No worries. There's a whole row of rental pickups out there. And these days, all you need to hotwire a car is a computer and a little know-how. I'll be fine. Besides, once I tell Avery what we've found, you can bet Tyler will make a beeline over here. There's no way she'll be able to resist a room full of stuff that goes boom."

* * *

The warehouse was at the end of a rutted road on a man-made peninsula lined with similar buildings, all of them in disrepair. Simon drove slowly, he and J.J. keeping their eyes peeled for any sign of activity, but the place remained eerily quiet, the harbor glistening gray in the fading twilight.

"Looks deserted," J.J. said, putting voice to Simon's thoughts.

"All the better for us to get in and out and find something to lead us to Joseph Isaacs and the people he's been working with."

"I don't know. It just feels too quiet, if that makes any sense."

"It does. Especially considering the reception we've gotten the last two times we've followed a lead. But the only prayer we have of catching these people is to keep pushing."

"And when they push back?"

"We push that much harder. I know it's tough, and I wouldn't blame you if you wanted to call it quits. Especially considering everything that's happened." He held his breath, not really certain what answer he was looking for. But if he'd thought about it, he'd have known there was only one possibility. This was J.J. after all.

"I'm here for the duration," J.J. responded, her chin shooting up, the motion a sure sign that he'd angered her. "I knew when I went to work for Homeland Security that it was possible I'd wind up in dangerous situations. I just didn't expect it to be like this." She paused, clearly considering her words. "You know, here—"

"With me?" he finished for her. "I know. And I know it's hard."

"But we're both professionals, so we'll get through it."

Simon's guilt surfaced again. What the hell was he thinking? There's no way she would ever have voluntarily agreed to partner with him. Let alone pick up where they'd left off ten years ago, before she and Ryan…he let the thought drop. As much as he wished he could turn back time, handle decisions he'd made differently, it wasn't possible.

His mother hadn't been a model parent, but in rare moments of lucidity, she'd always said that a person made his or her own bed, and that there was no changing it after the fact. At least in this one thing, she'd been right. And besides, even in better times, he'd never been the man J.J. had wanted. It had always been Ryan.

And Simon had never been the kind of man to settle for being second-best.

He pulled the SUV into the shadow of the building across from the warehouse and turned off the motor.

"So how do you want to handle this?" she asked, her mind clearly back on business. "Do you want to wait for backup?"

"Doesn't seem necessary," Simon said, getting out of the SUV and pulling his weapon. "Like you said, the place seems to be deserted. But if you want, I can go ahead and scout it out while you check in with Avery?"

"No way," she said, as she too exited the vehicle, gun at the ready. "You're not going in there without me."

He smiled, thinking that she was a hell of a lot better at this kind of thing than she gave herself credit for.

The warehouse, at the end of the row facing the harbor, was smaller than the others. It was fronted by two cargo bays and a small door at the top of a short flight of stairs.

They approached the first bay, guns drawn, not willing to take any chances, but it was locked from the inside.

The second bay was also locked. So they headed up the stairs to the door. As expected, it, too, was locked. And while Simon could have made short work of the lock with a well-placed shot, it was also barred from inside, which meant there was no access here either.

"So what next?" J.J. asked, her back to the wall as her gaze swept across the empty street and adjacent warehouses.

"We need to find another way in."

"I agree," she said, "and the only way to do that is to check out the rest of the building's perimeter. So in an effort to cover ground more quickly, I'm thinking we split up and head down each side of the building. If we're lucky, we'll find some other way to get inside."

"I don't know. Seems like it might be better if we stay together." He knew he wasn't making sense. If it had been anyone but J.J., he'd have thought it was an excellent idea to split up. Which smacked of chauvinism—and something else he wasn't even going to try to put a name to.

"It's your call," she said with a shrug, her expression hard to read. "But I still think it's the best thing to do."

"Yeah, I guess you're right. So we'll split up and meet in back unless we find a way in."

"Okay." She nodded, suppressing a smile, already moving toward the metal stairs.

"Hang on," he said, his fingers closing around her shoulder as she turned again to face him. "I want you to keep your eyes open. All right? If there was someone here, I think they'd already have shown themselves, but it never hurts to be too cautious."

"I'll be careful," she replied, her eyes meeting his. "I promise." She smiled, and he relaxed his grip, knowing that he had no right to try to hold her back, and yet still wanting to be the one to protect her. It was a modern-day conundrum. But he knew he had to let her go.

"So if you do find a way in," he said as she started down the stairs, "hold position and wait for me. Got it?"

"Loud and clear." She stopped, giving a mock salute, and then took the final two stairs and disappeared around the south corner of the building.

Still fighting misgivings about leaving her on her own, Simon headed around the north end, moving in a crouch, gun at the ready. In the distance, he could hear the sounds of the harbor. The plaintive cry of a seagull, the tremulous bass of a tugboat, and the hollowed-out clanging of rigging against masts floating across the water from the boat basin on the Manhattan side.

Otherwise it was quiet, the shadows starting to lengthen as the sun set behind him. The passageway between the two warehouses was narrow, a battered hurricane fence separating them. He moved forward, stopping once to check out a locked door, also barred from the inside, and then to examine what looked to be the entrance to a cellar. It, too, proved to be securely closed without offering a way in.

The building's windows, some of them tantalizingly broken, ran along the upper floor, with no easy access. Even with a ladder, they'd be difficult to reach, and the few scattered crates he'd found were too rotten to hold his weight even if carefully stacked.

Hopefully J.J. was having more luck. She'd always been the innovative one. He remembered once when he and Ryan had been goaded into accepting a hare-brained challenge issued by some upperclassmen, it had been J.J. who'd figured out how to accomplish the task without breaking their necks.

Close by campus there was a railroad tunnel running through the surrounding hillside. Extending about half a mile, it was old and narrow, but still in use. And it wasn't uncommon for kids to try to traverse it, the risk being that if you were caught by a train, there was nowhere to hide. Of course there were schedules, but the trains, mostly carrying cargo, were never on time.

Anyway, he and Ryan had set out for the tunnel, arriving at one end, the upperclassmen waiting at the other. It had been late at night, but only fifteen minutes before the train was due. J.J. had shown up just as they were starting out. Ryan had waved her off, saying that the tunnel was no place for a girl, but she'd ignored him, instead presenting them with a blueprint of the tunnel she'd found somewhere online.

The salient point was that there was a catwalk above the tracks, and by accessing it, they could walk the tunnel without fear of being caught by the train. And that's exactly what they'd done. All three of them.

And when, about ten minutes in, the train arrived— early—they'd held position, waiting for it to pass. He could still see J.J.'s eyes sparkling in the beam of their flashlights, her hair blowing behind her, exhilaration etched across her face as the train rumbled by beneath them. Watching her unadulterated joy had almost been more rewarding than seeing the frightened faces of the upperclassmen when they'd finally emerged from the tunnel, sans J.J., who'd gone back the way they'd come so that he and Ryan wouldn't lose face.

Jillian might have changed her name, but she was still the same woman. He'd been lucky to have her in his life then, and he was lucky that she was here now. No matter what lay between them.

With a sharp exhalation, Simon pulled his thoughts away from the past, focusing on the here and now. He'd reached the end of the warehouse with nothing at all to show for it. The backside, like the front, sported two bays. But the doors here were rusted, the salty sea air chiseling away at them.

There was no sign of J.J. And after a thorough check, no way to open either of the back bay doors, despite their dilapidated state. The smaller door, however, was another matter. It was standing open, its padlock lying on the ground in pieces.

He hadn't heard a shot, which meant that it couldn't have been J.J. So that meant that someone had broken in before them. Frowning, he ignored the urge to head inside for a look, remembering that he'd promised J.J. he'd wait. So instead, careful not to turn his back to the opening, he moved to the far corner of the building to check for her.

There was no one there. And suddenly, his mind trotted out the image of J.J heading up the stairs to Lester's apartment, leading with his gun—a Glock 19, complete with silencer.

Damn it all to hell. He'd told her to wait.

A rush of irritation pushed away all thoughts of her ingenuity as he headed back to the door, the evidence clear now that he knew what he was looking for. J.J. had shot off the lock. And then, clearly disobeying orders, she'd gone inside without him.

CHAPTER **14**

The warehouse was dark, the back entrance leading to a warren of hallways and deserted office space. Jillian knew she should have waited for Simon, but once she'd opened the door, the lure had been too much. She promised herself she wouldn't go far. Just a quick look and then she'd double back and wait.

He'd always hated her impetuous side, warning that it was going to get her in trouble one day. But so far, life had proved him wrong. It was only when she'd elected to play it safe that she'd wound up in trouble.

Maybe if she hadn't been so quick to take a backseat to Ryan...but there was no point in what if-ing herself to death. She sure as hell wasn't going to let herself wind up in that position again. She inched forward, gun still drawn. The irony of her thoughts didn't escape her. In electing to walk away from Simon and whatever it was that had happened last night, she was taking the safe route. The risk was Simon.

So maybe she wasn't so fearless after all.

Ahead of her, a shadow moved, and she strained, listening for some sign that someone was out there. But everything was quiet. She reached for a light switch, but the light above flickered once, popped, and then went black again.

So she took another step forward, stopping at the corner, her heart pounding in her chest, everything seeming overly loud in the still of the warehouse. Back to the wall, she counted to three and then swung into the intersecting hallway.

It was empty, the fading light from a window at the end of the passageway making the lengthening shadows seem to shimmy. She released a breath she hadn't realized she'd been holding, relief making her giddy.

Then something behind her shifted, the sound of leather against concrete sending her spinning around, gun leveled at the darkened hallway she'd just left.

"Don't shoot." Simon stepped from the shadows, one hand raised. "It's just me."

"Mother of God, Simon, I could have killed you." She lowered the Glock, her hand shaking. "What the hell were you doing sneaking up on me like that?"

"Trying to figure out where the hell you'd gone." Even though they were whispering, she could hear the anger in his voice. "I told you to wait for me."

"I know." She shook her head in apology. "But I figured I'd just a have a quick look while I waited."

"Rookie mistake," he said, his mouth drawn tight, a muscle in his jaw twitching. "And a surefire way to get yourself killed."

"I'm sorry." She took a step toward him. "I should have waited. I guess I got a little carried away."

"You think?" he said, as he came to stand beside her. "Look, J.J., I'm not trying to bust your chops. I just want you to be careful."

"And I was—being careful, I mean. I was only going to come a little way in and then go right back. You just got here sooner than I expected. And for what it's worth, I'm glad you're here. This place may be empty but it still gives me the creeps."

"You see anything at all?" he asked, his jaw relaxing.

"No. So far all the rooms I've passed have been empty."

"Which means we were right, and the place is deserted."

"Maybe," she acknowledged, "but there's not a lot of dust or debris either. Basically, compared to the outside condition, this place is clean as a whistle, which wouldn't be the case if it had truly been empty for a long time."

"You think someone has been in here to empty the place out?"

"It's possible, or maybe they just didn't need the offices. If they were simply using this place to offload cargo, then they probably wouldn't have use for any additional space. Just the storage area."

"All right then, let's check it out. I'm guessing this hallway should open out into the warehouse proper."

"Any word from Avery?" she asked.

"No. But I'm not getting any cell reception. Must be something to do with the water. Or the buildings. Or maybe it's just a dead zone. How about you?"

She pulled her phone from her pocket and turned it on. "You're right. I don't have any bars either."

"It shouldn't matter. He'll see our SUV when he gets here, so he'll know we've gone inside."

A cloud drifted across what was left of the sun, the hallway growing even darker. "We're losing daylight fast," Simon said. "I think we'd best get moving if we want to be able to see where we're going."

"Agreed." She tightened her hand on her gun as they moved forward, Simon turning on his tac-light so that they could better see the hallway in front of them.

There were a couple more empty rooms and a final passageway that led off toward the north side of the building and more offices. Then, at the end of the hallway, a set of double doors that presumably opened out into the warehouse itself.

Simon held a hand up to stop her from pushing through the doors, switching off his tac-light. "Better we go in dark," he said. "Just in case. Once we're sure it's clear, I'll turn the tac-light back on again."

She nodded and moved so that her back was to the adjacent wall. He did the same on the other side and then with a silent count of three, they swung through the doors, weapons drawn.

The movement of the doors sent a few stray pieces of paper scuttling across the floor. But nothing else moved. "Looks like we're alone," Simon said, holding up his hand to stop her as she moved toward the light switch. "Better let me make sure first. You stay here."

The room was probably half the size of a football field, with a vaulted ceiling, exposed rafters, and at strategic intervals, the large concrete and steel beams that supported the structure. On three sides, there was metal grating that made up the floor of a loft of sorts. A staircase about halfway along the far wall provided access.

Simon made his way slowly around the perimeter

of the building, and Jillian kept her eyes trained on the grating overhead. There was still no sign of life, except for the occasional soft scurrying of what she could only assume were rats.

Jillian kept a tight hold on her gun, only relaxing when Simon called "clear," striding across the warehouse again, this time stopping to flip on the lights. The overhead lighting didn't do much to eliminate the shadows, but it had the same effect as whistling in the dark, and Jillian lowered her gun, bending to pick up a piece of paper on the floor.

"Anything?" Simon asked, coming to stand beside her, his nearness comfortable and unsettling all at the same time.

"No." She shook her head, reminding herself that she wasn't a teenager anymore. "Just an old takeout menu. Feel like a burger?"

He shot her a smile and then turned full circle, his eyes still scanning for any signs of activity. "There are some crates over there. Maybe they'll yield something more interesting," he said, already heading that way. Above them, the windows rattled as the wind picked up.

Jillian followed him, moving backward to keep an eye on the warehouse behind them. Better safe than sorry. "You find something?" she asked, as she drew nearer to Simon and the crates, her eyes still on the upper level of the warehouse.

"Nothing of value. The crates are empty except for some of the packing. And if there were bills of lading, they're long gone."

She lowered her gun and turned around for a look. "The synthetic straw looks similar to what we found inside the crates in the storage unit. But I'm figuring it's pretty standard stuff."

Simon reached out and lifted the first layer of straw. "It might not be hard proof, but these indentations definitely indicate there were weapons stored here."

She shifted so that she could see better. "Machine guns?"

"Looks like it to me. PKs, maybe."

"Russian, right? The same as the ones we found in the storage unit?"

"Yeah, and if I had to call it, the same as the ones we found in Afghanistan. Although without an actual weapon, there's no way to know for certain."

Behind them, the wind whistled through a broken window, the sound eerie in the half-light. Jillian spun around, lifting her gun again as more paper rattled across the floor.

"It's nothing," Simon said, his mind still on the empty crates. "Just the wind."

"I know. But it's still creepy." She shivered despite herself, her eyes moving again over the upper level, not really certain what she was looking for. Then, when everything remained quiet, she bent down to retrieve the scrap of paper that had landed at her feet.

"Another menu?" Simon quipped, but Jillian shook her head, moving into his light so that she could see the writing more clearly.

"No. It's a shipping label. For artwork. Some statues originating out of Malaysia."

He moved over so that he could see, too, standing close enough that she could smell the sharp scent of his cologne and feel the rise and fall of his breathing. "Does it list a port of entry?"

"Not that I can see." She frowned. "And there's not a stamp or anything."

"So how about an end destination?"

"That part's been torn away. Along with the recipient's name. But I can still make out the name of the shipper." She moved the label farther into the light so that he could see it.

"Joseph Isaacs," Simon said, lifting his gaze to meet hers. "Looks like we were right. Isaacs and Lester have been smuggling arms through this warehouse."

Behind them, the harbor side bay doors rattled as one of them slid upward. Simon and Jillian swung around, almost in unison, Jillian reaching for her gun. But before she could take aim, she was blinded by several sharp beams of light. Blinking, she tried to figure out what was happening, but before she got the chance, something whizzed past her ear, and Simon grabbed her arm, jerking her down behind the crates.

"Looks like we've got company," he said, "And they sure as hell aren't a welcoming committee." As if to underscore the point, a barrage of bullets strafed the floors and walls, some of them slamming into the crates they were hiding behind.

"So what do we do?" she asked, nervously clutching the Glock as another round of shots was fired.

"Fight back," he said, as if it were the most obvious of choices. And she supposed for him, it was.

Sucking in a breath for fortification, she nodded, gun ready, waiting for Simon's signal. His gaze locked with hers for a moment, and then he signaled "go." Popping up from behind the crate, Jillian fired a couple of rounds in the direction of what she now recognized as car lights, praying that she'd managed to hit one of the bastards. Unfortunately, the lights made it impossible to see anything clearly.

Another bullet whizzed past her ear, and with a mumbled curse, she dropped back down beside Simon. "How many do you think there are?"

"Judging from the trajectory, I'd say at least three of them. Maybe more. And if we can't hold them off long enough to think of a way out, I'm afraid they're going to close the distance."

"How about ammo? I don't suppose you have any extra."

"I've got one extra clip. The rest is in the SUV, but they'll cut us down before we can make it that far." He nodded toward the front bays.

"So we're trapped."

"Looks like it," he agreed, popping up to get off another round.

She followed suit, this time holding her shot until she saw a shadow detach from the bright lights. She thought she heard a gasp of pain. "I can't be sure," she said, as she dropped back beside Simon, "but I think maybe I hit one of them."

"That's my girl." He grinned. "If we're going to get out of this alive, we've got to make every shot count."

"The lights make it impossible to see."

"So we even the odds. You any good at sharpshooting?"

"With this?" She raised an eyebrow as she looked down at the Glock. "I wouldn't hold your breath. But I did manage to hit the guy, so what have you got in mind?"

"Shooting out the lights. It'll mean using a fair amount of the shots we have left, but if we can manage to cut even one, it'll help with visibility and make it that much harder for them to maneuver."

"All right. Do we take turns or go for it all at once?"

"No guts, no glory." Again she could see him smile, and with a silent count of three, they both pushed up from behind the crates, firing.

She could hear the answering barrage, but shut the sound out of her mind, concentrating instead on the beams of light. She heard the report from Simon's gun, and one of the lights disappeared.

"Bingo," he breathed, as she took her shot. Unfortunately, the light stayed the same. So she sucked in a breath and fired again. This time she heard the splintering of glass and another of the beams went black.

But the bullets were flying now, and she was forced to duck back behind the crate, the sound of metal burrowing into the wood making her stomach lurch.

"Simon," she hissed, "get down."

He shook his head, his eyes never wavering as he took another shot. And then another. And then two more. And suddenly the warehouse was plunged into shadowy darkness. Only a tinge of gold remained in the west windows, the light playing to their advantage since the intruders had come in from the east.

Still, they were outgunned and almost out of ammunition.

"Okay, if we're going to make a move, we've got to do it now," Simon said. "Before they have a chance to regroup. They have no idea that we're running low on ammo, so they'll move cautiously until they're sure. That should buy us a little time."

She nodded, waiting for him to elaborate.

"We can either head for the bay doors and hope to hell

that we can get them unlocked or go for the entrance to the hallway where we came in. The problem there being that we'd be coming out on the same side of the warehouse as our enemies."

"Well, when you put it like that, neither option seems all that palatable. Is there a door number three?"

"Not that I can see." He shook his head. "Unless you want to rush them."

"Doesn't seem like the smart alternative. What about the loft? The stairs are just across from us. If we make it, we'll have a lot more room for maneuvering."

Simon looked up, his expression calculating. "It might work, especially if we can figure out a way to go out one of the windows."

"It'll be a hell of a drop, but it might be worth a try." She tried to keep her voice steady, but it trembled anyway.

"If I remember right," he said, his gaze dropping back to hers as he pulled out the extra clip and switched it for the spent one, "there were some crates piled against the wall on the north side near the front of the warehouse. We'll have to make it the full length of the loft, but if we do, the crates ought to help break our fall."

"I don't see that we have a choice."

The night exploded again with gunfire, this time closer as their enemies took advantage of the dark to close the distance. Then their flashlights went on, the beams not nearly as disorienting, but still preventing clear vision.

"If we're going," Simon said, returning fire, "we should do it now. You go first, and I'll cover you."

Jillian nodded, already on her feet. She sprinted for the staircase as Simon engaged the gunmen, stopping only when she gained the relative safety of the stairs themselves.

Then, using the last of her ammo, she provided cover as Simon ran toward her, bullets exploding at his feet.

"All right," he said, his breath warm against her cheek as they huddled beneath the stairs, "you start climbing, and I'll be right behind you."

Moving on winged feet, she started up the stairs, the metal risers clanging with each step. The shooters quickly readjusted their trajectory, a barrage of bullets slamming into the stairs. Then, just as she neared the top, a face appeared.

Not a friendly one.

She tried to stop, to reverse direction, but the man was already leveling his weapon, the flashlight in his other hand spotlighting her like a frightened ingénue on a Broadway stage. She froze, heart pounding, and then the sharp report of a gun was followed by the man above her tumbling over the railing.

Score one for the good guys.

But then the staircase exploded with light again. They'd run out of time.

"Move," Simon said, grabbing her arm and yanking her back down the stairs again, bullets ricocheting off the metal with a zinging sound.

As soon as they reached the bottom steps, they jumped to the floor, heading for a group of oil drums located next to what looked to be a generator. Their assailants' gunshots whizzed alarmingly close to Jillian's head.

She zagged in the other direction, trying to avoid the continuing gunfire. Then Simon grabbed her arm, pulling her behind the steel expanse of one of the support beams. She dropped to the floor, gulping for breath. It wouldn't work forever, but for the moment, it provided safe haven.

"I'm not sure that we have any choice but to make a run for it now," Simon said, his mouth close to her ear, his voice so low it was almost inaudible.

"Bays or hallway?" she asked, still fighting against panic, her quick response earning her a reassuring squeeze on the arm. There was something to be said for screaming in fear, but now wasn't the time. If they made it out of this in one piece, *then* she'd fall apart.

"Bays. We can use the support beams for cover. There's no way we'll be able to get the big doors open fast enough, but if we head up onto the loading dock, we might have time to get through that door. Unfortunately, there's no cover. Which means we'll be sitting ducks."

"I'm out of ammo. How about you?"

"I've got one round left."

"Well, if you can, save it," she said, already tensing for their mad dash. "You might need to shoot off a lock."

"Roger that." He nodded with the ghost of a smile and then, with a last reassuring squeeze, motioned her to go. She took off at a dead run, not daring to look behind her. The bullets were flying everywhere. Simon might have taken a man out, but it seemed there were plenty more left to give chase.

She made it maybe ten yards before she felt a sharp sting in her left shoulder. Sliding behind a support beam, she checked her arm, her fingers coming away sticky with blood.

"You hurt?" Simon asked, sliding in beside her.

"It's just a graze. Tore my shirt and scraped off some skin but that's all. You think we can make it the rest of the way?"

"I don't see another alternative," he said, his tone gruff. "I'm sorry I got you into this."

"You didn't. I'm the one who came in without backup, remember?"

Another gunman emerged from the shadows almost directly in front of them, but Simon reacted immediately, pivoting so that he could get the shot. The man teetered for an instant and then fell, his body landing hard on the cement floor. Two down, but they were out of ammo.

And worse they were out of options. Their adversaries were closing ranks.

"I still say we make a break for the door," Simon said, his gaze locked on the advancing tac-lights.

"I'm with you," she said, her false bravado exposed by the shaky sound of her voice. The enemy lights inched closer, the gunfire resuming, and it took every ounce of strength she possessed to force herself out from behind the support beam. "What was it you said?" she whispered as she tightened her muscles in anticipation. "No guts, no glory?"

She sprinted for the loading dock, the distance seeming insurmountable. Bullets strafed the floor and clanged off the pillars. Then suddenly, one of the bay doors shattered as an SUV rammed through it, metal tearing and wood flying everywhere as all hell broke loose.

Bullets slammed into the vehicle as it swerved to a stop, Nash hanging out the passenger window, firing a machine gun. The back door swung open, Drake shooting over the top of the frame. "Hurry," he said. "We can't hold them off forever."

For a moment, she stood frozen, stunned by the latest turn of events, and then Simon was there, grabbing her arm and pulling her forward. Just as they reached the SUV, something whistled past them, slamming into the loading dock, the whole thing going up in flames.

"Grenade launcher," Drake said as they slid into the backseat. "Sons of bitches are upping the ante."

"Everybody inside?" Avery asked, already flooring the SUV as he turned sharply back toward the shattered bay door from which they'd emerged.

"Roger that," Drake said, slamming the door shut. "Let's get the hell out of here."

Another grenade exploded just to the right of the SUV, and Nash dropped back into the seat, still firing the machine gun out the window. "I second that motion."

Avery pressed the pedal to the floor, and the SUV lurched forward, wheels spinning against the debris, and then they were flying forward through the bay door and into the New Jersey night. As they roared down the road away from the warehouse, the night sky behind them exploded, fire licking up from the front and sides of the warehouse. The weathered old building shuddered as the flames spread, consuming the building with a malevolent greed.

"What the hell was that?" Drake asked.

"Oil drums," Simon said. "Fuel for the generator. I'm guessing they must have hit them with a grenade by mistake."

"You think they made it out alive?" Jillian whispered, only vaguely aware that she was clinging to Simon's hand.

"Not if we're lucky," Simon said, with a twisted smile.

CHAPTER **15**

Köln, Germany

"It might not have turned out exactly as planned," Michael Brecht said, as he stood at the window in his office staring out at the Kölner Dom, the spires of the cathedral brightly lit against the night sky, "but we've achieved our goal nevertheless."

"But despite everything, A-Tac survived. And now they know everything about Lester and Isaacs. And probably Rivon's connection as well."

"Stop worrying, I've already closed that loop. Made it an endless circle, leading exactly nowhere. Rivon has always been problematic. He was never the team player his brother was. We'll be better off without him."

"And Isaacs?" Gregor asked.

"He still has a job to do," Michael shrugged, turning to face his number two. "But make no mistake, my friend. In our business, everyone is expendable."

"So you're not worried about A-Tac?"

Michael laughed, the sound bitter in his ears. "I'm

always concerned about their involvement in anything we do. But since we can't seem to stop them, our next best option is to use them. Which is exactly what I intend to do. I've managed to stay one step ahead of them thus far, and I'm not anticipating that changing any time soon. Avery Solomon isn't a fool, but he's never been a match for me."

"There are some who think you've gone too far." Gregor at least had the grace to look uncomfortable with the pronouncement. "That your obsession with A-Tac is going to be your downfall."

"Well, it's a good thing I'm running the show then, isn't it?" Michael forced a smile, even as he balled his hands into fists, swallowing his anger. There was nothing to be gained by letting his temper get the best of him. It wasn't the first time he'd heard the sentiment. And he doubted it would be the last. But he'd be damned if he let it come true.

"Despite A-Tac's interference, the first two stages went off exactly as intended. And the third and fourth have been carefully planned. All we have to do now is wait. A-Tac will be so busy trying to deal with the fallout from our newest attack they won't realize it's not the true objective until it's too late."

"All right, everybody," Avery said, his big voice booming out into the brownstone's parlor, "I know it's really late, and that we've all been through a lot. But we need to debrief while it's all still fresh in our minds."

"I don't think I'm going to be forgetting any of it any time soon." Simon sat with his foot propped up on a chair, his leg throbbing with pain that felt like a red-hot poker jamming into his upper thigh.

"No kidding," Drake said, his gaze shooting over to J.J., who was sporting a new bandage. "How's your arm?"

"Just a scratch," she replied. "Bullet only nicked me."

"Whoever these guys are," Hannah said, "they're not kidding around. If Avery and company hadn't arrived when they did, I don't like thinking about what might have happened."

"I just can't believe I missed all of it," Harrison grumbled, actually sounding disappointed. Which, Simon had to admit, would have been his reaction as well, had he been stuck in a storage unit while everyone else was off fighting the good fight. It wasn't the most rational of thoughts, but there you had it.

"Well, I'm glad you weren't there," Hannah interjected, her tone fierce.

"Actually, he was sitting on a different disaster," Tyler said, walking into the room with another filament-encrusted plastic box. "One of my techs found this in the storage unit, sitting in a back corner behind a crate." She held up an evidence bag containing what was clearly another bomb. "Same setup as the other three smaller bombs. Only this one didn't go off. The timer malfunctioned."

"And if it had gone off?" Drake asked with a frown.

"In close quarters like that," she said, dropping down into a chair, placing the bag on the table, "it would have incinerated anyone in the room."

"Yeesh, now I really wish I'd gone with them to the warehouse." Harrison pulled a face, his gaze dropping to the bomb. "Is that thing safe?"

"Yeah, I disabled it."

"Holy shit. So when was it supposed to have gone off?" he asked.

"When the three of you were all still there," Tyler said. "It was rigged to start the clock when the door was opened. But one of the wires wasn't fastened right, so even though the circuit was closed, there wasn't any contact."

"So we were supposed to have died before we had the chance to find any of the evidence." Simon sat back with a wince.

"Not necessarily you per se. I'm guessing that the bomb was rigged as a safeguard against anyone who might have stumbled into the unit. It was wired so that it could be disengaged with a remote. Meaning Lester or Isaacs would have been able to enter without triggering anything."

"But whether or not it was intended for us," Nash said, "it was another near miss."

"Looks like it." Tyler nodded, taking the bomb back from Harrison. "At least now I've got a complete bomb. Which means I'll be able to take it apart and hopefully figure out a hell of a lot more about the person who made it."

"What about the explosion in the warehouse?" J.J. asked.

She was sitting next to Simon, her hands on the table, her fingers only inches from his. She'd held his hand all the way back to the brownstone, only letting it go when Hannah had insisted J.J. take off her shirt so that she could bandage the wound. He knew it was just a reaction to everything that had just happened. But hell, he was human, and so he couldn't contain the small blossom of hope.

"You guys were right about the warehouse," Tyler was saying, "the explosion started with the oil drums. The hostiles must have hit them with a grenade. Either intentionally to try to kill you guys or to destroy evidence. Or maybe it was accidental—just fallout from the firefight."

"What I don't understand," J.J. shook her head, "is why they waited to use the grenade launcher. If all they were trying to do was take us out, it seems like that would have been a hell of a lot faster than a shootout."

"They had to know that we'd be sending backup," Nash said. "Maybe they were holding you guys off until the whole party was on the scene. Then they pulled out the big guns."

"You could be right. Although, as usual, they sadly miscalculated our ability to evade and survive." Drake grinned, then sobered. "So where did they come from anyway? I didn't see any other cars."

"They were in the rear, near the water," Simon said. "We shot out the lights. Although I never did figure how they got them back there."

"There weren't any cars." Tyler shrugged. "They were using boats. We found a mooring rope and some broken glass, along with some paint chips and a hunk of fiberglass on the quay. You evidently hit more than the lights. The water's only about five feet from the bay doors. I'm guessing that's how they got in and out so quickly."

"Well, bottom line, we still got out alive, and we found the weapons," Simon said. "Along with Isaacs and Lester's apparent ties to the same munitions. And unless I miss my guess, the Russian guns we found were from the same place as the crate we discovered in Afghanistan."

"Which does seem to tie the two together," Nash mused. "Now if only we can run Isaacs to ground."

"Maybe we'll get a hit off the prints I found in the storage unit. There were three good sets. We're running them now."

"So what's happened with Yusuf?" J.J. asked. "Have you gotten any closer to connecting Joseph Isaacs with an alias of that name?"

"No," Hannah replied regretfully, "I haven't even been able to find a Yusuf that ties to any of our players. And I've broadened the search as much as I can. But that doesn't mean I've given up."

"What about MI-6?" Avery asked, "You said they were sending a photograph. Do they have anything else on him?"

"No. He wasn't even on their radar. Which makes sense if he wasn't on ours." Hannah hit a key on her computer, and a photo flashed up on the monitor. "This is his passport picture."

The man looked older than the original picture Hannah had shown them. Grayer. He was thin, with a narrow chin and full lips. His hair was black, closely cropped, and curly. His eyes were close set and brown, with thick arching eyebrows. And yet, somehow the parts added up to an unremarkable whole. A man whom no one would notice. Someone who could easily blend into the background. It was a good look for an illegal arms dealer—or a terrorist.

"I ran facial recognition," Hannah continued. "But nothing popped."

"What about intersection with Lester?" Nash asked. "We know they both traveled a great deal. Anything that would put them in the same place at the same time?"

"Yes, actually, I was able to find some places where their paths seemed to have crossed," she said. "We know they were both art dealers so I started with conferences." She pulled up a document to replace the photograph of Isaacs.

"There were two of them," Harrison said, as usual working in tandem with Hannah. "One in Geneva and the other in San Francisco."

"Best we can tell, both of them were registered for each conference, and I verified flights for Lester to both Geneva and San Francisco at the appropriate times. But it wasn't as easy to confirm for Isaacs. Although I do have a record of him entering the country through New York with a continuing flight through to San Francisco for the U.S. conference."

"When was this?" Avery asked.

"Almost a full year ago, and I have a record of Isaacs leaving the country shortly after the conference had concluded."

"Anything to indicate that the two of them were together?" Drake asked.

"No. And the same is true for Geneva," Hannah said. "But I did some more digging using flight and hotel records for both Isaacs and Lester and I found two more intersections. The first a year and a half ago in Jakarta. It looks like both men were there at approximately the same time."

"Approximately?" Tyler queried.

"They overlap. Lester arriving first, staying for five days, and Isaacs arriving two days later and leaving six days after that."

"But that puts them in the city together for three whole days," Nash said.

"And one of the shipments in the storage unit was from

Indonesia," Simon added. "Does the date on the bill of lading corroborate the timing?"

"It does," Hannah said. "And a month later, they were both in Nicaragua. In Managua."

"There was a crate heading there as well," J.J. said.

"And Emilio Rivon's cartel operates out of that area." Nash leaned forward. "Did you find any connection to Rivon?"

"I did," Hannah said, sending another photograph to the overhead monitor. "And I've got pictures. It just so happened that we had a surveillance team in place. The CIA has been keeping tabs on Rivon's operation for a year or so now. This was from a meeting that went down last August. That's Rivon in the center."

The picture showed a group of five men, two of them obviously carrying weapons, sitting at an open-air café in what looked to be a large market in Managua.

"You can see Lester there in the seersucker suit." Harrison highlighted a man sitting across from Rivon.

"I didn't know anyone still wore seersucker," J.J. said. "I had an uncle who practically lived in it, but he was ancient." She frowned up at the photo. "I don't see Isaacs."

"Hold on." Hannah switched to a second picture. This time the men were standing up as a sixth man joined the group. "That's him there." She highlighted the man shaking hands with Rivon. "And you can just make out Lester standing beside him."

"So we know that the two of them were doing business with Rivon," Simon said.

"It would certainly appear that way. There are a few more photographs. The meeting lasted maybe twenty minutes. Unfortunately there was no audio, and as far as the team in Nicaragua was concerned, the meet wasn't anything to be concerned about."

"Had they seen Lester or Isaacs before?" Jillian asked.

"No. And they haven't shown up again either. These pictures were just part of the routine surveillance. They were only flagged when I started digging around about Rivon in connection with Isaacs and Lester."

"Hang on a minute," Simon said, still squinting up at the last picture. "Can you close in on the corner of the picture? The guy sitting at the far edge of the shot."

Hannah hit a couple of buttons, and the area in question was enlarged. And after a couple more keystrokes, the area came into sharper focus.

"Son of a bitch," Drake said, his chair dropping to all four legs. "That's Alain DuBois."

"Who is Alain DuBois?" Jillian asked.

"A man, working for the Consortium, who was involved with trying to get hold of a formula to aerosolize a biotoxin. His principal business was dealing with antiquities and art. He was our only lead into the organization itself. He fell off the grid after one of their operations went sour, but we managed to hunt him down. Unfortunately, before we could apprehend him, he was killed."

"By his own people," Harrison added. "Another successful effort to cover their tracks."

"But you're sure he was tied to the Consortium?" J.J. prompted.

"Absolutely," Avery confirmed. "We believe he was included in the upper tiers of the organization."

"So now we have a definitive tie between the Consortium and Rivon. Not to mention Lester and Isaacs." Simon was still staring at the photograph.

"Which means finding Rivon is almost as important as finding Isaacs," Tyler said.

"I've already put the word out to bring him in," Avery said.

"I'm afraid that's going to be a bit of a problem," Hannah said, looking up from her computer with a frown. "Rivon is dead."

"What the hell?"

"I just got a text from our people on the ground in Nicaragua. Looks like someone blew the hell out of the whole compound. Rivon and his second in command were among the casualties identified. According to this, it happened about an hour ago."

"Who is the report from?" Nash asked, pushing back from the table as Hannah flashed a video of Rivon's walled retreat. The entire place was lit up like a Christmas tree, fire and smoke billowing from every angle.

"Trevor Billingsly."

"Good man," Avery said. "I trust his word. If he says it's so—it's so."

"So what the hell happened?" Drake asked.

"Looks like the place was strafed," Tyler said. "From the amount of damage, I'd say at least two planes. Or maybe a drone."

"Well, according to Billingsly, their intel points to a rival cartel."

"The timing seems a bit suspicious," J.J. said. "Seems more likely that whoever is pulling the strings in all of this realized we'd discovered the link to Rivon. Which would mean he'd become a liability."

"Damn it." Drake pushed to his feet, his obvious

frustration mirroring everyone else's. "These bastards always seem to be one step ahead of us."

"All the more reason for us to dig in and figure out the endgame," Avery said.

"Well whatever it is," Simon frowned, still staring up at the fiery remains of the compound, "it's got to be something big."

CHAPTER 16

Jillian tossed and turned, pounding her pillow into submission as if success would allow her at last to sleep. But she'd spent enough sleepless nights to know that it was probably hopeless. Her arm ached. Her ribs ached. Even her hair seemed to be hurting.

She rolled onto her back, her good arm behind her head as she watched the shadows play across the ceiling. Outside the brownstone window, the street was fairly quiet. But she could hear the sounds of traffic in the distance. Even at this hour, the city was still awake.

After the debriefing in the war room, everyone had headed out to work. Tyler and Nash back to the warehouse. Hannah and Harrison already huddled in the corner of the parlor with their computers, shutting everyone else out. Drake had disappeared down the stairs into his basement bedroom, carrying a large stack of file folders. Simon and Avery had been cloistered in the kitchen, deep in conversation about the attack at the warehouse.

She'd been invited to join in, but had declined, having already relived the incident more than she could ever have imagined. She'd craved the warmth of a shower and the comfort of bed, just for a little while needing to put everything behind her. To pretend, at least for a few hours, that her life wasn't surrounded with death threats and explosions.

She wondered, not for the first time, if living constantly with this sort of thing was why Ryan had changed so drastically from the man she'd married. Or maybe it had always been there, and the violence he'd seen had just brought it to the forefront. She sighed, listening to the distant wail of a siren. Or maybe she'd just buried the truth—ignored the signs and made excuses so that she could continue to see Ryan as she wanted him to be.

Someone like Simon. It was all so twisted together.

Angry at herself for wallowing, Jillian threw back the covers and sat on the side of the bed. Her travel clock glowed green—and indicated it was well past the middle of the night. Which meant that sleep probably wasn't coming. Better to make good use of her time. She'd take another shower and then see if Avery or Hannah or someone needed her.

She stripped off the sweats she'd been sleeping in and headed for the door, wearing only a camisole and panties. Then stopped as she passed the mirror over the bureau, her eyes drawn to the woman reflected there.

Her hair was tangled from sleep, her face pale, dark smudges under her eyes, testament to everything she'd been through over the past few days. She'd dodged death more than once now. If it hadn't been for Simon . . .

She closed her eyes, her mind conjuring the memory

of his strong arms wrapped around her. She shivered, remembering the feel of his hands against her skin, his mouth tracing a hot, wet pathway from her lips to her breasts. Then her mind drifted farther back in time, and she remembered that night—her first. She could feel the texture of the hairs at the nape of his neck. The silky skin of his chest. The brush of his whispers against her lips. She could smell the sharp, clean scent of him.

The past and present blended together.

Nothing had changed.

Everything had changed.

With a swallowed moan, her eyes fluttered open, and she forced the thoughts away. She'd made her decision. She walked to the bedroom door and stuck her head out. The room was empty, and despite the wash of disappointment, she knew it was for the best. Crossing the room in two strides, she reached for the doorknob, but instead it swung open, and her hand met hard flesh.

Simon's.

She tried to swallow. Hell, she tried to breathe, her heart pounding so loudly that she was certain he could hear it. Her mind screamed retreat, but her feet were having none of it. Forcing herself to lift her eyes, her gaze collided with his, revealing both passion and need. Raw and hungry.

He held out his hand, the gesture both asking and commanding. And in that instant, she knew she didn't have the strength to say no. Despite her declarations to the contrary, she still wanted him. And though she knew she'd regret it tomorrow, in this moment, with his hand outstretched and his soul in his eyes, she realized she didn't give a damn.

She felt his fingers close around hers as his towel
dropped to the floor, and he drew her into the moist,
steamy sanctuary of the bathroom. Still holding her hand,
he reached behind him to turn on the taps, the sound of
the running water sensual as it cascaded against the tiles
of the stall.

The steam curled around them, as he traced the line
of her bottom lip with his thumb, her skin hypersensi-
tive, as if she'd finally come alive. She lifted her arms as
he pulled off her camisole and removed her panties, his
palms hot against her skin. Then with a slow smile, he
pulled her into the shower.

For a moment they stood, water coursing down around
them, electricity arcing between them, connecting them.
And then with a groan, he crushed her to him, his mouth
slanting over hers, his kiss hard and possessive.

She ran her hands along the scars on his back, reveling
in his strength. Steel tempered by a life she could only
begin to imagine. Simon was a warrior. And the thought
should have scared her. But as his tongue plunged deep
into her mouth, all she felt was desire. As if they'd been
kissing like this forever. As if he was her home and she'd
been gone for such a very, very long time.

The rational part of her brain knew that it was chemi-
cal. That his hormones were affecting hers. That she was
responding to something genetic, something hardwired
into them both at birth. And yet somehow it didn't matter. It was as if he were a part of her. Something she'd
cherished, then lost, and then found again.

Clearly she was crazy, but standing here in the swirling mist, she didn't care. All she wanted was this moment
and this man. He ran his hands along the curves of her

body, fingers exploring, missing nothing. And she greedily accepted his kiss. It crossed her mind that this was what it was supposed to be like. This unending need. A desire so strong she thought surely it would kill her.

His fingers found her breasts, stroking, squeezing, and still his tongue demanded more. She felt as if he were sucking the very life from her body, demanding everything she had to give, and yet she offered it willingly.

He turned her then, her back pressed against him, his penis hard against her, the water massaging her breasts and stomach. His lips found her neck, and she arched against him, reveling in the feel of his mouth and his hands. His thumbs moved in slow circles against her breasts until she moaned. Then one hand slid lower, her body braced against him as he stroked her inner thighs, slowly at first, teasing her, and then he slipped his fingers inside.

She whimpered and pushed against him as he caressed her sensitive nub. Then he slid one finger deep inside, stroking, his other hand tightening on her nipple as he rolled it between his fingers, the sensations combining, threatening to drive her over the edge. Her body trembled with need as the water continued to caress them. He licked the tender whorl of her ear, his tongue rough and gentle all at the same time, and then suddenly he pulled the lobe into his mouth, sucking deeply as his finger stroked inside her.

For a moment, he held her suspended on feeling, then he pulled away, turning her to face him, his mouth crushing down on hers as he shifted again, lifting her up onto the seat built into the shower stall. She bit at his lower lip, then thrust her tongue deep into his mouth, relishing the taste of him. Then he broke free, his mouth moving lower, tasting first her neck and then her breasts, his insistent pull sending shards of heat rippling through her. And she tipped her head back, wanting more, the water only adding to the seduction.

He caressed first one breast and then the other, laving each, and then tracing a fiery path downward, across her stomach and then her belly button, his mouth leaving a hot, wet trail for the water to wash away. Then, bracing her against the water-warmed tiles, his hands cupped her bottom as he slid lower still, lifting her up, his tongue parting the soft folds, flitting across her clitoris, sucking and teasing.

She squirmed against his lips and tongue, knowing that she wanted something more, but unable to stop him, her body responding like a well-strung instrument. Faster and faster his tongue moved, and she dug her fingers into his shoulders, thinking that she'd never found this kind of sexual release before.

His mouth pulled and teased and suddenly she came, her mind exploding with color and light as he drove her higher still, demanding something she'd never given anyone before. And for a moment, she hung on the precipice, afraid. But then she let go, her body breaking into pieces, pleasure indistinguishable from pain as she surrendered to his touch.

And surprisingly, instead of feeling spent, she only wanted more. With a smile, she buried her face in his hair, caressing the contours of his neck.

Then she slid down, sitting on the shower's bench, reaching for him. Pulling his hips to her mouth. At first, she just explored the contours of his hard, muscled body but then she let her tongue trail along the velvety strength of his penis. She heard the sharp intake of his breath and smiled, secure in her power. Then, with the water still pounding around them, she took him in her mouth, stroking with her tongue.

His hands dug into her shoulders as she began to move faster. And then with an audible moan, he forcibly lifted her up so that she was standing on the shower seat. Pulling her close, he took possession of her lips. She pressed closer, opening her legs, locking them around him so that the head of his penis pushed against her center.

"Now," she whispered, wanting him more than she'd ever wanted anything in her life. "Please, Simon, now."

For a moment, he pulled back, his eyes searching hers. And then with a crooked smile that cut through the defenses she'd spent years building, he thrust inside her, filling her to bursting. She closed her eyes, surrendering to the sensation as he started to move within her.

Slowly at first and then building faster and faster. Deeper and harder. His body moving within hers, their union becoming more important than breathing. And suddenly they were one, striving to reach higher still. As if together they were somehow capable of more.

And then, with the shower softly raining down upon them, bound together in a dance older than time, she called his name, their bodies joined, their hearts beating in unison as the world splintered into sensation. Magic beyond anything she could have ever believed possible.

Jillian sat on the edge of her bed, reaching for her boots, thinking that she'd totally screwed up everything. One look at Simon standing in that shower and she'd caved completely, losing every ounce of self-restraint she'd ever possessed. No matter that she'd told him there was no future. That she'd walked out the door yesterday morning intending to never look back

One look at his—admittedly smoking hot—body, and she'd folded like a stack of cards, letting her desire get the better of her. And now, *now* she had to face him—again. Tell him that it had all been a huge mistake. That she'd only given him her body and not her heart.

Which would, of course, be a lie.

She'd lost her heart to Simon over a decade ago, and even though he'd chosen Ryan, and she'd essentially done the same, her feelings for Simon hadn't changed one iota. Whatever the hell an iota was. She jerked on her left boot, wishing that the last two nights hadn't been wonderful. But there was no denying that they had been. Making love with Simon had been sublime. Superlative. Absolutely amazing.

Damn the man.

She blew out a breath and stuck her foot into the other boot. Now there was going to be a price to pay. Hers. It wasn't that she wasn't liberated. This was an age when people could sleep together without emotional entanglement. Men and women, yes. Her and Simon, no.

At least not her.

Maybe that's what was making her the most crazy. The irony of the situation. All those years ago, he'd been the one to run for the hills. God, she'd been so inexperienced. And she'd had such a crush on him. And so one thing had led to another.

It had been spring of their senior year. There'd been

a party. In some guy's off-campus apartment. She was supposed to have gone with Ryan. But at the last minute, he'd bailed. And in a fit of pique, she'd gone with her roommate.

It was a ratty old place on the railroad tracks. And they were serving hurricane punch. The kind that you made in trashcans with fruit juice and Everclear. She smiled at the memory. The stuff was pretty damned potent. And before she'd known it, her head was spinning.

She'd looked for her friend, only to find her out back on the picnic table—with the host. Not wanting to ruin a good thing, Jillian had decided to head home on her own. But on her way up the stairs to retrieve her coat, she'd run into Simon. He'd had his fair share of punch, too. And what started with a search for her coat had ended with them kissing, their combustion then every bit as passionate as their exchange last night.

She remembered him pushing her against the wall, his hands everywhere, touching everything. And she remembered the feel of her palms against his chest, his heart beating next to hers. Then they'd moved to a bed, and as things progressed, she'd thought that everything was exactly as it should be.

She hadn't hesitated for a moment. And she'd had no regrets. Until Ryan had called out from the stairs, and Simon had jerked away, the magic of the moment evaporating just like that. He'd helped her pull her clothes into place with a mumbled apology. And then Ryan had walked in. Even though the two of them had pulled apart, it was fairly obvious what had happened.

The next morning she'd expected Simon to call. Expected him to have felt the way she did. That she and

Simon belonged together. But she never heard from him. At least not concerning that night. In fact, from that moment, everything had been different.

They never talked about it, any of them, but the dynamic had changed. Ryan and Simon were still friends, but a wall had gone up between her and Simon. It was as though the whole night had never happened. And even though she knew now her hopes had been naive, she still hadn't really gotten over the hurt. Her heart had belonged to Simon almost from the moment she'd first met him. And their night together had only served to reinforce the point.

Which made her next move really stupid. Ryan pretended nothing had happened, and, angry at Simon, Jillian had gone along with the ruse. And when he'd asked her to marry him a few months later, she'd said yes. An act of defiance that she'd ridiculously hoped would goad Simon into action.

But nothing had happened, except that she'd become a bride. Simon standing silently next to Ryan as she'd walked to the altar. And somewhere along the way, she'd traded her dreams for a nightmare. Maybe what happened between them had been her fault—at least in part.

Of course, marrying Ryan had meant that Simon was still a part of her life. Albeit a fleeting one. He hardly ever spent time with both of them, and never with her alone. It was as though he'd cut her out of his life as much as he could without losing Ryan.

And for the most part, she'd accepted the fact. Until she finally forced herself to face the truth about Ryan. To accept that her husband was never going to stop hitting her. She'd so desperately needed someone to confide in. But by then, Ryan had cut her off from almost everyone. So she'd called Simon. But he'd shut her down cold. Not even giving her time to explain.

She'd hated him for that. So lost in her own fear and disbelief that she blamed him for what was happening. If he hadn't rejected her, then she wouldn't have married Ryan and her life wouldn't have turned to a living hell.

But that hadn't been fair. Simon had no idea what was going on. And her choices were certainly hers alone. But from that point on, she'd avoided him. Even at the funeral, she'd kept her distance. Certain that they were better off apart.

And now, here she was, in exactly the same place she'd been in that night at the party, and this time, just as the last, it was Ryan who was standing between them. Only now, she was going to be the one to walk away. She was going to be the one to save herself. Protect her heart.

She didn't need Simon. Or the memories he evoked. She wasn't that girl anymore. She'd survived hell since then. And she wasn't going to let herself lose what she had gained.

Fortified, she stood up, squaring her shoulders as she walked into the sitting room, determined not to let him change her mind again.

"There you are," Simon said from the sofa, where he was sitting with a cup of coffee. "I wondered if you were going to stay in there all day."

His sensual smile sent shivers of heat washing through her, but she bit her lip, the resulting pain helping her to stick to her resolve.

His expression sobered as he studied her face. "I think we need to talk," he said, motioning to the place next to him on the sofa.

Ignoring the invitation, she shook her head. "There's nothing to talk about."

"But we—" he started, clearly confused by her tone of voice.

"Made a mistake," she finished for him, struggling to keep her composure. "I told you I can't do this." Her voice almost broke, and she clenched her fists, determined to finish the thought. "No matter how good we are in bed, Simon, this just isn't going to work."

"Actually, I thought it worked pretty well," he said, one side of his mouth lifting, even though his gaze remained concerned.

"I'm serious, Simon. We can't do this again."

"And what if that's not what I want?" he asked, his expression turning obstinate.

"Well, maybe it isn't about you."

A flash of confusion laced with pain crossed his face, and she hated herself for causing it. But it was for the best. It wasn't as if he loved her. And she needed to protect herself.

He opened his mouth to respond, but the door behind them opened with a bang.

"I'm sorry," Tyler said, frowning as she looked first at Simon, then Jillian, and then back to Simon again, "I didn't mean to interrupt, but something's come up. Hannah's found evidence of a new threat. And Avery wants everyone in the war room posthaste."

Tyler shrugged apologetically and then turned to go,

and Jillian practically sprinted after her, but Simon managed to catch up with her at the door.

"Don't believe for a minute that this discussion is over," he whispered, his words sending a shiver coursing down Jillian's spine. Her heart fluttered with hope even as her mind insisted that she keep her distance.

CHAPTER **17**

Women were fucking impossible to figure out. Simon dropped into the chair next to Drake, wondering how in the hell he and his wife had ever managed to get together, let alone make a baby.

He understood that there were issues between the two of them—Ryan principally—but that didn't change what had happened between them last night. And it sure as hell had been about a lot more than sex. He wasn't certain what he wanted to do exactly, but pretend that it hadn't happened wasn't on the list.

He'd let her go once. Out of some sense of loyalty to Ryan. And he'd regretted it pretty much ever since. Then she'd chosen Ryan, and he'd accepted the fact. Even if it meant he'd had to stay away from her for fear that either she or Ryan would figure out how he felt.

And once Ryan had died, he'd accepted the fact that she'd no longer be a part of his life. That she'd never be able to forgive him for what happened to her husband.

But based on her comments the other morning, she didn't blame him. Which certainly didn't excuse his actions in Somalia. But that wasn't what was standing in their way. So what the hell was the problem? How was it that Ryan was still keeping them apart? There had to be logic there somewhere, but he'd be damned if he could see it.

Hell, maybe she was right. Maybe they were better off letting it go. Maybe she still loved Ryan too much to let anyone else in.

Jealousy reared its ugly head, but Simon shoved it aside. He'd yielded to Ryan in life. And he'd kept his distance. But last night—and the night before—he hadn't been able to stop himself. He simply hadn't had the strength to say no.

Even though he had no idea where they were headed. He damn sure wasn't going to let Ryan stand between them again. For better or worse, if there was a chance with her, he wanted to take it.

"Dude, you don't look so hot," Drake said, with a frown.

"I'm fine," Simon bit out, the edge in his voice belying the words.

"I can tell." Drake nodded, his expression growing speculative. "This wouldn't have to do with a certain blonde, would it?" He nodded across the room at J.J.

"Yeah, maybe," Simon groused. "I just don't understand women."

"Welcome to the club, bro," Drake said, his grin commiserative. "I'm here to tell you it doesn't get any easier."

"Great. That makes it so much better." Simon sighed, watching as J.J. sat between Nash and Tyler, the three of them in deep conversation about something.

"Hey," Drake said, his voice dropping to a conspiratorial whisper, "for what it's worth, I think she's a keeper. Which makes all the frustration worthwhile. All you've got to do is hang in."

"Yeah, well, I'm not sure that's an option. There's a lot of shit in our past. And it may not be something we can get over, you know?" He'd said more than he meant to, but Drake was a good friend. And hell, it was nice not to feel like he was on his own.

"I do, actually. Madeline and I started out on opposite sides of the fence, and it took a lot of work to get us together. But it happened. And now, honest to God, I can't imagine my life without her. So do what you've gotta do."

"Easier said than done." Simon sat back, trying not to stare at J.J.

"Okay, people," Avery said, pulling everyone's attention to the front of the room. "We've got a situation."

Simon pushed all thoughts of her aside, the familiar prebattle rush of adrenaline surging in the wake of Avery's words. They'd been right. This wasn't over.

"I've found intel suggesting there may be an attack planned for Yankee Stadium," Hannah said.

"Something to do with the game, I'm assuming?" Drake asked, leaning forward with interest.

"What game?" J.J. asked. "Isn't it a little late for baseball?"

"For the normal season, yes," Avery answered. "But this is the playoffs. American League Championship Series."

"Yankees against the Rangers," Drake added. "Although it should have been the Angels. Anyway, the series is tied at three and three which means this game will decide who wins the pennant."

"The stadium will be filled to the rafters," Tyler said.

"Something close to fifty thousand people," Nash agreed. "It could be the perfect storm."

"Except that there'll be security out the wazoo," Simon said. "Especially after what happened at the seaport."

"That's true," Avery agreed. "And the mayor is already ordering more. But since we've taken the lead in handling the other attacks, he wants us on board as well. Figures since we're already up to speed with everything, we'll be in a better position to spot something off."

"Well, there are certainly worse things than being assigned to attend a championship baseball game," Harrison said, exchanging a high-five with Nash.

"When is the game?" Jillian asked, shrugging when both Nash and Drake looked at her in surprise.

"This evening," Avery answered. "So as you can see, we're working at a disadvantage timewise."

"So, Hannah, how credible is your intel?" Simon asked, shooting a glance in Jillian's direction, frustrated when she ducked his gaze again.

"About as good as it gets," Hannah was saying. "I've got verification from the FBI, Homeland Security, and our people in Langley. And all sources are in agreement."

"And the specifics?" Tyler asked.

"There's where it gets a little vague," Hannah said. "Unfortunately, we only pick up bits and pieces and then try to fit them into some kind of coherent message. We know that there's been chatter concerning a third wave hitting the city."

"The first being the hospital and the second the

seaport, I take it." J.J. was chewing her bottom lip, a habit Simon had always found sexy, but it also meant that she was trying to make sense of something.

"That's what we're figuring." Hannah nodded. "And there's the intel pointing to the possibility of an attack on the stadium. Which would fit the idea of a high-profile target. And then to top it off, we've got credible proof that Isaacs is in the state."

"We found this photo of him," Harrison said, putting a picture up on the monitor. "This was taken at the border crossing at Trout River coming from Canada into New York." He hit a button, and the camera lens zeroed in on a man in a sedan being waved through the border crossing. Isaacs looked much the same as he had in the photos with Lester. "It's a rural area, so the customs procedures tend to be more lax. We're not sure why there isn't a paper trail of the entry, but as you can see from the photo, it's definitely Isaacs."

"When was this?" Nash asked.

"Just over a week ago," Hannah replied.

"Have you got anything else?" Jillian asked.

"We've got him going through a toll booth near Albany five days ago." Harrison put another photo up on the screen, this one a lot more grainy than the first, but still clearly Isaacs.

"But after that we've got nothing."

"What about tracking the car license?" Tyler asked, nodding at the sedan pictured on the monitor.

"Seemed like a good approach," Hannah said, her tone rueful, "until the state police found it abandoned at a roadside rest stop. The place wasn't manned, and the car was parked out of range of the security cameras at the

bathrooms. So it was a dead end. I've got people searching the security footage at all the bridges and tunnels into
the city, but it's going to take time, and we're not even
sure what kind of car we're looking for."

"Well, given Isaacs's relationship with Lester, and
Lester's ties to everything else that's happened," Harrison
mused, "I think it's safe to assume he's here in the city
somewhere."

"Quite possibly finalizing plans for an attack on the
stadium," Tyler said. "So why doesn't the mayor just cancel the game? Wouldn't that be easier?"

"For us, yes. But there's a hell of a lot of money
involved. And unless we can show the mayor definite
proof that there's going to be an attack, he's willing to
take the risk. The financial losses outweigh the potential
downside."

"Our politicians protecting their asses," Drake said.

"Well, in this case, I think he's making the right
decision." Avery shrugged. "We get threats like this to
the city all the time. And most of them never amount
to anything. If he called a stop to major activities every
time there was a threat, the city would be constantly shut
down."

"Yeah, but this is different," Simon said. "There have
been two actual attacks over the past week. Not to mention all the shit we've been through."

"Agreed. But I think the mayor believes that we're on
top of it. And that whatever was planned may have been
aborted."

"I wouldn't want to bet my life on that," Nash said.
"But I get the point. Now it's our job to make sure that
the mayor isn't wrong to put his faith in us."

"Well, it's not as if we won't have backup," Drake added. "Like you said, with all the recent activity, the FBI and Homeland Security will be there in force. Not to mention pretty much the entire NYPD. If that isn't a deterrent, I don't know what is."

"So how are we going to handle this?" Tyler asked.

"Hannah and Harrison are going to stay here and keep digging to try to turn up something on Isaacs and his whereabouts. They'll also monitor the chatter for any other possible suspects." Avery leaned forward, hands braced on the table, the gold band he wore on his little finger catching the light. "Tyler, I want you and Nash to recheck the warehouse and the storage facility to make sure we didn't miss anything that might give us a clue to what Isaacs and his people are planning."

"Copy that," Nash said, already pushing away from the table.

"Drake, you and I will head over to Lester's gallery and take a last look there in the hopes that maybe there will be some sign of Isaacs. Simon, I want you to head for the stadium. The chief of security will be expecting you. And Jillian. You go with him. I know you'll want to liaise with the team from Homeland Security. Then, when the rest of us are finished, we'll head over and meet you both there."

Simon nodded, already on his feet, striding across the room to catch up with J.J. as the others moved out of earshot. "You going to be all right with this?" he asked, not really certain he wanted to hear the answer.

"Of course," she said, her gaze questioning.

"Well, after everything you said—" he started but she cut him off with a wave of her hand.

"I said I didn't want to sleep with you, not that I didn't want to work with you. I want to see this through. And there's no one else I'd rather be paired with. It's just that I want to keep it professional. Okay?"

It sure as fucking hell wasn't. But now was definitely not the time to share the thought. There'd be time for talking later. Right now, they had a job to do. And, damn it all to hell, no one was going to mess with the Yankees on his watch.

CHAPTER **18**

Okay, I've got a confession to make," Jillian said, eyeing Simon over the top of her soft-drink cup. "I've never been to a baseball game before."

"Seriously?" His surprise was almost priceless.

"Well, if you count Little League, then maybe. Otherwise, no."

"That's just un-American," he said, then flinched, the perilous nature of the present situation giving new emphasis to the sentiment. "Sorry. Bad choice of words."

She shrugged and laughed, grateful that despite the tensions of the morning, they'd settled into familiar banter once they'd reached the stadium. At the moment, they were standing at the entrance to section 420C just behind home plate. From this vantage point, they had a bird's-eye view of the entire stadium.

There were security people stationed in each section, as well as at intervals along all the concourses. She and Simon had been assigned to patrol the grandstand level.

And so far, except for a couple of drunks and a rowdy Texas fan, there hadn't been any trouble.

Avery was set up with other top brass from Homeland Security and the FBI in a command center close to the broadcast booth. Nash and Drake had flipped for the field level, Drake winning with a whoop, and Nash grumbling all the way to the main level where he, too, was patrolling. Men and their sports. Tyler was acting as a runner between the two, working both levels, and from what Jillian could see, enjoying herself.

It was the top of the seventh inning, and the Yankees were up by two. And although spirits were high throughout the stadium, the game itself seemed to move incredibly slowly. Simon assured her that it was indeed exciting if you understood it. But she didn't, and now was certainly not the time to try to learn.

They were all wired for sound, connected to each other with comlinks running through the command center. While A-Tac maintained a separate channel, they could be connected at a moment's notice with the rest of the various personnel should the situation warrant it.

"I think I'm going to go downstairs and check out the concourse," Jillian said, as the crowd erupted with what sounded like a resounding boo but, according to Simon, was actually "Boone"—one of the relief pitchers.

"I'll come with you," Simon offered, pulling his attention reluctantly away from the game. "Fingers crossed, this will be over soon."

"You talking about the Yankees, or the threat?" she asked with a smile as they walked down the steps.

"Both." He grinned, and she felt her heart lighten. No matter how difficult things were between them, she was glad that there was still a connection. When this ended, she'd be reassigned back to Washington, but, at least in the moment, they were still friends.

She tossed the cup into the trash as they hit the pavement of the concourse and nervously ran her hand across the butt of her gun. So far there hadn't been any sign of a threat, but there was still time. This late in the game the vendors on the concourse were shutting things down, and most of the fans were in their seats. Which made it easier to survey the area for anything out of place.

Most of the high-end stores were located on the lower tiers, fans there paying a ridiculously high price for seats and therefore presumably better able to spend on extras. Seriously, for that kind of money, Jillian would rather take a trip to an island somewhere. Blue water, palm trees, sand, and...

"You guys seeing anything?" Nash asked, his voice jerking her away from an image turning decidedly X-rated. Clearly her imagination hadn't gotten the memo regarding Simon.

"Not a damn thing," Simon responded. "If Isaacs is here, I'd say he's focused on the game."

"Smart man." Drake's voice echoed across the airwaves. "Just a few more good pitches, and we're into the top of the ninth."

"Drake, I assume you're still keeping an eye out?" Avery's tone was fierce, but there was a hint of laughter as well.

"I am indeed." He sighed. "You know the operation is always number one with me. Besides, it's not the Angels. Anyway, at least for the moment, we're clear down here."

"We're also batting zero," Tyler said, as Nash groaned.

"But in the infamous words of Yogi Berra, 'it ain't over till it's over.'"

Everyone laughed, then the comlinks went dark as they turned back to the business at hand. Jillian and Simon headed for the far right side of the concourse. They passed a couple of security folks, acknowledging them with a nod. Then, just as they reached the end, and a crowd of rowdy fans spilling out of one of the stadium's private clubs, Jillian frowned as a man broke away from the group.

"Over there," she whispered, her hand on Simon's arm. "Moving through the crowd in the direction of the escalator." She nodded toward a dark-haired man in a bulky jacket. He was walking with purpose, ignoring the other revelers, but stopping every now and again to check out the crowd.

"Same height and coloring as Isaacs," Simon said as they moved forward, her hand still on his arm as they smiled and pretended to be engrossed in each other. "Keep acting casual, but let's try to close the distance."

They sped up the pace as the man broke free of the crowd, striding toward the escalator, which was running down now that they were in the final innings of the game.

"Nash?" Jillian called softly into the comlink. "We're coming your way. Got a guy acting suspicious and about to enter the south escalator. Could be Isaacs."

"Copy that," came the reply. "We're at the opposite end of the concourse, but we're on the way."

"Keep back for now," Simon interjected. "We don't want to spook him. So far, he hasn't made us. We'll keep you advised."

"We'll be listening. And we'll close the distance just to be sure."

The man walked into the open area fronting the escalators, then stopped for a moment, adjusting something inside his jacket. The bulky outline reminding Jillian of the bomber Simon had chased before.

"You thinking what I'm thinking?" Simon asked, clearly reading her mind as he reached for his weapon.

"His jacket looks just like the guy at the seaport's."

Simon inched closer, just as the man looked up, eyes narrowing as he saw Simon reaching for his gun. For a moment, the man froze, and then he bolted for the escalator, jumping over the railing to disappear onto the moving stairway below. But in the second before he disappeared, Jillian got a good look at his face. It wasn't Isaacs, although the guy obviously had something to hide.

"Son of a bitch," Simon cursed, sprinting for the escalator and vaulting over the side in pursuit, Jillian following behind him.

The man had a fairly good-sized lead, but Simon was taking the moving stairs two at a time. Jillian hurried to follow, but moved carefully, fearful that if she fell, Simon would have to stop to make certain she was okay.

Simon lifted his arm, trying to get a shot, but before he could manage, the man jumped the last five risers, hitting the bottom and rounding the corner into another boisterous crowd of tipsy Yankee fans. A huge screen on the wall above them showed that the game was still in the top of the ninth.

"Where the hell did he go?" Simon asked, sliding to a stop, gun concealed now near his pants leg.

Jillian stood on tiptoe, scanning the crowd. "Over there," she said, catching sight of the man as he pushed through the crowd just beyond the bar. He turned back for a look over his shoulder, spotted Simon, and began to run.

Simon sprinted forward, pushing people out of the way.

"Simon's in pursuit," Jillian cried into the comlink. "They're heading for the far side of the main level. Is there an exit that way?"

"A staircase," Drake replied. "I'm heading there now. Worst case, I'll cut him off before he has a chance to clear the field level and get outside."

"Copy that," Jillian said as Simon, along with the man in the jacket, disappeared into the now surging crowd. On the screen above, the Yankees were all spilling out onto the field, high-fiving and chest bumping each other, the game clearly over.

"Where'd they go?" Nash asked as he appeared beside her, raising his voice to be heard over the screaming crowd.

"I've lost sight," she said, "but they went that way." She pointed toward the far side of the concourse, now filling with fans as they vacated their seats, still whooping and hollering. "Wait a minute. There they are." Simon emerged from the bar crowd, headed toward a hallway leading to the back of the concourse. And just ahead of him, rounding a corner, she could see the man in the jacket.

Nash began pushing his way through the crowd, and she stuck close, following in his wake, knowing that she'd never make it through in time on her own. Finally, they broke free, and both of them began running. Simon was out of sight by now, but they followed his path into the corridor leading to the bathrooms.

They were still ahead of the crowd, but if the man was in fact wearing a bomb, it wouldn't matter. As they approached the two doorways, there was still no sign of Simon or the man in the jacket, and no other way out.

"You take the ladies'," Nash said. "I'll head for the men's."

She started to protest, knowing full well that they were most likely in the men's bathroom, but then stopped. If this guy was who they thought he was, there was no room for error. Pulling the Glock, she rounded the open doorway into the ladies' room. It was long and narrow, with stalls opening to the right and sinks with mirrors on the left.

Keeping her back to the wall, she moved along the line of stalls, kicking the first one open. And then the second and third. Only six more to go. Behind her, a woman walked into the bathroom, but Jillian waved her back, still moving along the line of stalls, kicking each door open in turn. Finally, she reached the last one, and after swinging the door open, determined that it, too, was empty.

Wild goose chase. Hopefully Simon and Nash were having more luck.

She was just starting to turn back when a shadow detached itself from the corner behind the last stall. Something hard hit her from behind, and she was sent sprawling to the floor, managing to hold on to her gun only through sheer force of will.

Rolling to her knees, she drew the gun level, pointing it at the now fleeing man's back. "Stop or I'll shoot," she yelled, her finger already tightening on the trigger. The man froze, back still turned, then one hand started reaching into his jacket.

"Don't do it," she said. "Unless you're ready to die right now." It was an empty threat if he was the bomber, but it was all she had. If she shot him, the odds were he'd still have time to detonate before dying. "I want you to lift your hands in the air. And turn around slowly."

Again the man made a move for his coat, and this time Jillian fired.

The bullet went wide as the man hit the floor, then rolled to his feet again, turning, a gun in his hand. For a moment, everything seemed to move in slow motion. The man fired, and Jillian dove to the floor, getting off a second round, but knowing that the trajectory had been off.

Then the man lifted his arm, and Jillian struggled to line up her shot, knowing she only had a second at most. But then suddenly another shot rang out, the man crumpling to the ground, the gun clattering against the tiled floor.

"Are you all right?" Simon asked, rushing over to her side, his face etched with fear. "Did he hurt you?"

"No." She shook her head, a combination of adrenaline and fear making her shake now that it was over. "You got here in time. What about the bomb?"

"There isn't one," Nash said, kneeling beside the body as Simon slipped an arm around Jillian, helping her to sit up. "Looks like he was concealing a bunch of signed baseballs." He held one up, then moved so that they could see that the inside of the man's coat was lined with little pockets, most of them holding a ball. "Counterfeit from the looks of them. Probably was hawking them to fans."

"Explains why the jacket was so bumpy," Simon observed.

"But why would he risk his life for something like that?" Jillian asked, taking Simon's arm as he helped her to stand.

"Depending on what he was selling them for, he could

have been charged with a felony," Nash said, "but I'm guessing the wild dash into the bathroom was more about this." He opened his other hand to reveal a plastic bag filled with white powder. "Looks like cocaine, but we'll need a lab to confirm it."

"Everyone okay?" Avery said, appearing in the doorway, followed by a uniformed policeman who walked over to the body.

"Yeah, boss," Nash replied, pushing to his feet after handing the drugs over to the police officer. "Looks like we've caught ourselves a drug addict, among other things. But no bomb. And no Isaacs."

"Well, considering the potential for disaster, I'd say that's a good thing."

The four of them walked out of the bathroom, a group of police and other assorted security people waiting just outside. And beyond them, a group of curious baseball fans.

"It's okay, people," Avery said, as usual assuming command. "Everything's been taken care of." He and Nash stopped to confer with the ranking Homeland Security agent.

Simon, his arm still around her, pulled her over to a quiet corner close to the stands, his gaze colliding with hers, his expression colored with worry. "Are you sure you're all right?" He framed her face with his hands, searching her eyes.

"I'm fine. I promise. Probably a couple of new bruises. I'm sorry, I should have got the guy, but he caught me off guard. I'd cleared the stalls so I thought the place was empty. If you hadn't gotten there when you did..." She trailed off, still shaken.

"You'd have shot him. I just moved things along a little more quickly."

"You saved my life," she whispered, thinking that it was getting to be an all too common occurrence.

"Again..." He smiled, his train of thought following hers. "But then you'd have saved me, too, if the situation had been reversed."

"Yes." She nodded, thinking that she should break the contact, but not actually willing to do it. "I would have."

Behind them in the stands, the remaining crowd was going wild, the Yankees lined up in celebration, air cannons firing confetti into the stands. Red, white, and blue bits of paper rained down everywhere.

"Which is why we make a perfect team," Simon whispered, bending his head closer to hers. For a moment, she thought he was going to kiss her, and by God, even though she knew it was a mistake, she was going to let him.

But instead, he slid his arm around her again, turning her back toward the crowd gathered near the escalator, as the confetti twirled and drifted to the floor around them.

"What do you say we call it a day and head for home?" he asked, his arm tightening around her. "Looks like we've made it through the game without an attack. And it seems as if Avery's got everything in hand."

She wished she could say the same. But her emotions were running the gamut from elation to despair. If this was really over, then she'd be leaving New York. Which should be a good thing. Except that there was a part of her that wanted to stay—with Simon.

CHAPTER 19

Jillian sat on the sofa in the sitting room, curled up under an afghan. They'd stayed at the stadium long enough to verify that things had quieted down and there was no sign of further threat. They'd closed the bars and restaurants that were still open and escorted the stragglers from the stadium. Then they'd worked to hurry the players and journalists along, the NYPD playing the heavy. And finally, with Avery's blessing, Simon had driven J.J. back to the safe house.

She probably ought to be in bed, but her mind was still running a mile a minute, replaying the events of a few hours ago. She could still see the guy leveling his gun, feel the wave of certainty that this was it. That she was going to die. But then Simon had been there, doing what was necessary to keep her safe. Riding to her rescue once again.

And yet even though she knew in her heart that Simon wasn't Ryan, she couldn't shake the conviction that if she gave in to him, she'd be falling into the same trap. Making the same mistakes all over again. Giving in to a man who lived his entire life surrounded by violence. How could it not spill over into everyday life?

She pushed her hair out of her face with a sigh, snuggling deeper into the comfort of the afghan, feeling as if she were being torn in two. She wanted him so badly. But she was afraid. Afraid of herself. Afraid of her feelings for Simon. Afraid of . . . hell, everything.

Ryan had taken so much from her, and she'd let him do it. Which meant that the biggest loss of all was that she no longer trusted her own instincts. At least not when it came to believing someone. Really, truly believing.

"I hope you still drink bourbon," Simon said, his voice startling her from her reverie. It was almost as if she'd conjured him. "I thought maybe we could use a drink after everything we've been through."

"You thought right." She nodded, pushing off the afghan as she took the glass from him. "And yes, I still love bourbon."

A smile ghosted across his face as he sat down next to her. He looked tired, and she resisted the urge to reach out. To try to ease his pain. But she couldn't stop herself from asking. She'd seen the awful scars on his leg the night before. Seen him wince even in the heat of passion.

"Are you hurting?"

"Always," he said, his mouth twisting with grim acceptance. "It's just going to be a part of my life. The new norm."

"I'm so sorry. I can't even imagine . . ." She trailed off, unsure of what to say. There really weren't words.

"I was lucky. I know soldiers who've come home with

a hell of a lot worse. And some of them," he paused, looking down into his drink, "like Ryan, didn't come home at all."

Silence stretched between them. It seemed that no matter what they said or did, the past was always there between them—waiting to rear its ugly head.

"J.J.—" he started then stopped, lifting his gaze to meet hers on a deep sigh, "we need to talk."

"I know." She nodded, taking a sip of her drink. "But it isn't going to change anything."

"Maybe not, but I think it's important to get it all out in the open. If we have any chance of putting this all behind us, we've got to be honest with each other."

"Sometimes honesty is overrated," she said, thinking about Ryan, about the real truth.

Simon leaned back against the windowsill, his expression resolute. "So if you don't blame me for Ryan's death, then why the cold shoulder? Why the distance when things have been so amazing between us?"

She knew it was time for the truth, but he was already shouldering the blame for Ryan's death, and she hated the idea of adding to his burden. He didn't deserve that. And she knew that he'd blame himself for what had happened to her for exactly the same reason he held himself responsible for Ryan's death.

Simon was an honorable man.

"It's just too much, too soon. I was afraid you'd hurt me again. And I couldn't deal with that. Not now. Not after Ryan . . ." She almost said too much, but caught herself, instead taking a long sip of bourbon.

"I hurt you?" He sounded puzzled. And she almost laughed. Something that had been so much a part of her daily thoughts had meant so little to him he'd completely forgotten.

"Yes. After the night when we first..." She trailed off, embarrassed. "In college. You and I, we..."

"Oh, my God, you're talking about ten years ago? But you—" He broke off, shaking his head, clearly not sure how to deal with what she was saying.

"I was what?" she asked, her throat tightening, heart pounding.

"You were with Ryan. We never should have... I mean... Jesus, J.J., I.." Pain and remorse and regret played across his face like an emotional marquee.

"But we did. And it was..." It was her turn to trail off, tears pricking the backs of her eyes.

"Fucking amazing," he finished for her. "I remember."

"But you picked Ryan," she said, clenching her fists to keep from crying. Angry that she was still so locked in the past.

"What the hell are you talking about? *You* picked Ryan. You married him."

"Because you acted like it hadn't meant anything. You blew me off."

"I didn't blow you off," he said, his voice lowering to almost a whisper as he stared down into the depths of his glass. "I walked away. You were drunk. And I took advantage of you. I was being a total prick."

"I wasn't that drunk. And did it never occur to you that maybe I wanted to be taken advantage of? Specifically by you?"

"No." He shook his head. "It didn't. Like I said, you guys were dating. He was in love with you, J.J. And I thought you were in love with him."

"Even after we were together?"

"Yes. What else was I to think? You stayed with him. Hell, you married him."

"Because you rejected me. When we made love, it meant something to me. And when you acted like it never happened, it tore me apart." Again she was saying more than she wanted to, but he was dredging up old wounds, and she was angry.

"Jesus, J.J.," he said. He was still using her old name, but somehow in the moment, it didn't rankle quite as much.

"I'm sorry. I know it's all screwed up. And it was my fault. I just—God, you'd think this would be easier after all this time, but I cared about you so damn much. It was always you, Simon."

"Then why marry Ryan?"

"I don't know. Maybe because you didn't want me, and he did. I was young and really insecure. More so than you can possibly imagine. And he was always so attentive. He made me feel important. Like I was the center of his world. And I'd never felt like that before. But then, that night, when you and I were together, even though I knew what we were doing was wrong, it felt so damn right. I'd wanted you for so long."

"I wanted you too." He said the words so softly she almost didn't hear them. "But Ryan was my best friend."

"And so he got everything he wanted. And we…" she cut herself off, still not willing to share the worst of it with him, the need to protect him—to protect herself—so powerful it overrode everything else.

"Talk to me, J.J.," he said, his eyes full of questions. "I understand that I hurt you. But it was a long time ago, and we're together now. We've been given a second chance. And yet, you still want to walk away. I think I deserve to know why."

"I told you, it's too soon. I gave up a lot when I got married." At least that much was the truth. "And I just found myself again. I don't want to lose that."

"You don't have to. I'm not asking you to change. I think you're pretty fucking amazing just the way you are."

"You say that now, but guys like you expect your women to fall in line. Follow the rules. Live according to the military code. And I'm just not sure I'm willing to do that anymore."

"What the hell are you talking about? Guys like me?" Jillian stepped back, his anger almost palpable, but she forced herself to hold her ground. She wasn't going to back down for anyone ever again.

"Military men."

"So what? You're lumping us all together?"

"No, I...it's just..." God, she was digging herself a hole there was no escaping from.

"Talk to me." He reached for her hands, but she pulled away, too agitated to let him soothe her. "Was it something else that I did?" The anger was gone now, his voice colored with dismay and regret.

She couldn't stand it. None of this was his fault. At least not directly. "No. Simon, it wasn't you. It was Ryan."

"Ryan?" If the moment hadn't been so serious, his surprise would have made her laugh.

"My life with Ryan was hell, okay? Complete and absolute hell. And there's a part of me that's glad he's dead. And I feel so damn guilty about it that most of the time I want to crawl in a hole and die."

"J.J., I don't understand." He looked almost as confused as she felt.

"Jillian," she said, automatically, "I'm not J.J. anymore."

"Okay," he said softly. "Jillian. Talk to me sweetheart. Give me the chance to understand."

"I tried that five years ago, and you didn't even bother to call me back."

For a moment he looked totally confused, then understanding dawned. "We were shipping out. I couldn't call. Besides, I was determined to keep my distance. I still cared about you. A lot. And I didn't want my feelings to mess things up for you and Ryan."

"Oh, God," she said, burying her face in her hands. "If you only knew how impossible that would have been."

"So tell me what happened."

She lifted her head on a sigh. "But you and Ryan were so close, and I..." She trailed off, words failing.

"Ryan is dead, Jillian. Whatever it is you have to say, it can't hurt him anymore. So just tell me."

She pulled in a fortifying breath, accepting that he wasn't going to let it go. Knowing that it would be easier for him to understand her decision if he knew the full truth. All of it.

"Ryan had issues. I think he always did. In the beginning, it was jealousy. Even before we started dating, he was possessive. And he wasn't very forgiving if he thought I was even looking at someone else."

"Did he know about what happened? With us that night, I mean?"

"I think so. At least I know he hated it when we were together. Especially when we were alone. But we never really talked about it. And once I made up my mind to marry him, I thought it would get better."

"But it didn't."

"No." She shook her head. "He was always looking over my shoulder. He didn't want me to do anything without him. And when I'd try to do something on my own, he'd find a way to sabotage it. To keep me home with him. At first I thought it was sweet. I mean, what girl doesn't want to be cherished? But little by little, I realized everyone else was gone from my life. Even you disappeared."

"J.J.—*Jillian*—you have to know that I had no idea. I only stayed away because I thought it was for the best."

"I know. And I'm sure Ryan found ways to make you believe that was true." She took another sip from her drink, needing fortification. "Anyway, I got a reprieve, you guys deployed for the first time. And I convinced myself that the whole thing had been my imagination. That I just needed to work harder at my marriage, to make him understand that I was loyal and that I loved him."

She leaned back against the sofa, memories threatening, the pain, both physical and emotional, still with her, an unending reminder of everything that had gone wrong. "But after you guys got back from that first tour, it was worse. *He* was worse. Different. War changes a person. I know that. I saw it firsthand with my dad."

"He was in the Army, right? A Ranger?"

"Yeah. Although I never saw that as a good thing. My dad was a volatile guy by nature. And he always had a tendency to take it out on my mom. But after he'd spent a couple of tours on the front lines, he got worse. It was mainly verbal…I don't know that he ever actually hit her, but—"

"Oh, my God, Jillian, are you saying…" His hands

clenched as he took in the enormity of what she was telling him.

She nodded, tears filling her eyes. "Ryan hit me."

"Starting after Iraq?"

"More or less." She shrugged, unable to look him in the eyes. No matter how many times she'd been told it wasn't her fault, she couldn't shake the idea that she'd made it happen somehow. "He hit me once before we were married. But we were fighting, and he was so sorry after the fact. But then after we moved to the base, it was like I couldn't do anything right. He'd just get angrier and angrier, and then he'd...he'd...hit me."

"But I never saw any sign. I never even knew there were problems."

"Mostly because you weren't around. But also because he played the perfect husband when we were with other people. He didn't want anyone to know and neither did I. Especially not you. I was so ashamed." She winced with the memory.

"I'm the one who should have been ashamed. I should have known. Here I've been going on about our amazing connection, and I couldn't see what was happening right in front of me." He shook his head, his hands still clenched, his eyes filled with disbelief. "He always talked about you. About how much he loved you. About how you were his whole world."

"I think he did love me. In his own way. But something inside him was broken. And going to war only made it worse."

"And did you love him?" he asked, the question catching her by surprise.

She paused for a moment, ordering her thoughts. "I

was really young. I don't know that I truly understood what loving someone really meant. But I suppose, on some level, I did love him. Or at least the man I thought he was. And I tried to be a good wife. It just wasn't enough. And he didn't know how to deal with the rage. So he took it out on me."

"And it kept getting worse."

"Yes. Every time he'd come home on leave, he was a little quicker to rile. And his anger became more violent."

"And you think it might have been worsened by PTSD."

"The thought crossed my mind, but he wouldn't even entertain the idea. I think he was afraid they'd drum him out of the SEALs."

"He was probably right," Simon said.

"Being in the SEALs meant everything to him. But even if they'd been okay with it, I don't think he'd have gone for help. He didn't believe he was the problem. As far as he was concerned, it was all my fault. And after a while I started believing that, too." The tears were falling in earnest now, dripping off her nose.

"And when you reached out to me, I wasn't there."

She shrugged, not knowing what else to say. "It had been a particularly bad fight. He...he pushed me down the stairs. I hit my head really hard and broke my wrist. And I knew then that if I didn't get out, sooner or later, he was going to kill me. Only I was so ashamed and so afraid. I didn't know what to do. So I called you."

"And I was so busy trying not to deal with my feelings, I left you out there on your own. I feel like such an ass."

"You had no idea what was going on," she said, surprised to find she wasn't angry at him any longer. "And

even if you had, I don't know that it would have played
out any different. I was going to tell him I was leaving
when he came back from this last tour...only he didn't
come back. And then everyone was going on and on
about what a hero he was."

"And you knew differently."

"I was so confused. I mean, on the one hand, he was a
hero. He died saving those women. But on the other hand..."

"He hit you."

"Not exactly the easiest of paradoxes."

"So why didn't you tell me then?" He reached for her
hands, and this time she didn't pull away.

"You had your injury. And your career. And besides,"
she allowed herself a little smile, "I was still angry at you."

"And I thought it was because you blamed me for his
death. God, Jillian, I'm so fucking sorry."

"It wasn't your fault."

She released a breath, feeling as if a weight had been
lifted. She wiped away her tears. And then his head
jerked up, his gaze colliding with hers.

"When you flinched—the day I caught you by surprise
in here—you thought I was going to hit you. You were
afraid of me."

"In the moment, yes," she said, hating the look of
shock on his face, "I was afraid. But it was just a reaction.
It wasn't about you."

"But that's why you wanted to end things. You're
scared that I'm going to do what Ryan did. That because
I've been over there, and seen what I've seen, that I'll
eventually take that out on you."

"Maybe. Yeah, I'd be lying if I said the thought hadn't
crossed my mind. But you also have to know that in my

heart I know that you'd never hurt me. Not intentionally. Not like that."

"So then—" He shook his head, clearly confused.

"I wanted to end things because I'm afraid. I'm afraid of making the same kind of mistake. Afraid of trusting my choices and finding out that I'm wrong. I barely survived Ryan, Simon, I can't risk that happening to me again." She sucked in a breath, lifting her chin, knowing that now was the time for complete honesty. No matter the consequences.

"And most important," she stared down at her hands, her heart pounding, "I'm afraid that whatever this is you feel for me—whatever is happening between us now— that knowing the truth about me will kill it. That you'll be as disgusted with me as I am with myself. I should have been stronger. I should have fought harder. I let him take everything from me."

"Look at me," he said, cupping her face with his hands. "Jillian, look at me. What happened to you wasn't your fault. And nothing you've told me changes the way I feel about you. I let you go once because I was young and stupid. But I'll be damned if I'm going to let you go again. If it takes fifty years for you to be sure you can believe that, then so be it, I'll be here waiting. I'll give you all the space you need, but I am not walking away again."

She searched his eyes, recognizing suddenly that this was one of those moments when a single decision had the power to shift their entire lives forever.

"I don't need space," she said, fighting against her battling emotions. "At least not right now."

"So what do you need?" he asked, his fingers warm against her cheeks.

"You," she whispered, "I need you."

CHAPTER 20

You're sure?" Simon whispered, his body already tightening with need. Nothing she had said tonight had changed the way he felt about her. In fact, if anything, he only cared about her more. As a girl, she'd been witty and idealistic. Beautiful inside and out. But only a wisp of the woman she'd become. Strong, resilient, a force to be reckoned with—the reality of the woman even more intoxicating than the memory of the girl.

Her gaze collided with his, her eyes hungry. "I want you," she repeated, on a soft exhalation of breath.

For a moment, they stood absolutely still, the only sound in the room the rise and fall of their breathing. And then with a strangled moan, she threw herself at him, pressing against him, twining her fingers through his hair, urging him closer.

When it came, the kiss was like an explosion, heat rocketing through him with the power of fission. What was it with this woman? She touched him, and everything disintegrated in the path of his overwhelming desire for her. He had wanted her from the first moment he'd seen her again. And being with her the past two nights had only ramped up his need.

He trailed kisses along the line of her jaw and the soft skin of her neck. She trembled at the touch, and he smiled, then moved his mouth lower, his tongue circling one taut nipple beneath the thin material of her camisole.

She sighed, arching her back, offering herself to him. He reached for the hem of her shirt, pulling it over her head, her nipples heading into little balls, his mind going into overdrive as the lamplight washed against her skin.

Then with a crooked smile, she returned the favor, undoing the buttons on his shirt, her fingers grazing the skin beneath. Finally, she pushed the shirt from his shoulders, her breasts pressing against his chest, the friction sending blood to his groin, his penis throbbing in anticipation. Then her lips found his again, her kiss a wicked combination of come on and surrender. He opened his mouth, welcoming her inside, using touch as a silent language, neither advancing nor retreating but instead joining together in a tempestuous dance of emotion and sensation.

His hands moved in slow, languid circles across her back, the silky feel of her skin adding fuel to his rising passion. With a groan, he pushed her backward toward the table by the wall, lifting her so that her legs straddled the corner, his mouth crushing hers, drinking her in, his need for her laid bare. She pulled him closer, clearly wanting him as much as he wanted her.

He trailed hot kisses down her neck to the valley between her breasts, and then slowly, he shifted to take one nipple into his mouth, biting softly, her answering moan sending liquid heat coursing through his groin. He circled her aureole with his tongue, then drew it farther into his mouth, sucking until she pleaded with him for more.

Happy to comply, he slid his hands under the elastic of her sweats and panties, caressing the soft skin at the juncture of her thighs.

"Oh, God, Simon," she whispered, her voice shaking with need. "Give me more. *Please.*"

Unerringly his fingers found the nub that marked the center of her desire. He circled it lazily, still sucking at her breast, her hair draped around his head like a curtain.

Then with a final kiss, he shifted back to her mouth, two fingers sliding deep inside her, his tongue mimicking the rhythm. He fed on her pleasure, relishing the movement of her body against his as she strove to find release.

His mouth and hands possessed her, and she cried in frustration when he released her, but he just smiled, his eyes locked with hers as he knelt beside the table, pulling off the rest of her clothes, and then pushing her knees open. Her eyes widened, but then, with a sigh, she leaned back to brace herself on her elbows.

He lifted her left leg over his shoulder and softly kissed the tender skin of her inner thigh. With a soft cry, she reached for him, urging him forward.

She tasted both sweet and salty, and he relished the power he felt in taking her to the edge of the precipice. He drove his tongue deep inside her, feeling her contract against him. He tasted her, drinking her in, his hands caressing her as his tongue moved in and out, driving her higher and higher until she lifted off the table, crying his name.

He stood then, gathering her trembling body in his arms, realizing that he, too, was shivering. But hers was from climax, his was from white-hot need. She rained kisses on his face as he carried her into the bedroom, her body rubbing tantalizingly against his erection as they moved.

He released her, letting her body slide against his. She stood for a moment, then softly smiled, holding out her hand, the gesture a reflection of the night before—their roles reversed now—the invitation hers.

He reached for her, and she closed the distance between them, pulling his pants from his hips, her fingers still trembling. He covered her hand with his. "You're sure?" he asked, repeating his earlier question, even as his mind rebelled against the possibility that she'd say no.

"From here on out," she whispered, reaching up to brush her lips against his. "Nothing between us but honesty." It was a new beginning. A covenant. And with a groan, he pulled her hard against him, accepting what she offered, raising the ante with the fervor of his kiss.

They backed farther into the room, arms locked around each other, her hands sliding along the muscles of his chest, the contact setting his synapses on fire. She teased him then, running her tongue along the edge of his nipple, laughing softly when it tightened under her touch. Then she dropped her hand, stroking first the ridge of his stomach and then the hard length of his penis, squeezing and stroking in a way that threatened to unman him on the spot.

"Jesus, Jillian." The words ripped out of him on a sigh.

And she laughed, tightening her hold, the strokes longer now, faster. And he pulled away, swinging her into his arms again, his mouth slanting over hers for a kiss.

He reached the bed, and they fell back against the sheets, legs tangling together, as she straddled him. She leaned down, her hair tickling his neck, her lips caressing the rough beginnings of his beard. Then she was everywhere, kissing and exploring, leaving nothing untouched, unloved. She paused when she reached his scar, and, without meaning to, he held his breath. Then she reached out to tenderly stroke the injured muscle, bending down to press her lips against it, her touch almost reverent.

Trembling with the sheer power of the feelings she evoked, he rolled over, pinning her beneath him, wanting nothing more than to feel himself deep within her heat. Catching her gaze, he waited, poised above her. And she nodded, opening to him, and with one swift move, he buried himself deep inside her, the contact beyond all imagination.

There was passion reflected in the depths of her eyes, passion and something else, something so tender it almost took his breath away. Slowly, almost languorously at first, he began to move, each slow thrust tormenting and delighting them both.

With a moan, she arched upward, driving him deeper, the storm reaching a crescendo. They moved together faster and harder, each stroke ratcheting them higher.

Simon closed his eyes and let himself go, surrendering to the moment. Together they moved in a sensual spiral, higher and higher, until they found release, the climax more amazing than anything he'd ever believed possible.

And in that moment of ecstasy, he held on to the fact

that it was his name she called, his body she clung to—
his soul she held in her hands.

Simon sat in front of the fireplace, wondering if Avery's
well-stocked safe house ran to a pile of wood. Then rejected
the idea as too much trouble. Instead, he poured himself
another glass of whiskey. It was late and dark, the moon
having set hours ago. He'd come downstairs to think.
Needing the space. Trying to absorb everything that Jillian had told him. While it might not affect the way he
felt about her, it totally changed everything he knew to
be true. Ryan had been his best friend, and yet, clearly,
he'd never known the man. Which didn't say a lot for his
powers of observation.

Jillian had been crying out for help, and he hadn't seen
a thing. In fact, he had gone to extremes to avoid being
alone with her. His pride had left her vulnerable in a way
he would never have imagined.

And Ryan. Who the hell had he really been? Certainly
not the hero everyone was making him out to be. And
yet, even as he had the thought, Simon knew that it was
more complicated than that. But if Ryan had hurt Jillian
then there was no forgiving the man. Which was a stupid
thought. Ryan was dead. What the hell did he care if
Simon forgave him?

Which, for a moment, illustrated the precarious feelings Jillian had been dealing with for years. And his heart
ached for her, some part of him wanting nothing more
than to erase all the pain. But he knew that it wasn't possible. So he was sitting here, feeling impotent. No matter
the reason, he'd lost a friend tonight. A man he'd thought
he'd known.

Then, to top it all off, there were his feelings for Jillian. Tonight when they'd made love, it was different from before. The connection stronger, deeper than he'd ever imagined possible. And yet, she'd made it more than clear that she wasn't ready for a relationship. Hell, she might never be ready. Especially with him. After all, he, more than anyone, stood as a reminder of the past.

Not to mention the fact that he lived life straddling the line between good and evil. Fighting to keep the world a safer place. It sounded noble. But it wasn't. The truth was that he was an adrenaline jockey. A man who loved living on the edge. And Jillian had spent every day with the fallout from that kind of life.

God, it was screwed up.

Or maybe he was just making it so. Relationships had never been his strong point. If nothing else his past with Jillian proved the point.

He drained the glass and started to reach for the bottle to pour some more.

"I see you're having trouble sleeping, too," Avery said, his big body filling the doorway of the parlor. "Want some company?"

"Sure. Grab a drink." He waved at the bottle on the table in front of him. "I was just about to have another."

"Anything particular on your mind?" Avery asked, as he poured for them, then handed Simon his glass. "I know you well enough to know that you're not the type of man to lose sleep over a mission. So what gives?"

"What would you do if you discovered someone you thought of as a friend, someone you thought you really knew, was in fact something else altogether? It changes everything."

"And nothing," Avery said, with a shrug, his words sounding cryptic. "You know that we had a mole inside A-Tac."

Simon nodded, taking a sip from his glass, the whiskey bitter against his throat. "He killed another team member. Hannah's friend. Right?"

"Yeah. But the hard part of it all was that he was our friend, too. *My friend.* I cared about him every bit as much as I did Jason." Avery paused, swirling the golden liquid in his glass. "So when he betrayed us, it was almost impossible to accept. Either we'd all been fools. Or he wasn't the villain he seemed."

"So how did you deal with the contradiction?"

"Well, on the surface, there was no question that he'd become the bad guy. Hell, he murdered Jason."

"Which made you fools," he stated, not really liking the direction the conversation was going.

Avery smiled. "In part, I suppose. But as with most things, the answer isn't black or white. It lies in the middle somewhere. And it was only when I allowed myself to accept both sides of Emmett—the part that had been my friend and the part of him that turned against us—that I was able to come to terms with it. The Emmett I knew wasn't the same man who betrayed his friends. Somewhere along the line, something changed. It doesn't make what he did all right, but it makes it easier to live with."

"So you've forgiven him?"

"I'm afraid I'm not that big a man," Avery said, twirling the gold ring he wore on his little finger. "But I'm working on it. And you should, too. What happened between Ryan and Jillian wasn't your fault."

"How did you..." He trailed off, not sure that he was really surprised. It wasn't the first time Avery had seemed to be omniscient.

"When someone comes into the unit, I make it a point to know as much about them as possible. Jillian has done a good job of keeping her private life just that. But I can be pretty determined when I have to be. Maybe that's the lesson I learned from what happened with Emmett."

"Or maybe sometimes even you can't know everything." Simon took another sip, staring down into the bottom of the glass. "I just don't know how to process it all, you know? I thought I knew Ryan so well. How can I have missed something so monumental?"

"We see what we want to see."

"Only now, she's back in my life, and everything I thought was true turns out to have been a lie. Finally it's my goddamned turn with her, but things are so fucked up I don't know if it'll ever be the right time. He hurt her, Avery, and I just stuck my head in the sand."

"Did you know it was happening, Simon?" Avery asked, his big voice gentle.

"No. Of course not. If I had, I would have stopped Ryan. Taken her away. I don't know—done something."

"Well, then you don't have anything to feel guilty about. You weren't there. You didn't know. And you just said that you'd have done something if you did."

"But she tried to tell me, and I blew her off." God, he sounded like a total jerk.

"It isn't the same. You couldn't have known."

"But what if it's too late?" he asked, realizing that he was terrified that the words were true. "What if it's all just too much?"

"Then you'll have to learn to live with it. But from what I've seen, that's not what Jillian's feeling at all."

"I don't know," Simon said. "Maybe I'm the one who needs the space. To sort all of this out. To figure out how I really feel in light of what's happened. It's not like I was looking for a relationship. It just sort of fell in my lap."

Avery absently turned the ring on his finger again. "I didn't have very long with my wife, Simon. We'd only been married a few months when she was killed. And I'd give anything to be able to turn back the clock and skip over all the bullshit and insecurities and just tell her I loved her and wanted to live my life with her. We'd have had years instead of months. So don't make the mistake I did. Don't let fear dictate your actions. Celebrate what you've got. Revel in it. Because you never know when it could be taken from you."

"Where have you been?" Jillian asked, her eyes fluttering open as she felt Simon crawling back into bed. "I woke up, and you were gone."

"I couldn't sleep," he said, his eyes turning silvery in the starlight. "And I didn't want to wake you."

"Well, I'm glad you're back." She smiled as she reached for him, realizing that she meant every word. "The bed felt empty without you."

He settled in beside her, framing her face with his hands, and then his mouth slanted over hers, the moment before contact seeming to last an eternity. Finally, their lips touched, and something inside Jillian combusted, a fire blazing with the frenzy of unbridled passion.

It was almost as if it were only the two of them, bound together by the kiss. She threaded her hands through his hair, pulling him closer, opening her mouth, delighting in the taste of him.

He dropped his hands, one sliding to the small of her back, urging her closer still, the other cupping her breast, rolling her nipple between his thumb and forefinger, the exquisite pressure triggering ripples of heat, pooling between her legs. And then his lips were everywhere, her eyes, her cheeks, her ears and her neck, licking, stroking, his tongue setting her nerves on fire.

She grabbed his head then, forcing a kiss, her tongue sliding deep into his mouth, wanting to possess him as he had possessed her. They rolled over until her body was beneath his, his penis hard against her belly. Fumbling in her need, she wrapped her legs around him, opening herself for him as he thrust into her, each time deeper, the two of them struggling for rhythm, striving for release.

Pleasure surpassed itself until it bordered on pain, every muscle responding to her need. He kissed her face and breasts, biting her nipples, and using his hands on her hips to thrust harder—and then harder still.

She screamed his name, certain now that she was riding a wave of pure passion, and then the world split into white-hot light, and she forgot where he ended and she began, wanting only for the pleasure to go on forever.

Shaking now from the sheer joy of it, she drifted slowly back to reality, his skin hot against hers, his breathing ragged, their bodies still connected.

Then, gently, he rolled to his side, holding her close, as if she were the most precious thing in the world. His kisses now were almost reverent, his hands and his lips moving over her in a leisurely exploration that sent spirals

of sensation dancing through her as her body reawakened
to his touch, the banked heat beginning to build again.

He kissed her shoulders and the soft skin along the
inside of her arms, stopping to leisurely suck on each of
her fingers. Then he kissed his way across her belly, giving equal attention to her hand resting there, then up the
other arm with tiny kisses that led to her ear, his tongue
tracing the whorl, then drawing her earlobe into his
mouth, the gentle sucking sending her squirming against
the bed.

With a smile, he slid lower, kissing the tender skin of
her feet and ankles, moving ever so slowly upward, ratcheting her need with every stroke, every kiss, his hands
clearing the way— massaging, kneading, exposing nerves
she hadn't even known she possessed.

And then just when she thought she couldn't possibly
feel any more—when she was certain he'd satiated every
part of her—he pushed her legs apart, his hair tickling
the skin high on the inside of her thighs. One minute she
closed her eyes in anticipation, and the next she was arching off the bed, his hands holding her hips in place as he
sucked her tender nub, each stroke of his tongue sending
her closer and closer to the edge.

She threaded her fingers through his hair, urging
him onward, her mind splintering with her rising desire.
Burning hot color formed behind her eyelids. She was
close, so close... and then he was gone.

The cold air taunted her.

She opened her mouth to protest, but he was there
again, thrusting inside her. She lifted, taking him deeper,
wanting nothing more than to be a part of him, her need
for him overriding everything else. They moved together,

the friction unbearable, her pleasure and his coming together into a crescendo unlike anything she'd ever experienced.

For a moment, she was afraid, frozen on the edge of nothingness. And then she could feel his fingers linking with hers, and she let go, the world disappearing into the fury of their climax. She closed her eyes, letting sensation carry her away. And just for the moment, she forgot about her doubts, allowing herself to believe that as long as they were together, they could overcome anything.

The pounding seemed to match the throbbing pain in his leg. Simon stretched, trying to alleviate it, but nothing seemed to help, the sound growing louder and louder. And then suddenly he pulled through the misty cotton of sleep, coming fully awake as he realized someone was knocking on the door.

Beside him, Jillian's eyes flew open, her face still foggy with sleep. "What is it?" she asked, her voice coming out a hoarse whisper as she pushed to a sitting position, the sheet held chastely over her breasts.

"I don't know," Simon said, already out of bed, pulling on his sweats. He crossed the room and opened the door to find Hannah on the other side, her eyes reflecting something just this side of panic.

"I'm sorry to bother you guys." She shot a regretful look over his shoulder at Jillian, who was standing now, still wrapped in the sheet, her face mirroring his concern. "But this can't wait."

"What is it?" Jillian asked, coming to stand beside him as if it were the most normal thing in the world for the two of them to be in bed together.

"The air cannons," she started, her words coming out in a tumble, "at the baseball game."

"The confetti?" Simon asked, his mind racing at the expression on her face.

"Yes." Hannah nodded. "It was laced with anthrax. There are already at least ten reported cases. And we're expecting more. You guys were there when they went off. So you were exposed. You need to get to the hospital to get tested as quickly as possible."

"You never know when it could be taken from you." Avery's words from last night rang in Simon's ears as his gaze locked with Jillian's, his heart twisting as the full ramifications of Hannah's news hit home.

CHAPTER 21

The overhead light in the hospital containment room was blinking on and off with annoying regularity. Dressed in scrubs, Jillian paced back and forth, watching out the windowed door for some sign of activity. The doctor had told her they'd be back in half an hour, and it had already been well over an hour. And she was going crazy. Isolated without any way to contact the rest of the team.

She and Simon had been separated on arrival. She'd been taken to a decontamination chamber and then a doctor had examined her mouth and nose, taking samples and leaving her to wait. They'd taken her cellphone and left her alone with her tumultuous thoughts.

There hadn't been time for talking. They'd wanted to avoid any further contamination of the brownstone. So they'd thrown on their clothes and driven to the hospital. The rest of the team had traveled separately, so she hadn't seen anyone since leaving Simon at the entrance. And now the suspense was killing her, imagination far worse than anything reality could dish out.

From an intellectual point of view, she knew that even after exposure to anthrax, there was a good chance of survival if the patient was removed from the source of contamination and treated with antibiotics. But emotionally, her mind insisted on replaying the moment when she and Simon had stood amid the falling confetti, the air quite possibly filled with anthrax spores.

How the hell had they missed it? There'd been so much security present. Of course, they'd also missed a drug dealer with a gun. She ran a hand through her hair, wishing to hell someone would come and tell her what was happening. Or at least let her see Simon.

The most frightening thing about all of this was the idea that she and Simon had only just found each other again. She knew that there was validity in her need to move slowly—to be certain before taking the leap into another relationship, but just at the moment, none of that made any sense. Life was short. It could end at any moment. Especially in their line of work. Caution was a waste of time.

She should have told Simon how much being with him had meant to her. Should have told him that she wanted to give them a chance. No matter how scary it was to say the words out loud. The truth is that she'd loved him for such a very long time. And now, suddenly, he was here. And although he hadn't told her he loved her, he'd certainly made it clear that he wasn't going anywhere.

So maybe she was being foolish to try to keep him at arm's length. Maybe it was time to let go of the past and grab on to the future. That is if they had one.

She blew out a breath, taking her hundredth turn around the room. She was talking crazy. The only people who died from anthrax exposure were the immuno-compromised. Which wasn't anyone on the A-Tac team. Of course if the anthrax had been upgraded, modified to make it more deadly...

She stopped in front of the door, slamming her hand against the window, her stinging palm somehow making her feel better—more alive. She sucked in a breath, relieved to find her lungs still clear, no sign of pulmonary damage. She might be scared shitless, but she was breathing just fine. And facts always outweighed irrational fear, except that her fear apparently hadn't gotten the message.

She closed her eyes, leaning her head against the cool glass, thinking of Simon. He'd been through so much. The attack in Somalia, the loss of Ryan and most of his team. The damage to his leg. Losing his place with the SEALs and then her revelations about his best friend. And now this.

Please God, she prayed, let him be all right. Let them both be all right.

The doorknob rattled, and she jumped back as a nurse pushed the door open.

"Ms. Montgomery?" the woman asked, consulting a clipboard in her hand.

Jillian nodded, her heart in her throat.

"I'm sorry it took so long. As you can imagine, we've been overwhelmed with potential victims. But I'm happy to tell you that there's no sign of your having been exposed to the anthrax."

"And my friend?" she asked, unable to make herself say Simon's name.

"I'm afraid I can't tell you anything," the woman said with an apologetic shrug, her mind clearly already on her next patient. "But you're free to go. Your personal effects should be at the front desk."

Jillian didn't even stop to say thank you. Just ran out into the hall, checking rooms as she passed them, her heart pounding as her mind teetered on full-blown panic. And then she saw him. Standing at the end of the hall with Avery.

She opened her mouth to call his name, but nothing came out, the relief washing through her so powerful she thought she might collapse on the spot. But then he was there, his arms around her, his lips against her hair.

"Thank God, you're all right," she whispered into his chest, relishing the rise and fall of his breathing. "I was so frightened."

"Me, too," he said, pulling her tighter against him. "But it's over. And we're going to be okay."

She nodded and stepped back, hating to break contact, but needing to see his face, to reassure herself that he was telling her the truth. "You're sure?"

"I promise," he said, his lips tipping into a smile. "Never been better. The doc released me. I was just signing myself out."

"And the rest of the team?" she asked, the new worry sending her heart pounding again. In such a short time, they'd all come to mean so much to her.

"Everyone is fine. Apparently the upper-level cannons weren't contaminated. Only the ones on the field level."

"But Drake was—"

"On the middle deck with us," he said, tucking a strand of hair behind her ear. "He came up when he heard about the shooting. Well before the air cannons went off."

"Glad to see you're all in one piece," Avery said as they sprang apart, Jillian feeling her cheeks going red. "Don't move for me. Truth be told, I'm tempted to hug you guys myself. It's been a really long couple of hours."

"So any idea how many people were exposed?" Jillian asked, still holding on to Simon's hand.

"We don't know yet," Avery said. "It'll be awhile before we have a clear picture. And once we have more details, we'll have to decide how much to tell the press. But for the time being, the stadium staff is working to contact attendees. Especially those in the sections we believe were most affected."

"So what happens for now?" she asked.

"We get you checked out of the hospital and then head back to the brownstone," Simon said.

"I already took care of it," Avery assured them as they moved down the hall toward the entrance to the ER. "If it's okay, I'll catch a ride with you guys. The rest of the team is already en route, but I didn't want to leave until everybody had been cleared."

There was something comforting in the fact that Avery had waited for them. And even though she wasn't an official member of A-Tac, for the moment she felt like one.

"Do we have any idea how this happened?" Simon asked as they walked through the sliding doors.

"Not yet," Avery replied. "But Hannah and Harrison are already on it. And we'll all be working around the clock until we figure it out."

"So what have we got?" Simon asked as he and Jillian walked into the de facto war room.

Hannah was sitting at the dining table with her

computer. Harrison was in the corner at the computer console, working with both a laptop and an iMac. Nash and Avery were standing near the head of the table discussing something while Drake flipped through the contents of a manila file folder. Tyler was the only one missing, but Simon assumed she was probably still at the warehouse where they'd gathered all the bomb components.

Basically, ignoring the fact that they'd just been through decontamination proceedings at the hospital, it looked like business as usual.

"Glad to see you got a clean bill of health," Hannah said, looking up with a grin. Today her glasses were fuchsia, her hair streaked a brilliant, but clashing, shade of orange. "I'd have hated to have to move to a hotel."

Simon shuddered, thinking that it would have meant a hell of lot more than just moving if they had actually brought the spores back to the brownstone. But since everyone was clean, it was a moot point.

"Now that everyone's together," Avery said, nodding at the table as they all moved to find chairs, "we'll get started."

"So do we have any idea how many people were affected?" Jillian asked. She'd changed to a pair of jeans and a T-shirt, the outline of her breasts proving to be quite a distraction. Simon swallowed and forced himself to lift his eyes, only to find Drake grinning at him across the way.

"Still no final totals," Avery said. "But we've got twenty-five patients at the hospital in the city and another fifteen who've been admitted at various regional facilities. And something like ninety who've been checked and released either because they're clean or because they didn't have any preexisting conditions that might complicate recovery."

"By my count," Simon said, "you've only accounted for a little over a hundred people who've been checked out. There were over fifty thousand at the stadium. And even if the upper deck can be counted out, that's still at least twenty thousand people."

"Well, that's a bit of good news, actually." Hannah leaned back with a sigh. "For whatever reason, only two cannons were actually seeded with the anthrax. Both of them in the right infield covering about five rows in three sections. So no more than one hundred or so with direct exposure. The adjacent areas may have had some minimal contact, but the CDC is saying only about 200 to 225 people total."

"So we dodged a bullet," Nash said.

"A big one." Drake tipped his chair back, his brows drawn into a frown.

"Have there been any fatalities?" Simon leaned back, rubbing his throbbing leg, the activities of the past few days wreaking havoc with his damaged muscle.

"Not yet," Harrison said, "but patient zero isn't looking good. He was sitting in the direct line of fire. And he has existing respiratory problems."

"But if he was patient zero, then that means he was treated early, right?" Nash asked.

"Yes. And that should help." Harrison was reading something on his computer screen. "In fact, I just got an email, and it looks like he's turned the corner. So maybe we're going to get lucky. He was definitely the worst off of the people who were admitted."

"So this guy coming into the hospital was the first clue we had that there might be a problem?" Drake asked.

"Unfortunately, yeah," Hannah said. "Although right after that, the forensics lab for the NYPD discovered that the cocaine we found wasn't cocaine at all."

"It was anthrax." Nash shook his head in disbelief. "And I almost opened it for a taste to confirm."

"Thank God you didn't or we'd all have been exposed," Jillian said. "I guess the baseballs were just a cover. So you're thinking that since he was carrying the anthrax, that makes him the one who seeded the cannons, right?"

"It would seem so," Avery acknowledged. "Although there's still a question of access."

"So why limit it to just two cannons?" Drake asked.

"Maybe we interrupted the process," Simon suggested. "If we hadn't made the guy as acting suspicious, then he'd have managed to seed more of them."

"I don't buy that," Avery said. "Not that your stopping him wasn't a good thing, but I'm guessing the seeding had to have happened a lot earlier than that. By the time you saw him, the game was practically over. Seems a little last minute for something so critical."

"Any idea who this guy was?" Drake asked.

"Yes," Hannah said. "And I finally got an ID on the seaport bomber as well." She hit a key and two photographs flashed up on the screen. The men, both of them young, were clearly of Middle Eastern descent. The one on the left, with the scar, was the man Simon had faced off against at the seaport. "Aamir Hassan and Saed Rahimi. Aamir," Hannah indicated the bomber with her laser pointer, "is a student at Manhattan Community College. He's first-generation American. His parents are from Afghanistan."

"I'm assuming he wasn't on any watch lists or you'd have been able to ID him sooner."

"Exactly right. Kid was a model citizen. Parents, too. I don't know that I'd have ever found him if it hadn't been for his cousin here." She moved the pointer until it illuminated Saed. "Saed is Afghani. Arrived here about six months ago and has been driving a cab. He also has nothing in his background that raises a red flag."

"But I thought you said that Saed led you to Aamir."

"As an alien working in New York, Saed's got a file. Nothing damning in it, but it was easy enough to tag who he was. And then with a little more digging, I discovered that Saed was admitted into the country under the sponsorship of his aunt—Aamir's mother."

"They're cousins," Jillian said. "That's why I thought I recognized Saed at the baseball game. It wasn't that he looked like Isaacs; it was that looks a lot like Aamir."

"Except for the scar, they could be brothers." Simon nodded. "So if they were both clean, then how did they wind up in the middle of all this?"

"That's where it really gets interesting," Harrison said, as usual picking up on Hannah's thread. "Turns out that they have another relative in common. A second cousin through their mothers." Hannah put a third photograph up on the screen. It was slightly blurry, but Simon didn't need a clearer picture to know who it was.

"Kamaal Sahar." He leaned forward, frowning up at the photo. "We're talking the same guy who was running the terrorist camp in Afghanistan. The one intel has linked to the Consortium."

"Exactly." Hannah nodded. "And thanks to some emails Harrison was able to snag off of Saed's computer, we know that he has been in constant contact with Kamaal."

"So we've managed to connect at least some of the dots," Harrison said. "Although there's nothing in the emails that directly connects to the attacks on the seaport or Yankee Stadium."

"Still it's a coincidence that we can't afford to ignore," Jillian insisted. "If Saed and Aamir were working for Kamaal, then that ties them and the two attacks, at least indirectly, to the Consortium."

"Yeah, but even if we agree that Kamaal's terrorist cell is responsible for the seaport bombing and the anthrax attack, we've still got nothing to connect them directly to Isaacs and Lester," Drake concluded. "All we've really got is another piece to one hell of a confusing puzzle."

"The weird thing about it," Jillian said, chewing on her bottom lip, "is that there's such an uneven mix of sophistication and naïveté. Getting past security at the stadium would require someone with both knowledge and connections. But getting caught in the bathroom with a Ziploc full of anthrax is amateur hour."

"So maybe the guy panicked and deviated from the plan," Simon suggested. "Maybe he got cut off from his assigned exit, and he was doing an end run, trying to get the hell out of the stadium."

"Well, he had to have some smarts," Nash said. "He managed to get past five national organizations and their supposedly unimpeachable security."

"Actually, I think it was as simple as using the pyro-technics company for access." Hannah hit a key on her computer, and one of the stadium security feeds was broadcast up onto the screen.

The footage showed a large truck being waved through one of the gates onto the field. "The truck belongs to Fire and Ice, a company in New Jersey that handles pyrotechnics for major events in the tristate area. F&I for short. They've been working in the area for years and have a solid reputation, including passing routine personnel background checks initiated by the FBI and Homeland Security."

She fast-forwarded the video and then froze it, zooming in on a man emerging from the truck.

"That's Saed Rahimi," Avery said.

"Yeah." Simon frowned up at the still. "And he's wearing an F&I uniform. So was he working for the company? You said he was driving a cab."

"He was." Hannah nodded. "And I double-checked, and he definitely wasn't listed as an F&I employee or on the security clearance list for the job. But look at this." She zoomed in again on the still shot of Rahimi, closing in on the name badge displayed on the pocket of his uniform.

"Robert Kahn," Nash read. "So Rahimi was posing as someone else. Do we know what happened to the real Robert Kahn?"

Hannah started to say no, but Harrison interrupted her, his eyes on the iMac's screen. "Actually, they just found him."

"And I take it the news isn't good?" Avery asked.

"No." Harrison shook his head, still reading. "He was found in his apartment in the Bronx. Single shot to the head. ME says he's been dead at least twenty-four hours."

"When was the footage shot?" Jillian asked.

"About three hours before the game. Just before the

stadium opened," Hannah said. "The schedule notes it as the final review of the cannons and their operating system."

"That's why he was by himself in the truck," Drake observed. "And why there wasn't anyone to question his identity."

"So we know how he got in. And that he had the opportunity to seed all the cannons if he'd wanted to. Which sure as hell doesn't explain why he only did two, and why he showed up after the fact, out of uniform, carrying a bag of anthrax." Simon slammed a hand down on the table, frustration getting the better of him. "Jillian is right. It doesn't make any sense. Even if he was a low-level player."

"Do we have a record of his leaving?" Drake asked. "Or at least the truck?"

"Yeah. He was clocked out about an hour later. So that means he had to have come back."

"Or maybe somebody else was already inside, and he's the one who drove the truck away?"

"Actually, I think you might be right about that," Hannah said as more footage flashed on the screen. "This is from the video taken just before the truck left." Again she zeroed in on the man in the driver's seat. But it wasn't Rahimi.

"Son of a bitch," Simon said. "That's Isaacs."

"What the hell is he doing there?" Nash asked.

"And more important—how did he get inside the stadium?" Jillian was staring up at the screen, shaking her head in amazement.

"Unfortunately," Harrison said, "absent additional evidence from the security cameras, that's probably a question only Isaacs can answer."

"I wouldn't hold my breath waiting for his cooperation," Tyler said, striding into the room, as usual toting
a bag full of God knows what kind of ordnance. "I got a
print off the car bomb." She sat down at the table, reaching into the duffel to produce a small piece of metal in a
plastic bag. "This is a piece of the trigger. And the print
on it belongs to Isaacs."

"Which means he was making the bombs," Jillian
said, finishing the thought.

"And makes it even more important for us to run the
bastard to ground," Drake added.

"Well, unless you've got a secret for resurrecting the
dead I'm not aware of, I don't think that's going to be
possible." Tyler sighed, leaning back in her chair. "A
couple of hours ago, the NYPD got called to the scene
of an explosion. A house in Queens. The place was
destroyed, but there was a body, and they managed to pull
a fingerprint."

"Let me guess—" Simon said, "the print was a match
to Joseph Isaacs."

CHAPTER 22

Köln, Germany

I still don't understand why we didn't take out more people," Gregor complained as he sipped cognac in front of the fire in Michael's study. The two of them had retired to the comfort of cigars and Courvoisier after hearing the news that the attack on Yankee Stadium had gone off without a hitch.

"Because it was never the plan. We needed for the authorities involved, particularly A-Tac, to believe that they'd thwarted the worst of it. That they'd won the day. Victory makes people careless."

"But it seems like killing or injuring a stadium full of people would have far better suited our purposes than a single death."

"Yes, well, maybe on the surface. But think of a chain of dominoes. If you were to drop something on them, explode them as it were, some of them, at least, would still remain standing. Isolated, but still strong. And the incident, though frightening, wouldn't guarantee their destruction. But if you arrange the dominoes properly and then knock over just the one—all of them fall. And the impact is far more disastrous."

"So the first moves we've made have been about setting up dominoes?" Gregor asked, his big face awash with confusion.

"Yes. We've set everything in its proper place. The last being the attack on Yankee Stadium. After 9/11, a series of protocols were developed for the city. Standard operating procedures that are activated in the event of a threat."

"And these standard operating procedures include all international agencies." Gregor smiled, comprehension dawning. "The summit will be moved."

"Precisely. And we'll be ready."

"And if A-Tac figures it out?"

"They won't." Michael took a sip from his glass, heat from the cognac searing his throat and spreading through his chest. "They'll be trying to make sense of what has no real meaning. And in the meantime, our people will do their jobs, and with a single domino—we'll change history forever."

"I know it seems impossible, but all the things that have happened in the past few days have to fit together somehow. There's a complete picture here. We're just not seeing it." Jillian sighed in exasperation, looking across the brownstone's library at Simon, who was sprawled across a wing chair. The two of them had been going over details, trying to make sense of the seemingly nonsensical. But so far, they had nothing.

Harrison and Hannah were still in the dining room,

Harrison watching the security tapes again while Hannah searched through the chatter for someone claiming responsibility for the latest attack. Nash and Tyler had headed over to the house in Queens to recheck the scene for anything that the NYPD had missed while Drake and Avery covered the same ground at Saed Rahimi's apartment.

"You think there's still something more looming out there?" Simon asked.

"I don't know." Jillian shook her head, focusing on the whiteboard where she'd written a chronology of events. "I just can't help thinking we're missing the forest for the trees."

"I'll admit that it does seem a waste to have gone to all this trouble and not actually make much of a stir."

"Which is, of course, the horrible thing about all of it really," Jillian said, with a sigh. "For the people killed or injured in the crash at the hospital and the explosion at the seaport, or the people going through the scare of testing for anthrax, this is a tragedy. But in the grand scheme of things, the events don't seem to be making headlines other than as failed terrorist attempts."

"Well, it certainly scared the bejeezus out of the city. And despite the fact that most folks are assuming that all this is over, New York is still under an elevated alert, governmental agencies are scrambling to make sure they're secure, and every potential target in the area is still under observation—so things are definitely not business as usual."

"Agreed, but it still feels like there's something more." She crossed her arms, frowning down at him.

"Okay," Simon capitulated, his expression turning

serious. "Let's take it from the top again. Maybe if we diagram it out."

"All right." Jillian nodded, erasing their list and grabbing a marker. "We start out with the helicopter crash. We know that was the intended target, and we know, from personal experience, that they were successful with their plan." She wrote the word helicopter and circled it.

"Well, I'd argue that they weren't completely successful, since we're standing here talking about it," Simon offered.

"True. And maybe that's where things started to go wrong. If we hadn't been on site, then maybe they'd have gotten away with their plan to make it look like an accident."

"Which might explain why they started attacking us directly." Simon nodded.

"Starting with Fulton Street and the seaport bombing." She wrote seaport and circled it and then added a satellite bubble, labeling it "apartment."

"Okay, and then following that line of thought, we've also got the other direct assaults on A-Tac." Simon was sitting up now, hands on his knees as he studied the board.

Jillian added the events at the gallery, Lester's apartment, the storage unit, and the warehouse to the board, circling each event with lines connecting the gallery to the storage unit and the warehouse.

"We know Lester set us up at Fulton Street," Simon said. "And when that failed, it makes sense that he'd have led us into an ambush, even if he did do it posthumously."

"Okay, I'm willing to accept that pretty much everything involving Lester was meant as a diversion for us. Something to keep us away from whatever the real goal was. But we've still got the air cannons at the game." She made a third main circle and connected it to the seaport since Aamir and Saed were clearly linked through their connection with Kamaal.

"But again," Simon said, frowning up at the diagram, "like the other events, it lacked in shock and awe, which is generally the point of a terrorist attack."

"Exactly, I mean, why only two cannons? And why not go to the effort to obtain weapons-grade anthrax? It has a much greater potential to be lethal."

"I'm not sure I have an answer when it comes to the cannons, but as to the anthrax, the way I understand it, it's damn near impossible to obtain, especially in quantity."

"Yes, but if this is really the Consortium, and they're as powerful as you guys make them out to be, then it seems to me like they'd find a way. Or use their sources to manufacture it. The point being that exposing a couple hundred people to what is an admittedly scary but ultimately nonlethal dose doesn't strike me as making a grand statement."

"So maybe the incident at the stadium was meant as a diversion, too?" he offered.

"But a diversion from what?" she asked.

"I think maybe I can answer that." Hannah walked into the room, taking a seat on the sofa, her eyes on the board. "Nice diagram. I should have thought of doing it myself."

"So what did you find?" Simon prompted.

"Something that might mean nothing. But I was digging through some older chatter from around the time you guys were in Afghanistan. I thought maybe there was talk in there somewhere about the plan for New York. And I found a reference to Yusuf."

"Joseph Isaacs?"

"No." She shook her head. "In fact, it isn't a reference to a person at all. It's an operation. Operation Yusuf. The first reference I found was vague, so I dug back even further. And it turns out that there have been rumors about it for quite a while, but they were unsubstantiated and therefore mostly ignored by the analysts. I never saw them because I wasn't looking back that far."

"So what's it supposed be, this Operation Yusuf?" Simon asked.

"That's just it." Hannah sighed. "We don't know. The only definitive thing they've been able to suss out is that it's meant to be a doomsday scenario. Something that leads us into World War III, and that it's named for the prophet Yusuf."

"Who is?" Simon asked.

"Joseph from the Bible," she said. "Jacob's eleventh son. He plays a more important role in Islam than he does in Christianity, but the story is virtually the same."

"It's the Technicolor dream coat, right?" Jillian said, her mind working to fit this latest piece into their admittedly puzzling puzzle.

"Exactly." Hannah smiled.

"Well, maybe you'd care to fill in the unenlightened?" Simon urged, looking at them both as if they'd gone crazy.

"Well, the Technicolor dream coat is a reference to a Broadway musical loosely based on the story," Hannah said. "But in short, Joseph was the favorite son of his father. Which royally pissed off his brothers. And when his father gave Joseph this really rocking coat, it was the final straw. The brothers decided to kill him, but at the last moment, they relented and sold him into slavery instead. Then they took his coat and dipped it in animal blood and told dear old dad that Joseph was dead."

"Nice family," Simon observed. "So what happened?"

"He lived as a slave in Egypt for a time and wound up on the wrong side of a very enamored queen. When he rejected her, she had him imprisoned. Meanwhile, the pharaoh, or king, depending on which version of the story you're reading, had a bad dream. In it, he saw seven skinny cows and seven fat ones, and he couldn't for the life of him figure out what was going on."

"But then he remembered that one of Joseph's many talents was the ability to interpret dreams," Jillian said, picking up the story. "So he had him brought up from the prison. And Joseph told the pharaoh that the dream meant that he was going to have seven years of prosperity followed by seven years of drought, and that he should prepare his kingdom accordingly."

"And the old guy did just that," Hannah continued, "thus avoiding the worst of the drought. And as a reward, he set Joseph free. And ultimately, Joseph returned home, much to the joy of his father. Then he forgave his brothers, and they, too, rejoiced in his return."

"Although if you ask me," Jillian said, "I'm thinking the last bit was wishful thinking on Jacob's part. Seriously, would you be pleased to see the guy you sent into exile return to hearth and home?"

"Anyway," Hannah smiled, "the long and short of it was that Joseph had foreseen the homecoming in a dream he had as a child. And so his life had come full circle."

"Nice story," Simon said, "but what the hell can that possibly have to do with what's been happening here?"

"I don't know," Hannah said, "but the name Yusuf was in the notebook you retrieved from Afghanistan. The same one that had the schematics of the hospital the helicopter hit. And we've believed from the beginning that there was some kind of big operation in the works."

"Like World War III," Jillian mused, with a frown. "That's what you said about Operation Yusuf. That it was about starting World War III. So what if this isn't about ideology at all? What if it's about business? The Consortium's business."

"Selling illegal weapons," Simon said.

"And keeping business booming," Jillian agreed. "War for war's sake. It'd be win/win for the arms cartels. Just look at what happened with 9/11. We were so angry we went to war in two different countries. And those wars dragged on for ten years."

"Only now, they're ending," Hannah said, clearly considering the notion. "But there are other wars. Look at all the new uprisings in the area centered on the Arab Spring."

"Yeah, but so far America has resisted becoming involved in any major kind of way," Simon argued.

"But if we were provoked," Jillian responded, "it would escalate all over again, one small event setting off a chain reaction that leads to something even bigger."

"Like the assassination of Franz Ferdinand of Austria and how his murder ultimately led to the beginning of World War I," Hannah offered.

"So in this case, we're saying that in provoking the U.S., the Consortium goads us into war, which in turn will mean the rest of the world becomes involved. And with the world at war, the arms dealers stand to make that much more money," Simon said. "The only problem here is that we don't have a cataclysmic event."

"What if it hasn't happened yet?" Jillian suggested. "What if the original diversions weren't intended to keep us away from the stadium, but to keep us from having the time to look too deeply into the first two events?" She studied the diagram, trying to order her thoughts. "Maybe the anthrax attack was meant to cause a reaction. Something that would set in motion a chain of events that somehow leads us to the Consortium's endgame."

"But what?" Simon asked.

"I don't know. But it has something to do with the first attacks. I'm sure of it." Jillian sat down on the sofa, still staring at the diagram. She'd drawn the circle representing the hospital crash to the left and the one for the seaport bombing to the right. Everything else was located below the two of them. For a moment, she felt nothing but frustration, and then suddenly it was clear.

"It's the location. It's got to be the location." She jumped up, adrenaline surging as she pulled out her iPad. "The hospital is located on the Upper East Side just behind the FDR."

"And the seaport is south of that, but also on the FDR," Simon said.

"And both the crash and explosion knocked out a portion of the highway." Hannah joined the party excitedly. "They've closed it from Seventy-sixth all the way to the Brooklyn Bridge."

"So something in between is the target," Simon said. "Something that, if successful, has the potential to lead to major world war."

"Operation Yusuf." Hannah nodded.

"It's the UN," Jillian said. "Something important must be happening at the UN. The building is almost halfway between the two closures on the highway. And more important," she enlarged the photo on her iPad, turning it around so that Simon and Hannah could see the Secretariat, "the FDR runs directly beneath the building."

CHAPTER 23

The Secretariat had been built in 1952, and despite ongoing restoration, not much had changed since then. Simon followed behind Jillian as they were led along an upstairs corridor lined with the lavish gifts from various countries over the years, a sign of posturing dating back to just after World War II. Whatever elegance the building had once had, it had been swallowed by years of bureaucracy.

Although he wasn't a political man, Simon knew that, despite the best of intentions, corruption and infighting had left the organization functionally impotent. Still, the idea behind the union of nations was a sound one. And despite the lack of efficacy, he recognized the value of continuing the exercise, even if its chances of success were futile.

"This is Ms. Giovanni's office," the man who'd been guiding them said. "She'll be with you in just a moment." He nodded to two chairs arranged in front of a partner's desk. "Can I get you something to drink while you wait?"

Simon bit back a curt reply. No point in antagonizing anyone. But just trying to get an audience with an under-undersecretary had been like cutting teeth.

"We're fine," Jillian said as she sat down in one of the chairs. "Thank you."

She'd always been the one to soothe ruffled feathers. His mostly. But sometimes when he'd pushed too hard, she'd cleared the way for him as well. He smiled over at her, thinking how much better his life was with her in it.

They hadn't had time to themselves since arriving back at the brownstone, but when this was over, he intended to talk to her. To convince her to give him a chance. Life was too damn short to let past mistakes stand in the way.

"I'm sorry to have kept you waiting," Ms. Giovanni said as she walked into the room, her tailored suit clearly expensive. She had short bobbed hair, accentuated with diamond ear-studs so large they had to be the real thing. Clearly, he'd underestimated the pay scale at the UN.

"We've only just arrived," Jillian said, standing up to shake her hand and introduce the two of them.

Ms. Giovanni sat behind the desk, and Jillian sat down again. Simon, as usual feeling jumpy in a formal setting, chose to remain standing.

"So, my understanding is that you're here about a potential security threat?"

"Yes," Jillian said. "We believe that someone here at the UN may have become a target of a potential act of terrorism."

"And do you have any idea who it might be?" she asked without any visible reaction, the lack of emotion showing that this wasn't the first time she'd been presented with this kind of information.

"Actually, we're still unclear on the details, but we believe it is a credible threat. Our best guess is that it will involve someone from outside of the country."

Ms. Giovanni smiled. "You just described most of the people in this building."

"What my partner meant to say," Simon said, dispensing with pleasantries, "is that we believe someone important has been targeted. Someone who is probably only here for a short period of time. Maybe just for a meeting or vote."

"Well, it can't be a vote." Ms. Giovanni shrugged, her posture making the gesture almost regal somehow. "We aren't in session, and there are no delegates in town."

"But you do have meetings?" Jillian pressed, her cheerful façade slipping a little due to Ms. Giovanni's obvious lack of interest.

"Of course." The woman shrugged again. "But none of them are happening today. In light of the elevated threat to the city, the secretary general suspended all business. Particularly any meetings that might put a visiting dignitary at risk. It's standard protocol."

"Are there people still in town who were planning on attending the meetings?" Simon asked.

"There are always dignitaries in the city," she said, "and more often than not, they have some business with us. But we have excellent security and are hardly in need of help from the locals. I appreciate your concern, but I assure you that we have things well in hand."

"And I assure you that unless you want an international incident on your hands, you need to cooperate with us." All signs of congeniality were gone. In fact, Jillian's eyes were flashing with anger. "We are not locals, Ms.

Giovanni. We are Homeland Security. And despite the fact that this is international soil, you are still within the borders of the United States, which gives me the right to require you to answer our questions."

To the woman's credit, she didn't even blink, but Simon could feel a subtle shift in the tension stretching between the two women. Jillian had made her point.

"What is it you want from us?"

"We need a list of every high-level meeting that's been canceled as well as any that may have been moved or rescheduled within the next few days. I'll also need a list of those attending the meetings, their country of origin, and their position with the UN."

"Is that all?" the woman asked.

"No," Jillian replied, and Simon bit back a smile. In truth, he was enjoying the show. Ms. Giovanni had met her match. "We'll also need detailed information on the purpose of each of those meetings."

"Some of that is classified," Ms. Giovanni protested. "This is an international organization, and as such, you can imagine that there are dealings here that would best be kept out of American hands."

"Last I heard, America was the single largest contributor to your organization, 22 percent of your regular fund and 27 percent of the peacekeeping budget. Not to mention the land on which this building sits. I think that gives us the right to be concerned about the security of members who may be under threat while visiting New York. I don't give a damn about state secrets, Ms. Giovanni. We just need to identify the potential target so that we can eliminate the threat."

"Perhaps if you give us the intel you possess, we can take over the investigation."

"Not going to happen," Simon said, cutting the protest short. "But I do promise that we'll keep you apprised of what we find out. As a matter of diplomacy."

"So if we could have the list, please," Jillian said, her tone dropping back to conversational.

Ms. Giovanni typed something into her computer terminal and a printer against the far wall sprang to life. In less than a minute, she retrieved a stack of papers, holding them out to Jillian. "I'll hold you to your promise to keep us in the loop, and I trust you'll be sure that the list is disposed of in a secure fashion when you've finished."

"I'll shred it myself." Jillian took the papers, and after shaking hands again, they retreated, battle won.

"Well done," Simon said, as they walked into the elevator and Jillian pressed the button for the basement. "You were a warrior in there."

"I hate women like that." Jillian shrugged, a perfect imitation of Ms. Giovanni, and Simon laughed.

"You really are magnificent." He watched as she ducked her head, but he could see her smile. "So where are we going?"

"We passed an empty office on the way in. In the public section near the coffee shop. "

"Wouldn't it be better to get ourselves back on U.S. soil?"

"I'd prefer it, quite honestly, but we can't afford to waste any more time. And just in case Ms. Giovanni is trying to keep something from us, I want to be here where we still have access."

The elevator doors slid open, and they walked out into the lobby, past the coffee kiosk, to a door leading to a small, clearly unused office. There was a desk and two chairs, but nothing else of consequence.

"It might be easier to just have Harrison hack into their computers."

"Talk about starting an international incident," she said as they walked inside, shutting the door behind them.

"Not possible. Harrison is way too good to be caught. But I'm pretty sure Avery would frown on the idea. So we'll try your way first."

After they sat down, Jillian pulled out her iPad, opened the FaceTime app, and then chose Harrison's name from a list of contacts.

Simon shot her a quizzical look as she propped the tablet up so that they both could see the screen. "I thought we'd agreed that we weren't going to call upon Harrison's unique skill set."

"I'm not asking him to hack anything, but he and Hannah are a heck of a lot faster looking things up than we are. I figure it'll make the search to identify the target go more quickly."

Thirty minutes later, they'd eliminated three-quarters of the list. Half because the meetings and the people involved weren't high-profile enough to provide the impact that would make an attack worthwhile. And the other quarter because, once their meetings had been canceled, the people involved had left the country.

"This is going nowhere fast," Simon said, frustration replacing the surge of adrenaline he'd felt after the meeting with Ms. Giovanni.

"We've still got a couple more to check out," Jillian said. "It just takes one. And I know we're on the right track."

"Well, this one looks like a possibility." Simon ran a finger beneath the listing. "A peacekeeping meeting concerning the genocide in the Sudan."

"Yeah, but the principals aren't even in the country," Hannah said, her voice sounding tinny as it was projected over the tablet's speakers. "It was originally scheduled as a video conference. And I can't find any sign that it has been rescheduled."

"The last one doesn't look much better." Harrison's face swam into view as he moved in front of his computer's camera. "It was meant to be a reception for a visiting dignitary, but it's been canceled."

"Which dignitary?" Simon asked.

"It doesn't say here," Jillian responded, a little line forming between her eyes as she studied the information. "You finding additional information there?"

"No," Hannah said. "And it's weird I haven't had any trouble accessing additional information about the other meetings."

"How did you manage to get a password for the UN's computers anyway?" Simon asked her.

"Friend of a friend. I've found it pays to get to know the techs at Langley. Anyway, I couldn't have accessed anything if the files had been password protected. I'm just logged into the UN's online information system. They track meetings there."

"So why isn't this one listed?" Jillian asked, clearly still perturbed.

"I don't know, but I'd say it's a red flag," Simon said.

"Great." Jillian sighed. "So now we have to go back to Ms. Giovanni."

"Hang on," Harrison said. "I think I just found her files."

"Harrison, I told you no hacking." Jillian looked over at Simon for support, but he just shrugged.

"Technically, I'm not hacking. I already had a way in, remember? I just sort of managed to sneak around a few proverbial closed doors." They waited for a moment, the sound of Harrison's keystrokes carrying across cyberspace. "Okay, I think I've got something. She's got a file for the event. But it's encrypted."

"I am so not explaining this to Avery if we get caught," Jillian said, still looking to Simon. But he was enjoying the whole thing way too much to protest. And besides, he had a gut feeling they were about to find what they were looking for.

"I'm in," Harrison said. "You should be able to see the file on your screen now, too."

As promised, a document opened. Simon peered over Jillian's shoulder, trying to ignore the tug at his groin as he inhaled her perfume.

"There must be a mistake." Hannah was obviously reading from her end as well. "This isn't a reception. It's a summit."

"And a hell of one at that," Simon said with a low whistle. "I knew there'd been chatter about the Palestinians and the Israelis resuming peace talks, but I had no idea they'd actually been scheduled."

"This isn't just the Palestinians." Jillian leaned forward, her face reflecting her surprise. "Several of the attendees listed are ranking members of Hamas."

"So this is a big thing," Hannah said. "But there's no one named Yusuf. And aside from the obvious Jewish/Islamic connection, I'm not sure what the tie-in to Joseph would be."

"Still, you've got to admit it's a big fucking deal," Simon said.

"Yeah, but it was canceled," Hannah reminded him.

"Which puts us back to square one, I'm afraid." Harrison sighed. "I'll close the file so that your Ms. Giovanni won't realize we've been in there."

"No, wait a minute," Jillian said. "I recognize one of the names. Bilaal Hamden."

"I know it, too," Harrison agreed, the sound of typing coming from the screen again. "I'm pretty sure he's the son of a high-ranking member of Hamas."

"I don't see another Hamden on the list," Simon said.

"He wouldn't be there," Harrison continued. "He's an old-timer. Was a big player about ten or fifteen years ago. He's got to be like seventy."

"I remember the story now," Jillian said. "The kid, Bilaal, was part of the Palestinian Resistance Movement. And he was killed in action. But then like six years later, it turned out that he hadn't died at all. He'd been taken prisoner. And then there was one of those prisoner release things, and he was part of the trade."

"Right." Harrison nodded, his face back onscreen again. "And his father was totally stoked. It was like his son had risen from the dead."

"And to top it off," Jillian said, "if I'm remembering right, he made inroads with his captors and gained their respect. I think he saved an Israeli kid or something. That's one of the reasons they let him go. It was big news at the time."

"Which would, of course, make him a valuable asset for any attempt at peace talks. He'd be the ideal negotiator." Simon felt anticipation rising.

"Anyone else seeing a similarity here to another lost son?" Jillian asked, excitement coloring her voice.

There was silence for a moment and then Hannah let out a whoop. "Joseph. Oh, my God, Bilaal is Yusuf."

"It fits," Jillian said. "And if you think about it, what better way to instigate an incident whose ramifications would certainly threaten the world as we know it. Bilaal is a hero among his people. And he's respected by certain parties within Israel. But if he were killed in a meeting with Israelis taking place on U.S. soil, you can bet your bottom dollar the entire Arabic world would want retribution. And they'd look first to their sworn enemies. The Israelis—"

"—and us," Harrison finished for her. "We'd be drawn right back into the heart of a war in the Middle East. "

"It's Operation Yusuf," Jillian continued. "It has to be. But if it's going to work, they can't just bomb the meeting or crash a plane into the building. They can only take out Bilaal. It has to be an assassination."

"I think you're right," Hannah agreed. "And all the other stuff that's happened was designed either to facilitate the strike or to keep us from figuring out what was really going on."

"Well, they damn near succeeded there," Simon said. "But no matter what they were planning, the meeting has been canceled. So the threat, if there was one, has been eliminated."

"Except that it hasn't," Harrison asserted. "Look at the last page of the document. At the very bottom. There's a date and an address. They didn't cancel it. They moved it. And buried the details in the fine print. So much for standard operating procedures."

"Well whatever the original intent, the meeting is happening today at three." Jillian leaned closer to the screen, her expression grim.

"That's in less than twenty minutes," Simon said. "If they're sticking to the original schedule, Bilaal is giving the opening statement."

"Which means there's no time." Their eyes met across the table. "We need to let them know."

"I'm trying to contact security at the summit," Harrison replied, "but there's no one answering. Looks like someone's jamming signals. Unless they are trying to make a call, they won't even realize the phones are down."

"What do we know about the location?" Jillian asked, pushing to her feet, tablet in hand.

"The building is on the East River in Murray Hill," Hannah said. "It's mixed use, commercial and residential. The UN maintains a conference room there. And it looks like you were still right about the FDR. According to my information, the building straddles the highway just like the UN. You guys are only like ten blocks away. If you hurry, you can make it."

CHAPTER 24

The Essex Arms had been built at the turn of the century, its graceful lines indicative of the financial wherewithal of the original tenants. But at the moment, Simon wasn't interested in architecture.

The UN conference suite occupied both the third and fourth floors of the building. What had originally been two apartments had been combined to make the main conference room with a mezzanine built above it in the back to house the translation booths.

The suite was accessed by a private elevator. Entrance required a passcode, which Hannah had provided before they'd lost telephone contact, the lines still jammed. Simon and Jillian stood in it now, watching as the numbers slowly inched upward.

"We're going to have to move quickly," Simon said, checking his watch. "There won't be a lot of time for explanations. We've got to size up the situation and identify the interloper before he has the chance to get off a shot."

"My guess is he'll be in the mezzanine. It'd provide the best angle for a shot."

"I agree. According to the blueprint Hannah downloaded, access is up a set of stairs in the back of the room to the right. If necessary, we'll split up. One of us will stay with Bilaal while the other heads for the mezzanine, hopefully cutting the shooter off. But with communications down, if we have to move fast, UN security isn't going to know who we are."

"Which means they could mistake us for hostiles." Jillian nodded. "But I don't see that we have any other choice."

"Hopefully, we'll have enough time to explain ourselves, but just in case, be ready. And follow my lead." He drew his weapon as a bell dinged and the doors slid open.

They stepped out into a short hallway with a single door at the end.

"I'd have expected there to be security," Jillian said, pulling the Glock from its holster.

"Despite what Ms. Giovanni said, security at the UN is notoriously lax even for something as delicate as this. And besides, according to public record, this meeting isn't even happening."

"Yes, but I'm thinking this is our missing link. Moving this meeting had to have been a result of the attacks on the city and the elevated terror alert. Maybe not a perfect example of standard operating procedures but probably a predictable one," Jillian said as they moved to flank the door. "Which means that there had to have already been a plan in place to move the meeting here should something happen to compromise the security at the Secretariat."

"And if the Consortium has someone on the inside, they'd have known that."

"So clearly there's a reason why they wanted the meeting moved here. Easier access or maybe even less security."

"Unfortunately, we don't have time to figure it out. You ready?"

She nodded, and on a silent count of three, Simon reached for the door and swung through it, weapon raised, Jillian following right behind. In front of them, just to the right of a set of double doors, a man in uniform jumped to his feet, eyes wide with surprise as he reached for his gun.

Jillian held up her credentials as Simon lifted a finger to his lips.

For a moment, he thought the guard was going to refuse to cooperate, but then he nodded, and both men lowered their guns.

"Has the meeting started?" Jillian asked, keeping her voice almost to a whisper.

The man nodded. "About two minutes ago."

"And Bilaal Hamden? Is he in there?"

"Yes. I saw him myself." The guard frowned, his eyes still on the gun in Simon's hand. "What's this all about?"

"We have reason to believe that someone inside is planning to kill Bilaal."

"Impossible," the man said. "The only way inside is past me. And everyone attending was cleared, first through the UN and then through me." He waved a hand at a list on his desk.

"Then you've got a mole." Jillian reached past him to pick up the list, scanning it quickly. "I can't be sure, but I don't see any names that weren't in the original file."

"Is your radio working?" Simon asked the guard.

"As far as I know." He retrieved it, holding it out for Simon to see.

"Is there someone in there you know you can trust?" Simon continued.

Confusion and doubt washed across the man's face.

"Look," Simon cajoled, "I realize we're asking you to take a leap of faith here, but if we're wrong then there's no harm done, but if we're right, then you'll be helping us save a life."

"All right. Yes. There is a guard inside that I trust. His name is Mikhail."

"Great." Simon nodded. "Quickly now, see if you can raise him on the radio. Tell him you're bringing in some last-minute guests. We don't want to alarm anyone."

The man pressed a button on the radio, speaking quietly in what appeared to be Ukrainian.

"English," Simon ordered.

"It doesn't matter," the guard said. "It's not working." He spoke again into the radio, this time in English, and then held it out for them to hear. A burst of static filled the room.

"They must be jamming the radio frequency as well," Simon said, his mind turning over alternatives. The idea of walking into the room blind did not appeal, but they really had no other choice. At least they'd had a chance to study the blueprints. "Is there another way into the room besides through those doors?"

"No." The guard shook his head apologetically. "There's only one way in. It was designed that way for security."

"All right, then we'll just have to go in blind," Simon said. "I assume you know how to use that gun?"

"Of course." The guard was back to indignant.

"Okay then—" Simon paused, his eyes dropping to the man's ID badge, "Danya, we're going to count on you for backup." He waited while Danya drew his pistol and then looked to Jillian. "You ready for this?"

"Absolutely," she said, already moving toward the double doors. "And like you said, if things go south, we'll split up."

"You go first." Simon waved the guard forward. "They'll be expecting you."

Danya looked for a moment as if he was going to balk, but then, with a nod, he pushed through the doors, careful to keep the gun out of sight.

As if on cue, the man standing at the podium off to Simon's immediate left introduced Bilaal. A young man in a business suit and traditional kaffiyeh rose from his seat on the dais, his broad smile filling the room as he lifted a hand in greeting.

Across the room, another security guard started toward the door and the newcomers, but Danya waved him off with a shake of his head. Jillian moved farther into the room, keeping close to the wall, her eyes scanning the attendees for signs of danger.

Simon, his gun held down at his side, lifted his gaze to the mezzanine. The glare from the room's chandelier bounced off the soundproof glass of the two translation booths situated on either end of the little balcony. In the middle, a narrow, open hallway connected the two rooms, the head of the staircase just visible at the center of the hall.

Bilaal began to speak, and all other noise in the room dropped to a hushed whisper. Above, in the hallway, something moved, light bouncing off something metal.

"Gun," Simon yelled, already in motion as he ran toward the dais and Bilaal, taking the stairs two at a time, his mind registering Jillian running for the staircase and the assailant as he leaped into the air, the sound of a shot ringing through the room.

His body slammed into Bilaal, driving the younger man to the ground, the two of them rolling off the dais onto the floor behind it. For a moment, the room went silent, and then it erupted with cries of panic as terrified summit attendees dove for shelter.

"Are you hurt?" Simon asked, as he rolled off the Palestinian, wincing as red-hot pain shot down his injured leg.

"No." Bilaal shook his head. "I am all right. But what happened?"

"Someone tried to kill you," Simon said, fighting off the pain to look up toward the mezzanine where the shot had originated. There was no sign of the assailant or of Jillian. His gaze dropped back to Bilaal. "Do you have bodyguards here?"

"Yes." The man nodded to two burly men pushing their way through the panicked crowd.

"Good. I'm going to need you to go with them. They'll get you out of the building safely. My people should be downstairs by now. They'll make sure you're all escorted to safety."

"What are you going to do?" Bilaal asked.

"I've got to help my partner," he said, the word taking on a new depth of meaning as he thought of Jillian. "She's gone after the shooter."

"I can help," the young man said, clearly eager for payback. "I have been trained. And I owe you my life."

"You owe me nothing." Simon shook his head. "If half of what I've read about you is true, you're the hope of the future. So go, now. Be safe."

Simon pushed to his feet, stumbling slightly as his leg protested. Damn it all to hell. Calling on every ounce of training he'd ever had, he pushed aside the pain, focusing instead on the mezzanine, watching for any sign of movement.

Then as soon as he was certain Bilaal was safely surrounded by his own men, Simon took off, heading for the staircase, ignoring the ripping pain accompanying each step. There'd been no further shots. But there was also no other means of escape, which meant the assailant was still up there—with Jillian.

About halfway up, he forced himself to slow his pace, not wanting to walk into an ambush. Behind him a stair squeaked, and he spun around, leading with his gun, but it was only the guard, Danya.

"What are you doing here?" Simon asked.

"I thought I could help," the man offered, lifting his hand to show that he still had his gun.

"All right." Simon nodded, motioning them both upward again. "But keep as quiet as possible. The guy up there is cornered, so he's bound to be spooked."

They covered the last of the stairs, and then together moved into the hallway, turning back to back in a slow circle trying to assess potential danger. But the hall was empty.

"Can you handle the room on the right?" Simon asked, shooting his gaze in the direction of the translation booth.

Danya nodded, already moving out, staying in a crouch as he made his way forward. Satisfied that the security guard knew what he was doing, Simon turned toward the other translation booth, inching forward, leading with his gun.

He paused at the open doorway, and then, heart pounding, swung inside. The room, like the hallway, was empty. On a sigh of pure frustration, he turned back in time to see Danya emerging from the other booth, shaking his head. They met in the middle, Simon spinning around, trying to find some other method of egress.

On the back wall, there was a shallow closet crammed with equipment and heavy metal shelving. There was no way it was big enough to hide a grown man, let alone a man holding a woman hostage. His imagination intent on presenting the worst-case scenario, Simon moved to the railing, looking down into the now almost empty conference room.

There was still no sign of Jillian.

He forced himself to replay the image he'd seen as he'd jumped to protect the Palestinian. She'd been running for the stairs. He'd actually seen her start up as he'd slammed into Bilaal. So she simply had to be up here somewhere.

He turned back to face the empty hallway, his mind spinning, his heart twisting in pain. Where the hell had she gone?

Jillian wasn't sure where she was exactly. Only that she'd followed the assassin after she'd seen him disappear behind a metal shelf in the back of a closet and had emerged into what appeared to be a passageway running behind the walls of the conference room's mezzanine.

The wallpaper was old and peeling, and some of the exposed boards in the ceiling and floor were rotted

through. Whatever the original purpose of the passageway, it had clearly been abandoned long ago. And
it wasn't easy to make progress, but she knew the man
couldn't possibly be that far ahead of her. So she quick-
ened her pace, shining her penlight ahead of her and
keeping her back toward the wall as she picked her way
around the rotting debris.

A part of her wanted to turn back. To wait for help to
arrive. But she'd seen Simon diving for Bilaal and knew
that his safety was their primary objective. Which meant
that Simon couldn't possibly come to her until he knew
for sure that Bilaal was out of harm's way. So waiting
would mean losing the killer. And she couldn't let that
happen.

She slowed as she approached a junction in the passageway, holding position for a moment, then risking a
look around the corner. Another hall stretched off to the
left, this one continuing straight ahead. Peering in both
directions, she strained for some sign of which way the
shooter might have gone, but everything was eerily quiet.
So she headed left, praying that she'd chosen correctly,
knowing that she couldn't afford to let the killer get too
far ahead.

There were openings along the way. What appeared
to have once been doorways. But all of them were either
boarded up or sealed off with heavy metal grating. And
everything was caked with dust. She rounded a second
corner, this time hitting a dead end, the wall abruptly
terminating into a huge pile of debris.

With a sigh of frustration, she turned back, hurrying
until she reached the intersection, this time continuing to
follow the original passageway. It twisted and turned for

another hundred feet or so with only two doors along the way. Both of them sealed shut.

At one point, she came to a huge section of the floor-board that had fallen through, and she had to brace herself against the wall to inch by. Once safely on the other side, she questioned her sanity, but quickly pushed the thought aside. There wasn't time for second thoughts. If she didn't keep moving, the killer was going to get away.

Just ahead, a large wooden archway loomed out of the shadows, fading brown paint covering the rotted surface. Beyond the arch, the hallway veered sharply to the right, and Jillian sucked in a breath, preparing to step around the corner, gun leading the way.

But just as she tensed to move, something hit her from behind, and she fell to her knees, her gun clattering across the floor, disappearing into the shadows.

"Get up," a deep voice ordered, a hand yanking at her hair.

She kicked out, fists flying, trying to get a hold on her assailant, but the man quickly pulled her against his body, one arm circling her neck. She jerked her arm back, intent on slamming him in the gut with an elbow, but he only tightened his hold, pinning her in place.

"Do that again and you're dead," he said, his voice cold and flat. "The only reason you're still alive is that, should I need it, you'll provide a handy ticket out of here. But make no mistake, if you cause me any problems at all, I won't hesitate to kill you."

CHAPTER 25

Simon slammed his hand into the wall, anger and frustration threatening to overwhelm him. He'd looked everywhere, and there was no sign of her. And no sign of any other way they could have gotten off the mezzanine. It was is if they'd simply disappeared into thin air.

He'd sent Danya back to get help. The rest of the team should be onsite by now. But there wasn't time for him to wait. Jillian needed him now. There had to be another way out of here. He just needed to find it.

He blew out a breath, forcing his heart rate to slow. Anger wasn't going to help anything. He had to focus. He'd searched every inch of both sound booths as well as the walls lining the hallway. There was no sign of a door—hidden or otherwise. Which left the closet.

Still fighting off the pain in his leg, he stepped inside the tiny space, the back wall lined with metal shelving. Every shelf was overflowing with junk. There appeared to be no room for egress of any kind. But appearances could be deceiving, the voice in his head whispered.

Simon pressed forward, shoving aside a broom and a mop so that he could move all the way to the back of the closet. And it was then that he realized the shelf wasn't actually sitting against the wall. Instead, it was about two feet in front of it, and directly behind it, centered in the damn wall, was a hole about four feet wide and six feet high.

"Son of a bitch," he whispered as he pushed through the hole and stopped on the other side, the phone in his pocket vibrating. Activating the Bluetooth headset, he answered. "Kincaid."

"It's Hannah." The sound of her voice was like manna from heaven. "Harrison managed to get around the jamming."

"Jillian is missing," he said, pulling out his gun and switching on the tac-light. "She's just disappeared."

"I know. I'm downstairs. The security guard you sent filled me in. Have you made any progress?"

"Yeah, I'm in some kind of passageway, I think. I got here through a closet. It must be how the assassin got in. And why Jillian's disappeared. I'm guessing she's following the shooter."

"Makes sense," Hannah said. "There's a whole series of passageways running behind the walls of the building. I've got the blueprints in front of me. Originally they were designed as a network for servants. A way for deliveries to be made without being seen. They were abandoned years ago."

"So which way do I go?"

"Straight ahead," Hannah said. "There'll be a turnoff

in a few yards, but ignore it. You're headed for a staircase
just on the other side of an archway."

Simon nodded, fighting to keep from running, the rotting floorboards combined with the pain in his leg making it impossible to maneuver as quickly as he'd like. At
one point, he had to edge around a large hole where the
floor had given away all together, but once on the other
side, his light picked up the archway.

"I'm here," Simon said. "What now?"

"There should be a sharp turn to the right, and then
just beyond that, you should see a doorway leading to a
set of stairs."

He maneuvered around the corner, but stumbled as
his foot hit something. Stopping, he bent down, his light
sweeping across the floor, his heart stutter-stepping when
he recognized a gun lying next to the baseboard. The
same make as the one Jillian was carrying.

"I've found what looks to be her gun." His voice fal-
tered as he picked it up and slipped it into his pocket.
"But there's no other sign of her."

"Well, at least we know she came this way. Which
means we're on the right track." Hannah's tone was
businesslike, but he could tell that she was as worried as
he was.

He swept the light across the hallway again, and
finally satisfied that it was truly empty, he ran forward,
not caring about the danger anymore, sliding to a stop
again when he found the door to the stairs. "Okay, the
stairs are here, just like you said."

"Go down," Hannah said, her voice crackling a little as
he began to make his descent. "Just keep moving until you
get to the very bottom. You'll be in the basement of the

building, but still in the hidden passageway. According to the blueprint, the hall at the bottom will terminate at a door leading outside the building—directly onto the FDR."

"So that's how he got in," Simon said, taking the stairs two at a time, careful to keep his light trained on the risers to make sure he didn't fall through a rotten one.

"Yeah. On a normal day, you couldn't possibly access it without risking death by traffic accident. But with the highway closed, it makes for a perfect way in and out. And the damn thing was sealed up so long ago, I doubt anyone has thought about it in years."

"Well, thank God we found it," Simon said, as he passed the first floor landing still heading down. "If we're right, and that bastard's got Jillian, I don't have much time to find her. He'll only keep her alive as long as he's worried about being intercepted." The thought sent a cold spike of fear stabbing through him, but he shook it off.

"I think I'm near the bottom of the stairs." He rounded the final turn and stopped, the steps abruptly ending, the bottommost risers completely rotted away.

Shining his light on the floor below and using the railing to push off, he leaped down, landing hard, but staying on his feet, fighting through another surge of searing pain. "Okay, I'm here," he said. "Which direction?"

"With the stairs directly behind you, turn right," Hannah instructed. "Any sign of Jillian?"

"Nothing so far," he said. "In fact, except for the gun, there's been no sign of anyone. How much farther?"

"About ten yards. You should be able to see the door any minute."

"I've got it," Simon said, breathing hard as he threw it open, the bright sunlight making him squint.

It was weird stepping out onto the highway, even without cars. The road stretched across with three lanes on
each side, and he stopped for valuable seconds trying to
decide which way to go.

"There's a pier just across the highway and down to
your right," Hannah said, and he silently blessed her for
reading his mind. "It's a water taxi landing, but it hasn't
been running since they shut the FDR down. However,
there are some private docks as well. And if I was trying
to make a quick escape, that's where I'd head."

Simon nodded, already heading across the lanes
for southbound traffic, then running down the median
toward the landing before crossing the final northbound
lanes. There was a running path on the far side, and,
ignoring the protesting pain, he accelerated into a full-out
sprint when he hit the asphalt. Ahead of him, he could
just make out two figures struggling as they moved across
the landing toward a large cabin cruiser anchored just off
a small jetty.

"I think I see them," Simon said. "They're heading for
a boat. I'm closing the distance, but I don't think I'll be
in time."

"Just keep moving," she urged him. "Drake and Avery
are coming in just down from the pier. They were heading for the highway from the access ramp on Thirty-
fourth. So at least you'll have backup."

"Won't matter if he gets her on that boat before I can
get there."

As Simon rounded the corner onto the landing, he saw
the figures ahead of him detach, one of them clearly trying to pull away. He lifted his gun, but the distance was
too great and the bodies too close together. Out of the

corner of his eye, he saw Drake and Avery, but they were even farther away than he was.

The two figures continued to fight, and Simon managed to close the distance enough so that he could see the sun glinting off Jillian's hair. And then the man she was fighting grabbed her by the waist, hoisting her up and over the railing onto the cruiser.

Simon fired, but the shot went wide, and the man leaped over the railing and onto the boat, the motor roaring to life as he pulled the first mooring rope free. Simon couldn't see Jillian, but he could see the killer, the man concentrating on the second rope, the tension from the boat pulling it taut, making it more difficult to untie the knot holding it in place.

Taking advantage of the moment, Simon pushed forward, his injured leg muscle screaming with pain, but he ignored it, his only thought to reach Jillian. He was probably less than fifteen feet away when the rope suddenly gave, and the boat was free, roaring away from the dock.

Jillian felt the boat moving beneath her and struggled to push to her feet, to fight to escape. She knew that the farther the boat got from shore, the more likely her fate was sealed. The killer had his back to her, coiling up the mooring ropes, but there was nothing at hand to use as a weapon. The deck was empty. And he was twice her size. Better to just use the opportunity to try for the side. If she could jump into the water, maybe she'd have a fighting chance.

Eyes glued on the man in front of her, she pushed to her feet, using the side of the boat to balance herself, fighting against a wave of dizziness. She'd hit her head when he'd thrown her on board, and her vision was blurry, her mind foggy. But fear urged her onward, a shot of adrenaline temporarily giving her a boost.

With both hands on the railing, she climbed up, lifting a leg to throw it over, but before she made it, the boat jerked forward, and she fell backward onto the deck again. The man grabbed her around the shoulders, pushing her toward the front of the boat as it pulled away from the jetty.

Glancing behind her, she saw Simon standing on the quay, and just for a moment, her heart filled with hope, and she opened her mouth to scream. But before she could utter a sound, the world went black, her last cognizant thought that she'd never told Simon how much she loved him.

"Over here," Drake called, but Simon barely heard him, his mind on Jillian and the rapidly departing cruiser. Leveling his gun, he shot after the boat, knowing he was too far away to hit it, but needing to do something— anything—to make him feel less impotent.

"Simon," Drake said again, this time his voice cutting through the haze of self-pity and rage. "Come on. Avery's commandeered a boat."

The words sank in, registering, and Simon spun around in time to see Avery maneuvering a small speedboat next to the jetty. Drake was already climbing aboard. Crossing the distance in two strides, Simon jumped onto the back of the boat just as Avery hit the throttle, and the little racing boat began to skip across the water in pursuit of the cruiser.

"We have to hurry," Simon yelled above the noise of

the engine, knowing it was a blinding glimpse of the obvious, but his frustration made the words still necessary. "If they make it into the harbor, we don't have a chance in hell of catching them."

Avery nodded, gunning the engine as Simon made his way forward to stand beside Drake, all three of them watching the cruiser in front of them.

"How are we fixed for weapons?" Simon asked, pulling his gaze back to Drake.

"Just handguns." Drake shrugged. "I didn't realize we'd be hitting the high seas. Do you have any idea about the people on board?"

"No. Just that there are at least two of them. And they were planning on escaping across the water."

"Which means they're probably prepared." Drake nodded, clearly considering the situation. "With your leg, can you still swim?"

"Yes," he replied, studying his friend, trying to follow his train of thought. Hell, he'd swim across the fucking harbor if it meant he could save Jillian.

"So if Avery could pull alongside, even for a minute or two, we could try to board the ship and take them out that way."

"If I'm going to get close enough for you to get on board," Avery said, his attention still locked on the cruiser as they began to close the distance, "I'll need someone to provide covering fire. Or you'll both be dead before you hit the deck. Which means only one of you can make the jump."

"Well, it's going to be me," Simon said. "It's my fault she was up there on her own. I should have had her back."

"You were tasked with protecting Bilaal. And that's

what you did." Avery's tone brooked no argument. "Splitting up so that Jillian could intercept the assassin was the right call. Under the circumstances, there was no other way to handle it."

"But if she dies..." He trailed off, just the idea untenable.

"She's not going to die," Drake said. "She's got us. And we never leave anyone behind. You're sure you're up for the jump?" Again Drake shot a look at Simon's leg.

"I'm positive." Simon nodded, pushing aside his fears, concentrating instead on the cruiser and the quickly narrowing distance between it and the speedboat.

"As soon as they realize we're in range," Avery said, "they're going to open fire. If we're lucky, it'll just be the one shooter. The driver's up top so there's no way he can get off a shot. But for all we know, the damn thing is crawling with men and guns."

"I'm betting they're alone," Drake offered, drawing his gun and moving to stand beside Avery behind the boat's windshield. "Makes more sense for a getaway. And if they were to get caught, there would be fewer chances for successful interrogation."

"Well, let's hope you're right," Simon said.

"Go ahead and move to the back." Avery motioned with one hand. "I've almost closed the gap. I'm going to do a test run to see what kind of firepower we're up against, and then I'll pull away long enough for you to get in place."

"Copy that," Simon said, tucking his gun firmly between his jeans and the small of his back.

"Once you're there, I'll pull back into range and give you a sign when you're good to go. We won't be able to

stay with you. We don't have enough ammo. But we'll
hang in as long as we can."

"No worries. I'll signal you when we're in the clear."

"Happy hunting," Drake called, as Simon made his
way to the back of the boat.

Avery maneuvered the little craft closer, and as
expected, bullets started to fly. Drake returned fire, and
Simon focused on the cruiser, trying to pinpoint the number and location of guns.

"Looks like I was right." Drake turned back with a
smile, as Avery reduced the throttle and the speedboat
pulled out of range. "Just two hostiles. That ought to give
you a fighting chance."

Avery lifted a hand to signal Simon to get ready. He
pulled back the little door that closed off the railing
and stepped up onto the fiberglass edge of the boat, his
muscles tensing in anticipation. Beneath his feet, he could
feel the roar of the engine as Avery throttled it forward,
the boat skimming across the water, quickly closing the
distance again with the cruiser.

The gunman on board opened fire. Drake shot back,
and Avery tried to hold the boat steady as he pulled
alongside. Simon pushed off the edge of the speedboat,
diving over the aft railing of the cruiser, landing on the
deck, and rolling to his feet.

Avery held the speedboat in place, the sound of gunfire
popping over the water. Simon knew he only had a few
minutes before Avery had to disengage and the gunman
came looking for him. He needed to find Jillian—fast.
And the best bet was the cabin.

Fortunately, the door to the cabin was on the starboard side. And based on the trajectory of the bullets, the

shooter had been on the deck somewhere midship, port side. The guy captaining the boat was in the control station, with access to the rest of the boat via a ladder on the starboard side. But it was situated toward the bow, so with a little luck, Simon would be able to gain entrance to the cabin without coming into the direct line of fire.

Leading with his gun, he rounded the corner, keeping low, and in just a few seconds, he'd reached the hatch. With a last look both fore and aft, he slipped inside, the sound of gunfire still echoing through the air.

The cabin was on the small side, with stacking bunks on one wall and a tiny galley on the other. A table sat in the middle of the floor, a set of blueprints spread across the top. There was no sign of Jillian, and Simon fought a wave of fear. She was here somewhere. He just had to figure out where. He crossed to the back of the cabin and a small storage area. On the floor was a second hatch, this one closed.

After checking behind him again, he reached down to pull it open, revealing a second narrow storage space that ran the length of the boat. Holstering his gun, he climbed down the ladder, heart pounding, as he searched the cramped space.

At first, he thought she wasn't there. But then he saw a hand extending from underneath a tarp, and his stomach lurched, his heart twisting as he pulled back the plastic sheet and knelt beside her, reaching for her arm, praying to find a pulse.

He slid his finger across the inside of her wrist. For a horrifying second, he thought she was dead, but then he felt the beat of her heart as it surged through her veins, pulsing against his finger.

"J.J.," he whispered, sliding an arm beneath her head. "Sweetheart, can you hear me?" She had a hell of a bruise on her forehead, the deep purple already spreading across her temple. "J.J—Jillian?"

"It's okay, Simon. You can call me J.J." Her eyes fluttered open. "But only you." The words came out on a breath of air, like a sigh, and he smiled. Despite their precarious position, everything suddenly seemed right in his world. "Is it over?"

"I'm afraid not," he said, brushing the hair from her face as he helped her to sit up. "We've still got to get out of here. You think you can walk?"

"Yes, definitely." She nodded, her voice sounding less foggy as she tried to push to her feet.

"Hang on. Let me help you."

He stood up and then reached down to pull her gently to her feet. "I'm going to go first, in case we've got company," he said, nodding toward the hatch behind him. He waited for her agreement and then pulled his gun and climbed back up into the cabin.

After making sure they were still alone, he reached down and helped her up and out.

"So what next?" she asked, her eyes clearer, her voice strong.

"Now that I know you're okay, I'm going to find the asshole who did this to you." He reached over to touch the purpling skin on her temple.

"I'm going with you," she said. "No way am I getting separated again."

"All right," he agreed. "But you stay behind me, okay?"

"I promise." She held up two fingers, Scout style.

They made their way back onto the deck and retraced his initial steps back to the stern. Then, after signaling her to wait, he cautiously inched around the corner to the port side. There was no sign of the shooter, and everything was quiet, which meant that Avery had been forced to drop back out of range.

Something behind him shifted, and Simon swung around, gun leveled, to find the assassin standing near the corner of the cabin, one arm around Jillian's neck, the other pointing a gun at her head.

"Drop it," he said, his gaze locking on Simon's. Neither man moved—seconds stretching to what seemed like hours. "Drop it," the man repeated. "Or I'll kill her."

"And then you'll die," Simon said, playing for time, trying to figure a way out. "So nobody wins." He let his gaze fall to Jillian, and she lifted her chin, then wiggled her fingers, pointedly revealing three. Simon tightened his grip on the gun, his mind clicking into gear as Jillian's fingers started to disappear. Three...Two...

One.

Jillian threw back an elbow, the punch landing squarely in the assassin's gut. He jerked back, his gun hand dropping away, and Simon took the shot, praying to everything out there that was considered holy.

For a moment, he thought he'd missed, and then the assassin's gun clattered to the deck, and he fell forward, pulling Jillian with him. Simon crossed the distance in seconds, freeing her from beneath the dead man. "Are you all right?" he asked, wondering how many more times he was going to have to ask her that question.

"Yeah." She nodded, her breathing still coming in gasps. "I'm okay. That was a hell of a shot."

"It was a hell of an elbow." He wanted nothing more than to pull her close, to hold her forever, but there was still the matter of the man at the helm of the ship. If they could take him alive, maybe they could get him to talk. And gain information that might finally put a face on the Consortium.

"Come on," he said, glancing over her shoulder to see that Avery and Drake were still with them. "We've got to try to capture the guy up top."

"I don't think that's going to be possible." She shook her head, her eyes going wide again.

He turned around, his gun still in his hand, but at the sight of the man standing near the bow, he knew that a bullet wasn't going to do any good. It was like the same song, second verse. The jacket pulled wide, the twisted smile. The bomb strapped around the man's waist.

"Son of a bitch," he whispered, reaching out to grab Jillian's hand. "Don't these fucking people ever quit?"

The man at the bow lifted his hand, his finger on the detonator, and Simon ran for the side of the boat, dragging Jillian along with him, the two of them diving over the railing as the autumn afternoon exploded into a fiery ball of light.

Simon hit the water hard, the cold knocking the breath out of him as he plunged into the murky depths. He struggled to orient himself, panicking when he realized he could no longer feel Jillian's fingers locked with his. Frantically, he flailed through the darkness trying to find her. But there was nothing—no one. Still, he kept pushing himself deeper, trying to find her, until, lungs bursting, he gave in to self-preservation and kicked for the light.

Gasping for air, he treaded water, calling her name, turning in circles, trying to find her. And then she was there. Surfacing beside him, sputtering as her hair fanned out around her in the water.

He locked his arm around her, pulling her close, her body shivering against his. The remains of the cruiser burned off to the right, ash and burning debris still raining down from the sky. But Simon could also hear the sound of Avery piloting the speedboat closer, rescue imminent.

"It's okay, baby," he whispered. "It's okay. It's over. And we're alive."

She nodded, leaning her head against his chest, still sucking in air. Then she tipped her head back, her lips tilting in a tiny smile. "And we're still together. And after all this time, that has to mean something, right?"

"It means everything, sweetheart," he said, brushing his lips against her hair, relishing the feel of her heart beating against his. "Absolutely everything."

EPILOGUE

Köln, Germany, two weeks later

Michael Brecht twisted the browning rose bloom, snapping it off the plant. He'd been thwarted by A-Tac, again. It was as if Avery Solomon was always there, looking over his shoulder, waiting to swoop in at the last minute in his goddamned white hat.

He grabbed another stem, popping the dead flowers off the rose bush with a zeal that went beyond deadheading. He'd made his plans so carefully. Even when things had gotten out of hand, he'd maintained control, only to lose it when it had mattered most.

A thorn dug into his thumb, and he swore, sucking away the blood as someone behind him cleared his throat.

Gregor.

Michael stifled a sigh and turned around, surprised to see that his number two was not alone. Anthony Delafranco was supposed to be in Nice. The Consortium had business there. Delafranco, one of the Consortium's founding members, was supposed to have been on point.

"Is there a problem?" Michael asked, his senses on high alert. A second man—armed—stood behind Delafranco. Michael recognized him as Delafranco's bodyguard. Nothing unusual in that, but something felt off somehow.

"Nothing that we can't handle," Delafranco replied, his expression guarded as he studied Michael. "There's nothing new on Isaacs, I'm assuming?"

"No. But I've got some of our best men looking. The Americans are still asserting that it was his body found in the aftermath of the blast." Michael shifted so that he could meet Gregor's gaze, but the big man was staring off at the horizon, apparently not feeling the same degree of trepidation. "But Isaacs is too good at what he does to have let himself be blown up with his own bomb, and he's definitely not the type to martyr himself by committing suicide."

"Agreed," Delafranco said. "But then how do you explain the body?"

"If I had to call it, I'd say it was Stoltz's. After all, he was tasked with taking Isaacs out. And we haven't heard from him since. I'm guessing Isaacs left some kind of trace—something to throw A-Tac off. Something to make them believe it was him in the fire instead. They'd have no way of knowing about Stoltz and so no reason to dig beyond the surface evidence."

"Yes, but A-Tac seems to make a practice of doing exactly what we think they won't."

The words were galling, but true. And Michael had learned a long time ago that the only way to fight fire was with fire. It was time for a showdown. To end things once and for all. "Even if they do figure it out, Stoltz will only be another dead end. And we'll find Isaacs. And when we do, he'll cease to be a problem as well."

"And A-Tac?" Delafranco asked. "Thanks to your actions, they're more interested than ever in destroying everything we've worked so hard to build."

Anger flared, and Michael closed his fists, striving to maintain calm. "You leave A-Tac to me."

"Unfortunately, that's not going to be possible, Michael." Delafranco shrugged, the Walther in his hand glinting in the sunlight. "I'm afraid, my friend, that your time with the Consortium has come to an end."

Sunderland College, one month later

Jillian and Simon stood near the picnic table in Avery's backyard, the smell of ribs and BBQ chicken filling the evening air. Everyone was present and accounted for. Madeline, Annie, and Alexis back from California. And Owen and Tucker back from —wherever—it was classified.

They'd spent the last four weeks trying to find answers in the aftermath of all that had happened. But there had been little to go on. Questioning Aamir's parents had been a dead end, the couple clearly unaware of their son's militant leanings. And backtracking on Saed's movements had proven equally futile, the trail growing cold in the mountains of Afghanistan along with all traces of Kamaal.

Not surprisingly, the remains of the boat had yielded nothing. They had found .22 caliber brass casings on the floor of the UN's conference room mezzanine, a choice of weapon that was obviously meant to have incriminated

Mossad had the assassination of Bilaal been successful. And despite hours poring over pictures of potential killers, no one had been able to identify the man who'd tried to kill Bilaal and held Jillian hostage.

Thankfully, though, Bilaal had been saved and, with him, the hope for a lasting peace in the Middle East. There was still a long way to go, but with him as part of the process, there was a real chance of success. He was turning into a true Yusuf, crossing cultural lines with charm and an innate goodness.

The FDR had reopened, as had the seaport. And the Yankees had gone on to win the World Series. With the deaths of Lester, Rivon, and Isaacs, their network seemed to have dried up. Which was at least a small success. But overall, though the Consortium had lost this battle, the final outcome of the war had yet to be decided.

"So, if I can have everyone's attention," Avery said, breaking into Jillian's thoughts, his smile warm and inclusive.

She'd been surprised at how easily the team had accepted her as a part of their family. Of course, it was mostly due to the fact that Simon had made his feelings for her more than clear. But she also felt as if she'd earned her place—on her own merit. And that meant more to her than she could ever have thought possible.

"We're here tonight to honor Jillian and Simon." Avery's voice filled the backyard, and everyone grew quiet.

"Not exactly necessary," Simon insisted from his perch on the edge of the table. "After all, this was a team endeavor. Anything we accomplished was part of a group effort. Any victory belongs to all of us."

"Spoken like a true kiss-up," Harrison heckled, as Drake and Tucker exchanged grins over the grill where they were manning the meat.

"The two of you," Avery continued, shooting a sharp look in the other men's direction, "were the ones who put yourselves directly in harm's way to protect Bilaal. Without your quick thinking, the man would surely be dead, and America would potentially be on the brink of war. The way I see it, you both deserve more than a medal."

He reached into his pocket, producing two small velvet boxes. "And so on behalf of the United States government, I'm very pleased to present you both with the Intelligence Star. I don't have to tell you what an honor it is to be recognized in this way." He opened each of the boxes and held them out for Jillian and Simon while the others lifted their beers and cheered.

"But I'm not even CIA," Jillian protested. Actually, she wasn't even with Homeland Security anymore, but they hadn't told anyone yet.

"As far as Langley is concerned, you were acting as a member of this unit, which makes you CIA," Avery assured her. "And well-deserving of the honor."

"Well, if you ask me, these medals belong to all of us," Simon reiterated, still looking embarrassed as he rose to his feet.

"No worries." Tyler laughed, her arm linked through Owen's. "This is the only time you'll ever actually see them anyway. They give them to you and then take them away. After all, technically, we don't exist—which means we can't risk having something as auspicious as a medal hanging around. So enjoy the moment."

"I knew there had to be a catch," Simon said. "Oh, well, easy come, easy go. I've got all the reward I need right here." He slipped an arm around Jillian, and her heart flipped over in her chest. The man had always had that effect on her, and now he always would.

Harrison smiled and pulled Hannah closer. Madeline and Alexis, now visibly pregnant, soothed Bree, who was clearly not as enthralled with the proceedings as the grown-ups. Annie and Nash moved over to their son, the three of them starting an impromptu game of Frisbee. And Drake, sporting an Angels cap, was squirting water on a burst of flames coming from the grill as his brother gave him a hard time.

After everything that had happened, things seemed absurdly normal. But then maybe that was the way it was supposed to be. The hard stuff, the difficult bits, just a blip in what was otherwise a perfectly ordinary life. Jillian sighed. Just at the moment normalcy sounded like heaven.

"If you guys have a minute," Avery was saying, "I've got something else I need to say."

Jillian settled on the picnic table next to Simon, lacing her fingers with his.

"I wasn't kidding about your being a part of the team, Jillian. I want you here, permanently. So I talked to the brass, and they've authorized me to offer you a position. I'm sure you've heard us talking about Lara Prescott." Avery paused to take a sip from his beer. "Among other things, she served as the team's medical officer. And as you also may know, she's taken an indefinite leave of absence. So long story short, we need someone to take her place, and we'd like that to be you."

"Did you know about this?" Jillian asked, turning to Simon.

"No." He shook his head, holding up his hands in denial. "Not a thing. Avery is pretty good about playing his cards close to the vest."

"I didn't want to say anything until everything was approved," Avery said. "So what do you think?"

Jillian glanced over at Simon, wondering if this new offer would change anything. They'd talked and talked about their options and where they wanted to go next, not only with their relationship but with their lives. And while she wanted to be with him, it was important that she have a life of her own as well. And A-Tac was Simon's world.

"I think J.J. has already made another commitment," Simon said, reaching for her hand, telling her with just a touch that nothing had changed. Decisions about her life would always be hers.

"Please tell me it's not with Homeland Security." Avery frowned. "I'd hate to think we're losing you to them."

"No." Jillian smiled, loving that she was wanted, but equally pleased with her decision. "Although the director did play a part in it. I've decided to go back to medical school. And he pulled some strings to get me into Cornell. I start in the spring. And though your offer is tempting, the truth is that, while I want to save lives, I'd rather do it in an OR than in the field. I'll leave that to you and Simon and the rest of the team."

"And you're sure it's what you want?" Avery asked.

"Very sure. Between Cornell and Simon, I feel as if all my dreams have come true." She squeezed his hand, feeling absurdly happy in the moment.

"Well, I can't say that I'm not disappointed," Avery groused, "but I understand the choice. And I'm happy for you. And after you graduate, if you change your mind, there will always be a place for you on my team."

"That means the world to me, Avery," Jillian said.

"I'm afraid you're going to have to do without me, too, boss," Simon said as she turned to look at him with surprise. "My leg isn't going to get any better. And if I learned one thing out of all of this, it's that you have to grab on to the things that matter while you've got the chance. And for me," he looked down at her, his eyes full of love, "that means being with J.J.. So I'm going to move to the city with her."

"But you can't resign," Jillian protested. "You love A-Tac."

"I do. And assuming Avery's willing, I think I can still be of use to the unit, helping with logistics when I'm needed. But beyond that, I think maybe it's time for me to reinvent myself, too."

Jillian felt tears welling in her eyes. She'd never have asked him to choose. But he had anyway. And he'd chosen her.

"So am I still on the team?" Simon asked. "Or did I just quit?"

"I'm happy to have whatever you've got to give me, Simon," Avery said, his face breaking into a smile. "And I wholeheartedly support your decision. Most people don't get second chances, and the two of you need to cherish the fact that you've been given one. Next to that, nothing else really matters."

Simon walked across the back patio, the autumn night crisp and sweet. The BBQ was still winding down, his friends huddled in groups around the backyard, their voices carrying on the soft breeze. J.J. was sitting on the porch swing, the last of the light caressing her golden hair. He dropped down beside her, relishing her warmth as she leaned against him with a contented sigh.

"Happy?" he asked, already knowing the answer, but loving the sound of it anyway.

"Incredibly." She sighed, cuddling closer, then tipping her head back so that she could see his eyes. "And you?"

"Beyond belief," he said, stroking her hair. "I think I've always loved you, Jillian Montgomery. Starting that first moment I saw you at orientation in college. Avery was right. Most people don't get a second shot. But you've given me one, and I intend to spend the rest of my life proving that you made the right decision."

"You don't have to prove anything, Simon." She lifted a hand to caress his face. "It's enough just to know that you love me."

"And that I do, sweetheart," he said, with a smile, as he pulled her onto his lap, his lips slanting over hers. "That I do."

Don't miss the next novella in
Dee Davis's thrilling A-Tac Series!

Please turn this page for a preview of

Dire Distraction.

Köln, Germany

'm afraid, my friend, that your time with the Consortium has come to an end." Michael Brecht stared down the muzzle of Anthony Delafranco's gun, anger mixing with surprise. He wouldn't have believed his friend capable of such betrayal.

But he recognized the determination in Delafranco's eyes, even as he saw the slight movement of his hand tightening on the trigger. Michael dove for the ground as the quiet garden exploded with gunfire. Pea gravel scraped across the skin on his forearms as he fell, Delafranco's first shot going wild. Behind him, Michael could see his associate Gregor struggling with Delafranco's bodyguard. And as Delafranco tried to readjust the trajectory, Michael scrambled for cover, wishing to hell he had his weapon. This wasn't the way he'd planned for it to end.

More shots rang out and Michael flinched, then blinked as Delafranco's gun fell from lifeless fingers, his body crumpling forward, blood staining the gravel walkway.

Gregor stepped from behind a rose bush, still holding his gun, the bodyguard's lifeless form stretched out beside him.

"You okay, boss?" Gregor asked, kicking away the bodyguard's weapon and bending to check for a pulse. There was no need to check on Delafranco. His blood and brain matter had been sprayed across the roses like macabre graffiti.

"Is he dead?" Michael asked, brushing the gravel from his pants, his gaze still on Delafranco.

"Yes." Gregor stood up, holstering his weapon. "We'll need to get the bodies out of here as soon as possible. We don't want any unnecessary questions."

"Agreed. You can call Stephan. He's discreet. And he'll make sure there's nothing for anyone to find."

"Still, you'll have to explain Delafranco's death to the Council."

Michael reached out to pluck a wilted rose from its stem, thinking about the group of men he'd hand-picked to help lead the Consortium. "Eventually. But for now, we'll just let them believe he's disappeared."

"There will be questions."

"That's to be expected. And I trust that you and Stephan will leave a trail of answers. Delafranco would never have dared to try this if he were on his own," Michael admitted, the taste of the words bitter in his mouth. "I need to know who was acting with him. And then we can weed out the rest of the traitors. Once that's done, I'll make sure the others know the real truth. That I created the Consortium. And that I'm the one in charge. And should anyone else try to interfere, he'll meet the same fate as Delafranco."

"As you wish," Gregor said, nodding his agreement.

"But what about A-Tac? Delafranco was right. They are going to continue to be a problem."

"Not to worry. I've got plans for them too. All that remains is to activate the file I embedded in the hard drive I had Kamaal Sahar leave behind at the camp in Afghanistan. And when Avery Solomon and his merry band find it, the wheels will be set in motion. He'll come running, and vengeance will be mine."

Sunderland College, New York

All right, chow is served," Avery Solomon said, setting a platter of burgers on the game table in his living room. "First pitch is in five. So fill up your plate and grab a seat."

"Angels are going to kill," Drake Flynn said, sliding two burgers onto his plate along with a healthy serving of potato salad. "Just so you guys are prepared." He settled on the sofa and reached for his beer.

"In your dreams, surfer boy." Nash Brennon laughed, dropping into an armchair as strains of the Star-Spangled Banner resounded from the surround-sound system. "Yankees rule."

"Most of the time. But this year your pitching sucks, and we've got Pujols."

"And not much else," Avery said, settling into a chair. It was good to have some down time. Of late, it seemed like the team had been spending a hell of a lot of time chasing after ghosts. Most of them sent by their nemesis, a secretive arms cartel known as the Consortium. And despite the fact that they'd managed to win most of the battles, the cost had been high.

Too high, if he had to call it.

But it was what it was, and there was nothing he could do to change the past. Best to focus on the future. And on the moment, the things that made it all worthwhile: baseball, beer, burgers, and good friends.

"Where's Harrison?" Nash asked, taking a sip from a bottle of Shiner Bock. The beer, a Texas import, was a favorite. And Harrison, recently back from a job consulting with drug enforcement agents about an operation on the Mexican border, had brought Avery a case. "I thought he was supposed to be here."

"He is." Drake nodded. "But he also just got back from almost a month on an operation. And if Hannah is anything like Madeline, let's just say absence really does make the heart..." he trailed off, waggling his eyebrows for effect.

"Jesus, Drake." Nash blew out a disgusted breath. "Do you ever think of anything besides sex?"

"Yeah. Baseball and beer." Drake grinned, lifting his bottle. "The trifecta, of course being all three at once."

"Good luck with that," Nash snorted, shaking his head.

Avery watched his friends, suddenly feeling too damned old. This business had a way of sucking the life right out of you, particularly when they were dealing with the Consortium. He took another sip of his beer, turning his attention to the TV. The first Angels batter was up to face C.C. Sabathia on the mound for the Yankees.

Behind them, the doorbell rang.

"Harrison," Nash said, shooting a sideways glance at Drake as he bit into a burger. "Told you he'd be here."

"It's open," Avery called. C.C. threw a curveball for strike three.

"Sorry I'm late," Harrison said, something in his expression sending alarm bells jangling. "I was working and sort of got sidetracked." He held up a mangled-looking black box, his eyes telegraphing regret.

"Dude, you're not supposed to be working," Drake protested. "The Angels are playing the Yankees. Where I'm from that's almost sacrosanct."

"Big word, Drake," Nash said, turning to look at Harrison, his eyes narrowing at the sight of the black box in Harrison's hand.

Apparently Avery wasn't the only one to sense that something was up.

Never late for the party, Drake swiveled around, looked first at Harrison, then at Avery, and then back at Harrison again, the game forgotten. "You've pulled something off the drive."

The mangled hard drive had been recovered in an abandoned terrorist encampment in Afghanistan. A-Tac had received intel about the possibility of a Consortium-funded operation, but when they'd arrived, the camp had been abandoned, everything of consequence removed or destroyed.

Except for a notebook that had helped them stop an assassination attempt. And the remains of the hard drive. Avery hadn't doubted for a minute that if there was recoverable information, Harrison would find it. But he'd also been fairly certain that there wouldn't be anything left to find.

Clearly, he'd been wrong.

"I'm sorry," Harrison said. "I know the timing sucks." As if to underscore the sentiment, the solid swack of bat meeting ball echoed through the room, but nobody turned to look. Not even Drake. "But you're going to want to see this."

Harrison's gaze locked with Avery's, and suddenly he wasn't all that certain he wanted to know. But there was nothing to be gained in putting off the inevitable. Whatever the Consortium had in store for them next, he was ready.

"Okay then," Avery said, switching the TV off with the remote, then pushing the burgers out of the way as they all gathered around the table, "what have you got?"

"It's a little startling." Harrison paused, clearly searching for the right words. "And kind of personal." His gaze met Avery's. "You might want to hear this on your own."

Avery shook his head, crossing his arms over his chest. "We're all family here. So tell us what you've found."

Harrison hooked the box up to his laptop and hit a key. A woman's face filled the screen. Her dark hair curled around her face, brown eyes glittering with some unshared emotion, her generous mouth giving nothing away.

Avery's heart stopped. His breath stuck in his throat. And he felt as if someone had just kicked him in the gut.

She was dressed in fatigues, standing next to a bearded man leaning against a desk, his hand resting intimately on her knee. "Sweet Jesus," Avery said, the words strangled. "This was on the backup drive we found in Afghanistan?"

"Yeah." Harrison nodded, his face filled with worry. "I was just as surprised as you are."

"Is that?" Drake said, turning to Nash, who was staring open-mouthed at the photograph.

"Yeah." Nash nodded. "Martin Shrum. Avery's old

partner. From before A-Tac days. And Evangeline, Avery's wife. But I thought she was—"

"Dead," Avery finished, emotion cutting through him as he caressed the ring he wore on his little finger. "She is. For almost fourteen years now."

"Yeah, well, Avery, there's more." Harrison clicked the picture so that it zoomed in and then moved it so that they could better see the desk behind the two people. "Look at the wall." He enlarged the picture again.

"It's a calendar," Drake said, stating the obvious.

Avery's blood ran cold, his eyes reading the date, his mind trying to process the seemingly impossible.

"Holy shit," Drake continued, his incredulity only adding to the surrealistic horror of the moment. "It's dated December of last year."

THE DISH

Where authors give you the inside scoop!

♥ ♥ ♥ ♥ ♥ ♥ ♥ ♥ ♥ ♥ ♥ ♥ ♥ ♥ ♥

From the desk of Katie Lane

Dear Reader,

Have you ever pulled up to a stoplight and looked over to see the person in the car next to you singing like they're auditioning for *American Idol*? They're boppin' their head and thumpin' the steering wheel like some crazy loon. Well, I'm one of those crazy loons. I love to sing. I'm not any good at it, but that doesn't stop me. I sing in the shower. I sing while cooking dinner and cleaning house. And I sing along with the car radio at the top of my lungs. Singing calms my nerves, boosts my energy, and inspires me, which is exactly how my new Deep in the Heart of Texas novel came about.

One morning, I woke up with the theme song to the musical *The Best Little Whorehouse in Texas* rolling around in my head. You know the one I'm talking about: "It's just a little bitty pissant country place…" The song stayed with me for the rest of the day, along with the image of a bunch of fun-loving women singing and dancing about "nothin' dirty going on." A hundred verses later, about the time my husband was ready to pull out the duct tape, I had an exciting idea for my new novel.

My editor wasn't quite as excited.

"A what?" she asked, and she stared at me exactly like the people who catch me singing at a stoplight.

She relaxed when I explained that it wasn't a functioning house of ill repute. The last rooster flew the coop years ago. Now Miss Hattie's Henhouse is nothing more than a dilapidated old mansion with three old women living in it. Three old women who have big plans to bring Miss Hattie's back to its former glory. The only thing that stands in their way is a virginal librarian who holds the deed to the house and a smokin' hot cowboy who is bent on revenge for his great-grandfather's murder.

Yes, there will be singing, dancing, and just a wee bit of "dirty going on." And of course, all the folks of Bramble, Texas, will be back to make sure their librarian gets a happy ending.

I hope you'll join me there!

Best wishes,

Katie Lane

♥ ♥ ♥ ♥ ♥ ♥ ♥ ♥ ♥ ♥ ♥ ♥ ♥ ♥ ♥

From the desk of Amanda Scott

Dear Reader,

What happens when a self-reliant Highland lass possessing extraordinary "gifts" meets a huge, shaggy warrior wounded in body and spirit, to whom she is strongly attracted, until she learns that he is immune to her gifts and that her father believes the man is the perfect husband for her?

What if the warrior is a prisoner of her father's worst enemy, who escaped after learning of a dire threat to the young King of Scots, recently returned from years of English captivity and struggling to take command of his unruly realm?

Lady Andrena MacFarlan, heroine of THE LAIRD'S CHOICE, the first book in my Lairds of the Loch trilogy, is just such a lass; and escaped Highland-galley slave and warrior Magnus "Mag" Galbraith is such a man. He is also dutiful and believes that his first duty is to the King.

I decided to set the trilogy in the Highlands west of Loch Lomond and soon realized that I wanted a mythological theme and three heroines with mysterious gifts, none of which was Second Sight. We authors have exploited the Sight for years. In doing so, many of us have endowed our characters with gifts far beyond the original meaning, which to Highlanders was the rare ability of a person to "see" an event while it was happening (usually the death of a loved one in distant battle).

It occurred to me, however, that many of us today possess mysterious "gifts." We can set a time in our heads to waken, and we wake right on time. Others enjoy flawless memories or hearing so acute that they hear sounds above and/or below normal ranges—bats' cries, for example. How about those who, without reason, dream of dangers to loved ones, then learn that such things have happened? Or those who sense in the midst of an event that they have dreamed the whole thing before and know what will happen?

Why do some people seem to communicate easily with animals when others cannot? Many can time baking without a timer, but what about those truly spooky types who walk to the oven door just *before* the timer goes—every time—as if the thing had whispered that it was about to go off?

Warriors develop extraordinary abilities. Their hearing becomes more acute; their sense of smell grows stronger. Prisoners of war find that all their senses increase. Their peripheral vision even widens.

In days of old, certain phenomena that we do not understand today might well have been more common and more closely heeded.

Lady Andrena reads (most) people with uncanny ease and communicates with the birds and beasts of her family's remaining estate. That estate itself holds secrets and seems to protect her family.

Her younger sisters have their own gifts.

And as for Mag Galbraith… Well, let's just say he has "gifts" of his own that make the sparks fly.

I hope you'll enjoy THE LAIRD'S CHOICE. Meantime, *suas Alba!*

Amanda Scott

www.amandascottauthor.com

♥ ♥ ♥   ♥   ♥   ♥

From the desk of Dee Davis

Dear Reader,

Sometimes we meet someone and there is an instant connection, that indefinable something that creates sparks between two people. And sometimes that leads almost immediately to a happily ever after. Or at least the path taken seems to be straight and true. But sometimes life intervenes. Mistakes are made, secrets are kept, and that light is extinguished. But we rarely ever forget. That magical moment is too rare to dismiss out of turn, and, if given the right opportunity, it always has the potential to spring back to life again.

That's the basis of Simon and Jillian's story. Two people separated by pride and circumstance. Mistakes made that aren't easily undone. But the two of them have been given a second chance. And this time, just maybe they'll get it right. Of course to do that, they'll have to overcome their fears. And they'll have to find a way to confront their past with honesty and compassion. Easily said—not so easily done. But part of reading romance, I think, is the chance to see that in the end, no matter what has happened, it all can come right again.

And at least as far as I'm concerned, Jillian and Simon deserve their happy ending. It's just that they'll have to work together to actually get it.

As always, this book is filled with places that actually exist. I love the Fulton Seaport and have always been fascinated with the helipads along the East River. The buildings along the river that span the FDR highway have always been a pull. How much fun to know that people are whizzing along underneath you as you stare out your window and watch the barges roll by. The brownstone that members of A-Tac use during their investigation is based on a real one near the corner of Sutton Place and 57th Street.

The busy area around Union Square is also one of my favorite hang-outs in the city. And so it seemed appropriate to put Lester's apartment there. His gallery, too, is based on reality—specifically, the old wrought-iron clad buildings in SoHo. As to the harbor warehouses, while I confess to never having actually been in one, I have passed them several times when out on a boat, and they always intrigue me. So it isn't surprising that one should show up in a book.

And I must confess to being an avid Yankees fan. So it wasn't much of a hardship to send the team off to the stadium during a fictional World Series win. I was lucky enough to be there for the ticker-tape parade when they won in 2009. And Boone Logan is indeed a relief pitcher for the Yankees.

I also gave my love of roses to Michael Brecht, dead-heading being a very satisfying way to spend a morning. And finally, the train tunnel that the young Jillian and Simon dare to cross in the middle of the night truly does exist, near Hendrix College in Arkansas. (And it was, in fact, great sport to try and make it all the way through!)

Hopefully you'll enjoy reading Jillian and Simon's story as much as I enjoyed writing it.

For insight into both of them, here are some songs I listened to while writing DOUBLE DANGER:

"Stronger," by Kelly Clarkson
"All the Rowboats," by Regina Spektor
"Take My Hand," by Simple Plan

And as always, check out www.deedavis.com for more inside info about my writing and my books.

Happy Reading!

Dee Davis

♥ ♥ ♥ ♥ ♥ ♥ ♥ ♥ ♥ ♥ ♥ ♥ ♥ ♥ ♥

From the desk of Isobel Carr

Dear Reader,

I have an obsession with history. And as a re-enactor, that obsession frequently comes down to a delight in the minutia of day-to-day life and a deep love of true events that seem stranger than fiction. And we all know that real life is stranger than fiction, don't we?

RIPE FOR SEDUCTION grew out of just such a real-life story. Lady Mary, daughter of the Duke of Argyll, married Edward, Viscount Coke (heir to the Earl of Leicester). It was not a happy marriage. He left her alone on their wedding night, imprisoned her at his family estate, and in the end she refused him his marital rights and went to live with her mother again. Lucky for her, the viscount died three years later when she was twenty-six. And while I can see how wonderful it might be to rewrite that story, letting the viscount live and making him come groveling back, it was not the story that inspired me. No, it was what happened after her husband's death. Upon returning to town after her mourning period was over, Lady Mary received a most indecent proposal...and the man who made it was fool enough to put it in writing. Lady Mary's revenge was swift, brutal, and brilliant. I stole it for my heroine, Lady Olivia, who like Lady Mary had suffered a great and public humiliation at the hands of her husband, and who, also like Lady Mary, eventually found herself a widow.

And don't try finding out just what the poor man did or what Lady Mary's response was by Googling it. That story isn't on Wikipedia (though maybe I should add it). You'll have to come let Roland show you what it means to be RIPE FOR SEDUCTION if you want to find out.

Isobel Carr

www.isobelcarr.com